Praise for *Kissing Kosher*

"Powerfully heartwarming, passionate, sometimes painful, but endlessly entertaining." —M. J. Rose, *New York Times* bestselling author of *The Jeweler of Stolen Dreams*

"Full of heart, wisdom, and poignancy without sacrificing the fun." —Felicia Grossman, author of *Marry Me by Midnight*

"Daring, poignant, brutally honest but also exquisitely romantic!" —Holly Cassidy, author of *The Christmas Wager*

"Long after I finished *Kissing Kosher*, I found Avital and Ethan taking space in my head." —Marilyn Simon Rothstein, author of *Crazy to Leave You*

"This delicious romance is more satisfying than the best dessert." —Amanda Elliot, author of *Best Served Hot* and *Sadie on a Plate*

"Mix a backstabbing babka war, a romance, and a dose of real life pain. Bake until the tension is thick—and you get this soulful novel." —Rachel Barenbaum, author of *Atomic Anna* and *A Bend in the Stars*

"This proudly Jewish and sexy romance highlights the importance of finding joy even in the most painful of times." —Meredith Schorr, author of *As Seen on TV* and *Someone Just Like You*

"Propulsive, sexy, brutally honest, and overflowing with heart and hope." —Lynda Cohen Loigman, bestselling author of *The Matchmaker's Gift* and *The Two-Family House*

"A beautiful babka of a book, with multiple layers tied together by a romance that is as sweet as it is vulnerable." —Stacey Agdern, author of *B'Nai Mitzvah Mistake*

Kissing Kosher

JEAN MELTZER

mira

Recycling programs
for this product may
not exist in your area.

ISBN-13: 978-0-7783-3440-8

Kissing Kosher

For questions and comments about the quality of this book, please contact us at
CustomerService@Harlequin.com.

Mira
22 Adelaide St. West, 41st Floor
Toronto, Ontario M5H 4E3, Canada
BookClubbish.com

Printed in U.S.A.

Also by Jean Meltzer

The Matzah Ball
Mr. Perfect on Paper

For my father
Dr. Jeffrey I. Meltzer
July 16, 1947–March 26, 2022

TEVET

(December–January)

ONE

Avital Cohen wasn't wearing underwear.

Standing behind the front counter of Best Babka in Brooklyn, holding their signature pink box in one hand and a pair of tongs in the other, she tried to ignore the pain radiating through her lower abdomen. Despite the fact there was a line spreading around the block, and Shabbat was less than four hours away, the middle-aged woman with streaks of purple in her hair was taking her sweet time.

"I've got three black-and-white biscotti," Mrs. Purpleman said, speaking into her cell phone. "Four confetti rugelach, one challah...I know, I know, but Alyssa is on one of her health kicks, again."

Her name wasn't Mrs. Purpleman. It was just one of many nicknames that Avital had created in order to remember customers. Mrs. Purpleman was, in fact, Mrs. Perlman, and Avital had come up with the name because she wore her hair styled into a bob and dyed a deep maroon. The effect of which always managed to look purple.

Mrs. Purpleman had been a longtime customer of Best Babka in Brooklyn, arriving like clockwork every Friday morning to stock up on Shabbat goodies for her family.

"But if I buy two challahs," Mrs. Purpleman sighed heavily into her cell, "she'll say I'm not validating her feelings..."

Avital glanced down the long line and wondered when Mrs. Purpleman—a professional go-getter when it came to lengthy and irrational amounts of indecision at the counter—would finally notice the eye rolls behind her and make a choice.

"Well, how do you think she'll feel about some apple cake macaroons?" Mrs. Purpleman asked into her phone.

Avital interrupted. "Those are really good."

She looked up. "Really?"

Avital began loading three cookies into the box. "They're always a huge seller on Fridays," she said, putting a fourth into the box that was angling in the direction of Mrs. Purpleman. "Can I help you with anything else today?"

"Oh." Mrs. Purpleman placed one finger on her chin. "Well, I guess not..."

All at once, she felt bad for losing her patience.

Normally, Avital was good with the clientele. She could typically deal with indecisive customers and long lines and the *total* lack of smiles or gratitude that came with the Shabbat rush hour...but today, she was once again dealing with a flare-up of her chronic-pain condition.

Since being diagnosed with interstitial cystitis two years ago at the age of twenty-two, her life could be boiled down to one phrase. She came, she saw...she realized she needed to pee and quickly stopped whatever she was doing in order to find a bathroom.

"Tell you what," Avital said, grabbing two pink boxes

tied up in white twine from a shelf behind her. "Why don't I throw in two pumpkin-spiced babkas for free?"

"For free?" Mrs. Purpleman asked, confused.

"I know I'm rushing you here," Avital said, bouncing up and down in her spot. "It's just… It's an emergency, Mrs. Perlman."

Mrs. Purpleman finally twisted in her spot and noticed the line. "Oh, Avital—" she said, touching her heart, embarrassed "—I'm so sorry, I didn't even realize!"

"It's okay."

"No, no…" She shook her head, apologizing profusely. "My husband always says, 'Goldie—you take too much time with everything. Just make a decision!' I don't know why it's always so hard for me. I just get nervous, you know, and Alyssa is going through this whole phase, where everything I do is wrong…"

"I know, Mrs. Perlman," Avital said, gently, before angling to move her along. "You have a good Shabbat, okay? I'll see you next week."

Handing the box to Tootles at the front counter, Avital began calling out the order. "One pound marzipan," she shouted over the hum of the crowds, "Three black-and-white biscotti, four confetti rugelachs, one challah, four apple cake macaroons."

"What about the babkas?" Tootles called back.

"On the house," Avital said, and swiftly began taking off her apron. Her break came just in time. Her twin brother, Josh, had just returned from his lunch break. *"Baruch Hashem,"* she said, handing her apron to him.

"That good today, huh?" Josh asked sympathetically.

"You have no idea."

Avital escaped through the back door, sprinting down the

hall toward her office, where she could enjoy the privileges of an attached private bathroom.

As she closed the door behind her, the vent fan and light turned on, buzzing into a familiar hum. Considering how much time she spent there, her mother had tried to spruce up the place—make it feel more homey and comfortable—with the addition of fancy pink soap and a small dish full of potpourri. Instead, all the floral scents really managed to do was seep into her frizzy hair and make her smell like cherry cough syrup.

Sitting down on the toilet, Avital shut her eyes and tried to breathe though her pain. The burning, aching pressure increased. Her stomach cramped. Really what she needed to do was to take the day off. Lie in bed, with ice between her legs and a heating pad on top of her belly, drowning in *rescues*, the colloquial term for the over-the-counter medications and nontraditional remedies used when the pain was at its worst.

Unfortunately, going home was not an option. Even though she had specifically returned to work at Best Babka in Brooklyn for the familial benefit of taking off as needed—a luxury not afforded to most anyone living with chronic pain and chronic illness—they were desperate. With its lines out the door and rapidly expanding social-media presence, the bakery needed support staff as much as it needed flour.

A small whine of pain escaped her lips as she finished her business. She waited for relief, for the feeling of *better* to return to her body…but her pain was relentless. That was the hardest part of it, really. The fact that it never stopped. The fact that it just went on and on, sometimes shifting form but never being eradicated completely.

Returning to the front counter, she found both Tootles and Josh sweating bullets, working hard to fill orders. As general manager, Avital didn't often work the front counter, but

Sara, one of their bakers, had a custody hearing in Manhattan to attend that day.

Avital threw on an apron and scanned the line. Though it seemed impossible, the crowd cramming the front entrance had doubled in size during the three minutes she was stuck in the bathroom. Avital grabbed a pink box.

"Next!" she called out.

A woman with a baby angled on the edge of her hip stepped forward.

"What can I get you?" Avital asked.

"Two challahs," Mother Russia said, the thick accent that had earned her the nickname from Avital, evident in her voice. "Six honey cookies, one black-and-white cheesecake, and a mandel brownie."

Upside: Mother Russia was always decisive. She came in, ordered quickly, and left. She also never smiled or said thank you, which, weirdly enough, actually felt like a gift. Avital didn't have to fake wellness. She didn't have to smile through her pain. She could be just like Mother Russia, totally unconcerned about American social norms.

"Anything else?" Avital said.

"No," Mother Russia said, catching the teething giraffe just before it fell to the floor.

"Great."

Avital handed off the box to Josh. She was just about to call out the order, when the sight of a young man—pushing his way through the crowd—caught her attention.

Holy pumpkin-spiced babka.

Avital faltered. The tongs dangled unused in her hand. Her lower lip parted from the top, jaw dropping. The long line dissipated into silence. There were twenty-five people waiting at the counter, but her eyes were transfixed on the stranger.

He was exactly her type. Square shoulders. Tangled dark curls that lifted like swirls of icing off a perfectly molded face. The most gloriously prominent nose. He was a recipe of charm, all plated together by a navy blue peacoat and gray fitted trousers. He made his way through the crowd, tapping old ladies on the shoulders to offer apologies as he squeezed past.

She couldn't help but be curious. Avital knew most everyone who came into the shop on Friday. They were locals and diehards. People who—like her own family—never skipped a Shabbat.

And then, Prince Charming cut the line.

Her ire began to rise. There was nothing she hated more, on a busy Shabbat afternoon, than a person who cheated the system. Prince Charming suddenly morphed into Sir Cheat-a-Lot.

"Excuse me," Avital said, pointing her tongs at his head, "there's a line."

Sir Cheat-a-Lot smiled nervously. "Uh, no, I... I don't think..."

"Yeah," Avital said, rolling her eyes. "I know. Your Shabbat dinner is *very* important. Far more important than the other three hundred people waiting before you." She turned to Mrs. Grossman, waiting patiently with her pocketbook, directly behind him. "Can I help you today, Mrs. Grossman?"

"Oh yes," the old woman said, leaning over the counter. "I'll take four black-and-white cookies..."

Avital grabbed a pink box. Sir Cheat-a-Lot decided to tempt fate, and her patience, on a high-pain day.

"I'm sorry," he said, his perfectly adorable cheeks turning red in the process. "I think you're misunderstanding my intention here."

Avital didn't have time for this. She glanced over to Rafi,

a plump middle-aged Israeli they had hired for security, and waved him forward.

"Rafi!" Avital shouted. "Can you please show our guest where the line begins?"

"Not a problem, Avi," Rafi said and moved to escort the trespasser outside.

Avital returned her attention to dear, sweet Mrs. Grossman. Rafi grabbed the young man by his arm. But Sir Cheat-a-Lot shrugged out of his grasp and reached into the backpack he was wearing, pulling out a piece of paper.

"I'm here for the job interview," he said, speaking quickly, waving it in her direction.

Avital stopped serving Mrs. Grossman. "What?"

"My name is Ethan Rosenberg," he explained, nervously glancing toward Rafi. "I have an interview scheduled with the general manager here at two thirty. I believe her name is—" he glanced down at his sheet to double-check "—Avital Cohen. We confirmed via email on Monday."

Avital squeezed her eyes shut, wanting to die of embarrassment.

She had completely forgotten.

Then again, she had been up all night—every hour, on the hour—using the bathroom, only to return to bed, exhausted and miserable, with pelvic spasms that didn't let her sleep. Was it any wonder she was forgetting job interviews with desperately needed help? Or that the hours were painfully and purposefully slipping by focused on other things?

Avital waved Rafi off. Then, handing Mrs. Grossman off to Josh, she directed her attention back to the handsome interloper. "Come with me," she said, raising the entrance to the front counter.

She had to press her body all the way back to allow him to pass. The wool of the merino sweater he was wearing be-

neath his coat—his broad and apparently extremely fit chest—
swiped against her own.

"Sorry," she said, straightening her back. "It's...tight."

"No problem." He grinned.

She blanked. She knew there were words in her vocabu-
lary, and that she was supposed to be using them, but all she
could focus on was his scent. He smelled incredible. Like the
leaves of a freshly cut eucalyptus plant, woodsy and delectable.

It was not like her to get so flustered around a man. She
considered herself far too practical to be the type of woman
who gave in to romantic whims. But he had this bold sort
of confidence in the way he walked, and his sense of fashion
was impeccable...and all that masculine energy, brushing up
against her, reminded her that she hadn't had sex in years.

It made her feel vulnerable. Exposed.

Avital thought back to his résumé. "I'm sure you're used
to working in much bigger places."

"Bigger isn't necessarily better," he said, as if anticipating
her own misgivings. His voice was deep and dreamy. "There's
a lot that can be learned from working in more challenging
spaces."

He was saying all the right things.

He was stoking her imagination, too.

Avital needed to get a grip. Especially since her twin
brother was side-eyeing them curiously from the counter.

She waved Ethan to follow, leading him down the hallway
and back to her main office in order to begin his interview.
Even though she knew—as sure as the burning pain radiating through her lower abdomen—that there was no way in
olam haba she would ever hire him.

TWO

Ethan Lippmann was walking through enemy territory.

Following after Avital Cohen, passing through hallways, he couldn't help but sneak a peek at the space. Best Babka in Brooklyn was a thriving bakery in full swing. In one area, employees in branded T-shirts pounded dough on steel countertops. In another, a woman in a long black skirt counted out hundreds of challahs, traditional braided breads, placing them into plastic bags for sale.

Dotting every hall were signs of their success. Platters of baked goods were stacked up by an exit, waiting to be picked up by delivery drivers. Bags of challah were being stacked up for last-minute Shabbat pickups. What filled the majority of the space, however, and damn near overran every free inch, were pink boxes, each one a receptacle for their well-known pumpkin-spiced babka.

"You guys are certainly busy," Ethan said.

"And getting busier," Avital admitted.

Ethan had to be careful with the next question. "Is it all because of your babka?" he asked, feigning ignorance. "I've heard all about your world-famous pumpkin-spiced babka from my friends at culinary school." It was a lie, of course. Ethan had never been to culinary school. He didn't even know how to cook.

"We're known for a lot of things," Avital said.

"Of course."

"But obviously, our pumpkin-spiced babka—created by my grandfather, Chayim Cohen—is what we're most famous for. It's our anchor recipe, the thing that brings new customers in. What keeps them coming back is all the rest," Avital said as she bent down to push a stack of pink boxes out of the way.

The place was a fire hazard.

With luck, they would burn themselves down.

Since he was twelve, Ethan had heard about the Cohens from his grandfather, Moishe Lippmann. It was like a bedtime story in their family. A retelling that occurred every Passover Seder so that each generation would remember. *Chayim Cohen had attempted to ruin his grandfather by throwing him out of the business they had built together. Chayim Cohen hated the Lippmanns and riddled their lives with frivolous lawsuits and one-star reviews. Chayim Cohen didn't even bother to pick up the phone or send a shiva platter when Ethan's parents died.*

This was not corporate espionage. This was not revenge between two rival families, each hell-bent on torturing the other. This was Chayim Cohen getting what he deserved.

Whether or not Ethan agreed with his grandfather's sentiment really didn't matter. He was twenty-four years old, and as the oldest surviving grandson, he was heir to the Lippmann empire. That position came with certain responsibilities. Not only to his grandfather, but to the company he had spent every summer working at since he was fourteen.

Lippmann's. Anyone Jewish would have heard of them. In a world of Twinkies and Ding Dongs, they were the only mass-produced kosher baked good to line supermarket shelves. Since 1962, you could walk into any Jewish home, in any state or neighborhood across the country, and see their quintessential yellow-and-blue boxes stacked on the counters.

Most often, with a knife still left in the box and all the best parts of the dessert picked off and eaten. The point being, they were not just well loved and well-known for their delights—their black-and-white cake or their pumpkin crumble doughnut—they were part of Jewish culture.

Unfortunately, the modern age had brought with it a host of troubles for Lippmann's. The world had changed, and with it, their consumer base. For one, there were way more options for kosher baked goods. In addition, families had become less interested in lining their kitchen counters with processed foods. With the advent of social media especially, everyone wanted the homemade and artisanal goods they saw on Instagram.

It was a sad reality showing in Lippmann's numbers. Despite all their best efforts to retain distribution partners and increase sales, the Lippmann's corner of the baked-goods market was rapidly shrinking. They needed to come up with a plan.

Ethan had his own ideas about how to revitalize his grandfather's company. He spent months scouring numbers, searching for sales reports, taking meetings. But whatever Ethan proposed, Moishe rejected it outright.

Then, one day—like a bush burning in the middle of a desert—Moishe saw an ad in the local Jewish paper. Best Babka in Brooklyn was looking for help. All at once, the memory of the long-standing feud between their two families rose to the surface once more. The old curmudgeon came up with an idea.

All Ethan had to do was infiltrate the business of his longtime enemy and steal the recipe for their world-famous pumpkin-spiced babka. After which, Lippmann's would replace their once popular pumpkin crumble doughnut with pumpkin-spiced babka, saving their corporate empire while also putting Chayim Cohen, and Best Babka in Brooklyn, out of business forever.

Whether or not Ethan liked the idea—or frankly, thought it was a good one—was irrelevant. His grandfather had given him a task. You did not disappoint Moishe Lippmann. The man had not become a billionaire by having long, heartfelt talks about feelings with his grandsons.

"I apologize for not realizing who you were before," Avital said.

Ethan felt his heart skip. "Who I was?"

"I had completely forgotten about you coming in for an interview today."

Ethan was relieved that he had misunderstood.

Still, the comment made him nervous. At any moment, someone could identify him.

He tried to remind himself of the positive. His legal name was Ethan Rosenberg, which he had kept after his father died. He had spent hours wiping clean the Lippmann's corporate website and social-media feeds, removing any pictures of himself. He had even set up a fake address to use on employment papers, an easy-enough task when your company had corporate apartments. As for references, he had handled that, too, outsourcing the task to a service he had found online.

The lawyers had assured him that what he was doing wasn't illegal, even if he felt it was unethical. But what could he do? Moishe wasn't content to send some stranger in to do their dirty work. A stranger could never be trusted like family.

Ethan understood the importance of loyalty. What he was

not expecting, however, was Avital Cohen. Based on his grandfather's retellings, he would have been less shocked if his interview was with some screeching Demogorgon. Alas, Avital Cohen was no horror show. Much to his dismay, she was attractive.

Ethan was drawn to her blue eyes and the way they'd lingered on his own when he entered the establishment. For one iota of a second, he had thought that she was also attracted to him…but then he realized she was calling security.

Walking behind her, his eyes continued trailing the length of her form. She was striking, with blond hair spun into wayward and frizzy curls. High cheekbones. She was also quite tall, with legs that immediately made him wonder how long it would take to run his tongue up them.

He shook the thought away. Avital was the enemy, after all…and he was here on a mission.

He searched for reasons to reject her. For one, she was the worst-dressed woman he had ever laid eyes on. Beneath a T-shirt, which read *I Danced My Socks Off at Rachel's Bat Mitzvah*, she wore a white cotton skirt decorated with ruffles.

The pièce de résistance, however, came at her ankles. For some reason, she had seen fit to wear Birkenstocks paired with pink Wigwams. In truth, it looked like she got dressed in the dark.

Beyond the fact that her choice of outfit was totally inappropriate for the weather—she would most certainly die of hypothermia in such attire—the ruffles in her skirt seemed purposefully designed to tease him. Despite wanting to keep his eye on anything but her tuchus, he couldn't help but find himself lingering on her hips. The hip-to-waist ratio she was sporting seemed impossible.

But even beneath the oversize clothing, he could see it. Though he loathed himself for admitting it, she was exactly his type. Despite her overall thin form, she was still inappropriately wide in all the right places. He could imagine himself gripping those hips, pulling her closer to him.

And then, Avital stopped. Full-on came to a complete standstill in the hallway. Pressing one hand against the brick wall, she bent over halfway, before taking deep and staggered breaths. Had he been walking any quicker, he would have run directly into her delicious-looking back end. Not that he would ever consider bumping rumps with Avital. One did not bump rumps with their mortal archenemy.

The way she had stopped and then keeled over without any explanation left him perplexed. He had no idea what she was doing. None. But the anxiety he was a pro at hiding beneath a confident exterior began to peek through the cracks.

Did she recognize him? Did she know he was really a Lippmann? His grandfather would never forgive him if he failed at this task...and then what would happen to his siblings?

Perhaps his younger brother, Randy, would be okay, cut off from the family fortune. But his older sister, Kayla, needed full-time and round-the-clock care. She lived in an expensive, privately funded assisted-living center in Upstate New York. It was Kayla, especially, that kept Ethan toeing the line when it came to his ironfisted grandfather.

Ethan rubbed the back of his neck. "Excuse me, Avital?"

"What?"

"Is everything okay?"

It seemed like a reasonable question, but she answered it with the most resounding *Uuugh* he had ever heard in his life. And then, Avital pushed off the wall and began sprinting.

"Can you move quicker?" she shouted back at him.

"What?" Ethan asked, bemused.

"Quicker!" she snapped.

Ethan nearly died tripping on a pile of pink boxes, trying to keep up with her.

Finally, she brought him to her office. Just like the rest of the bakery, the large room with a desk and attached bathroom was a mess. Papers littered the room. Boxes of shipping labels, bags of holiday decor and more pink boxes plagued every available inch of space.

Avital pointed to a chair in front of a desk. "You can just take a seat."

"Thank—"

He did not have time to finish the thought. Avital squeaked around on her sandals, disappearing down the hall. Ethan did as she had instructed, taking a seat. He waited. And waited. After a solid five minutes of solitude, boredom got the best of him. Ethan pulled out his phone to find three dozen text messages from his grandfather.

Did you see Chayim?

Where is the recipe?

WHY IS THIS TAKING SO LONG, ETHAN?!?!?!

I knew you would disappoint me.

He closed the phone. Moments later, Avital came sprinting back through the threshold of her office.

"Sorry about that," Avital said, taking a seat at her desk, barely making eye contact.

Ethan forced a smile. "Not a problem."

The rest came in an almost rapid-fire succession of facts. Without coming up for air, Avital explained who she was, a brief history of Best Babka in Brooklyn, and why they needed help. Whatever attraction he had initially felt for her dissipated. In addition to being the worst-dressed person on the planet, she was also the most inhospitable woman he had ever met.

"You studied culinary arts at college?" she asked.

"That's correct."

"And you're experienced with baked goods?"

"I was trained at the New York Institute of Culinary Education," Ethan said, working hard to win her over. "And did two years at Le Beurre in Paris. My main body of expertise is in French desserts, however. I did invent my own ice cream once."

"Ice cream?"

"Who doesn't like ice cream, right? For Rosh Hashanah, I made a delicious apple and honey—"

"We don't make ice cream here."

Ethan bit back his annoyance. "I'll keep that in mind."

It was not going well.

Avital sighed, short and resigned. "Look," she explained succinctly, "I appreciate you coming out for this position. Obviously, you're qualified. I would even venture to guess you're overqualified."

"So that means I'm hired?"

"No."

She shifted in her seat, before once again closing her eyes. Ethan swallowed the insult. Her entire body language screamed that she wanted this interview over as quickly as possible. Like every second sitting there with Ethan was making her miserable. What was this woman's problem?

He was normally quite good at molding himself into whatever people wanted from him.

"I'll be quite honest with you, Ethan," she said, finally reopening her eyes, huffing out a determined breath. "Your résumé is great. Better than anyone else's I'm looking at for the same position. But my fear is...you won't be happy here. I worry that you'll find the work beneath you. And no one gets a chance at making a specialty dessert without proving themselves in the trenches first."

"I'm happy to prove myself in the trenches," Ethan defended. "And I *completely* understand that I'll need to work my way up. But Ms. Cohen, there is no other bakery in the entire world known for their unique and inspired artisanal take on kosher baked goods. The stuff you come up with is genius. It's brilliant! Sure, I can go back to Paris, or Israel, or Los Angeles, study under some great pastry chefs. But I want to learn from the best. The best is right here in Brooklyn... with you."

He realized he was laying it on thick. But Ethan was desperate. Her terse tone and unfriendly demeanor told him that he was unlikely to get the position. He couldn't let that happen. He would do anything—say anything, too—to walk out of here knowing he got the job.

Avital considered his statement seriously. "You definitely have passion."

"I am *full* of passion."

"But what we *need*," she said, meeting his eyes directly, "is someone to help make pink boxes. Clean bathrooms. Mop floors. Yes, there's a chance that after a few months you can move up to the position of baker, or even design one of our weekly specialty desserts...but the majority of this job is going to be spent on support and custodial work."

Ethan met her decisiveness with a strong uptick of his chin. "That's my favorite type of work."

"It also requires standing on your feet for long hours at a time. As you can see, we get very busy here. Especially before Shabbat and holidays, but really...for anyone who works at Best Babka in Brooklyn, there's never a break. You'll come in early and you'll stay late as needed. We close early on Friday, and every Shabbat, and for all the Jewish holidays. We do a special event on Purim, though...for the neighborhood."

"I understand."

"We're also a kosher bakery," she said, still firmly determined to play devil's advocate, "which means that you can't bring any outside food into our store for meals. You are, however, welcome to eat whatever we make. And you're welcome to bring home any extra at the end of the week, as well. Do you have any questions for me?"

"When can I begin?"

Avital didn't crack. "I have a few more people to interview."

It was not what he was hoping to hear.

Still, he was determined to win her over. He needed this job. His grandfather was depending on him. Opening the door to the office, Avital began ushering him out.

It was then that he smelled it. Beneath the scent of butter and fresh baked challah was something distinctly pleasant. And feminine. It took Ethan a few moments to place it, and then he remembered. *Cherry Blossoms.* She smelled like cherry blossoms. Standing so close to Avital, breathing her in, Ethan was instantly transported back to Kyoto and the trip he had taken to Japan during his first year of boarding school. He forgot who he was, melting completely.

Avital led him back through the front entrance. "Thank you—"

"I'm sorry," Ethan interrupted her, "are you wearing perfume?"

"What?"

"It's just..." Ethan said as he blushed "...you smell kind of like cherries."

Her face scrunched up around her nose. Her eyes narrowed. Picking up one of those pink boxes filled with ready-made babka, she slammed it into a brown paper bag, before holding it out to him like a bar mitzvah party favor. "Thank you for coming in today. Feel free to take one of our world-famous pumpkin-spiced babkas with you on the way out."

"Thank—"

Ethan didn't have to finish the thought. Avital disappeared down the hall.

Shaking it off, Ethan headed for the exit. Emerging from the bakery, he found the gray winter skies now shifting into hues of pink, and the line in front of Best Babka nearly cleared out.

In its place, families had appeared. Rushing past him loaded down with bags, pushing baby carriages, they made their way home to prepare for Shabbat. Across the street from him stood the empty store once known as Greatest Babka in Brooklyn.

Old newspaper clippings covered the front windows. A large lock and chain secured the entrance. He could just make out the lettering of the name above the first floor, now faded from so many years of neglect.

It had been his grandfather's store.

Fifty years ago, Moishe Lippmann had bought the building after his partner, Chayim Cohen, had kicked him out of their dual ownership in Best Babka in Brooklyn. Perhaps it was not the wisest idea to build a kosher bakery, whose specialty was babka, across the street from his ex-partner, but Moishe had had no choice.

He had a wife and small daughter at home to support. Besides, Moishe figured being across the street from his main competitor was the equivalent of selling umbrellas in a rainstorm. People were coming for babka, anyway... It was the type of savvy thinking that, eventually, made his grandfather a billionaire.

It was also the beginning of a rivalry that would encompass three generations.

A winter wind brought Ethan back to his senses. Checking to make sure that the coast was clear, he did a quick dip around the corner and down three blocks to where Moishe, his grandfather, was waiting for him in a black limousine.

THREE

Avital was hiding in her main office.

Laying her head on her desk, the stack of résumés piled up like a pillow beneath her forehead, she couldn't stop obsessing about Ethan Rosenberg. He was super hot, overqualified…and he had just called her out for smelling like a toilet.

Maybe she was being ridiculous. Maybe the whole cherry comment was meant to be a compliment. Perhaps it had nothing to do with the oodles of cherry potpourri and cherry-scented hand soap her mother stockpiled the bathrooms with at Best Babka.

The remark—*along with the man*—had triggered her very deepest fears. She would never find love, she would never be normal, because she couldn't have sex.

Opening a drawer, she pulled out a plastic food-storage bag before heading to the small fridge-and-freezer combo she kept in her office. Filling it with ice, she returned to her chair, laying down a towel.

She glanced toward her door, which was closed, but unlocked. Normally, she would have the good sense to secure her privacy. Today, however, she was just too exhausted.

Bringing her attention back to her bag of ice, she placed it in the center of her chair. Then, she lifted her skirt, before taking a seat directly on top of it. The constant burning she always felt—the feeling of a fifty-pound bag of flour using her pelvic floor as a shelf—was now replaced by an icy stinging.

Placing her hands on her lower belly, she breathed deeply. Closing her eyes, she recalled a guided meditation she often did, focusing on opening her pelvic floor.

It wasn't working.

Outside her closed door, she could hear the voices of the staff dwindling as they shut down and closed up early for Shabbat. She knew she should get up, help her Best Babka family with closing. She knew she should check on Ethan Rosenberg's references, too—but her pain was at an all-time high. In the process of simply surviving, she wasn't giving her best self to anyone.

An email pinged its arrival on her screen. Avital opened her eyes and, sitting up, angled her body toward the desktop. She was expecting to find a note from Josh about reordering supplies. Instead, she found an email from Kallen Art Gallery.

Her heart pounded against her chest. Avital inched her fingers toward that email, opening it up.

Dear Avital Cohen,

Thank you for sending us your submission, LA Voices. While we see merit in your work and particularly liked your strong use of lighting throughout your photography, we unfortunately have to be extremely selective in who we choose for our gallery. At this time, we will not be pursuing a relationship with you.

Pamela Jones-Reznick

Acquisitions Director, Kallen Art Gallery

Her stomach roiled. Rejected, *again*. The sadness she had bitten back all day now had ample ammunition to surface.

All Avital had ever wanted to be was a photographer. But ever since developing chronic pain, her well of artistic inspiration had run dry.

Returning to the email, she analyzed every word of it. She read it over and over, until the bag of ice she was sitting on began melting.

It was clearly a form letter. But even though it had come with a compliment, she couldn't help but focus on one line. *At this time, we will not be pursuing a relationship with you.*

It felt like a much grander statement on her life.

Avital thought back to the photos she had sent as part of her submission. She couldn't really blame Pamela for rejecting her. Avital wasn't sending out her best or latest work. She was simply rehashing old stuff, sending out photographs that she had taken for fun and practice while living in Los Angeles. There was nothing about her images that screamed *art*. They didn't have a cohesive voice or central theme, all things acquisitions directors looked for when choosing to display new talent.

She had considered taking new photographs, but she had run into a few problems. For one, her camera was broken. She had damaged the power button on it during her cross-country move from California to New York. She also had no idea what to take pictures of. Maybe it was because she had been born and raised in Brooklyn, but everything in her life felt *so* familiar—the bakery, her family, the dreadful New York winters. Nothing seemed to move or inspire her. Because everything in her life was buried under the relentlessness of chronic pain.

Instead, she sent out her old stuff. She spent whatever little money she had left after medical care and high deductibles to afford high-gloss paper and pay for postage. And she did it, over and over again—racking up seventy-six rejections in the process—out of some desperate, frantic need to hold on to the past.

To hold on to some semblance of who she was before chronic pain changed everything.

Closing the email, she made her way over to the Best Babka Instagram account. Scanning the photos, she came to this week's specialty item, developed by Josh. It was tahini challah, which when pulled apart, oozed rich hazelnut halvah. It had three thousand comments. Avital scanned the most recent ones.

OMG. NEED!

When are we going to be able to order pumpkin-spiced babka online?

Do you ship?

How much for shipping?

TAKE MY FIRSTBORN CHILD!

At least people on social media liked her photographs.

Avital turned off the comments in preparation for Shabbat. Working at Best Babka had never been her dream, but she was proud that her business savvy had developed growing opportunities for both her family and the people of her community. Glancing over to the stack of applications sitting on her desk, her mind wandered back to Ethan Rosenberg. They desperately needed help—and frankly, more space—if they ever wanted to expand into the online world of shipping baked goods across the globe.

Not that anyone in her family was really thrilled with the idea of expanding.

Part of what made Best Babka so special was their artisanal and homemade take on traditional items. Expanding into shipping, into online goods and services, meant taking the thing that made them unique—and their personal values as a family regarding the food they baked for other people—and shoving their recipes full of stabilizers and preservatives.

Plus, they were all so swamped with what they currently had on their plate—lines out the door, eager online fans, and a very real lack of space and help in the back kitchen—that most of them couldn't bear the thought of adding one more to-do on to their already overloaded schedule.

Still, Avital couldn't help but think about the empty storefront across the street. The one that had once belonged to Greatest Babka in Brooklyn—and Moishe Lippmann—before he had gone off and become a zillionaire by doing the very thing that Avital was considering. It would be the perfect location to begin experimenting with expanding their business. She could already envision the lines of perfect pink boxes, tiny logo stickers, and shipping labels, filling the empty space.

Unfortunately, even if Moishe Lippmann were willing to sell to them, she would have to convince her brother. He was her fifty-fifty partner after their parents had handed the business over to them when they'd retired.

A knock on the door drew her attention back to reality.

JEAN MELTZER

"Who is it?" Avital called out.

Josh opened the door. Peeking his head through the threshold, he kept one hand on his knitted *kippah* in order to keep it from falling off. Like Avital, he was five foot seven. Unlike her, he was pudgy. And bald. The front of his forehead, once loaded with thin blond hair, was now a landing strip of pink.

For this reason, her brother was often overlooked by women. He was average in the looks department. Average in his dreams. Average in his career goals. But Josh had the biggest and best heart.

"You okay?" he asked.

Avital thought about the half-melted ice she was sitting on. "Not really."

She gave him a brief rundown of the afternoon's events. Her pain. Her epic disaster of an interview with Ethan Rosenberg. Her rejection from Kallen Art Gallery. Josh pursed his lips, taking it all in. Maybe he didn't share her hurt directly, but he always empathized with her.

"What can I do to help?" he asked seriously.

"Remind me that it gets better."

He met her eyes directly. "It gets better," he said. "It always gets better."

Avital nodded.

There were days where she still couldn't believe this was reality. She had never heard of chronic pelvic pain before she began to experience it. No one ever warned her, or told her, that vaginas—and their corresponding parts—could simply stop functioning. She was a young woman, reasonably healthy, in the prime of her life.

Indeed, for most of her life, Avital had been completely normal. Aside from painful cramps, and some truly terrible mood swings during her cycle, she managed. She did what all

34

women with dysmenorrhea did: kept a stockpile of NSAIDs, heating pads, and emergency chocolate in her bedroom.

But then, one morning while working her first big-girl job as an assistant photo editor at the *Los Angeles Times*, she woke up to what she felt was a urinary tract infection. Eight rounds of antibiotics and three specialists later, she knew whatever was going on was not some simple UTI. Her journey with chronic pelvic pain had begun.

Avital spent the next year maneuvering through the medical system. Yet, every doctor she saw seemed to have a different diagnosis. There was endometriosis, fibroids, ovarian cysts. Some called it vulvodynia or pelvic-floor dysfunction. Some regaled her with theories regarding embedded infections and chronic UTIs. Eventually, those same doctors offered up treatments. Painkillers that made her groggy. Hormones that put her into chemical menopause. Transvaginal ultrasounds and MRIs. Surgery.

She got used to lying on her back, her feet wedged into stirrups. She got used to disappearing into the ceiling while doctors poked and prodded. That was the funny thing about chronic pain. It didn't disconnect her from her body. Instead, it made every single second of her life about her body. She couldn't escape the never-ending reminders of her pain if she tried.

But oh, how she tried.

She was stricter than a rabbi when it came to staying on the IC diet, and drinking alkaline water, the somewhat disputed method of consuming only low-acid foods and drinks recommended by her urogynecologist.

She meditated regularly and sat on tennis balls during yoga classes aimed at pelvic health. When that didn't work, she consumed hundreds of dollars a month in all-natural but completely untested supplements. Marshmallow root. Aloe vera pills. Vaginal probiotics. At one point, thanks to advice of some online medical experts, she even tried ozone therapy. For three hundred dollars a pop, after insurance, a doctor blew air straight up her hoo hah.

Like many folks dealing with the onset of chronic illness, she had hope—this great and unfettered optimism—that she would one day wake up normal again if she could just find the right treatment.

There was no cure. While some of the treatments helped, nothing completely eradicated the constant ache she lived with. There were bad days and better days, but rarely did she experience pain-free days.

Despite all her best efforts to win the war against her own failing body—despite the fact that she was trying not to make her disease her identity—she kept getting worse. Some nights, the fear that accompanied the realization that nothing she did was working was more awful than the pain itself.

"Come on," Josh said, patting her on the back supportively. "I'll give you a ride to Mom and Dad's for Shabbat."

"What about closing up?"

"All handled." He smiled, gathering up her bags for her. "Nothing left to worry about."

Avital sucked back tears. She was so grateful for the love and support of her family. She was so grateful that her twin had a sixth sense about her pain and went out of his way to help her.

Feeling relieved that the cash register had been emptied and the counters wiped down by someone other than her, she rose from her seat. The half-melted ice bag slid down her legs and onto the floor. It landed with a loud *kerplop* between her leather Birkenstocks before jiggling like Jell-O in front of her feet.

"You know what—" Josh said, after a thoughtful moment "—I'm just gonna let you pick that up."

Avital couldn't help herself.

For the first time all day, she laughed.

FOUR

Ethan slid down into the back seat of the limousine. Moishe Lippmann—founder and CEO of Lippmann's Baked Goods—fixed Ethan with an unhappy scowl.

"Well?" Moishe said, the words curling between his teeth. "How did it go?"

"Great," Ethan lied.

Moishe was eighty-six years old and as set in his ways as the many wrinkles that lined his face. It was odd that Moishe had insisted on accompanying Ethan to his job interview at Best Babka.

The old man rarely left the sixteen-bedroom estate where Ethan and his younger brother—along with a full-time staff—lived. In recent years, his health had been failing. Ethan's grandfather, who had once seemed an immovable force in his youth, now needed to walk with a cane. He took blood-pressure medication and had developed adult asthma.

Moishe called over his shoulder, "Take us home."

Stephen, their driver, responded, "Yes, sir."

As the car started off, Moishe raised the privacy divider between them and Stephen. His grandfather had that strange glint in his eye again. It was the same twinkle that had appeared when Moishe had first approached Ethan with his mission.

"And what about Chayim?" Moishe asked.

"I interviewed with the granddaughter."

Ethan wasn't sure why he called her *the granddaughter*. But he felt the need to place some emotional distance between himself and Avital.

"I don't care about the granddaughter," Moishe spat back. "I want to know about Chayim! Is he old? Is his skin covered in shingles and pockmarks? Does he smell like eucalyptus sucking candies and rotting adult diapers? Tell me, Ethan! I want to hear that the disloyal bastard is spending his last days crying into his pumpkin-spiced batter!"

Ethan, like always with his grandfather, worked to keep his true feelings hidden behind a frozen facade.

The drive from Best Babka to the Lippmann family compound in Westchester normally took an hour. Unfortunately for Ethan, it was Friday. Traffic out of the city was at a standstill.

There were about ten million things Ethan would have preferred to be doing right now. Queuing at the DMV. Filing tax returns. A colonoscopy without anesthesia. Instead, he was stuck spending quality time with his grandfather.

"I don't believe I met him," Ethan said flatly.

Moishe grumbled. "And the job... When do you start?"

"She said she'll make her decision shortly."

"So you didn't get it?"

Ethan knew he needed to tread carefully. "I'm certain I will get the job, Grandpa."

"I'm certain you'll be a giant disappointment."

Ethan felt a stab but said nothing.

Ethan had been a part of Lippmann's since he was fourteen years old, when upon his return from boarding school, Moishe had announced that he would be spending his summers working as an intern at Lippmann's corporate headquarters in Manhattan.

Whether or not Ethan had any personal interest in taking over the family business was irrelevant. His grandfather was the legal guardian of Ethan and his two siblings, Randy and Kayla. Ethan had to obey. It was a trajectory that had followed him his whole life.

As a young man, Ethan continued to do everything his grandfather demanded of him. He went to undergrad at NYU Stern and got his master's in business from Wharton. He didn't play sports or have hobbies or see friends. All of that, Moishe had informed him early on, was irrelevant. He didn't get paid a salary. Instead, all his money was tied up in Moishe's assets.

But Ethan—as his grandfather constantly reminded him— was well provided for. He wanted for nothing. He had access to credit cards with no defined limits. He had a full-time house staff that met every one of his whims. And yet, it was a life of luxury that he never wanted.

The day Ethan lost his parents was the worst day of his life. The five of them had been vacationing at their lake house upstate. At the time, he was twelve years old, and the plan was for Ethan to return to the city in order to meet with his bar mitzvah tutor.

He didn't want to go back to the city to study boring Hebrew. He was having fun, playing in the lake, hanging out with friends. He threw a fuss. He kicked and screamed— running away to hide with Randy—before, finally, his parents gave up. They made the executive decision to leave Ethan and his younger brother behind with a nanny while they went into the city for the day.

It was still hard to believe what had happened to them.

His father had his pilot's license. He was a reasonably experienced flyer. But for some reason—some random event Ethan would never understand—weather conditions shifted. His dad lost control of the plane. They crashed shortly after takeoff into a wooded area. Kayla was the only one to survive.

After his parents' deaths and Kayla's injury, Ethan tried to make sense of what happened. He spent hours scanning pages of the Torah, looking for some explanation from the universe. When that didn't work, he turned to science. He went on the internet. He found statistics on small-plane crashes and learned that the odds of dying in one were one in ten thousand. But even then, why his family?

Ethan couldn't bring back his parents. He couldn't take back the traumatic brain injury that Kayla had woken up from the accident with. But after the crash, Ethan felt guilty. *He should have been on that plane. He should have died alongside them.*

He knew it wasn't a rational thought. But the guilt took root inside him and without anyone there to help him navigate his feelings in a safe manner, it began to grow.

Somehow, it was his fault his parents had died. It was his fault that Kayla was permanently disabled. He became obsessed with the idea that he needed to be good. As if success and obedience could absolve him of the crime of surviving.

But mainly, and though he loathed himself for indulging in such sentimentalities, what he really wanted was Moishe's love and approval. As if winning over Moishe, turning him into a grandfather who would accept him, would mean that he was worthy of the life that had been granted to him in his parents' stead.

"What's that?" his grandfather said, pointing to the brown bag sitting at Ethan's side.

"Oh." Ethan picked it up. "It's from Best Babka. It's their pumpkin-spiced babka. Apparently, you get it as a parting gift after an interview."

Moishe waved his wrinkled fingers at Ethan. "Let me see."

Ethan handed him the bag. Moishe reached inside and, finding the pink box, opened it up and tore off a piece of babka. Thick layers of oozing chocolate dripped onto his hands, while tiny crumbles of sugar and cinnamon and babka dough fell around his lap and seat. Moishe took a bite of the babka and after a few moments of chewing, quickly declared it the worst thing in the world.

"Blech!" Moishe shouted, spitting the masticated bit of babka in a clump on the limousine floor. "Disgusting! People eat this stuff?"

"It seems so."

Moishe tossed the bag back to Ethan. "Did you try it yet?"

"No."

"Try it," Moishe ordered. "Tell me what you think."

Reaching into the bag, Ethan took a bite. A rush of sensations, sweet and delicious, found their way to the forefront of his taste buds. His entire body zinged with pleasure. His soul lifted. His mind wandered into the strangest hallucinations: fluffy clouds made of chocolate-and-cinnamon, and a rainbow appeared, and at the end, there was a pot full of pink boxes.

No wonder their pumpkin-spiced babka was causing folks to form lines around the block.

The stuff was addicting.

"Well?" Moishe grumbled. "What do you think?"

Ethan lied, "It's terrible."

Still, the knowledge that he likely did not get the job was weighing on him. Ethan ran one hand through his hair. For the next part, he needed to tread carefully. "I was wondering if you had a chance to look at the proposal I left you last week."

"What proposal?"

"I left it with Stella." Surely his grandfather's executive assistant had passed it along.

"I read it," his grandfather grumbled.

"So you know that Healthy Farms Brands is interested in creating a new line with us."

"What are you trying to say, Ethan?"

"I'm just wondering if a recipe for pumpkin-spiced babka is the best option for rebranding our company going forward. Perhaps what our company needs, beyond corporate espionage—"

The words were enough to open the floodgate. "What our company needs?" Moishe spat out. "Tell me, Ethan, how could you possibly know what *my* company needs?"

"If you would just look at the projected numbers—"

"You," his grandfather continued, "who have disappointed me your entire life. You, who have never once lived up to the expectations I have placed on you. I sent you to the best schools. I gave you the best of everything. I took you in... when nobody else wanted you. And how do you repay me?"

Ethan said nothing in his own defense. He was used to his grandfather just losing it on him. He'd lost count of all the terrible things he had heard from the older man over the years. Getting beat on emotionally by Moishe was par for the course, as expected as the sun rising each morning. Perhaps it had been different with his mom and dad...but if it was, he didn't remember it.

All his memories of gentle kisses and soft words had been replaced by Moishe's shouting.

"You're afraid," Moishe huffed. "You would rather be a

nothing than take care of your family. And what about me, Ethan? You think I like it? Having an embarrassment as my eldest grandson? Taking care of your useless, druggie brother? Paying for your sister's exorbitant twenty-four-hour care? When it should have been you! It should have been you that died on that plane! Somedays I wish it were—"

His grandfather started coughing. Ethan moved to his side, helping Moishe pull his inhaler from his pocket. His hands were thin and shaky. Combined with the movement of the car, he was having trouble getting it into his mouth.

"Here," Ethan said, gently guiding the inhaler to his lips. Moishe took three deep puffs. Soon, he was back to breathing normally.

"You need to stop getting yourself so worked up," Ethan said.

"Don't tell me what to do," Moishe snapped at him.

"It's not me," Ethan reminded him. "It's your doctors."

"Those doctors are useless," Moishe said. "Besides, this is all Chayim's fault. He's still trying to kill me after all these years. You know, he never once…*not once*…called me after Lilly died."

Ethan had always wondered if his childhood would have been different if his grandmother hadn't died before Moishe took them in. He remembered bits and pieces of his *bubbe*, as she often came to their home in Manhattan and their lake house upstate to visit them. He remembered that she was all warmth and energy, and that his grandfather adored her.

But the loss of both his wife and his daughter had shaped Moishe. It had hardened him, too. He lashed out at everyone around him. Ethan, Randy, their staff…but he reserved his most vehement hatred for Chayim Cohen. In their household, his status as their enemy had become mythic.

"And your mother!" Moishe continued, shaking his head.

"He couldn't even bother to send a shiva platter when she died. When he had held her, rocked my own baby girl in his arms when we were both working at Best Babka together. He knew her, Ethan. You understand? He knew them both."

"I understand, Grandpa."

"No," Moishe said, growing more agitated. "What he sent me were lawsuits and fifty years of harassment. Tell me that doesn't deserve retribution. Tell me that the Cohen family doesn't deserve to suffer, like they've made us suffer, after all these years."

Ethan handed the inhaler back to his grandfather. "Either way, you don't need to worry…because I have it handled, okay?"

Moishe waved at Ethan dismissively. Ethan returned to his seat, and the limo fell into silence. Glancing out the window, he watched as the traffic of the city morphed into lush trees. In the distance, perched high on a hill, loomed the Lippmann family compound.

The huge estate overlooking the water had once belonged to a robber baron. The house had sat in disrepair for decades, until Moishe Lippmann arrived and bought the property. From there, his grandfather spared no expense turning it into the epicenter of Lippmann family life.

"You going to see Kayla tonight?" Moishe asked.

"It's Friday," Ethan said.

Moishe grumbled. "You spend too much time at that place."

The limo pulled up to two golden gates. Ethan felt his stomach turn. The gates swung open slowly, and the car proceeded its trek up a long path. He was home. The place where he and his brother had taken refuge after their parents had died.

But it never quite felt that way.

FIVE

One of the nicest parts about moving back home was Shabbat dinner on Friday evening. Sitting down at the dining-room table in her parents' house, across from her brother, Avital waited for her mother to finish ladling a heaping bowl of chicken soup from a large ceramic tureen.

For most of the week, Avital and Josh were in charge of food at the bakery. That all changed on Friday evening, when their mother—who had retired two years earlier alongside their father—insisted on cooking and serving the traditional Sabbath meal while Josh and Avital rested.

At the end of the table, and as patriarch of the Cohen family, sat Chayim Cohen. A white satin *kippah* dangled precipitously upon his head as he dug his spoon into a bowl of soup. Beside him, her father, Paul, was still buried in his prayer book, analyzing some line he had landed on.

"Margie," her father suddenly called, "can I help you in the kitchen?"

A resounding *no* exploded from everybody in the room. Her father shrugged his shoulders. "Suit yourself."

Avital breathed a sigh of relief. It was the strangest curse of her family. While the Cohen men had all seemed to inherit some extraordinary gift for baking, they had none of those same skills when cooking dinner. Her father was particularly terrible. He burned water. He oversalted all the rest. He had 210 different recipes for baked chicken that all tasted exactly the same.

"Avital—" Grandma Rose poked her head out of the kitchen "—did your grandfather drink his Ensure?"

Avital glanced over to her grandfather. Not surprising, his glass of red wine was nearly empty. The bottle of meal replacement he was supposed to be drinking—the one the doctor had said he needed to start consuming to keep his weight up—was still sitting untouched beside his bowl of soup.

Avital frowned. "I don't think so."

Grandma Rose threw down her dish towel and huffed her way over to the dining table. "Chayim," she said, shaking the untouched bottle to confirm for herself, "this happens every week. You start with the soup…and then you're not hungry for dinner. You need to drink two of these, two of these a day."

"I'm drinking, I'm drinking."

"You're not drinking."

Her grandfather took another bite of his soup. Avital couldn't be sure if her *zeyde* was playing at having a senior moment or simply ignoring her grandmother. She settled on the latter because almost as soon as she turned toward the kitchen, Chayim grabbed her hand. "Rosie, Rosie," he said, smiling in her direction. "Has anyone ever told you…you are the most beautiful woman on the planet?"

Even after fifty-four years of marriage, her grandmother

was swayed by his charms. "I swear," she said, swatting him playfully with the towel, "you are the most stubborn man on this entire earth. An old and stubborn mule…that's what you are!"

"Rosie, Rosie," he said and smiled back, pulling her closer to him and looking to his family. "Just beautiful, isn't she?"

Avital smiled watching them. This was why she loved Shabbat dinner with her family. This was why, even when she was in pain, she did her best to attend *some* of the meal. She knew that moments like this, with her grandparents and her parents, would not be forever.

At only seventy-eight years old, her beloved *zeyde* was slowing down. It was a combination of prostate cancer— slow-growing, but still—and a bad heart. Of course, he wasn't at any risk of dying tomorrow, but he was not the same man who had turned Best Babka in Brooklyn into the flagship kosher bakery it was today.

Suddenly, Josh snickered at something on his phone.

Avital glared across the table at him. "Who are you talking to?"

"No one," he said, quickly finishing what he was doing and shoving his phone back into his pocket. "Just…a friend."

Avital did not believe him.

While they weren't the most observant family in the whole world, they were traditional. They kept Shabbat and observed all major Jewish holidays, centering their lives around the lunar calendar. But despite running a kosher bakery and having gone to Jewish day school, both Avital and Josh used their phones, traveled, and watched television on Shabbat.

"Avi—" her grandfather waved one wrinkled hand down the length of the table "—pass me some challah."

Avital reached for the challah plate, where three different flavors of the traditional braided bread were now displayed.

They always had a plethora of baked goods left over from the store on Friday evening.

"Dill, cinnamon, or raisin?" Avital asked.

"Cinnamon," he said.

"Chayim." Grandma Rose peeked her head out of the kitchen. "You don't want cinnamon challah in your soup! Avi...pass him the dill."

"I want it," he insisted over and over, waving toward Avi. "I want it!"

"It doesn't go together, you ninny!" Rose shouted.

"Aaah!" he said, waving her off, "I know what I want, Rosie."

Her grandmother rolled her eyes and plopped down into the seat beside him. Avital took that as her cue. Ripping off a chunk of the cinnamon-swirl challah, she handed it to the old man. Digging it into his bowl, allowing it to slurp up a generous portion of soup and become soggy, he lifted the combination into his mouth. All at once, the white in his skin turned an off-color shade of green.

"Well?" her grandmother asked.

"It's not very good."

Grandma Rose sighed. "Let me get you a new bowl."

"Let me." Avital quickly rose to her feet. She was looking for a reason to stand up. Sitting, waiting for her mother to finish heating up the brisket, was causing all the muscles in her pelvic floor to ache. Taking the bowl and heading into the tiny kitchen beside her mother, she dumped her grandfather's cinnamon-chicken soup into the sink.

"Oh, Avi," her mother said upon seeing her. "I'm glad you're here." She turned to a smaller bowl of soup, sitting beside the larger one. "Now, this bowl...this bowl only has broth in it. No pepper or onion, okay?"

No taste, either. Avital couldn't help but think it. Still, she smiled, grateful that her mother, so thoughtful and doting, always went out of her way to cook IC-safe food for her.

Ever since Avital had been diagnosed with IC, she was supposed to be on a specialized diet. It basically eliminated anything that could be acidic or problematic for her already-damaged bladder lining. There were things that were obvious on the list, of course. Tomatoes. Wine. Chocolate and processed foods. But there were things that were less obvious, too. Onions. Sesame seeds. Hell, at the worst of her flares, she couldn't even tolerate spinach.

It honestly made no sense.

Who couldn't eat spinach?

The only thing Avital knew for certain about her broken body was this: she was used to being hungry. In the span of six months, she had gone from being a relatively *zaftig* Jewish girl to bordering on underweight.

Avital glanced back at the table where Chayim was waiting. "Maybe I'm the one who should be drinking Ensure?"

"Do you think you can handle it?" her mother asked hopefully.

Avital grimaced. "Definitely not."

Sympathetic, her mother laid a hand comfortingly on her rail-thin arm. "Well," she said, trying to sound positive, "don't you worry. I made you lots and lots of IC-safe foods to eat tonight. Enough for the whole week, too."

Avital nodded, gratefully. "Thanks, Mom."

And truly, she meant it.

It was so hard to manage chronic illness alone. She relied on her family to be her caregiver, to support her financially, to keep her fighting. But despite their constant, never-wavering support, there was always this fear tucked away, deep inside of her. What would she do as the years passed and she had to find ways to manage her long-term disability alone?

"Mom," Avital said, "I love you."

"Oh, honey," her mother said and squeezed her arm again, "I love you, too! We all love you. Now, go sit down! Let me be your mother and dote on my two little babies…just a little bit longer in my life."

Avital smiled. "Okay."

Finally, with soup served, and re-served, all around the table, the entire family sat down.

"So," her father said, digging into a chunk of boiled onion, "how did it go this week?"

"Pretty good," Josh said and began regaling them all with an update.

It was the usual types of stories. Avital told them about Mrs. Grossman, arriving like clockwork on Tuesday to complain about whatever she ordered the previous week. Josh gave them an update on the staff. But when the conversation veered toward the lines out the door earlier this afternoon, Avital felt the frustration in her gut growing.

"We really need more space," Avital spat out without thinking.

Josh stopped eating, his empty spoon lingering midair, between his bowl and his mouth. "You just finished interviewing prospective candidates today," Josh reminded her. "That will take some of the burden off—"

Her mother beamed. "How wonderful!"

"See anyone you like?" her father asked.

"There was a really interesting character who came in this afternoon, actually," Josh said, oblivious to the ire rising in her belly. "I think Avital was actually blushing when he came in."

"Oh, really?" Her grandmother's head was on a spigot between them. "Is he Jewish?"

"He looks Jewish," Josh said casually.

"You can't look Jewish," Avital said, annoyed.

"Of course you can look Jewish," her grandfather suddenly chimed in. "I look Jewish. Avital looks Jewish. Everybody Jewish...looks Jewish." He took another bite of his soup. "There! Argument resolved."

While the family continued debating looking Jewish, Avital shook her head. It was so unfair. She was the general manager of Best Babka in Brooklyn. She knew, better than Josh, better than her parents, exactly what their small family business needed. And then, finally—also, likely, because she was starving, eating bland broth, and still in pain—she snapped.

"It's not enough!" Avital said.

The entire table quieted.

"Avi," her father warned.

"No," she said, tossing down her spoon. "It's not enough, Josh! We have lines out the door. We have over a million followers on Instagram. Every day I am inundated...*inundated*... with messages about online orders. We are standing on the precipice of what could be a Cohen family baked-goods gold mine...and all you can think about is hiring extra counter help!"

"Because you just don't get it!" Josh said. "You've never gotten it, Avi." Josh threw the battle over to his father. "Come on, Dad, help me out here. You can't possibly agree with her."

Thankfully, Josh's efforts to enlist his father's help were all for naught. Once her parents had officially signed over Best Babka to their children, they made the wise decision to remain safely out of all business conflicts between them. Throwing his hands in the air in open surrender, her father made the motion of zipping his lips shut, before allowing them to continue without his help. Avital took the opening.

"If we could just think about expanding..."

"Every week," Josh groaned, throwing his head backward.

"We have the opportunity to do something really great

here," Avital defended. "We have the ability to make sure our products are on every shelf in every grocery store in America. Hell, maybe even the world."

"Careful, Avi," her mother said.

Avital glanced at her grandfather before whispering, "We just need...to talk to the man."

The building across the street. The building that belonged to their grandfather's archenemy. Avital knew that if they bought it, they could turn it into the epicenter of a thriving online business, shifting their small family-run company into an empire.

There were two major problems, of course. The first was that Moishe Lippmann would never, in a million years, sell it to them. Indeed, the man had left the storefront empty for over fifty years—with the words *Greatest Babka in Brooklyn* still emblazoned on the front—in order to mess with them.

But the main reason she couldn't even begin to draft up a business plan for a potential sale was far more simple. Josh— the other totally unreasonable and annoying half of their equal partnership—simply wouldn't hear of it.

"That building costs millions of dollars, Avi."

"We will make it back in sales."

"And what will we risk in the process, huh?" he said. "The business, the house, everything Grandpa and the family have built for five generations? Expanding means changing what makes us unique. It means stuffing our products full of preservatives, creating them on assembly lines...baking without passion, without love!"

"But we haven't even spoke to Moishe Lippmann."

Almost as soon as the words escaped her lips, she regretted them. Her father groaned, collapsing into both hands. Her mother rose from her seat, panic spreading over her round cheeks. Because Chayim Cohen, patriarch of the Cohen family, creator of the world-famous Best Babka in Brooklyn, could not hear that name without completely freaking out.

All reason flew out the window. No one could stop him now, as a bevy of torrid insults, wrapped up alongside decades of bad blood between them, exploded from his mouth.

"Moishe Lippmann!" his grandfather said, slamming his hand down on the table. "Moishe—that crook—Lippmann!"

"Chayim," her grandmother said cautiously, "please."

"Where are his pills?" her mother said.

"I think in the blue bag."

With that, her mother, father, and *bubbe* were scrambling through the house, looking for his heart medication.

"Do you know why that man never liked me?" Chayim said, continuing his rant. "You know why he's spent his whole life, going out of his way, to try to one-up me in every endeavor? Because I was a Cohen! Ever since Rosh Hashanah 1956—when the rabbi called me up to the bimah to do the blessing of the Cohenim—he's been jealous of me. That man could never accept being a Levi."

"Great," Josh said, throwing his arms up. "Just great! Way to ruin Shabbat dinner, Avi."

"Oh, screw you," Avital snapped back, before both she and Josh were racing to sit beside her grandfather at the table. "Please, *Zeyde*," Avital pleaded with the old man, stroking his arm and head like a small child. "Please don't get upset. We were just talking, okay?"

It was no use. Chayim continued rambling, tears forming in the corners of his eyes. "His whole life," he repeated. "Always trying to one-up me. Building that bakery across the street. Stealing my business. The Purim carnival!"

"Here." Her mother returned from the bathroom. "Here, Chayim," she said as she grabbed a glass of water, "take this."

With a little more pleading and prodding from the entire

Cohen family, Chayim eventually swallowed the pill. Avital counted the seconds. A few more tense minutes passed. Then, acting as if nothing was wrong, Chayim returned to slurping his soup. Any chance of veering into a Shabbat disaster had, thankfully, been averted.

"So," her mother said, fanning the sweat from her chest and brow, "who's ready for brisket?"

SIX

Ethan wasted no time escaping the clutches of his grandfather. Holding the paper bag of half-eaten babka in his hand, he raced up the grand staircase, toward his bedroom on the second floor. The residence he shared with his little brother, Randy, was in the corner wing of the house—on the opposite side of the compound from his grandfather.

Throwing open the door, he was greeted by a four-poster bed. On the wall, an oil painting of a man and his hound hunting stared back at him. Across from both, a heavy oak dresser—which had once belonged to Napoleon Bonaparte himself—loomed. The traditional style was not to Ethan's personal taste, but his grandfather had chosen the decor.

Ethan tossed that bag of half-eaten pumpkin-spiced babka onto his bed and set about changing into something more comfortable. Then he settled on finding his younger brother. It wasn't hard. Making his way down the hallway, he could smell Randy long before he ever reached his door.

Even though Randolph was not supposed to smoke bud in the house, his constant devotion to the green herb meant that he always reeked of weed. It infiltrated his clothing, his hair, his bedding...and from there, announced his arrival to everyone in a one-hundred-yard radius.

Ethan came to his bedroom door. Like always, it was closed. A trail of neon light peeked out from beneath. Ethan knocked on the door.

"What?" Randy shouted from behind it.

"It's me," Ethan said. "Can I come in?"

His brother did not answer him.

Freaking Randy.

Ethan opened the door anyways. It wasn't locked. *It was never locked.* Moishe had decided early on—for their protection, obviously—that the brothers shouldn't have locks on their doors. It made for more than one awkward situation growing up. But thankfully, Ethan—like his little brother—spent most of his youth in boarding school.

The primary difference being, while Ethan excelled—took first-place honors and stayed out of trouble—Randy was the opposite. By the time he was fifteen, Randolph Elijah Lippmann had been kicked out of, and funneled through, at least six different boarding schools. From there, he dropped out of college freshman year. Ethan was horrified. But his grandfather didn't bat an eyelash at having Randy return home.

"It's better this way," Moishe had told Ethan. "He'll be with the people who truly love him."

Entering Randy's room, his nostrils were assaulted by a cloud of putrid-smelling smoke. Ethan coughed, waving it away, trying to see through the haze. Finally, he found his little brother. Randy was sitting up on his bed, packing herb into a bong half the size of him.

"Duuude," Randy said without looking back. "Close the door! You know how Grandpa gets…"

Quickly, Ethan closed the door. Not that it would make much difference. His younger brother didn't seem to have one single talent in life except for when it came to cannabis. It wasn't just a hobby but a passion. He grew his own weed, converting a series of hydroponic planters he had bought off Amazon into a three-tiered shelving unit across the back windows, now covered in sheets, of his room.

The sight of those planters, lined up methodically and with such care, drove Ethan batty. If Randolph would just apply himself to something, anything, the way he did to cannabis, he would likely be a millionaire in his own right. Instead, he was the druggie loser of their messed-up family empire… with a serious failure to launch.

"What are you doing?" Ethan asked.

"What does it look like I'm doing?" Randy said, almost annoyed. "Research."

Ethan scoffed. "Research?"

"For my business," Randy said, taking a hit of the bong. The water inside the tube bubbled. "I'm doing a little R and R."

"R and D," Ethan corrected him. "The correct term is *Research and Development*."

"Yeah," Randy said, blowing out smoke in three perfect ringlets, "that, too."

Ethan waved another haze of skunky smoke away from his eyes. He was certain that just standing in this place, he was getting some sort of contact high.

"Randy!" Ethan said.

"What?"

"You can smell it down the hall, okay?" Ethan said, pointing toward his door. "Grandpa is gonna flip if—"

Randy interrupted him, "You're totally killing my high right now."

It was no use. Randy had never taken their grandfather, or his threats, seriously. But then again, Randy didn't live with the same pressures as Ethan.

"Besides," Randy said, eyes glazing over, "you know that Grandpa doesn't give a pumpkin crumble doughnut about me. You're the golden child, after all. You're the one who went to Wharton...heir to the Lippmann empire...most special and favorite grandchild destined to take over the family business. I'm just the spare in case something happens to you."

"You're not the spare."

"He literally calls me the Spare, Ethan."

Ethan chewed on his lower lip. His younger brother wasn't wrong.

"Look," Randy said, finally taking a moment off from getting high to formulate a point, "the old man is a tyrant, okay? You know it. I know it. Every single living thing in this house, from Freya to the... Wait, what was I saying again, man?"

"You were saying that every living thing in the house—"

"Oh, right," Randy interrupted him. "Everything living thing in this house—except you, apparently—knows one important fact about the great and mighty Moishe Lippmann."

"Oh yeah?" Ethan asked incredulously. "What's that?"

"There's no pleasing him, okay? He *likes* being disappointed in us. He *likes* being disappointed in *you* especially. Why do you think he's always threatening to throw us out while simultaneously forcing us to live in this big-ass and ugly monstrosity of a house? Because he's a control freak. The sooner you figure that out, the better."

"Grandpa has reasons for being the way he is," Ethan said.

"Yeah, yeah," Randy said, waving away Ethan's justifications. "Poor Grandpa was the child of Holocaust survivors who didn't know how to parent. Poor Grandpa was betrayed by his best friend and business partner, then lost his wife to cancer and his only daughter in a plane crash. And now, poor Grandpa is an abusive tyrant who makes everyone around him miserable. You know what I think, Ethan? I think poor Grandpa needs to go to therapy."

Randy huffed, annoyed. He was making fun of Ethan who had always understood Moishe's bad behavior as the by-product of transgenerational trauma.

Expulsion. Pogroms. The Holocaust. In every generation, some villain rose up, seeking to destroy them. And sometimes, the parents came home and—collapsing under all those generations of bloodshed, anti-Semitism, and disrupted family units—traumatized their children, too.

It was the dirty little secret of the Jewish world.

Abuse.

Beneath all those stories of picturesque Shabbat dinners, doting Jewish mothers, and high-education rates, the Jewish world had their own share of dysfunction. Ethan could still remember Kayla talking about the stickers left inside the women's restrooms at synagogue. The ones that gave women a number to call if they were experiencing domestic violence.

Still, Ethan tried to give Moishe some leeway. After all, he never hit them. Sure, he showed up randomly in their bedrooms in the middle of the night in order to berate them. He tore through the house, screaming and jumping up and down, occasionally breaking objects or throwing things. It was, to a twelve-year-old boy who weighed all of eighty-nine pounds, absolutely terrifying.

But like the old nursery rhyme about sticks and stones, names weren't supposed to hurt people. They weren't supposed to leave long-lasting scars, affecting your overall self-esteem along with your ability to bond and connect with others. Perhaps that was why Moishe felt so free in doling them out, and Ethan always found a way to forgive him.

"All I'm saying is," Ethan said, bending down to pick up Randy's dirty clothes and throwing them into a hamper, "Grandpa isn't all bad. He took us in when Mom and Dad died. He spent hundreds of thousands of dollars on Kayla's rehab and care—the best physical therapists, the best hospitals. He sent you to the best schools, too...before you messed it up. And he does love you, Randy. He loves all of us."

Randy put down his bong. "Do you really believe all that crap you're spewing?"

"Yes."

"Then, you must be higher than me," Randy said, taking another hit of his bong.

Ethan watched the bubbles rise up in his pipe. It was pointless talking to his little brother. Randy had nothing but anger and animosity when it came to their grandfather. Still, they were a family. Even though his parents were gone, he did his best to keep them a cohesive unit.

Ethan glanced down at his watch. "It's Friday. I'm going to go visit Kayla for Shabbat."

"So?"

"You wanna come?"

"Can't."

"Come on," he said, tapping Randy on the arm, trying to get him moving. "You haven't seen Kayla in over a month. She misses you, dude. Come out and see her."

"Dude!" Randy swiped his brother's hand away. "Can't you see I'm busy here? Besides, I've already got plans for Shabbat."

"Getting high alone in your room?"

"First off—" Randy put down his lighter "—this weed is totally kosher. Blessed by a rabbi and everything. Secondly, who are you to be so judgy about my Judaism?" He angled his lighter toward the metal apparatus on his purple bong. "*Bo-ee, Bo-ee*...come, my Shabbat Queen...in all your splendor."

Ethan knew that short of physically dragging his brother to the car, it was a lost cause. Randy was old enough to not only be stubborn, but fully dig his heels in.

Ethan knew the real reason Randy avoided visiting their big sister. It was the same reason his younger brother spent all his time getting high in his room alone. Going to see Kayla made what happened to them, the tragedy that changed their lives in an instant, real all over again.

They had never gone to therapy for that tragedy. The closest they had ever come to dealing with their emotions was coming back from the funeral, when Randy had started crying in the limo and Moishe had barked at him to knock it off.

"All right," Ethan said, heading for the door, "I'll tell Kayla you said hi."

Randy stopped him. "Wait."

Randy leaned over his bed frame, searching for something on the floor. After a few awkward minutes of grunting, he reappeared. In his hands, he held three empty Lippmann boxes.

"I saved these for Kayla," Randy said, offering them to him. "You can tell her they're from me...and I'll try to come next week, okay?"

Ethan took the boxes from his brother. "Thanks, man."

Randy nodded, before quickly escaping back into his bong. Ethan took the empty Lippmann's boxes and, after making his way back down the main staircase, found Stephen already waiting for him by the front door.

"Same place as usual, sir?" Stephen said, helping him into his coat.

"Yes," Ethan confirmed. "Thank you, Stephen."

Sure, Ethan's family wasn't perfect. They put the fun in dysfunctional and likely could have used a class on anger management. But like Randy saving up all those Lippmann's boxes for Kayla—or Ethan going undercover at Best Babka to help his grandfather—they were there for each other where it mattered. That was love, after all. That was family. And having already lost his parents to terrible circumstances, he was determined to hold on to them—no matter the cost.

SEVEN

With Shabbat dinner over—and her grandparents walked safely to their house one block away—Avital took refuge in her bedroom. Sitting at her desk, staring at the stack of résumés she had brought home with her from work, she felt terrible. It wasn't just her body that ached but her soul. She was missing something, broken. Like the Nikon camera with the malfunctioning button, sitting dusty and unused on the side of her desk.

She picked up the camera and examined it. She had worked an entire year straight, during college and in the campus cafeteria, to pay for that camera. And for what? A photography career that had gone nowhere. An office drawer full of rejections from the very worst galleries in the nation. She had returned home to live with her parents in the same bedroom she had inhabited in her childhood. And though she was grateful for the safety net her family lovingly provided in the development of chronic illness, she hated that bedroom.

Even though she had tried to reclaim the space by buying a new comforter and throwing out all her *chazarai* from high school, she still hated it. She hated the white furniture, purple carpet, and twin bed. She hated how it made her feel. Like a child. She lived at home, not by choice, not because she was saving up for some better adventure, but because chronic illness had robbed her of autonomy.

A knock on the door drew her attention.

"Yeah?" Avital called out.

"It's me," Josh said.

Avital glanced back to the lock on her door. "It's open," she said.

Josh pushed it open just a hair. "I'm heading out."

"Cool."

Unlike Avital, Josh shared an apartment with two friends in a trendier part of Brooklyn. Perhaps Avital would have liked to do the same, but all her extra income from the bakery went into medical care.

"Look," Josh said, stepping inside, "I don't want to fight with you, okay? And I do understand why you want to expand."

"It's fine, Josh."

"I just..." He huffed over the words. "It's not my dream for the bakery, okay?"

"I know."

Josh pursed his lips. They were more than just twins. They were best friends. But on this conflict, Avital knew that they would never see eye to eye.

The bakery had never been her dream. But Josh had always wanted to take over Best Babka. He had always wanted exactly what his parents had given them. A simple life, living a few blocks from where he worked, surrounded by friends and family. And there was nothing, absolutely nothing, wrong

65

with the life Josh wanted. It just didn't mesh particularly well with chronic illness.

For Avital, expanding meant making more money. Money represented safety. It meant being able to pay for your medicine when insurance suddenly denied you coverage. It meant living with less uncertainty. Money meant a higher quality of care, too. It was expensive to see the best specialists, eat the most wholesome and organic IC-safe foods, take all the supplements. Even her fancy alkaline water, which her doctors had told her to drink, cost three dollars a bottle.

Of course, money wouldn't cure her chronic pain. But she couldn't help but feel that having more of it would help level the playing field.

Josh stepped closer to her desk, leaning over her shoulder. "You checking out résumés?"

"Oh," she said, suddenly feeling caught, "yeah."

"Ethan Rosenberg," he read the name aloud. "Was that the good-looking guy who came in today?"

She pulled the résumé away from him. "He wasn't good-looking."

"Avi," Josh said, raising both eyebrows, "I'm straight as they come, but that dude was, objectively, really freaking good-looking."

Avital put his résumé back. "Good thing we're not hiring him for his looks."

"Good thing," Josh said, pulling it back out, scanning his credentials, "because Mr. Rosenberg might be more qualified than me. Le Beurre? Capitan in New York? They wouldn't even let me sweep the floor at those restaurants, let alone bake at them."

"He's overqualified."

Josh stared blankly. "I'm confused."

"This is primarily a custodial position. He'll be bored within a week."

"So what you're telling me," Josh asked curiously, "is we have a good-looking, overqualified person who wants to work at Best Babka for minimum wage...and we're not going to hire him because you've decided that he's too good to be true?"

Avital bit back her annoyance. It was more than that, obviously. It was this feeling, deep down inside herself. A feeling that had developed alongside her chronic pain. *Good things were meant for other people.*

Beyond her quarter-life existential crisis, there were practical matters to contend with. Namely, Avital was barely hanging on by a thread, as it were. She was falling behind on everything at Best Babka. Plus, her pain was getting worse. The last thing she needed right now was to hire Ethan Rosenberg—with his charming smile and his wellspring of passion—and have him quit on her the first day. She had lost her unbridled optimism right around the same time she had lost her faith.

Josh picked up the camera on her desk. Spinning it around in his hands, he analyzed the broken power button at the top.

"Avi," Josh said, handing it back to her, "don't give up on yourself, okay?"

Avital nodded. Message received, loud and clear.

EIGHT

Ethan arrived at Hebrew Home for Assisted Living later than he had intended. Swinging through the main doors, holding the three empty Lippmann's boxes in his hands, he came to the nurses' station. Unlike strangers to the facility where his sister lived, Ethan never had to sign in. He was a regular at this place. He came as often as physically possible, and everybody on staff knew him well.

"Hello, Ethan," Melinda, the nurse at the front desk, greeted him warmly.

"*Shabbat shalom,*" Ethan said, stopping to speak with her. "You're back?"

"I'm back!"

Melinda Shankman was small and thick, with large arms that matched the roundness in her cheeks when she smiled. Ethan had always considered her thick arms, along with her kindness, an occupational necessity. Over the years, they had found themselves having a friendly acquaintance.

"And with a tan?" Ethan couldn't help but notice. "I'm assuming Florida was good, then?"

"Beyond amazing," Melinda squealed before leaning over to whisper, "Plus, I met someone."

"Really?"

"Well, not in Florida," she said, blushing a little. "On the way to the airport."

Ethan was surprised to hear it. Melinda had been trying to find a love match on J-Mate for as long as he could remember. She had also regaled him with plenty of first-date horror stories. He was happy to hear that, finally, she had found someone worth her attention.

"Well, go on," Ethan said. "You can't start a story off like that and then leave me hanging."

"I don't know," she said, nervously shifting her weight onto the counter. "We only just met. I don't want to jinx it."

"All right," Ethan said. "I can respect that. And your sister and the new baby are good?"

"Oh my gosh." Melinda came further alive. "My little nephew is so cute."

Pulling out her phone, she quickly scrolled to the ten million photos she had taken of her sister's newborn. When she was done describing all the delights of his giggles and hiccups, Ethan headed off to find Kayla.

Making his way down the hallway, he passed a large gallery of windows and a dining hall, where the attendants were cleaning up from a Friday-night meal and Shabbat services. Sometimes, if Ethan came early enough, he would sit with Kayla and bang on the tambourine beside her, watching her sway and shriek with happiness. But tonight, given everything that had happened with his grandfather, Ethan was running late.

Ethan came to the door marked Kayla Rosenberg-Lippmann. Like always, it was open.

Stepping inside, he found his older sister sitting cross-legged on the floor. Her curly brown hair held back in a headband, wearing pink-and-white pajamas, she held a pair of children's scissors in her hands and was working hard to cut a small triangle from the edge of an empty Lippmann's box.

Across from her, laid out beneath the windows of her room, was a massive arts-and-crafts project of boxes. A mismatch of shapes lined the wall, held up by scotch tape, glue, and Popsicle sticks. Occasionally, she would intersperse some color into the design or a bit of tinfoil. It was a truly remarkable sight to behold, even if no one really knew what it was she spent so much time building.

"Guess what I brought you," Ethan said, dipping into her room.

Kayla looked up and, seeing Ethan holding those Lippmann boxes, immediately raced to take them from his hands. She placed them neatly in a pile with a dozen others, barely giving him a second glance.

"That's it?" Ethan teased her. "I don't even get a hug or a thank-you?"

She blushed, putting one finger in her mouth and coming over to throw her arms around him. It was an unusually receptive greeting from Kayla. Since the accident, Kayla was primarily nonverbal. She didn't always react to a comment or a question. Though, unlike the doctors, Ethan believed she was always listening. Whether she chose to respond or not was her prerogative.

"Those are from Randy," Ethan said, kissing her once on the head before letting her go.

Kayla returned happily to her place on the floor. Ethan

watched her from the threshold. It was Lippmann's boxes. *Always and only Lippmann's boxes.*

No one really knew why Kayla had become completely obsessed with them after the accident or what she spent countless hours creating in her room from them. Of course, every expensive doctor they brought in had some theory.

Most believed it had something to do with her acquired brain injury—a way to process the memories of the accident and make sense of the changes that had occurred in her life in the aftermath. Some believed she did it for the sensory benefits. That she liked the feeling of the boxes, the slow and methodical cutting, taping, and pressing down glue.

But Ethan had always felt that those same doctors didn't give Kayla enough credit. Yes, the accident had changed her. But his big sister had always been creative. Back in Manhattan, the walls of her bedroom had been filled with a variety of drawings. Though the majority of her doctors saw her arts and crafts as the by-product of a brain gone wonky, Ethan believed it was Kayla talking to him in her own way.

"So," Ethan said, taking a seat on the floor beside her, "remember how I told you about Grandpa's plan to steal the babka recipe from Chayim Cohen?"

His visits with his big sister always went the same way. She would sit beside him, working on her project, and he would tell her everything that was going on in his life. He'd fill her in on Randy and Moishe and the plans for the company, and Kayla would listen.

"Well," Ethan continued, "I went to Best Babka today, and I interviewed with—get this—the granddaughter of our family's archenemy, Avital Cohen."

Kayla continued cutting triangles, totally unconcerned. He debated telling her the rest. That his interview was a disaster. That he might not get the job. But he didn't want Kayla to worry. Even if there were plenty of things that kept Ethan up at night.

He worried that Moishe would get tired of covering her cost of care at the home. He worried that Moishe would prevent him from visiting her. Ethan didn't have power of attorney over Kayla. His grandfather did. With a swipe of his pen, Moishe could put Kayla someplace worse, someplace where people didn't treat her with the love and respect she deserved. He might do it to punish Ethan, but they both would suffer.

"Anyway," Ethan said, grabbing a pair of safety scissors to help her with cutting triangles, "I don't want you to worry. Everything is under control. It's like I promised you in hospital, okay? I'm always going to take care of you. I'm always going to be looking out for you...now that Mom and Dad aren't here."

He searched her face for a response, but she was too fixated on drawing a lowercase *t* on a tiny square backing of cardboard.

"Here," he said, steadying her hand inside his own. "Let me help you."

His phone vibrated in his pocket. Pulling it out, he found a Brooklyn number he did not recognize. Ethan scrambled to take it.

"Hello?" Ethan said.

"Oh," a chipper voice sounded at the other end of the line. "I'm sorry. I didn't actually think anyone would pick up. I hope I'm not calling too late. This is Avital Cohen, general manager of Best Babka in Brooklyn. You interviewed with me today."

Ethan's heart full on skipped. Rising from his seat beside Kayla, he angled his body toward the door, in order to give them privacy. "Avital, hi. And no...not too late. I was just thinking about you, actually."

"Oh." This news seemed to surprise her. "Really?"

"Your pumpkin-spiced babka is incredible."

"Right," she sighed. "My babka. Anyways, do you have a free minute to chat?"

"Of course."

"Well, I just wanted to call to tell you that I was very impressed with both your interview and your résumé. I talked it over with my partner, and if you're still interested in the position…we'd loved to offer you full-time employment at Best Babka as an assistant baker."

Ethan did a victory jump. "Really?"

"Yes."

"I'm super excited."

"Us, too."

She had the loveliest voice. Deeper than one would expect for someone her age, but almost weirdly melodic. He shook the thought away.

"So anyway," Avital said, returning them both to business, "I know you probably need some time before you start—"

"I don't need time."

"Oh." Avital paused. "Okay, then. Well, when would you like to begin?"

"When would you like me to begin?"

"I mean…as soon as possible would be great, but again—"

"Would tomorrow work for you?"

"Tomorrow?"

"I mean Sunday," he said, remembering that they were closed for Shabbat. "Would Sunday work for you?"

She teetered on her response. "Sunday's…great. How's six a.m.?"

"Six a.m. works for me."

"Great," she said. "Then, I'll see you on Sunday at six."

"Thank you so much, Ms. Cohen," Ethan said. "I promise. I won't disappoint you."

There was a pause before Avital said, "Avi."

"Excuse me?"

"You can call me Avi. Or Avital. Really, either is fine..."

"Avi it is, then," Ethan smiled. He didn't know why, but her words felt like an invitation to something more. "And I... I look forward to getting to know you better."

He waited for Avital to hang up before fully disconnecting himself. Whooping at the victory, he spun around on one foot, before burying his phone back in his pocket. The noise caused Kayla to look over.

"Guess who just got a job at Best Babka in Brooklyn?" Ethan asked.

Kayla blinked but otherwise seemed unimpressed. She returned to making paper cutouts. As for Ethan, something strange was bubbling around in his belly. A feeling arose, alongside the memory of her hips, sashaying so seductively beneath the white ruffles of a long skirt. Even though he hated the idea of going undercover at Best Babka, he was also weirdly excited for it.

NINE

It was still dark out when Ethan arrived at Best Babka. Hopping over puddles, he made his way down Flatbush Avenue, still nearly empty. Even though it was freezing, and the sidewalks were an icy mess, he was in a great mood. Glancing up at the sky, the stars were still shining. He marveled at how cool it was to be up early enough to see them—when he ran straight into a pole.

Or...what he thought was a pole.

Ethan looked down to see Avital, hands swinging in circles, her mouth formed into an O. She was falling. Her life flashed before his eyes.

The rest was pure instinct. He reached out, attempting to grab her by the arms. Sadly, his attempt to play the hero was all for naught. The new distribution of weight, in addition to his inappropriate shoes for the weather, spelled immediate disaster.

Ethan slipped on a patch of black ice, taking Avital down

with him. From there, they rolled three times—a tangle of arms, flailing legs, and choice words—before finally coming to a stop at the edge of a snowplow drift.

Ethan took a few moments to recover from the shock. Scanning his body, he was grateful that nothing seemed broken. Much to his good fortune, something warm, and soft, and *extremely* pleasing, had managed to break his fall...

Ethan swallowed, his eyes lowering.

Avital was lying facedown on the sidewalk, and he was pressed up doggy-style on top of her.

"Owww," Avital said.

"Oh God," Ethan said, scrambling to get off her, "I'm so sorry."

He reached down to help her up. And then stopped. Avital Cohen—*his boss, his enemy*—wasn't wearing underwear.

It was just a quick glance, but long enough to see that the pink-and-black leopard chiffon skirt she had been wearing during their fall had somehow managed to get wedged between her butt cheeks. One round and perfectly shaped pale half-moon gazed up at him. A tiny little freckle, the most delicious little dot of brown, sat off-center.

Red-hot embarrassment rose in his cheeks. That spark of something wonderful and pleasant returned, until there was no choice but to look away from her completely.

"Um, Avital," Ethan said, clearing his throat, "normally, in this situation, I would help you up...and I mean this in the most respectable way possible, but if your hands are working...you may want to adjust your skirt."

It took her a moment. Her hands moved from beneath her jacket to try to figure out what Ethan was talking about. "Oh God!" Avital groaned, pushing down her skirt. "Seriously!" Ethan heard her rising to her feet. When he was certain that she was decent, he returned his gaze to her eyes.

She did not look happy. But weirdly, staring into that ferocious set of baby blues, all he could think about was that freckle. That delectable freckle that made his body twinge and his mind wander into the most dangerous territory. This was the granddaughter of his family's archenemy, after all. And, though he was beginning to see this would be harder than he realized, he was here on a mission.

"I'm sorry," Ethan said, trying desperately to make this less awkward. "I didn't see—"

Avital cut him off. "It's fine."

"You're not hurt, are you?"

"Nothing more than my pride," she grumbled.

She was looking away from him, arms crossed against her chest, her eyes fixed on the front door of the bakery.

"Look," she said suddenly, "I don't know what you saw—"

"I didn't see anything," Ethan lied.

"But I have my reasons, okay?"

Ethan raised both hands in open surrender. "I'm just here to bake babka!"

Avital met him with a gaze that could cut through ice. *God, she was cold.* All the unfriendliness of their first meeting had now doubled after the embarrassment of their first-day foible. There was no coming back from this catastrophe.

"You're also here an hour early," she snapped back at him.

"I didn't want to be late."

"I told you six."

"Am I getting fired for coming in early?" he asked seriously.

"If you have trouble following directions, I'd prefer to know sooner rather than later."

Ethan choked on his response. Granted, he was here to steal her family's babka recipe, *and* he had just seen the outline of one perfectly formed cheek...but that was no reason not to be friendly.

"I—I…" Ethan stammered. "I can wait outside if you want?"

Avital pressed her lips together in a tight line. He could see her thinking about it. Ethan shifted his weight nervously. And then, thank God, a late-Hanukkah miracle occurred. Manna falling from the Heavens. The door to the bakery swung open.

The tiniest old man that Ethan had ever laid eyes on peeked his head outside. With wiry white hair framing his wrinkles, wearing a red apron with white flour streaked across the front and the sleeves of his white button-down rolled up to his elbows, he reminded Ethan of some fierce little gremlin. Yet, despite his tiny size—and an age equivalent to Ethan's own grandfather—he had forearms that could easily tackle a polar bear.

"Avi, it's freezing," the old man said, glancing between them. "What were you doing outside?

Avital turned her gaze to the old man. "I'm sorry, *Zeyde*," she said, her voice finally softening. "I had a run-in with our new employee." Thankfully, she left the explanation at that. "Ethan," she said, pointing with one hand toward the old man, "this is my grandfather, the legendary creator of Best Babka himself, Chayim Cohen. *Zeyde*, this is Ethan, our new hire—" Avital fixed Ethan with a wry smirk. "He's here early!"

"Ah," Chayim said, studying him. "Well, that's nice…but what are you both doing outside? Come in! Quickly! You'll catch your death out there."

Ethan trailed them inside, his heart racing. He could not believe he had just met Chayim Cohen. This was the man who had thrown his grandfather onto the street, leaving him destitute. This was the man who'd riddled them with frivolous lawsuits and left Facebook comments all over the Lippmann's social media pages that their pumpkin crumble doughnut gave him diarrhea.

He was not what Ethan was expecting.

"So, Ethan," Chayim said, squeezing his forearms to check their size, "you ready to work hard?"

Ethan forced a confident smile. "Always."

"Good," he said, like a war general about to lead an army, "because we need tough people in our kitchen. Strong people, too! Strong of character and heart. That's what it takes to be a Best Babka employee... Passion, but also courage."

"That's a job I'm ready for, sir."

It was a lie, obviously. Ethan's plan was to get in and out of Best Babka as quickly as possible. Indeed, he could already smell the scent of something warm and buttery emanating from one of the back kitchens. All he needed to do now was find that pumpkin-spiced babka recipe and snap a picture. Or watch them make it, taking copious notes along the way. But his plan had always been not to stay at Best Babka for more than a day or two.

"Please," Chayim said, his face wrinkling, "call me *Zeyde*."

"It means Grandpa in Yiddish," Avital explained.

"Everyone here calls me *Zeyde*." He beamed. "And that's how I like to think of myself. Grandfather to all...mother to none!"

Ethan wasn't sure what to say.

Avital stepped in to translate. "Grandpa likes to tell jokes."

"Oh," Ethan said, smiling back at the old man. "Funny! I get it."

He didn't actually get it.

"You know," *Zeyde* said, stepping in closer and peering into his face, "you look familiar."

The accusation sliced him. Ethan forced himself not to swallow.

He didn't look like his grandfather. He had taken after his father, inheriting his height and dark features. He had also taken every precaution in the world, as was needed in corporate espionage, to hide his true identity. Still, he found himself biting back nerves. Perhaps his grandfather's mortal enemy could smell the Lippmann in his blood.

"I know!" he said, pointing one finger at him. "I know! You look like that actor. Charlton Heston. A young Charlton Heston. Ben-Hur," he said, rolling the *r* with a tiny jump and one fist forward. "Oh, that man was a great actor."

Ethan blinked. He did not look anything like Charlton Heston.

Avital explained, "Grandpa thinks everyone looks like Charlton Heston."

"That's not true," *Zeyde* defended. "I only think the handsome ones look like Charlton Heston." He leaned into Ethan once again, patting his cheeks in a loving and friendly manner. "Very handsome. Very nice boy. Jewish?"

"Jewish," Ethan confirmed.

"Jewish!" *Zeyde* threw a victory fist into the air. "I knew it. Did you hear that, Avital? He's Jewish."

"I heard, Grandpa." Avital pressed her lips together.

"What's your favorite thing to bake?" *Zeyde* asked.

"Challah, of course."

"Challah!" *Zeyde* patted his cheeks again. "Good boy. Smart boy, too, this one."

It was another lie. Ethan had never actually baked before in his life. When he wanted something to eat, he asked Ivan—the Lippmann family chef—to make it. Aside from some tortilla chips nuked with tomato sauce he used to eat during late nights at business school, Ethan had no reason to step into a kitchen.

"You know," Chayim said, leaning into Ethan to whisper, "the thing about baking people don't realize, it's the basics that are most important. You can't make a good challah, you can't make anything else. Now, when I was starting out, there was this schmuck who thought he could make a challah better than me—"

"On that note," Avital quipped, clapping her hands together, bringing the conversation to an abrupt end, "I'm sure there's a babka burning in an oven that needs to be checked on. Grandpa—" Avital took her grandfather by the arm, gently leading him down the hall "—I'll be back to help you in a minute, okay? I'm just going to get Ethan started on some paperwork..."

"Sounds good, Avital," *Zeyde* said, doing a little prance down the hall. "I like this new one you hired, too. He's got good arms. Good, strong baking arms."

Avital returned from helping her grandfather, her smile fading.

"You can follow me," she said flatly.

Avital hid her true feelings behind the frozen facade of a professional. All she could think about—beyond the fact that her hoo hah was killing her—was that Ethan Rosenberg had just seen her ass.

She could only imagine what he thought. That she was a freak. That she had some sort of kinky, pantyless-boss fetish. That she spent all day, hidden away in her office, masturbating furiously. None of which was true. Avital couldn't remember the last time she let anyone, including herself, attend to her lady garden. But walking down the hallway with him, the embarrassment of the morning was heightened by just how good he looked. Wearing his stylish navy peacoat with a cashmere scarf slung around his neck, he looked like he was a model in some Parisian Fashion Week.

Avital felt like a full-fledged bridge troll standing next to him.

They came to her office. Avital went inside first, turning on the lights. Heading to a filing cabinet, she tried to find the paperwork for the new hires. And then, frustration. She groaned aloud, slamming the cabinet drawer shut in anger. The folder where she *always* kept the new hire paperwork was missing.

It was only a minor thing. She knew, logically, that it was only an inconvenience. But her pain was so bad she was having trouble walking. Ethan Rosenberg had seen her butt. And maybe it was missing paperwork to normal, healthy people... but to Avital, it felt like the universe was hell-bent on torturing her. She closed her eyes, determined not to lose her cool.

"Um, Avital?" Ethan said, breaking her train of thought.

"What?"

"Is everything okay?"

Avital turned to him, stone-faced. *Apologies. But the bridge troll will not be granting wishes today.*

"I can't find the paperwork," she said dully.

"Oh." Ethan smiled, breezy and warm. "Well, that's no problem. I can just come back later to do it."

He was so damn happy. It was five o'clock in the morning, in the dead of winter, and he was beaming like a bar mitzvah who had just finished his Torah portion. Nobody was naturally that chipper. *She hated him. Oh, how she hated him.* In her mind, she saw a thousand flying gummies—each wrapped up in plastic—popping him directly in the center of the forehead.

Okay, even Avital was with it enough to realize that her disdain for Ethan this morning was a bit much. Obviously, her bad mood had far more to do with her being exhausted and in pain than Ethan being a klutz.

She forced herself to focus on the positive. Their run-in

had been an accident. He was not a horrible human being, no matter how much he beamed before the sun rose or how good he felt—after two years without a man touching her—his full weight pressed up against her. She was, totally and completely, willing to let what had happened between them go.

And then, Ethan broke the eleventh commandment: *Thou shall not repeat, or ever mention again, our shared awkward moment.*

"I'd also like to explain about our run-in this morning," Ethan said.

Avital closed her eyes. "Please don't."

"You see," Ethan began rambling, "I took public transportation to work...and I didn't realize you needed a card... so I had to figure out where to get a card. And then, I got here an hour early because my brother told me that the bus schedule can be unreliable. I didn't want to be late, so I just gave myself extra time...but anyway, and starting tomorrow, I should be able to time it better."

She deadpanned. "Great."

"So we're good?"

"We were much better before you mentioned it again."

Ethan blinked, confused in her direction.

"Well, since I am here early—" Ethan clapped his hands together "—I'm happy to help in whatever way you need. If you want, I can even start helping you on baking some things..."

"Baking?" Avital smirked. "Really?"

"Sure." Ethan smiled warmly. "Challah, black-and-white cookies...your world-famous pumpkin-spiced babka recipe?"

She knew it. She should have gone with her first instinct. Ethan hadn't even been here a half hour and already he was looking for a promotion. Clearly—and despite the full warning that she gave him during his interview—he still didn't grasp how things worked at Best Babka. She attempted to be gentle, but firm.

"I do appreciate your efforts to come in early today," Avital said, forcing herself to sound friendly. "I also appreciate your offer to help in the kitchen. That's very kind of you. But as I mentioned in your interview, we don't need an extra person in the kitchen right now. What we need is someone to help with tasks around the store."

Ethan's smile faded. "Of course. I just meant—"

"I'm not done," Avital said, interrupting him. "And the reason I ask employees to come in at six a.m. is because we—*meaning members of the Cohen family only*—make our pumpkin-spiced babka at five a.m. daily. No one else is allowed in the building while it's happening."

"Oh." Ethan rubbed the back of his neck nervously. "I didn't realize the recipe was such a carefully guarded secret."

"It has to be. It's our anchor recipe," Avital explained. "It's the thing Best Babka is known for, and it's kept us in business, sustaining my family and our employees for three generations. If someone were to find out that recipe—or, worse, steal it and reproduce it—well, it could hurt us. It could even put us out of business permanently."

Ethan swallowed. "I can understand why you're so secretive about it, then."

Avital nodded. "Sorry to disappoint you."

She closed the filing cabinet drawer. "If you'd like to follow me, I'll show you what you'll be working on today."

TEN

The task which Avital set Ethan up with that morning had nothing to do with babka. Instead, he was relegated to a back hallway, where he was given the job of constructing a zillion pink boxes. After three hours of cutting and opening, pressing and sealing, Ethan was certain he had never worked so hard in his life.

He needed a break. Putting his X-Acto knife down, he stretched his arms above his head, cracking the joints in his shoulders. Avital was working in her office down the hall. He could hear her, tapping away on the keyboard. His mind began to wander. The image of her—facedown on the sidewalk, one round and perfectly plump butt cheek aimed up at him—caused a pleasurable sensation to spread through his lower extremities.

Strange that she didn't wear underwear.

Then again, he was attempting to understand the stylistic choices of a woman who paired pink Wigwam socks with

Birkenstocks, and in the middle of winter. Still, he tried to come up with some reasonable explanation.

Maybe she didn't like doing extra laundry. Maybe she was a minimalist. Perhaps she had held her underwear during some Marie Kondo–type method of decluttering and realized it didn't bring her joy. Either way, Ethan needed to stop daydreaming about Avital Cohen and her *bottomless brunch* and focus on finding that damn recipe.

"Oh, you poor bastard," a voice called out behind him. "Avital's got you on box duty, huh?"

Ethan turned to find a short, round man, bald as they come, wearing a knitted *kippah*. The glow of the overhead lighting caused a shine to angle from his head. "I'm Josh," he said, extending his hand, "Avital's twin brother, and dare I say it, the better-looking half of this operation."

Ethan put down his X-Acto knife to shake Josh's hand. "Ethan."

"Right, the overqualified pastry chef?" he said curiously.

"Excuse me?"

"I'm kidding, dude!" Josh clapped him on his shoulder. "Welcome aboard."

"Thanks."

"Anyway," Josh said, shrugging happily, "I'm here to take you to lunch."

The room where the majority of the staff took lunch at Best Babka was your typical workplace-gathering hot spot. A large counter across the wall, separated by a refrigerator and sink, was loaded down with coffee and bottles of water. In the middle of the room, set up buffet-style, were aluminum trays filled with a variety of foods. Just beyond that, at a long table, the employees of Best Babka were chattering away.

"So," Josh said, turning in the doorway. It was clear he had given this tour a hundred times before. "This is our employee kitchen. Every Best Babka employee gets a full hour off for lunch. We stagger those hours so that we never find ourselves shorthanded at the counter. For the next two weeks, you're officially on the first lunch shift. You can eat here…or outside our bakery. Just make sure you're back after an hour, because someone is probably waiting to take your place."

"Got it."

"Secondly," Josh said, moving to a large refrigerator, "you're Jewish, right?"

"Right."

"How much do you know about keeping kosher?"

"I keep kosher."

"Wait," Josh said, his voice rising one octave in surprise. "Really?"

"Is that unusual here?"

"Actually, yeah…" Josh said, crossing his arms and leaning back curiously. "Cool, man. I keep kosher, too. So does Avi. You go to day school?"

"No."

"Jewish summer camp?"

"No."

"Where you from?"

Ethan was getting nervous with his line of questioning. "Westchester."

"Oh." Josh beamed like they were old friends. "I know a ton of people from there!"

Josh began rattling off names—a whole litany of Dahlias, and Amys and Elissas, followed by Zimmermans and Kaplans and Levis—in some attempt to play Jewish geography. When he realized that Ethan genuinely did not know a single person he mentioned (and even if he did, he would never admit it, at the risk of being found out), he gave up on the whole endeavor.

"Ah, well," Josh said, shrugging his shoulders. "I'm sure if we did this long enough, we'd probably find out we're cousins."

"Probably."

"Anyway," Josh said, moving him over to the sink and refrigerator, "since you keep kosher, you're officially further ahead than most folks on their first day. Still, I'm gonna do my due diligence here."

Josh spent the next five minutes going over the basics of kosher law. He explained that there were three categories of kosher food: dairy, meat, and pareve, or neutral, items. He explained how plates and utensils changed status—a plate becoming dairy, for instance, because you set a piece of cheese upon it, or a fork remaining neutral because you have only ever used it on fruit. At Best Babka, they made dairy and pareve items. The latter, however, were made in a separate kitchen.

"Now," Josh said, "what working in a kosher bakery means for you is that, from this point forward, you cannot bring any food or drink in from the outside. If there is something you want, run it by Marty." Josh waved to an old man with eyebrows like caterpillars, watching from a metal chair at the side the room. "Marty is one of our three full-time and in-house *mashgiahs*. Are you familiar with what a *mashgiah* is?"

"They're like kosher police, right?"

"Man!" Josh said, shaking his head, amazed. "You are making my job easy here today. A *mashgiah* makes sure that we are certified to have our *hechsher*, or kosher status, for the Jewish community. A *mashgiah* does more than just make sure nobody mistakenly cooks a steak on one of our dairy stoves. They verify that all our items—the flour we use, the milk we buy, for instance—are certified kosher. They make sure we're checking our eggs for blood spots and the vegetables for bugs. And in the case of a mistake or an accident, they make the final decision on whether or not an item is still suitable for sale. So, for example, if a hot dog randomly falls into a pot of cream of mushroom soup, do we need to throw it out? Or, can we just remove the hot dog and still serve the dairy soup as kosher?"

Ethan grimaced. "Has that...ever happened?"

"Once," Josh said. "Not here, but between two rival kosher pizzerias in Queens."

"Wow."

"Oh, that's nothing," Josh said, stepping closer to whisper. "One day, I'll tell you the story of Moishe Lippmann, the sociopath who has been trying to put us out of business for over fifty years."

All at once, a dozen people shushed Josh into silence.

"Sorry." Josh leaned in closer to explain, "We don't really say his name around here. At least, not while my grandfather is still in the building. My *zeyde* gets *very* upset. Anyway, I don't want to bog you down with our whole sordid family history on your first day."

Ethan forced a smile. "Great."

"But back to the point of me giving you this whole spiel," Josh said. "Every employee of Best Babka needs to be careful about maintaining our *kashruth*. Not just because our Jewish community trusts us to provide kosher food but because if we lose our *hechsher*, we lose the ability to sell baked goods to the Jewish community."

"Got it."

"Good," Josh said, bringing Ethan over to the buffet table. "Because we at Best Babka understand that employees need to eat. In fact, I love eating! So we provide a kosher dairy lunch every day here for our employees. Mostly, its items we make and sell in the bakery. Though, we always try to provide a salad and fresh fruit when possible. Please eat whatever you like, and you're also free to bring any extra home with you for Shabbat on Friday. If you don't like the food here, you are more than welcome to go out to eat. There are lots of great restaurants along Flatbush Avenue. Just come back after your hour is up, and remember...don't bring anything back with you. Any thoughts, concerns, questions?"

"I don't think so."

"Great," Josh said, handing Ethan a plate. "Then, happy eating!"

Josh took off. Ethan found himself alone once more. Turning back to the cafeteria, his eyes scanned the room. Most everyone in the lunchroom was already engaged in some conversation. It made him feel terribly awkward. And then, Avital entered the room.

It was weird how his heart skipped a little, floated even, the moment she entered. The image of her rump—that enjoyable sensation in his lower extremities—arose once again. He reasoned that his attraction was purely logical. Getting closer to her, getting friendly with her, could help him succeed in his mission for his grandfather.

Ethan waved at her. Her eyes scanned the room—and he was certain they crossed his path—but instead of waving back, acknowledging him, she grabbed a plate and headed over to the buffet.

What was this woman's problem?

He decided to give her the benefit of the doubt. Stepping behind her in line, he was going to attempt small talk, when for no reason he could comprehend, she lifted the top of a steel pan before huffing loudly and slamming it back down. She repeated this pattern seven times in total, before finally filling up her plate with a boring old salad.

Ethan didn't understand. Even as someone hesitant to give

Best Babka credit, the food they were providing looked incredible. In one pan, tiny pizzas were loaded down with an assortment of mushrooms and caramelized onions. In another, mini quiches oozed with spinach and cream.

Ethan grimaced, concerned. "Is that all you're eating?"

Avital stopped midway through creating her mountain of lettuce. "What?"

Ethan smiled, trying to be polite. "You don't need to diet."

Avital did not blink. Did not move or bat an eyelash. It was then that he realized she might be misinterpreting what he was saying. He wasn't commenting on her weight. He was simply trying to tell her that he had already seen her half-naked, and from what he had seen, she was absolutely perfect. Still, the woman was shooting daggers at him, and he got the distinct impression she was considering homicide.

"Has anyone ever told you, Ethan," she said, her voice monotonous, "that it's rude to comment on what people are eating?"

With that, she spun away from him—dumped her entire plate of salad in the trash—and stormed out of the room. *Well, that went great.* Dragging one hand down his face, he began to regret ever agreeing to take this ridiculous assignment. He regretted meeting Avital, especially.

"Try a boureka," a gruff voice called out.

Ethan looked back—and then, all the way up—to find what could only be described as an elephant of a man. Standing over six feet tall, his head shaven and wearing what appeared to be a motorcycle vest, he had a menagerie of tattoos decorating his arms, hands, and neck.

Ethan swallowed. "What?"

"The bourekas," he said, opening one of the steel pans, before grabbing a set of tongs and loading six tiny triangle pastries onto his own plate. "Everybody loves the bourekas."

Ethan decided not to argue. Leaving the pizza behind, he grabbed a puffed phyllo pastry and attempted to slink away. Instead, the extremely large and intimidating-looking man called him back.

"Hey," he shouted, "where you going?"

Ethan squeaked out a response. "To eat?"

"You antisocial or something?"

Ethan wasn't sure how to respond. "I don't...think so?"

"Well, come on, then," he said, waving Ethan over to one of the tables crammed full of people. "We got plenty of room!"

Begrudgingly, Ethan took a seat. The Elephant squeezed down next to him.

"Tootles," he said, offering his hand.

"Excuse me?"

"My name is Tootles," he said, before nodding to the boureka on his plate. "Did you try it, yet?"

"No."

"Well, go on," he said, nudging Ethan on.

This guy seemed obsessed with Ethan eating bourekas. Still, he wasn't exactly eager to get into fisticuffs with an elephant. Picking it up, he took a bite. Ethan melted. His taste buds tingled, as he covered his mouth with his hand.

"Holy—"

"Right?" Tootles beamed widely, slapping him on the back.

"What do they put in this stuff?"

Tootles laughed aloud.

The food at Best Babka was beyond good. Every bite transported Ethan to his best memories. The sweet way Kayla trilled whenever she saw him. Cherry blossoms streaming down around him on a perfect spring day in Japan. Avital splayed out flat in the ice water, her pale rump shining bright in the dark. He really needed to stop thinking about his boss.

"Now, don't be so modest, Tootles," Josh said, appearing with his own plate, filled to the brim with bourekas, pizza, and salad. "Tootles made those bourekas himself."

"Really?" Ethan turned to him, surprised.

"Well," Tootles said and blushed in a way that made him appear only slightly less dangerous, "I had a good teacher."

"So, new man," an older woman with black hair tied back in a scarf called out to him from the end of the table, "what's your story?"

"My story?" Ethan said, somewhat caught off guard by the sudden interrogation. "I don't really...have a story."

Tootles took another bite of his boureka. "*Everybody* at Best Babka has a story."

Ethan shifted in his seat uncomfortably. His real story, of course, was far more complicated than the one he had invented for Best Babka in Brooklyn. He settled on telling the one he had concocted for his résumé.

"Well," Ethan said, squaring his shoulders confidently, "I studied French pastry-making at the New York Institute of Culinary Education. But being Jewish, I wanted to learn more about our background and heritage and appealing to the kosher market. The idea, too, of merging the old with the new appealed to me. I thought there was nowhere better to do that than Best Babka."

The table fell into a weird and uncomfortable silence. Ethan couldn't help but feel confused. Why else would anyone take a job at Best Babka in Brooklyn? They loved making baked goods. They wanted to learn more about working in, and being part of, a kosher bakery. Finishing his boureka, he turned back to Tootles.

"And you?" Ethan asked, trying to remember the rules of polite conversation. "What brought you to work here?"

Tootles spoke without missing a beat. "I was in prison."

Ethan nearly choked on his water. "I'm sorry... I don't think I heard you right?"

"Yep," Tootles said, totally unfazed by the question. "Ten years for armed robbery, possession with intent to distribute, and a few other undesirable mentions. After I got out... Best Babka was the only place that would hire me."

Josh pointed a half-eaten boureka at his head. "And it was the best decision we ever made! Seriously, Tootles...you got the touch."

A round of *Hear! Hear!* rose unanimously from the table. Ethan was still in too much shock to join in.

For one, he had never actually met someone who had been in prison before. He especially couldn't imagine his grandfather hiring a convicted felon to work in one of his businesses. Ethan envisioned it as a fluke. Some momentary lapse in what was otherwise sensible judgment. But then, going around the room, each person who introduced themselves *indeed* had a story.

There was Jose Morales, a self-described dreamer in his twenties, who had found his way to Best Babka part-time as a means to pay for college. There was Sara Riva Leah, who sat across from Ethan at the table, her curly black hair held back in a pastel scarf. She had left the Satmar community in Brooklyn—painfully making the decision to leave behind a wife and six children—when she transitioned.

Down at the end of the table, small and reserved, was Chaya Lieberwitz. Chaya was an *agunah*, or chained woman under Jewish law. After she left her abusive husband of ten years, he went into hiding in Israel, refusing to grant her a *get*, or written decree of divorce.

One by one, they told their stories. Rafi, the Israeli security guard, had lost everything to a gambling addiction. Marty, the in-house mashgiah, was born in a displaced persons camp after World War II. And of course, there was Tootles—and Samira and Philip—all of whom had spent lengthy amounts of time stoking very impressive résumés of criminal endeavors.

But among these stories of hardship were also victories. Jose had just been accepted into Harvard Law. Sara was in a loving relationship, not only with herself but with a new and fantabulous man. Chaya sat on the board of Unchained, an advocacy group that helped demand justice for *agunot*, fighting for them through social media, *get*-police, and the rabbinic courts.

Tootles, as it turned out, was apparently the Banksy of knitting cozies, leaving his yarn-art as an expression of freedom on stop signs and streetlamps all over New York.

It struck Ethan that these were all second-chance types. The kind of people no one else would hire. People with sketchy backgrounds, no employment history, no references. It made him wonder if Avital had even checked his references. But given what he was learning now from the staff at Best Babka, he had to assume not.

"So," Ethan said, surprised, "none of you had any baking experience when you started working here?"

"Nope," Tootles said. "But we all have a specialty now."

"A specialty?" Ethan didn't understand.

"Sure!" Tootles explained like it was nothing. "I make bourekas. Sara makes challah. Chaya's specialty is rugelach. Rafi makes cheesecakes. And every year, we have a big competition during Purim. We shut down the shop...and everybody comes in and bakes their specialty item. And you know what happens, Ethan? Guess!" Tootles hit him in the chest. "Go on, guess!"

"I wouldn't dare—"

"I'll tell you," Tootles interrupted him, a terrifying twinkle in his eye. "Whoever sells the most money worth of their specialty item gets to donate all the proceeds of that day to the charity of their choice. Isn't that just something, huh?"

Ethan breathed out a sigh of relief. "It is something."

"Rafi won last year," Chaya spoke up. "Made a pomegranate cheesecake that was so good Avi put it on the Shavuot *and* Rosh Hashanah menus. Rafi even got his recipe written up in the *Jewish World News*. Donated all the proceeds to some miniature-horse rescue out in Rhinebeck."

"I seriously wanted to shank you for that one, Rafi!" Tootles beamed.

"We take the Purim competition very seriously around here," Josh chimed in.

"I can see that." Ethan shifted in his seat nervously.

"So," Tootles said, lifting up one half-eaten boureka and jabbing it toward Ethan's eye, "I guess the real question for you—Ethan Rosenberg, fancy-pastry chef, with the fancy résumé, who wants to learn all about kosher Ashkenazi Jewish cooking—what is your specialty gonna be?"

Ethan considered the question. "I don't...know?"

"That's the right answer." Tootles beamed, clapping him on the back. "'Cause first, you gotta work your way up. You gotta make thousands and thousands of pink boxes and ribbons and deliveries. And then, only then, do you get to work in the kitchen."

Ethan pressed his lips together. "Thanks for reminding me."

With another round of laughter, the entire table began getting ready to return to work. Ethan was just about to follow them when Tootles leaned over him one more time.

"Oh, and new guy," Tootles said, pointing to the side where a trash can was beginning to fill up, "forgot to tell you. New guy is always in charge of trash." He pointed to a large blue bin, where the refuse of Best Babka was now overflowing like some kosher baked-goods volcano.

Ethan bit back a frown. "Great."

"Just take 'em to the dumpsters out back," Tootles said, pointing to one of the many back doors that led to a small parking lot outside. "They're about a block down. But here's the thing. Don't throw our trash in the neighbors'. They get really pissed, you know? We got a lot of trash."

"Got it."

Ethan rose and made his way to the front of that large blue container. Staring at that stinky, disgusting refuse sticking out from the top, he called back out to Tootles. "Hey, Tootles?" Ethan said. "You got, like…gloves or something?"

"You mean winter gloves?"

"No, like—" Ethan waved his hands "—rubber gloves."

Tootles cocked his chin backward. "What the hell you need rubber gloves for?"

Ethan shifted in his spot, embarrassed. "Never mind."

And then, for the first time in his life—*and with his bare hands, even*—Ethan took out the trash.

ELEVEN

"Hold up!" Ethan waved in the direction of the bus, before sprinting down the icy sidewalk. He had just enough time to fly through the double doors at the front before the bus rumbled to a start. "Thank you," Ethan said, out of breath. He attempted to find an empty seat, when the bus driver corrected him.

"Card?" she asked.

Ethan blinked, confused. And then, he remembered that he needed to *pay* for public transportation. He dug into his pocket, awkwardly fumbling with his wallet, before finding his MetroCard and sliding it through the receiver. The woman driving didn't even bother to affirm his payment with a polite nod.

It would take Ethan over an hour to get uptown to the location where Stephen would be waiting to take him home. It wasn't an easy commute. Certainly, a helicopter would have been far more reasonable. But Ethan was wary of casting suspicion.

Making his way down the aisle, he found an empty seat. Unbuttoning his jacket, he let his body breathe. He was exhausted. Every part of his body ached. But glancing around at his traveling companions, it seemed he was not alone.

Across from him, an older woman in a puffer jacket snored loudly. A few rows behind her, a teenager in a fast-food uniform disappeared beneath giant headphones. The bus came to a stop again, and a man boarded, holding three bags of leaking, stinking trash.

Ethan was aghast. He debated saying something, but what was the point? He was an alien who had crash-landed on a new planet. He added it to the list of oddities he had experienced on his first day out.

Getting trash on his shoes.
Using public transportation.
Eating lunch with a felon.
Making pink boxes.
Seeing Avital's tuchus.

Not that he completely minded the last one.

By the time Ethan returned home to the Lippmann family compound, it was late afternoon. Scanning the foyer for his grandfather, he was relieved to find the downstairs empty. Moishe hadn't come down for dinner yet. Quietly, Ethan sprinted up the stairs and toward his room.

Closing the door behind him, he took a seat on his bed and rubbed out a headache from his forehead. It had been a day. He needed sleep. He was also full-on starving.

He glanced over to the clock. Moishe always took breakfast at seven, skipped lunch, and ate dinner at five. Ivan was likely putting the finishing touches on some Eastern European delicacy.

Of course, going downstairs to eat with his grandfather was out of the question. As hungry as he was, Ethan couldn't bear the thought of a four-course meal full of criticism.

He settled on the next best thing. Opening the drawer of his nightstand, he searched for the babka that he had acquired during his interview with Avital. He had been going slowly with it, only allowing himself one or two pieces a day—delaying pleasure and gratification—in order to savor every morsel. He was certainly grateful for his willpower tonight, as it meant avoiding difficult questions from Moishe.

But as Ethan poked through the drawer, he realized something was wrong. The bag, the box...but most important, his babka...were missing.

"Randy!" Ethan shouted, throwing open the door to his brother's room. Randy was sitting on his bed, peering down into what appeared to be a petri dish. "Did you eat my babka?"

"No," Randy said without looking up.

Ethan searched the room, annoyed. Suddenly, his eyes landed on a brown bag, and a pink box, crumpled and empty on the floor. "Then, what," Ethan said, picking it up, displaying it as evidence between them, "is this?"

"Oh, wait," Randy said, considering the question. "I did eat your babka. Sorry, man. I totally forgot."

"Seriously?"

Randy shrugged. "Munchies, man."

Ethan couldn't believe his brother. "I've told you a thousand times not to go into my room."

"I needed something."

"What could you possibly need?"

"A shirt."

"You have hundreds of your own shirts!"

"But I needed one of yours."

"For what?"

"Duh," Randy said. "For my business."

"You don't have a business, Randy!"

Randy blinked three times in Ethan's direction. "Don't you work in a bakery?"

"We can only take home extra on Friday."

"Oh," Randy said, laying his petri dish down at the side. "Well, that sucks. Guess you're babka-out-of-luck, then."

Randy stood up. Ignoring Ethan, he moved to his computer, typing numbers into an Excel document on the screen.

"Randy," Ethan said, biting back his frustration. He could feel the urge to say something hurtful, something cruel, sitting on the tip of his tongue. But he didn't want to be like his grandfather. "I'm serious, okay? I'm killing myself here to keep Grandpa happy, and the least you can do for me is—"

"You want an edible, man?" Randy asked, interrupting.

"What?"

"It's good for stress."

"I'm not stressed out!" Ethan snapped at him.

Randy let the question linger in the air. "Suit yourself."

Randy returned to his computer. Ethan huffed. Maybe his little brother was right. Maybe he was stressed out. Ethan took a seat on the edge of Randy's bed.

"I'm screwed, Randy."

Randy turned around. "Screwed how?"

"Well, for starters," Ethan said, listing off his issues, "the recipe that Grandpa wants me to steal is a closely guarded secret. Only Cohens know it. Which means, getting it is going to be harder, and take longer, than I originally intended. It means having to stay working at Best Babka, getting to know these people, while simultaneously trying to find the damn thing…or trick someone into giving it to me."

"Oh wow."

"Beyond that," he said, "I saw Avital Cohen's ass today."

"Wait," Randy squinted. "What?"

"And I liked it," Ethan said, throwing his hands up in the air. "I liked her ass a lot!"

"Okay…well, I guess that's normal."

"But the bigger problem," Ethan said, his voice quieting with the admission, "is that they're not monsters."

"Who?"

"All of them," Ethan tried to explain. "The people who work at Best Babka. Josh. Tootles. Chayim Cohen."

Randy leaned in closer. "You met Chayim Cohen?"

"Yeah."

Randy cocked his head. "And?"

"He was normal." Ethan shrugged. "I mean… normal for an old dude."

"Whoa."

"And there was something else."

"Okay."

"Something that's bothering me." Ethan was almost afraid to say it aloud. "Josh, Avital's twin brother, said something when he was giving me a tour… He said Moishe Lippmann was a sociopath who'd been trying to put them out of business for fifty years. Which didn't make sense to me. Chayim is the one that's been obsessed with ruining Lippmann's. But it's like they have a completely different story than us."

Ethan looked up to see his brother, eyes narrowed intently on the center of Ethan's nose.

"Are you okay?" Ethan asked.

"Oh, sorry," Randy said, shaking off wherever he was, returning to their planet. "I was just wholly focused on this freckle you have on your nose."

Ethan sighed. "What am I gonna do, Randy? You know

what Grandpa is like when he sets his mind to something. If I don't find this recipe…"

He couldn't even say the words aloud.

Randy considered the question thoughtfully. "Well, maybe they wrote it down?"

"What do you mean?"

"It's a recipe, right?" Randy said simply. "Maybe it's in a cookbook somewhere. Or in a safe in someone's office? I mean…if the recipe is that valuable, they have to have it somewhere. So, while you're doing all these awful chores, go looking for it. Look everywhere. Look in places they don't want you looking. I'm sure you'll find it eventually."

It wasn't terrible advice.

Ethan returned to his room. But going to bed hungry that evening, he realized he didn't like it.

He didn't like being under the thumb of his grandfather. He didn't like having his siblings used as pawns. He didn't like having to make choices between the people he loved and his own personal-values system…but what did it matter? He was stuck. How could Ethan take care of anyone, independently and on his own, when all his money was tied up in the company his grandfather oversaw? When he didn't even know how to take public transit?

Ethan had spent his entire life in boarding schools, earning fancy degrees, working in the corporate headquarters of Lippmann's. He had a mansion over his head, a driver at the ready, and a credit card to use whenever he liked. It was a life of extraordinary privilege. But what Ethan realized that night—after his first day working in the real world—was all the things he was lacking.

TWELVE

Ethan arrived to Best Babka at exactly six on Tuesday morning, expecting to once again be working under Avital. Instead, he was handed off to Tootles. Standing over him at the front counter, arms crossed against his chest, Tootles's tattoo of Donald Duck flexed repeatedly in Ethan's direction.

"From this point on," Tootles had said, "you're gonna be my little buddy. And I'm gonna be your big buddy. Capisce?"

Ethan had full-on whimpered. "Capisce."

From there, it was a crash course on working hard for just above minimum wage. Whatever menial and horrible chore needed to be accomplished, Tootles put Ethan to the task.

Ethan cleaned counters, bathrooms, and windows. He learned how to take orders over the phone. He worked an entire day in what could only be kindly described as Dante's tenth circle of Hell—customer service.

As for Avital, the only time she spoke to him after that first day was when she located him in the hallway to finish filling out his employee paperwork.

Not that he hadn't been trying to get her attention. Whenever Avital would enter a room, he tried to catch her eye. When she was sprinting by him in the hall, he would say hello, only to have her ignore him totally. He couldn't decide if Avital was swamped, hated his guts, or was simply rude. The only thing he felt for certain was that she was unhappy.

In the meantime, Ethan did his best to take his brother's advice. He hunted for that pumpkin-spiced babka recipe. He fingered through the collection of Best Babka recipes that were posted on hooks, in laminated pages, on the walls of the kitchens. He casually questioned Tootles and the rest of the Best Babka staff during lunchtime breaks, seeing if their many years of working at the bakery would reveal some clue.

He had even gone online and considered purchasing a hidden camera—leaving it overnight to video the Cohen family secretly. But realizing that using one in New York State would change his actions from unethical to totally illegal, he quickly decided against it.

Finally, on Friday afternoon, with Shabbat looming, Avital appeared as he mopped floors in the hallway. Of course, she looked adorable. Dressed in a winter coat, hat and mittens, she also seemed ready to leave.

"Going home for the day?" Ethan asked, hoping to spark a conversation.

"No."

She left the statement at that. No explanation. No digression, either.

"I need you to help me with something while I'm out," Avital said.

Ethan attempted to crack a joke. "Hopefully, it's more pink boxes."

Avital didn't budge. "Pink boxes happen on Sunday."

"Great." Ethan pursed his lips. "Can't wait."

Avital waved for him to follow her. Walking him down the hall and up a set of rickety old stairs, she led him to the second floor of the building. The place was a mess. Whatever potential the small rooms on the second floor had once held, it had now devolved fully into storage. Containers, baking equipment, photo-staging materials, and Jewish-holiday decor crammed every free inch of space.

"Yikes," Ethan said and grimaced.

"Yeah," Avital sighed, pushing a box of vintage-looking cooking equipment out of the way. "It's on my to-do list to clean it up."

Avital brought him to a tiny room at the end of the hallway. Opening the door, he was less than pleased to discover three hampers full of towels, aprons, and Best Babka–branded employee wear. A dusty old industrial washer and dryer set, which had to be from the seventies, stood against the back wall.

"I need you to help me finish the laundry," Avital said. "If you could move over this wash when it's done, and then start that load over there—" She began to explain, pointing to buttons, showing him where the detergent and dryer sheets were.

"I got it." Ethan smiled, interrupting her halfway through her explanation.

"You sure?" Avital said. "It's kind of an old system."

"Avi," Ethan laughed at the insinuation, "it's laundry, all right? I've done it a zillion and one times in my life."

Avital took him at his word and left him alone on the second floor to get started. He turned to the machine.

He had never actually done laundry before. It was one of those things that came with being extravagantly wealthy. Like making your bed or cooking your own meal, there was always someone else to manage those normally important life skills.

Still, he couldn't just admit that to Avital. He didn't want her to think that he was a nothing and a disappointment. He was also not so far removed from reality to realize that having never done his own laundry at twenty-four years old was totally weird. Still, staring down at that monstrous machine, he felt his stomach turn a bit with anxiety.

There were so many buttons.

Way more buttons than seemed reasonably necessary.

Ethan called his brother.

"What?" Randy said, picking up on the first ring.

"I need to know how to do laundry," Ethan said.

"Why?" Randy asked.

"I don't have time to explain," Ethan said. "Just…go get Freya." Freya was their Scandinavian housekeeper.

"I mean," Randy huffed, annoyed, "I was kind of in the middle of something."

"Randy!" Ethan snapped at him, before bringing his voice down to a whisper. "You can go back to doing drugs later. Just help me, okay?"

"Fine," Randy said. "But you owe me another babka."

For the next few minutes, Ethan heard Randy searching the house. He talked to Stephen, Ivan, and Sandra, the gardener, before finally coming across Freya. Ethan could hear Randy on the other end of the line trying to explain the situation to her—Freya responding in a mixture of Swedish and English—before Randy returned to the line.

"She says to just bring it home," Randy said.

"I can't bring it home!"

"Hold on," he said, speaking to Freya again. "She says, 'I'll take care of it. Just bring it home.'"

He could hear Freya saying *No problem, no problem* on the other end of the line.

"That's not—" Ethan rubbed his temples, frustrated, before realizing this entire endeavor was pointless. It wasn't just Moishe who treated them like incompetent children, it was the staff, too. "Never mind," Ethan said. "I'll figure it out myself."

Ethan hung up the phone, then turned to face the contraption. Sure, he had never done laundry before…but how hard could it really be? The wash came to a standstill. Ethan took a deep breath and opened the top.

Victory.

He had figured the damn thing out.

From there, it was a bunch of best guesses before, somehow, the dryer rumbled to a start. He reached down to one of the baskets, throwing its contents in the machine, before grabbing the bottle of detergent.

He wasn't sure how much to use, so he just dumped some in. Not too much, of course: he didn't want to start some sort of bubble flood. He had seen enough movies to know that this was always how these situations ended for a main character. Finally, he spun the dial around. It clicked. The machine began agitating.

Look at that! He was a goddamn laundry genius.

Stepping back from the machine, hands on his hips, he felt extremely proud of himself. And then, knowing that Avital was away, he settled on doing reconnaissance. Ethan had scoured all of Best Babka for the recipe…but there was still one place he had not been able to look. Now the opportunity presented itself.

Returning downstairs, grabbing his mop and bucket where he had left it, he made a beeline straight for Avital's office.

★ ★ ★

"Okay, Avital," the nurse said, sliding the metal knob downward. "Looks like we're at one-twenty-four today."

Avital stepped off the beam scale and made her way back to the chair in the doctor's office. It had taken her three weeks to get a so-called emergency appointment with her urogyne-cologist, and she was determined to use every single second of it to advocate for herself.

"And what brings you in to see the doctor today?" the nurse asked, taking a seat across from her, opening her laptop on the counter.

Avital clutched her lower belly. "I'm in pain."

"I see here that you have a diagnosis of interstitial cystitis?"

"Yes."

"And that you had a laparoscopy last year?"

"Yes."

"And we didn't find endometriosis, right?"

"No," Avital said and then felt like she had to add more just so this nurse wouldn't think she was imagining things. "But I had a benign tumor...on my bladder."

"So we removed the fibroids," she said, jotting down some notes, "and the cyst on the right ovary...and the tumor, which was benign...and how is your pain today, Avital?"

Did this woman not see her, clutching her abdomen, on the verge of tears?

"About a six," Avital said through bated breath, "on Azo."

She left out the part about downing enough ibuprofen to euthanize a horse. She didn't want the nurse to think she was addicted, after all.

"Okay!" The nurse popped up from the seat with a pleasant smile, and then, taking the laptop with her, departed the room. "The doctor will be right in to see you."

Avital knew that the doctor wouldn't be right in to see her.

Just like she knew the reason for the nurse taking the laptop. Behind all the smiles and niceties of the medical establishment was the simple fact that they had all been trained, from their very first day of medical school, not to trust patients.

For the next twenty minutes, Avital stared at a painting of a woman in a lilac dress standing in the middle of a field of flowers. When she wasn't practicing for an argument, she was trying not to focus on her pain.

A knock at the door drew her attention away. Dr. Prikh, a small woman with pitch-black hair pulled into a tight ponytail, peeked her head inside.

"Avital!" Dr. Prikh said, immediately recognizing her longtime patient. "Good to see you again. How are you doing today?"

"Not great," Avital said through gritted teeth. "Kind of why I'm here."

Avital had found Dr. Prikh after two years of traumatic experiences, misdiagnoses, and four different specialists. She was also one of the few doctors willing to stop throwing hormones at her for clinical endometriosis and actually do surgery.

But beyond that, and what she liked the most about Dr. Prikh, was that she gave her honest answers. She didn't sugarcoat things. She didn't make everything about diet or meditation, or maintaining a positive attitude. When Avital had once asked her if her chronic pelvic pain would ever go away, she looked her straight in the eye and said, "No."

Avital had needed to hear it. She needed to hear that it wasn't her fault. She needed to hear that you could do everything right and still be in pain. Just like you could do everything wrong and get better. Chronic illness was chronic illness, after all. Not math. But today, more than an understanding ear, what Avital straight up needed was drugs.

Dr. Prikh took the seat across from her. "What's going on, Avital?"

Avital began. She told her how her pain, often tied to where she was on her menstrual cycle, was getting worse. She explained that she was trying so hard on her IC diet, barely eating anything, doing meditation and taking walks. And then, the tears started coming. She was scared, her anxiety around her pain...the fear that it would move beyond unmanageable...how would she survive? How could she function even ten more years in this constant never-ending hell?

Dr. Prikh listened sympathetically before responding. "Avital," she said, "is this better or worse than onset?"

Avital considered the question. Onset was a nightmare. Not just because her pain hadn't been managed, and she'd had to wait weeks upon weeks to get in to see specialists for testing before treatment, but because she'd had to maneuver the medical system for the first time in her life as a chronic-pain patient.

"I guess it's a little better," Avital said honestly.

"So there has been improvement?"

"There was, for a time...but the last two months have been really terrible."

"It sounds like you're in a flare," Dr. Prikh said thoughtfully. "But you also had a few fibroids, and they do grow back... Just in case, I think we should get you in for another transvaginal ultrasound."

Avital slumped in her seat. She despised transvaginal ultrasounds. The last one had triggered her vulvodynia so bad, she'd had to sit on a round butt pillow for three weeks.

Worse yet—the reality of the suggestion began spinning in her mind—even if her fibroids had grown back, she wasn't certain she could afford the cost of another expensive surgery. She had insurance through Best Babka, but it certainly wasn't great, and she was already struggling to meet her high deductible. She could ask her parents for help, obviously, but she considered that option an absolute last resort. Medical bills could throw families into bankruptcy, after all.

"And what do I do in the meantime?" Avital asked.

She scrolled through Avital's chart. "I see you're still on the Elmiron, and the birth control…and do you need a new prescription for ibuprofen?"

"That would be great."

"And how are you on the diazepam suppositories?"

"I'm all out."

Her doctor made another note in her chart. "Well," Dr. Prikh said, avoiding eye contact, "I can put in another prescription for that, okay?"

Avital shifted in her seat. "Would it be possible to maybe get more than ten this time?"

Dr. Prikh hesitated. Avital took a deep breath. She was ready to fight for her needs. "The thing is, we're super busy at the bakery right now…and I have all these extra responsibilities…and I just can't afford to be in this much pain right now. It's ruining my life. It's ruining *everything*. And I just think, if I could maybe have a few more pills so I can get through this flare…I think it would help an awful lot."

She stopped herself there. The worst thing a pain patient could be labeled was a drug seeker. Even though, in her mind, all she could think was *help me, please. Help me feel better. See me as a human being, as a person just like you, and help me find some semblance of a life again. I have done everything right.*

Dr. Prikh sighed heavily. "I can write you a prescription for thirteen pills, okay?"

"Only thirteen?"

"Believe me," she said, shaking her head, "I wish I could write you more, but unless you've got a terminal illness nowadays…doctors, and pharmacists, are under tremendous federal scrutiny. I'm sorry, Avital. I really am. But I won't be able to prescribe you any more than that."

"Then what am I supposed to do?"

"Continue what you're doing," Dr. Prikh said, rising from her seat. "Stay on the IC diet. Take the Azo and Uribel and ibuprofen for pain management. Hopefully, this flare you're currently in will pass. But in the meantime, get that transvaginal ultrasound, and come back in three months if the pain doesn't get better on its own, okay?"

With a gentle smile, Dr. Prikh left the room. Avital's eyes drifted back to that painting of a woman, abandoned to a field of flowers, and found it oddly appropriate.

Ethan did his best to appear innocuous. Lingering in the hallway outside Avital's office, he mopped the floors, offering a wide smile to whoever passed. When he was certain that he was past the point of arousing suspicion, he slunk inside.

He closed the door halfway behind him. And then, determined to keep up appearances, he mopped behind her door. He trailed the walls, whistling a happy ditty before finally landing at her desk. A quick glance toward the door told him that the coast was clear. Ethan bent down and opened the top drawer of her desk.

It was not what he was expecting.

The whole thing was loaded down with meds. There were giant wholesale-style bottles of ibuprofen and acetaminophen and at least six different boxes of some drug called Azo. There were also dozens of prescription bottles. Some empty. Some with only one or two pills left. He picked one up, reading the name on the white label pasted on the front: *methenamine*.

Ethan frowned. He didn't know what methenamine

treated, but it sounded illegal. Like one of those drugs Tootles must have sold before he went to prison.

A voice at the end of the hall brought Ethan back to reality. Quickly, he rose from the seat. Grabbing the mop, he returned to the action of mopping innocently. When he heard those voices drift and dissipate, he returned to the desk and opened the second drawer.

It was just as confusing. Inside were four different types of plastic freezer bags. *Yep. Definitely a drug dealer.* But then, right beyond the gallon bags, she had a lavender-scented pillow and four different types of Icy Hot Patches. He scratched his head, trying to understand, before giving up totally. He was running out of time. Ethan opened the third drawer.

It was then that he saw it. Sitting all alone, at the bottom of her desk, was a giant black binder. And not just any binder, either. He could instantly see that it was filled to the brim with papers. He felt certain, positive, that this very special binder in the bottom drawer of her desk *had* to contain the recipe. He couldn't believe he had found it. With shaking hands, he inched his fingers toward it, pulling it out and opening it up.

Instead, he found a photograph in black and white.

Three children, sharing water from a hose, stood outside the entrance to a homeless shelter. It was a compelling composition. Not just the joy of the children, the happy innocence to be playing around a hose on a hot day, but the background of poverty. The juxtaposition of the joy against the harshness of their daily life made his heart ache.

He went to put the image back when he realized he wasn't holding a cookbook at all. He was holding a portfolio.

He was holding Avital's art and photography. Ethan couldn't help himself. He forgot all about his grandfather's silly mission, collapsed into the chair.

The image was just one of many. Ethan continued flipping through. There was a close-up of an old woman, her wrinkled eyes sparkling with joy, each crease and crevice reminding him of the dips and depths of a rocky mountaintop terrain. Another was taken outside an old brick synagogue. Two boy chicks—Hasidic hipsters—smoked cigarettes, their *peyos* tucked behind their ears and underneath black hats. In another, a group of four college-age friends, clad in black leather jackets and black leather pants, waited for breakfast to be served in the booth of an all-night diner.

Ethan felt his heart lurch into his chest. Avital Cohen was so freaking talented.

She had a way of seeing people. She had a way of connecting to her audience through the camera. It impressed him to no end. He wished he had her gift for creativity. Whatever creative talents resided in Ethan had been squashed early on by a grandfather who deemed art, in any form, impractical. And yet, the photographs he was holding were not impractical. They were beautiful.

He couldn't help but wonder why she was working in a bakery, taking pictures of confetti challah for Instagram, instead of sharing her talents with the world. It was beneath that black portfolio that Ethan found his answer. Kept safely inside a manila folder were a stack of rejection letters from different galleries.

Ethan scoffed aloud.

Clearly, those galleries were filled with hacks.

He was just about to put her book of images away when one final photo caught his eye. His focus narrowed. His lower half responded. A small and pleasurable twitch caused his desire for her to grow.

It was a picture of Avital.

She was younger in the picture. Heavier, too. But he would have recognized her anywhere. She was sitting on the roof of an old station wagon. Covered in beads and wearing bell-bottoms, she threw her head back in open laughter, while her arms lifted up to the sun. She was also braless. He could tell because the tank top she wore was loose, and the faintest curve of a perfectly round breast peeked out. His eyes trailed down to her plump thighs.

It was a black-and-white image, almost vintage in its feel, but the sun shone down on her. A thousand tiny rays of light spread out from her heart, as if her smile was the center of the universe and all good things came from her. She looked happy. Free.

The dichotomy struck Ethan hard. Since starting work at Best Babka, he realized he rarely saw Avital smile. Not really. It made him feel bad for her. He couldn't help but wonder what had happened. But it seemed wrong to him—on some higher-plane, spiritual level—for someone this beautiful, someone this talented, to keep her creativity hidden from the world.

Ethan returned her portfolio safely to her drawer, when a commotion at the end of the hall caught his attention.

"Fire!" Chaya shouted, sprinting through Best Babka. "Fire on the second floor! Everybody out!"

THIRTEEN

Avital didn't go back to work right away. Instead, she went to the park a few blocks away from Best Babka, taking a seat on a bench. It was beyond freezing out, but she didn't care. She closed her eyes, allowing the chill to bite at her nose. It was so unfair. She was in pain. She was suffering…and once again, she was left to figure it out on her own.

Three months. She had already survived three weeks, and now, they were tacking on more time to her sentence? How could anyone—*especially a doctor*—ask any human being to survive like that? She didn't know what to do. She didn't know how to face the next three hours, let alone twelve weeks of living like this.

She was scared.

She didn't want to die. She loved life. Her family. Best Babka. Even looking around now—she loved the trees, and the grass, and the snow piled up from the winter around her. She worried a night would come where, abandoned by the medical community and unable to get support, she would see no other out to her chronic pain other than taking her own life.

Avital reached into her pocketbook. Searching for another dose of Azo, she was surprised to see her phone lit up by messages. Josh had called nine times. Quickly, she called him back. Josh picked up on the first ring. The words that came next were harried, frantic...but it only took one word to send a shiver down her spine. *Fire.*

Avital hung up the phone and raced toward Best Babka with full alacrity.

It was a scene out of one of her worst nightmares. Six fire trucks lined the street. Onlookers stood on the sidewalk, their phones pulled out, taking videos. Between them, scattered about on different parts of the street and sidewalk, the staff of Best Babka stood huddled in tiny circles.

"Josh!" Avital said, waving him over. "Over here."

Josh went to her, and the two immediately broke into a tight embrace.

"Everyone is fine," Josh confirmed.

"You sure?"

"Not to worry, Avi," Tootles said, stepping forward with Chaya and Sara. "I did a head count as soon as we got outside. Everybody is accounted for."

Avital breathed a sigh of relief. "And the store?" Avital asked.

"Still standing," Josh said, digging his hands into his pockets.

Avital shook her head. "But I don't understand. What happened?"

"We're not sure." Josh shrugged. "We were all down on the first floor, dealing with the midmorning Shabbat rush, when all of a sudden—"

"Smoke," Chaya said. "Smoke just started seeping downstairs and from every direction."

"I thought I was in a prison riot for a minute," Tootles said.

"Thank God for Chaya," Josh said, clapping her on the back gratefully. "She started running through the building, notifying everybody to get out. The fire department arrived shortly after."

Avital was speechless. In the blink of an eye, everything her family worked so hard for—everything her family loved, including the people inside of their business—could have been lost. Scanning the faces of the crowd, she did her own quick head count.

Josh, Chaya, and Tootles were now standing beside her. Rafi and Marty were nursing cups of Turkish coffee across the street. Then, her eyes landed on Ethan. He was sitting on the sidewalk, his legs splayed, his head folded into his hands.

"Excuse me," a firefighter interrupted them. Avital turned around to see a beast of a man, holding his helmet beneath his arm. "I was wondering if I could talk to the person in charge."

Avital took that as her cue. "That would be me," Avital said, turning around to her extend her hand. "I'm Avital, general manager of Best Babka."

"Jensen," he said, shaking her hand. "If you'd like to follow me, I can tell you a bit about what happened today."

Heading into Best Babka, Avital breathed a sigh of relief. The first floor was still in working order. But it was obvious that the fire had caught everyone by surprise. Pink boxes, half loaded with pastries, littered the counters and floors. In one of the kitchens, a refrigerator had been left open, ruining at least three days' worth of challah dough.

"As you can see," Jensen said, leading her up the staircase to the second floor, "you're pretty good on the first floor.

Not much damage, aside from a little cleanup. The second floor, however…"

Avital gasped at the sight. "Oh my God!"

It looked like the place had been straight up ransacked.

The boxes which had once lined the hallways had now been kicked over. A window was broken. There was a hole in the drywall the size of a crater. The worst part, however, was the laundry room at the end of the hall where large stains of black now painted the paneling and walls. She was speechless. Horrified. Completely overwhelmed.

"Hey," Jensen said sympathetically, "it looks a lot worse than it really is."

"I just…" Avital choked out the words. "I don't understand. What happened?"

"Well," Jensen said, grimacing a little. "It seems someone ran the dryer on your second floor with lint still inside it."

Her mind immediately went to Ethan. "What?"

"Most people don't realize it's a major fire hazard," Jensen said, bending down to showcase a patch of dust and string that had been burned to a crisp. "But the reason I wanted to talk to you about it is, first, you might want to speak with your employees about it, give them a gentle reminder that lint can actually be deadly."

Avital pressed her lips together in a tight smile. "I'll be sure to do that."

"Secondly," Jensen said, standing up to lay one hand on the appliance, "and the main reason I wanted to talk to you privately is this place is a bit of a mess. Your second floor, especially, is littered with stuff. That stuff could have prevented us from getting in or a person from getting out."

Avital closed her eyes, regret coursing through every bone in her body. She knew Jensen was right. The second floor of Best Babka had been a fire hazard for years. It had been on her to-do list to fix forever. But Avital had been so busy with just general maintenance, and surviving her chronic pain, that tasks such as organizing the upstairs had fallen to the wayside.

"Are you shutting us down?" Avital asked.

"No."

"Oh, thank God!" Avital clutched her heart, relieved.

"Look," he said sympathetically, "I know how rough you small businesses got it nowadays. And I also know that shutting you down means a lot of people who work for you won't be able to pay their bills this month. Beyond that, and for purely selfish reasons, everyone knows Best Babka has the best black-and-white cookies around."

Avital smiled. "True."

"Which is why I'm gonna let you off today with a warning."

"A warning?" Avital nearly hugged him.

"I'm giving you six weeks to get this place fixed, okay? Considering you've already got smoke damage on the second floor, and you're gonna need to replace your washer–dryer set anyways…now is the best time to do it. You can keep operating your business out of the first floor in the meantime, but nobody should be upstairs during working hours unless they are specifically cleaning this mess up. Got it?"

"I got it," Avital said.

"Good," he said, offering her a tiny smile. "Because I'm gonna come back in six weeks to do an inspection. Now if you don't have any more questions for me…you and your people have the all clear to return to work."

"Thank you," Avital said, shaking his hand once more.

Jensen departed with a quick jog down the stairs. Moments later, Avital heard the first fire trucks departing, and a rumble rolled through the building, as the staff of Best Babka returned to the building for the day.

Avital took one deep breath, by herself, at the top of the stairs. And then, scanning the damage one last time, uttered the only word that came to mind. *"Oy."*

FOURTEEN

It was not good.

Sitting in the lunchroom, long after the first floor had been cleaned up and the majority of staff had gone home, Ethan was a bundle of frayed nerves. Word had spread rather quickly that he was the one at fault for the fire. But even though every person at Best Babka had been decent about it—far more decent than his own grandfather would have been had he almost burned down the center of their entire livelihood—he still felt terrible.

He was hoping that by staying late he would have the opportunity to apologize to Avital. Instead, and like always, she disappeared into her office, shutting the door behind her. Four hours later, she still hadn't emerged.

"Relax," Tootles said, entering the room.

Reaching for a plastic cup, he filled it with water, handing it to Ethan. Ethan took it gratefully. Anxiously turning the cup in his hand, he tapped his foot repeatedly. Tootles slid down across from him.

"She's gonna fire me," Ethan said.

"She's not gonna fire you," Tootles said.

Ethan chewed on a fingernail. He wished he could believe Tootles. But all he really knew about making mistakes he had learned from his grandfather. Failure was always met with harsh words and terrible criticism. Disappointment was always met with awful consequences.

"You want a boureka?" Tootles asked.

Ethan stopped chewing. "What?"

"Bourekas always make me feel better."

"I'm good."

"Listen," Tootles said, leaning across the table. "I know Avital, okay? Nobody got hurt. The building is still standing. Yes, it could have been a disaster…but it wasn't, all right? Mistakes happen. Fires happen, too. I mean… I've almost burned down Best Babka about eight different times."

"Really?"

"No." Tootles grinned. "I'm just saying that to make you feel better."

With a pep to his step, Tootles departed for the evening. Ethan realized that it was only him and Avital alone in Best Babka now.

There was nothing left to do but face the inevitable. Gathering his courage, he headed toward her office. He was only inches from the closed door when a sound caught him off guard. Avital was in her office crying.

Leaning in closer, placing one ear against the shut door, he confirmed. Not just crying, but sobbing. He could hear her choking in between breaths and bellows of sorrow. Ethan knew that kind of pain.

Gathering his courage, he knocked on the door. All at once,

the sobbing went silent. He heard her rustle for something—drawers opening, a chair moving—before finally, she responded.

"Yes?" Avital shouted.

"It's me," Ethan said. "I was wondering if I could talk to you for a minute?"

Avital hesitated. "Fine."

Ethan opened the door. Face-to-face with Avital, his heart broke: he could see the hurt he had caused. Her eyes were bloodshot. Her entire face was puffy. It looked like she had been crying for hours. She was doing her best to hold back the floodgates, but it wasn't working. Almost as soon as he met her eyes, the sobbing began again.

"Oh gosh," Ethan said, racing to get her a tissue. "Let me help you."

"I'm fine," she said, waving him away.

"You're not fine."

"I'm fine!" she snapped at him, expelling a ball of snot into another tissue.

And then, Ethan just came out with it. "I'm really sorry about the laundry."

Avital looked up from her tissue. "What?"

"I'm sorry," he said, rambling, desperately trying to alleviate the situation. "I messed up. I didn't mean to almost burn down Best Babka. But I swear to God, Avital... I learned my lesson about the lint, and it will never happen again. I will work doubly hard, extra hours and everything, to make it up to you. I'll even pay for the damages out of my salary."

The admission seemed to work. Avital stopped crying long enough to meet his eyes.

"I'm not upset about the laundry."

"You're not?"

"No," she said, before adding, "well, I mean... I am upset

about the laundry and the fire...but I'm not upset at you, Ethan. It was an honest mistake, and I know you'll work hard to rectify it, okay?"

"So I'm not getting fired?"

"Not today, anyway."

Ethan couldn't help but feel relieved. Still, he couldn't be more perplexed by the whole situation. "Then, why," Ethan said, rubbing the back of his neck, trying to make sense of the situation, "are you sitting in your office crying?"

Avital sighed and rubbed her forehead. Meeting his gaze directly, she looked at him like some lost puppy dog, sad and confused. "It's complicated."

"Oh," Ethan said, surprised by her answer. "Well, I can do complicated."

Avital sighed. "I have a disease called interstitial cystitis."

Ethan shook his head. "I'm not familiar with it."

"It's a chronic-pain condition that affects the bladder. Actually, it's a whole bunch of other things too...fibroids, cysts, wonky cramps and spasms... Honestly, half the time my doctors have no idea what's wrong with me. But basically, I'm in pain. I'm in pain all the time."

"That sounds—" Ethan searched for a word "—horrible."

"It's not fun."

Ethan considered his last week at work. He had thought Avital was rude. He had thought she was avoiding him. He didn't realize she was in pain. But lining up all her oddities now, things began to make sense. The way she was always disappearing, sprinting through a conversation, or ignoring him. The whole lack of underwear, especially.

Ethan's eyes trailed down the length of her form. She looked tired. Her whole body, the way she slumped in her seat, reminded him of petals falling off a tree after the first full bloom of cherry-blossom season. He couldn't help but compare this Avital to the one hidden away in the bottom drawer of her desk. It seemed so unfair. It seemed so wrong, too.

Ethan ran his hand down his face. "I'm so sorry, Avi."

"Thank you," she said, finally meeting his eyes directly. "Believe it or not, that means a whole lot."

Ethan nodded. A moment of silence passed between them.

"Anyway," Avital continued, grabbing another tissue, "the reason I'm crying is because my pain has been getting worse. A lot worse. So I went to my doctor today, begging for help, begging for her to give me something to feel better...and she couldn't. *She wouldn't help me.* And then I came back to work, and Best Babka was on fire...and now, on top of being in severe pain, I need to call insurance and get new laundry units and clean up the entire second floor..."

The tears began falling again. Ethan stood to grab her another tissue.

"And I'm swamped, Ethan!" Avital said, growing agitated. "I'm completely overwhelmed and exhausted. And maybe I could handle it all if I wasn't flaring...but I'm in so much pain. I'm hurting all the damn time, and I don't know how to survive this. I don't know how I'm gonna be able to handle this, when I'm already hanging on to my sanity by the very tips of my fingernails."

Avital collapsed into her hands once more. Ethan swallowed. Seeing her cry brought his own feelings of being stuck—*of being squeezed*—to the forefront of his mind. Though his own hurts were not of a physical nature, he understood carrying a pain that no one else saw.

"If you feel that awful, Avital," Ethan said it gently, "why don't you just go home?"

"I can't."

"Of course you can," Ethan said, pointing out the obvious. "You're the boss."

"No," she repeated, more adamantly. "I can't. I have to file a claim with insurance, and I'm behind doing all the paperwork for tax season, and someone needs to go to Queens to buy more supplies at the wholesale market on Sunday...because Josh can't be trusted to go alone. And my brother, and my *zeyde*...but especially, the entire staff of Best Babka...they rely on me, Ethan. So I can't go home. I can't take the time off right now, no matter how sick I am, or how awful I feel, because all these people *need* me to be here."

Ethan felt his heart lurch into his throat. He couldn't say it aloud, of course, but he felt like he was talking to himself. Ethan knew the pressures that came with being heir to a baking empire better than anyone. He also knew what it meant to have people rely on you. He felt the same exact way about Randy and Kayla.

"Well, what do you need?" Ethan asked quietly.

Avital coughed through her tears. "What?"

"I mean, you keep talking about all these people needing something from you...but what do you need, Avital?"

She laughed, manic and wild, before answering. "I need another me."

Ethan considered her words. "Okay. Simple enough."

"What are you talking about?"

"Make me your right-hand man."

"I don't understand."

"You know," he said, trying to explain, "like an assistant, or an intern, or your very own personal manservant...whatever you want to call it. The point is, let me help you with all the things you need to do, whatever extras or difficulties feel overwhelming, until you feel well enough to get back on your feet again and tackle things on your own."

He wasn't sure why he was offering, but he could almost hear this tiny voice, whispering away in his brain. *See, Ethan?*

This is how a Lippmann operates. Infiltrate while she's down, become a trusted companion. Pretty soon, she'll be begging you to take that pumpkin-spiced babka recipe.

No, that wasn't it at all. Because when he looked at her—when he saw her crying—he wasn't thinking about manipulating her into giving him the recipe. He wasn't thinking about his clear physical attraction to her, the sight of her bottomless brunch on his first day of work, or the curve of her breast in a black-and-white image. *Though he did, truly, enjoy both.* All he could think about was that Avital was in pain. She was hurting. And Ethan, being a fellow human being with feelings, wanted to take that pain away.

Ethan found his footing. "Let me help you."

"You can barely do laundry," she reminded him.

"True." He smiled, coming in closer. "But I didn't have experience with laundry."

Avital gaped. "How can someone not have experience with laundry?"

"Long story," he said, quickly veering to a new topic. "But I do have a ton of experience with payroll, taxes, and ordering supplies."

"How are you at packing and lifting heavy boxes?"

"I love packing and lifting heavy boxes!"

Avital considered his offer. "I would need you to stay late. I can't risk losing an extra body during the day."

"Done."

"I'll pay you for the overtime, obviously."

"Great."

"It's not going to be fun work, either," she continued. "It's going to be long hours, late into the night, just me and you on the cramped and sweltering second floor. It gets really hot up there, too. *Really* uncomfortable. That's why we never use the space, to be honest. Some people think it's haunted, too."

"Sounds fun." Ethan found himself weirdly excited by the prospect. Though Avital—he couldn't help but think it—seemed desperate for Ethan to rescind the offer.

"I don't know," Avital said, still hesitating.

"Look," he said, pulling up a chair. "I know it's hard to rely on other people when you're used to doing everything on your own. I get it, okay? I'm the exact same way. But the way I see it, this is a win-win situation for both of us. I get to learn about the inner workings of running a thriving kosher family bakery, and you *need* the help. So let me help you, Avital. Let me be the guy who comes when you call and jumps when you need him. Besides, it's the least I can do for almost burning down Best Babka."

Avital laughed aloud at that one. Ethan couldn't help but warm at the sight of her. Her eyes drifted over him like he was some newfound curiosity. Her focus narrowed. The tiniest slit of a smile appeared in the place of that cute little frown. And then, likely because she was desperate and he was offering, Avital agreed.

"Fine," she said, shaking her head. "From this point on, you can be my official manservant."

FIFTEEN

Avital barely had time to shake the snow from her coat before her parents appeared. Even though Shabbat dinner was long over, they had clearly been waiting up in the aftermath of the news. When she stepped through the front entrance, they left their cups of tea on the living-room coffee table, racing toward the front door. Offering hugs and kisses, they apologized for never replacing the laundry unit upstairs and leaving the place a mess. Avital did her best to assuage their guilt.

"It's fine," Avital said over and over. "Really."

"Are you sure?" Her mother glanced between her and her father. "Because we're happy to start coming in and helping you clean up the second floor."

Her father frowned, forlorn. "Josh said it's a disaster. That it will take weeks to clean up."

"And you already have *sooo* much on your plate."

It wasn't really a plate as much as a pelvis.

Avital considered their offer. It wasn't a bad idea. The upstairs was littered with their crap, after all. *And her grandparents' crap.* If Avital wanted to be a total brat about the whole thing, she could easily demand they fix the whole place themselves.

The problem was…at least, for Avital…it sucked working that closely with your parents. She knew this from experience, having spent most of her life working after school at the bakery in order to help out.

Now, as an adult, already living at home with Mom and Dad, the last thing she wanted was to have them back in *her* building. She loved her parents, obviously. And she was grateful for them. But you didn't need to be a baker to know that spending 24/7 with your parental units was a recipe for disaster. Someone was likely to get murdered.

Besides, she already had a totally practical and clearly nonromantic offer of help from Ethan. Whether or not she found him wildly attractive was irrelevant. He was, from a purely logical standpoint, a much better choice of company.

"It's fine," Avital repeated. "Ethan, the new hire, has actually agreed to stay late and help me begin cleaning up. We'll have it fixed up in no time."

"Oh," her mother said, perking up. "Oh! That's wonderful."

"Yep."

"What a nice boy," her mother said, shaking her head.

"And a baker," her father reminded all of them.

Her mother squeezed her wrist, leaning in, but not bothering to whisper. "Bakers make the best lovers, honey."

"It's true," her father said, beaming with pride.

"Okay," Avital said, ready to end the conversation immediately, "on that note, I'm going to grab something to eat and head to bed."

Avital made her way to the kitchen. Grabbing some cold

chicken broth from the refrigerator and spooning it into a glass, she retreated to her childhood bedroom.

Taking a seat at her desk, she placed her glass of soup to the side. Today had been a whirlwind. Crappy doctors. Fires. *Ethan Rosenberg.* What was she going to do? How the hell was she going to survive working, all alone, on the cramped second floor with him? It was one of those things that led to flirting. Flirting could lead to kissing. And then, where would she and her broken-down cherry rugelach be?

Sighing heavily, she didn't want to deal with it now. For one, she didn't even know if Ethan liked her. Granted, she was attracted to him. But that didn't mean he was attracted to her. Likely, they would hang out together—night after night—and nothing at all would happen between them. She was just freaking out, spiraling into needless anxiety. She desperately needed to put him out of her mind and find a way to relax.

Avital glanced over to her bathroom.

Oh, how she would love to take a bath.

It had been almost a year since she had last taken a bath. Once she'd developed IC and the associated vulvodynia, she'd found that even water—everything from bath time to taking a cooling dip during summertime in a pool—could cause her to flare. For this reason, and like everything in life that had once given her pleasure, she avoided taking baths.

She couldn't help herself. She folded her chin into the palm of her hand, staring at the tub longingly. What would be the harm? She was already in horrible pain. Maybe if she were super careful, only spent five minutes maximum in there, she could enjoy the sensation without getting worse.

She decided to be brave. Heading to her bathroom, she grabbed a washcloth, cleaning out the bottom of the tub, making sure that any speck of dust—or chemical from a cleaning solution—would be eradicated before getting in. When she had wiped down every square inch of the porcelain tub, she turned on the water and began to undress.

She slipped off her socks, skirt, shirt, and bra. And then, totally naked, she caught her reflection in the mirror.

The sight startled her.

Avital had not actually seen herself fully naked in some time. Normally, she got up early and threw on clothes in a semiawake state—not caring about how she presented herself or the way she looked. But she was so thin now. Her ribs jutted out from beneath her breasts and peeked through the skin on her back. And yet, despite her clear downward trend on the BMI scale, the hormones she was taking to regulate her estrogen levels had changed her body.

She was twenty-four and emaciated, but somehow, her hips were wider. She had a strange buildup of fat around her thighs that when she bent over to inspect more closely, curdled like cottage cheese around her muscle. Her eyes wandered to her lower abdomen. Across her belly, at both the place of her navel and the spot right between her hip bones, ran two long and raised pinkish-purple scars.

The scars themselves didn't bother her. Everybody had scars. It was what they represented. Battle wounds. A never-ending war with her body. Hurt and trauma. *How could anybody love something that had hurt them so bad?*

The bath was ready. Avital turned away from the mirror. Resolving herself to bravery, she put one toe—followed by a whole foot—into the steaming water. *It felt remarkable.* Like Heaven. Absolute pleasure. She had forgotten how good hot water against her aching flesh could feel. And then, forcing herself to continue experimenting, she popped the other foot in. She now had both feet in the scalding water.

Oh, how she wanted more.

She began to inch down. To her thighs. Each centimeter

of skin feeling like another victory. And then, right before the hot water was to meet the tips of her labia, she stopped.

Whatever pleasure was there, waiting for her beneath that water, dissipated into fear. She was suddenly reliving two years of sleepless nights, writhing in pain. She remembered how bad it could get, none of her medicines working, having to wait weeks to see a doctor for a supposedly urgent appointment.

She became overwhelmed by the memories, all those medical traumas—feet wedged into stirrups, doctors poking her, crying out in pain during hydrodistensions and biopsies, all while those same doctors told her that her *pain was impossible*. But it was possible. Wouldn't she know, better than any doctor, if there was something hurting inside her own body?

She couldn't go through that again.

Avital rose from the water and quickly drained the tub.

Intimacy. That was the thing she really missed in her life since developing chronic pelvic pain. That was the feeling tumbling around inside her when she looked back at Ethan. She missed the feeling of being wrapped up in one person. She missed lying in bed with someone, tangled up in the sheets together, arms wrapped tightly around her own.

She missed sex, too. *Obviously.* But what she really wanted, beyond the memory of a pain-free touch and an orgasm that didn't induce a week's worth of burning spasms and pain, was the closeness that came from being in partnership with another human being. She wanted to find her person.

Being a pragmatist about these things, she understood that there were certain expectations that came with being in a long-term relationship with another human being. Like regular sex. Or having children. But even if she could get pregnant...she wasn't certain that she would want to.

The thought of having anything else pressing against her, causing more damage to her already broken body, was beyond unbearable. It was kind of Ethan to offer help. But even if she was attracted to him—heck, even if he were attracted to her—what did it matter? The ask, on both of them, felt too high.

SIXTEEN

Ethan awoke to find himself covered in a cold sweat. Sitting up in bed, breathing heavily, he reminded himself that it was just a nightmare. He was no stranger to them. Ever since his parents had died, they had been a constant in his life.

Rising from his bed, he went to the bathroom. Washing his face and getting dressed for the day, he forced himself to get a grip. *He had not been on that plane. He was not responsible for what happened. He was not a little boy anymore, his life spiraling out of control.* But catching his reflection in the mirror—trying to compare the memory of his parents against the image of the man he found there—he wasn't entirely certain that his last statement was entirely true.

Avital.

What the hell was he going to do about Avital?

He shouldn't have done it—offered to help her. He could tell himself that he was simply using her, trying to get closer to her in order to steal that recipe...but he knew that wasn't the truth.

There was just something about her. Some pull toward her he didn't fully understand. The way he had wanted to help her when she was crying. The admiration he had felt upon seeing her photographs. Her pale rump, shining up at him in the moonlight. He wasn't lying when he said he wanted to help her. He was also more than a little bit excited to finally be spending time with her.

But then, there was also Kayla. And Randy. There was all that guilt he held on to for surviving. *Because he wasn't on that plane.* And then, acknowledging that he was stuck, that he was a Lippmann, that he was building a house of cards that would, eventually and no matter what, come falling down around him, he realized that he didn't know what he was doing at all. He was totally and completely lost.

Dragging one hand down his face, he returned to his bedroom. Reaching into his nightstand, he pulled out two bags. The first one, knitted in yarns of gold, purple, and white, held his *tallit*, *kippah* and a *siddur*, or prayer book. The second one, made of crushed blue velvet, held his *tefillin*.

Opening the first bag, he placed the *kippah* on his head. Then, unfolding his large *tallit*, he said the blessing before wrapping it around his shoulders like a cape, letting it trail down to the center of his thighs.

He always liked the feeling of the *tallit gadol*. He remembered when his grandfather had first given the large prayer shawl to him. It had been on the occasion of his bar mitzvah, when he had turned thirteen years old, becoming an adult under Jewish legal tradition. Back then, the *tallit* had swum on his tiny frame. Now, it fit perfectly across his broad shoulders. Thinking back on the day, the pain of his parents' loss an ever-present reality in the empty pews and unfamiliar synagogue he was about to enter, he remembered what his grandfather had told him.

"Listen, Ethan," Moishe had said, before fixing the collar of his shirt and handing him his first tallit to wear, "what's the other option? Stand around and mope?"

That was the thing about Moishe.

For all his rants and tirades, he wasn't all bad.

Ethan shook the memory away. Reaching for the second bag, he opened it up. Inside, he found the set of small black leather boxes with corresponding leather straps, each containing scrolls of parchment inscribed with verses from the Torah.

He knew the pair he used were far too worn down at this point to still be considered kosher. The prayer scrolls inside each box, made of lamb skin and etched with ink by a special scribe, had certainly faded in their holy lettering, but Ethan didn't care. This pair of *tefillin* had once belonged to his father.

After his death, Ethan had inherited them in a box that Moishe had deemed important. Ironically, it had also been Moishe who had taught Ethan how to wrap *tefillin*.

Ethan was still in the period of mourning for his parents. Moishe was still in the period of mourning for his daughter. For the eight months that followed his bar mitzvah, Ethan would get up each morning with his grandfather and head to *shul*. Standing there beside him, both of them wrapped up in their rituals and patterns, the only words shared between them belonged to the ancient text of their prayer book.

For Ethan—and probably, for his grandfather—it was easier this way. Not having to talk about what had happened. Not having to find some common ground. They put on their *tallit* and *tefillin*, and opened their *siddurs*, and for that one hour each day, they had a way to confront the things that had hurt them.

That was the thing about loss. It was also the part the poets and authors tended to gloss over. Grief was survivable. Judaism had six thousand years of history that made death and dying more tolerable.

Ethan took out the box that would go on his left arm. Positioning it at the fleshy bit of his forearm, he pointed it across from his heart, tightening the knotted loop there. Bringing the strap below the elbow, he proceeded to wrap the leather around his arm seven times. Carefully, he kept the loops equidistant from each other, arranging them in a neat pattern, tightening them repeatedly by pulling and shifting, before finally placing the strap around his hand to rest.

Next, he took the box out for his head. Finding his hairline, he checked that the front was centered between the eyes and the back knot was positioned in the soft spot at the upper part of his neck, before bringing the straps around to the front, letting them fall over his pectoral muscles.

Finally, he returned to his left hand. Unwinding the strap, starting over, he began to form one of the names of God, *Shaddai*, around his finger. Looping three Hebrew letters across his fingers, he made a *shin*, *dalet* and *yod*, before stopping at his middle finger to recite a verse from the book of Hosea. *"I betroth you to me forever. I betroth you to me in righteousness, justice, lovingkindness, and mercy."*

It was such an intimate verse. It was such an intimate ceremony. Wrapping the leather around your middle finger, talking about betrothal, all while tangled up in a large white sheet literally the size of a blanket. He wondered if the rabbis had done it on purpose, if it was supposed to make you think of love, and passion…and maybe even sex. His mind wandered to Avital.

His body responded. Ethan looked down. *Great. Just fabulous.* What kind of horrible Jew got aroused standing before God? Ethan rolled his eyes up to the ceiling. "Sorry," he said, before adding, "but also…kind of your fault for making her so cute."

Ethan waited for a response.

When he didn't get hit by lightning, he figured they were cool.

Picking up his *siddur*, he put Avital firmly out of his mind and got on with his davening.

SEVENTEEN

Avital had chewed the tip of her plastic pen into a rectangle. Sitting in her office, staring at the glowing screen of her desktop computer, she was working hard at pretending to work on the budget. In reality, she couldn't stop thinking about Ethan. When was he going to get here?

"Hey, Avi. Happy—"

Avital spun around in her seat. When she realized that the male voice in her threshold did not belong to Ethan, her smile faded. "Oh," she said, disappointed. "It's you."

"Uh," Josh said, bemused. "Nice to see you, too."

"Sorry," Avital said, waving away any offense. "I didn't mean it like that. It's just... I've been waiting for Ethan."

"Oh yeah?" Josh smirked.

She rolled her eyes, spinning in her chair away from him. "I didn't mean it like that."

Entering the office, Josh took a seat in front of her desk.

"Just so you know," Josh said, lacing his fingers behind his head, "Mom says to tell you that bakers make the best lovers."

"Josh!"

"What?" Josh laughed. "You knew Mom was gonna call me first thing Saturday night and tell me about the whole Ethan Rosenberg offering to help you out with things situation."

"It's not even like that."

"I can see it now," he said, making a square with his hands like he were filming a movie. "Ethan, walking around shirtless, waving a wrench, talking about how he needs to get this tight screw loosened. In case you're wondering, Avi, you're the screw. You're the tightly wound thing that needs to be undone."

Avital crossed her arms against her chest. "Really?"

"We'll call it *Kissing Kosher*," he said and smiled, spreading his hands as if the title were up in lights on a billboard somewhere. "All the bagel chasers will love it."

"You're disgusting."

He tsked his teeth teasingly at her. Even if the idea of her and Ethan hooking up all over Best Babka were somewhat tempting...it was also ridiculous. The burning ache she currently felt between her legs, the spasms and the pressure, had nothing to do with desire. Still, if Josh wanted to spar over secret attractions, she was more than happy to throw jabs back. After all, she *lived* with their parents. She had heard more than a few rumors about Josh from *Ema* Cohen, too.

"Like you're one to talk." Avital snickered in his direction. "Don't think I haven't noticed you sneaking off constantly to talk to someone on your phone. Or texting beneath the counter when you think no one is looking. I'm docking your pay this week, by the way."

Josh beamed, clutching his heart. "She is worth every penny."

"Oh boy," Avital said, rubbing her temples. "It's been what...two weeks? So I'm assuming you're planning to propose to her this weekend?"

"Actually," Josh said, "I'm taking it slow with this one."

"Three weeks, then?"

Josh turned red as a cherry, but otherwise refused to offer any hints.

She was glad to hear her brother finally taking it slow with a woman. Josh was more than her twin. He was her best friend. He deserved a good woman. His problem was, however, that he wanted to be married—carting three kids to *shul* in a stroller—since yesterday. It meant he often rushed into relationships, even when they weren't the best fit.

She had seen him cry his heart out over a woman dozens of times. In truth, she was tired of him getting hurt. She felt the easiest way to avoid such a problem was not to rush into things. But Josh...he adored rushing.

"Tell you what," Josh said, smiling at her. "I'll promise to slow down...if you promise to speed up."

"Speed up at what?" Avital scoffed.

"You know," Josh said, demonstrating with his hands. "Doing the old *lulav*-and-*etrog* shake."

Avital shook her head. "Thanks for ruining Sukkot for me."

A knock at the door drew both their attention.

"Sorry to interrupt," Ethan said, "but I'm here to help Avital for the day."

Her stomach dipped. Ethan looked particularly stunning this morning. Perhaps she had been too distraught to notice it through her tears on Friday, but as he stood in her doorway, wearing a crisp button-down, sleeves rolled halfway up, along with tailored wool pants, she couldn't help but find her eyes wandering down the length of his form.

It was amazing how he could do that. Pull off that unassuming yet classic look. Like he rolled out of his bed with his hair perfectly disheveled, but smelling like Old Spice and without wrinkling his shirt.

"Right," Avital said. "Of course. Josh and I were just finishing up."

She waited for Josh to leave. When he did, she directed Ethan to the chair across from her. She shuffled some papers, making some comment about little brothers, before Ethan took a seat. Spreading his legs wide apart, he ran his hands down his thick thighs.

God. He had such beautiful thighs.

She could imagine all the things he could do with them.

She needed to get a grip. She reminded herself that she was his boss and there was nothing more to their relationship than that. That his eyes flicked upward and sank unwaveringly into her soul when he looked at her meant nothing. She was reading into things. She was seeing things. It was likely some sort of delusion, brought on by chronic pain, lack of sleep, and involuntary celibacy for the last two years.

"So," Ethan asked, "how are you feeling today?"

"A little better," she said.

"But not great?"

"I'm never really...great."

"Well," he said and smiled, "I'm happy I'm here to help, then."

Avital whimpered. Ethan was like finding a well in the middle of a desert. She hadn't realized till he was sitting there in front of her how much she needed someone to show up and just simply help her.

"So," Ethan said, breaking eye contact, "where would you like me to begin?"

"I have a list," she said, holding a paper up in the air.

"Great," Ethan said, rising to take it, "because I am a man who loves a good to-do list."

It was then that she saw the distinct impression of strap marks creasing his skin. All at once, she forgot about the list. She was completely transfixed, totally mesmerized by the sight.

"You lay *tefillin*?" she said, nodding toward his left arm.

"Oh," he said, moving to roll his cuffs down, "yeah."

Avital was sad to see him cover them up. *Beautiful.* They were so intensely beautiful. He was so intensely beautiful in them. The artist in her, the photographer, was not prepared to lose the image forever.

Avital swallowed. "I didn't realize you were religious."

"I'm not," Ethan said before backtracking. "I mean… I'm not really consistent with it."

"You don't wear a *kippah*, though?"

"Like I said—" he blushed, eyes lowering "—inconsistent."

"But you don't keep kosher?"

Ethan squinted. "I keep kosher."

A heat rose in her cheeks. This was bad. Terrible. Avital had a thing for hot and inconsistent but still decently observant Jewish men. She loved nothing more than a man sporting a *kippah*, quoting her verses from Talmud and Pirkei Avot. Once in Jewish summer camp, she'd caught sight of the older boys down by the lake laying *tefillin* while in their swim trunks one morning—and it basically ruined her for life.

She needed to stop talking Jewy with Ethan.

"Do you keep kosher?" he asked.

"It's kind of a moot point."

"Why moot?"

"Well, for one," she said, rolling her eyes to the ceiling, "I'd have to be able to eat more than four items." Ethan stared blankly. Avital realized he didn't know what she was talking about. "I'm on this awful specialized diet for my disease where I basically can't eat anything."

"Ah," he said thoughtfully, before adding, "so that's why you only eat salad at lunch?"

"Believe me," she sighed, "it's not by choice."

"But I noticed you called me on Shabbat?"

"I noticed you picked up."

His chin tilted flirtatiously. "Like I said... Inconsistent."

She knew she needed to end this line of questioning, immediately. But the *tefillin* straps—also, to be fair, the suggestive way he kept rubbing his thighs—were stoking her curiosity.

"So you're not *shomer Shabbat*?" she asked

"No."

"Do you light candles?"

"Not really."

"But you keep kosher?"

He shifted. "My dad kept kosher."

"*Kept?*" Avital blinked, surprised. "Your father passed?"

"Oh," Ethan said, sitting up in his seat. "No. I just meant... I grew up in a kosher home. My mom and my dad are both retired now and living in Connecticut. I have a sister there, too, actually. A whole big...loving family."

"That's nice."

He nodded. "I'm very lucky."

He was showing her his depth. It was the thing she had always loved about taking photographs. The layers. In her artwork, what was in the background was often more important than what was on the surface. Like *peshat* and *derash*, the two methods for reading sacred text, you had to look beyond the simplicity of the first layer in order to find the deeper, hidden meaning.

"So why do you do it?" she asked point-blank.

"What?"

"Why do you lay *tefillin*…and keep kosher…if you're so inconsistent?"

He took one deep breath through his nose before answering. "You know that old saying, *There's no such thing as an atheist in a foxhole*?" Avital nodded. "That's why."

Avital considered the statement.

"And what about you?" he asked. "Are you religious?"

It wasn't an easy question. "I used to be more observant," she admitted. "But not in the last few years."

"Why not in the last few years?"

She answered him honestly. "You know that old saying *There's no such thing as an atheist in a foxhole*?"

Ethan grinned. "Yeah."

"It's wrong," she said, meeting his eyes directly. "Atheists are created in foxholes."

The statement caught him off guard. Ethan cocked his head back and swallowed. "Hm," he said, thinking it over. He tapped his cheek a few times before looking at the wall. Moments later, he returned his gaze to her. His dark eyes were two narrow slits angled in her direction.

Avital felt like she had gone too far. "Sorry."

"Don't be sorry," Ethan said. His voice was clear. Firm. "I actually… I really like talking about this stuff with you."

A silence filled the room. His gaze tore through her. Things had just gotten way too intimate. She needed to find an escape route and quick. "Anyway," Avital said, reaching for her to-do list and waving it in front of him, "I should probably let you know what I need help with today."

For the next twenty minutes, Avital went over her list with

Ethan. In addition to Ethan's regular tasks, like making pink boxes and taking phone orders, he was going to head to the wholesale market to stock up on supplies. In truth, he was also there to accompany Josh, who often used the weekly run to garner inspiration, and ingredients, for the creation of a weekly specialty item.

"The thing you need to know about Josh," Avital said, "is he's very gifted in the kitchen. The specialty items he makes each week are always some of our bestsellers. But sometimes, his brilliant ideas are bigger than what he can realistically accomplish in a week. The way we've worked this out is he gets one item that's not on the list—*one*—under ten dollars, per run, per week. I love my brother, but I find he works better with boundaries."

"He can't be that bad?"

Avital sucked all the air back through her teeth. "Yeah... he can."

"*Oy.*"

Finally, with nothing left on the list to discuss for the day, Avital rose from her seat. Ethan followed suit.

"Of course—" she smiled, totally professionally "—if you have any questions or problems, my cell is at the top of the page. Feel free to call or text me."

Ethan folded the list in half, placing it into his pocket for safekeeping. He lingered at her desk for another moment—his face red, his eyes on the floor—before turning to exit. Avital couldn't help herself. Her eyes drifted down to where two perfectly round challah buns flexed in time with each other.

That tuchus, though.

And then, Avital stood up, closed the door to her office, and forced herself to get a grip.

EIGHTEEN

Ethan stood at the counter of the wholesale market in Queens, surrounded by aisles of dead fish, dead meat, and more cheese floating in containers of brine than he had ever seen in his life. It was loud. And smelly. And really freaking cold. But considering he had never been grocery shopping before in his life, he was surprised at how well he was managing.

What he was not managing well was his attraction for Avital. It wasn't just physical with her, but mental. He kept thinking about the conversation they'd had in her office. She was clever as well as lovely. She had caught him off guard with her comment about foxholes.

Meanwhile, he was lying to her.

Pulling his trolley full of food items off to the side, dragging one hand down his face, he tried to get her out of his mind by focusing on practicalities. Scanning the crowds and the vendors, he searched for Josh.

Ethan had last seen him almost an hour ago when they were

in the produce section. Josh had run off to poke and prod at a new shipment of dragon fruit, while Ethan was left stacking up fifty pounds of bananas. He had no idea why they needed so many bananas at Best Babka. He didn't recall banana bread or banana muffins on the menu. But when he checked Avital's list with Josh, her brother had confirmed that fifty pounds of bananas was correct.

After that, Ethan had basically been left on his own.

Standing there, he double-checked his list one more time to make sure that he had gotten everything Avital expected.

There were five fifty-pound bags of whole wheat flour. One fifty-pound bag of white flour. Enough herbs to start their own botanical garden. Fruit. Vegetable. Milk. *Crap.* He still needed cheese. Pushing his trolley down the aisle, following Avital's carefully laid-out map and instructions, he made his way to the cheese station.

"How can I help you today, sir?" a man in a white cap called over the counter.

Ethan checked his notes. "Sixteen pounds of feta."

"Which one?" he said, pointing with his tongs to the three dozen plastic bins of white cheese, swimming in brine, in front of him.

"I… I…" Ethan hesitated, staring down at his list. All it said was *feta.* He flipped through pages, searching for an answer. When that yielded no results, he looked behind him, hoping to find Josh. Alas, Josh was still missing. "Sorry," he said, moving to pull out his phone and call Avital. It was the last thing he wanted to do. He knew she was extremely busy.

"Who you with?" the guy asked.

"Best Babka," Ethan said, replacing his phone.

"Oh." Lucky for Ethan, he recognized the name immediately. "Avital and Josh's crew. No problem. You want the Machenzi family brand. Imported from Santorini, Greece. Good stuff. Kosher. Expensive. But only the best at Best Babka."

"So I'm learning," Ethan said.

The man turned away, heading for a refrigerator at the back of his stall. Pulling another large plastic bin out and opening the top, he grabbed a hunk of cheese and, changing his coat and gloves, laid it on a separate counter, cutting it with a separate knife.

"You new?" the man asked, looking back.

"One week in," Ethan explained. "I'm gonna be helping Avi out for a while."

"Good for you," he said. "Avi could certainly use it." That seemed to be the never-ending refrain when it came to her.

Taking the giant hunk of cheese, Ethan added it to the trolley. Now officially done with the shopping, he texted Josh a message that he was getting in line. Heading down to checkout, seeing the way the line snaked halfway into the market, he settled in for a long wait.

Suddenly, the sound of rattling—followed by someone calling his name—caused him to turn. Josh was coming his way. But he was pushing his own trolley, completely loaded up with stuff. Josh parked his trolley right behind Ethan.

"No," Ethan said.

"Come on," Josh whined. "I need this stuff."

Ethan glanced over his items quickly. He could make out three boxes of dragon fruit. Six boxes of asparagus. Some sort of wok, and a blow-up dinosaur doll. But it was the four packs of rib eye that completely threw him off.

"Josh—" Ethan shook his head "—why are you buying meat?"

"I have an idea."

Ethan bent down to inspect it. "This isn't even kosher."

"It's not?" Josh shook his head, surprised. "Oh, I guess I

got so excited about my idea I didn't even think to check. Anyways, I'm gonna get it." He went to push his cart forward again.

Ethan placed one hand out, stopping him. "No."

"But—"

"One item," Ethan said, remembering his lesson from Avi. "Under ten dollars. Let's try to keep it kosher, too."

Josh huffed, pushed his trolley back to return the items. He spent a few minutes, fist on his chin, picking through items, debating this dragon over that box of strawberries, before returning with a three-pound jar of maraschino cherries.

"Happy?" Josh asked.

Ethan checked the price. They were under budget. "Thrilled."

Josh put the cherries on the trolley, and the two men settled into waiting in line together. Ethan knew he should make small talk. Get friendly. *Ask about the pumpkin-spiced babka recipe.* But all he could think about was how he was standing next to Avi's brother. He wanted to ask questions about her.

"It's the key to a woman's heart, you know?"

Ethan squinted. "What?"

"Cooking for them," he said, nodding toward the cherries. "That's why I'm getting the cherries."

Did he really want to know about this? He wasn't sure. But they were standing there, surrounded by feta cheese and fish eyes, and Ethan got the feeling he was gonna get the story from Josh whether he wanted it or not.

"Anyway," Josh said, "I'm seeing this new girl. And she's kind of been my muse the last two weeks for developing all my specialty items for Best Babka. You see, every week, she tells me something new about her. For example, two weeks ago, we're talking about Passover, and she tells me how she

loved those chocolate-covered jellies on Passover as a kid...
You know, the ones that came in boxes?"

"Yeah, of course," Ethan admitted. "Everybody knows
them."

"So you know what I do?" Josh said, leaning in. "I make
her a chocolate cake. I make a jam, mixing fresh raspberries
and the insides of those jelly candies. Delicious, man. So it's
Saturday night, we're watching Netflix, feeding each other
pieces. She's got her head on my belly. Right here, you know?
And I'm rubbing her hair. Pure bliss, being like that with a
woman. I don't need anything else, you know?"

Ethan shifted in his spot. He didn't actually know.

"I don't." Ethan cleared his throat. "I'm not actually dating anyone right now."

"Oh," Josh said, turning down the corners of his mouth.
"Sorry to hear that, man. You know, Avi's single, too. *Anyway...*" He let the pause linger there just a little too long.
"Last week, she tells me about how, when she was little, they
would all go down to the Jersey Shore and her parents would
get her and her sisters Shirley Temples. So now I'm thinking,
I got to make her something with cherries. I was considering making her a cherry tart, but that feels too *goyishe*, you
know? Not Jewish enough. Too buttery. So I was wondering, because you're a pastry chef and all, trained at the top
restaurants, you got any ideas?"

Ethan worked hard not to show his true feelings. He knew
zilch about baking. Still, he needed to come up with some
reasonable response. It would look suspicious otherwise.

"Ice cream?" Ethan squeaked out.

"Ice cream?" Josh considered the idea. "We've never made
ice cream before at Best Babka."

"Oh."

"But never mind that," Josh said, tapping him on the chest. "Tell me what you're thinking."

Ethan swallowed. He wasn't thinking. That was the problem. He was more than happy to pick up a shovel and continue digging his own grave.

"You know," Ethan said, pulling his answer out of nowhere, "like a homemade cherry-vanilla ice cream…but load it with maraschino cherries, lots of whole pieces. And maybe…some white chocolate on top. Like in a shape."

"A shape?" Josh said dubiously.

He thought back to all those fancy restaurants he had eaten at over the years. There was always something sticking out of one of their desserts. He had no idea what those things were called, but either way, he was going all in on the hard sell now.

"Like a heart," Ethan said, spewing nonsense, "or uh, a seagull, 'cause of the shore. And since it's a play on a drink, you could maybe put some uh…those uh, sugar things…you know what I mean. Put some sparkly sugar things on there. The ones you can eat, though."

"You mean make my own edible sugar glass?"

"Exactly." Ethan forced a smile. He had no idea what edible sugar glass was. But still, he kept talking. He kept trying to sound like Ethan Rosenberg, someone who had spent his life in the most delicious restaurants, building amazing desserts. "And I suppose if you really wanted to go all out, you could pair it with some rosé."

"What do you mean?"

"Like a float, you know?" Ethan knew, as soon as he said it, that it was a terrible idea. "Like a Shirley Temple on the Jersey Shore. The rosé is the ocean, the homemade maraschino-cherry ice cream is the Shirley Temple, the edible glass is the ice cubes, and the white chocolate emerging from the top are the seagulls of the Jersey Shore."

Ethan waited, nervously. He waited to be called out. Found out. For Josh to realize, right then and there, that Ethan had absolutely no clue what he was doing. He was a disappointment. A failure. A nothing.

"Holy hell!" Josh said, clapping him on the back. "That's freaking brilliant!"

Ethan blinked. "It is?"

"No wonder you trained at the best schools."

Ethan forced a smile. "No wonder!"

"Why do we have you making pink boxes again?"

"I really don't mind the pink boxes."

"I don't know," Josh mused, placing his finger on the bottom of his chin. "Maybe I should talk to Avi about getting you moved up to baker sooner."

Ethan needed to get Josh off this train of thought as quickly as possible. "I don't think that's a great idea right now. We got a lot going on with the second floor."

Josh sighed. "You're right, man," he said, shaking his head, moving to give him a supportive squeeze of the shoulder. "And just so you know, I'm grateful you're gonna be helping my sister with the second floor. You have no idea how much this means to my family right now."

"Yeah?"

"We really owe you, my man."

Ethan swallowed. This was it. An opening. He knew he should ask about helping out with that babka recipe. *Take the burden off Avital, and all.* Instead, he found a totally different question emerging from his mouth.

"You said Avital's not dating anyone right now?" he asked.

"Nope," Josh said. "Hasn't really dated anyone for a while, actually."

"Huh," Ethan said, trying to act casual. "That's surprising."

"Right?"

"You would think someone like Avi would be dating. It seems like lots of people would be interested in her."

Josh leaned in to him fully. "Definitely. She has had *loads* of interest over the years."

The news made Ethan's stomach churn. He didn't like the idea of Avital getting *loads* of anything...from someone other than him.

Another lane opened, and Ethan and Josh unloaded their items onto the conveyor belt. When they were done, Josh took out the company credit card to pay. Ethan was just in the middle of jotting Avital a text, letting her know to add the cherries to the budget for the week...when another thought popped into his head.

"Hey," Ethan called out to Josh. "What about a ganache?"

Josh looked back from the register. "A cherry ganache?"

"No," Ethan said, thinking back to a time when he was in France. "A champagne ganache within the cherry ice cream. A surprise...like a wave, crashing along a shoreline, something she's not expecting."

"Wow!" Josh said, choking a bit on the words. "You *are* good."

Ethan tugged on the center of his shirt. He was good, wasn't he? He had designed his first real dessert. He had successfully completed his first real grocery shopping trip. He was helping out Avital. Maybe his grandfather was wrong. Maybe he wasn't a nothing, after all.

NINETEEN

"I need to tell you something, Avi," Ethan said, pulling a frog-prince stuffed animal out of a dusty plastic garbage bag. He waved the little froggy in her direction before tossing it to her. "Your parents are hoarders."

Avital caught the creature with both hands. They had been going at it like this for the last four hours. Pulling items out of rooms, sorting them into three bins of Trash, Keep, and Donate. Despite their nonstop effort, they had barely made a dent. The three rooms on the second floor, plus one laundry room, were still a full-fledged disaster.

"Excuse me," Avital said, turning the frog-doll around so she could wave its tiny green arm in Ethan's direction, "that would be an insult to my grandparents, who are also hoarders."

"So it runs in the family, huh?"

"God, I hope not."

Avital tossed the toy into a box marked Donations.

Ethan appeared around the stack of boxes he'd been crouching behind. Raising his arms above his head, he cracked the joints in the back of his shoulders.

"Does it always get this hot up here?" Ethan asked.

"Old building," Avital said, diverting her eyes. "Plus, with the ovens on all day... Heat just rises, you know?"

"It's practically steaming," he said, reaching down to roll up his sleeves. And then, as if a second thought had just occurred to him, he stopped. "Actually, do you mind if I just take my shirt off?"

Avital's eyes went wide. "Excuse me?"

"My shirt," he said, pointing to the neatly pressed button-down he was wearing. "I have a T-shirt underneath."

Avital swallowed. She didn't know why the question made her mouth go dry and her heart palpitate. It was a perfectly innocent and totally reasonable thing to do on the sweltering second floor.

"Of course." Avital smiled. "Wish I could take off some clothes myself."

Ethan's head snapped in her direction. "Excuse me?"

"I—I mean..." Avital stammered. "That's not... I just meant..."

"If you need to get naked, Avital," Ethan said, his tone flat, serious, "by all means...don't let me stop you."

She stopped stammering. Her eyes narrowed as she cocked her head sideways, trying to figure out his intent. He was so serious in his delivery that she wasn't at all sure if he was trying to be helpful...or genuinely joking. It wasn't until his corner lip edged into a smile that she realized he was kidding. Avital smiled, too.

"I thought you were serious for a minute."

"I have a very British sense of humor."

"Is that what they're calling it nowadays?"

"It's what I call it." He smiled.

"Ah."

She liked his weird, flat sense of humor.

Avital focused on her box, pulling out a three-foot plastic vine. Ethan returned to taking off his shirt. She tried to concentrate on the task at hand, but in reality she couldn't stop looking at Ethan in her peripheral vision. She was glued to him, pulled to him.

Starting at the top button, he worked his way down slowly, before removing it entirely. Smoothing out any wrinkles, he laid it on a banister at the side. He took one more moment to lift his arms and stretch, working out the muscles in his back and neck. This time, however, she found herself fully watching him. He moved like an Olympic swimmer, twisting his arms and waist, taut and elegant, before a race.

Ethan glanced over. Their eyes caught. Avital looked away.

"I don't know." Ethan dug back into a box and began rummaging. "It seems like there could be some real family heirlooms in here." When she looked over, he was holding a pair of pink fuzzy handcuffs.

"Ew!" Avital grimaced. "Trash."

With that, the two continued their relentless task of cleaning up. After another hour, Avital glanced down at her watch. "Maybe we should take a break. Get something to eat."

Heading downstairs, they found that the only person still working was Chaya, who was on bread duty. The bread dough at Best Babka was made in the evening, so that it had time to rise overnight. Ethan made his way to the kitchen, while Avital headed to her office.

For tonight's dinner, she would be having a lettuce salad, paired with gluten-free macaroni and cheese, baked salmon, blueberries, and a bottle of alkaline water. It was the most common dinner she had been eating for months, sometimes replacing the salmon with tilapia. Since fish was not considered meat under kosher law, and technically fell under the pareve, or neutral category, she could pair it with macaroni and cheese.

Avital finished heating up her meal and went back upstairs to the second floor. When she did, she was surprised to find Ethan sitting in the hallway, eating a half loaf of their world-famous pumpkin-spiced babka.

"Is that what you're eating for dinner?" Avital asked, surprised.

"You kidding me?" Ethan defended his choice. "Your babka is the best thing I have ever eaten."

Avital slid down beside him. Despite the cramped, hot quarters, despite the fact it would make far more sense to go downstairs where they could eat at a proper table, with plenty of room, across from each other, neither of them suggested it.

Ethan looked over. "And what are you eating?"

Avital showed him her plate.

"That all on your diet?" he asked.

"Yep."

"What isn't on your diet?"

She began to rattle off a list.

"Jeez," Ethan said. "So you basically can't eat anything we make at Best Babka?"

"Nope."

"Isn't that hard?" Ethan asked. "To be surrounded by all this food, all this temptation that you can't have?"

"It is," Avital admitted, "but it's less about the food…and more about what the food represents. Food is communal, right? It's sitting around sharing a meal with your friends. Or the experience of eating. The joy of it. The pleasure of tasting something remarkable…the first bite of a piece of challah fresh from the oven…or an oozing chocolate croissant.

When you can't eat, or experience that pleasure like normal people, you do feel a bit like your disease is a…a joy-robber."

Ethan had stopped eating his babka. His eyes were fixed, pensive. "A joy-robber, huh?"

She backtracked on the statement. "It's probably a silly way to describe it."

"It's actually a great way to describe it," he interrupted her. "Believe it or not, Avi… I know exactly what you mean."

His face was turned in her direction. The scent of him, the way he was sitting so close, made her breathless. Even with chronic pain, she realized, he made her feel good. It scared her.

"Anyway," she said, angling a piece of her dinner at him, "would you like some of my dinner? The Jewish mother in me feels the need to insist you eat some protein."

Ethan hesitated. Avital wasn't sure what she did wrong, but maybe she had misread the situation. She had thought that sitting upstairs together, sharing intimacies, meant that they were ready to share food.

"Sorry." Avital pulled back. "I agree it's not that appetizing."

"No." He started to backpedal, too. "It's not that. It's just… you can eat so little already. I'd feel bad…eating your food."

Her heart lurched. He was always putting her needs first.

"Really," she said, breaking off a quarter of her salmon, followed by a dollop of mac and cheese, "it's no big deal. I've been eating the same meal for weeks. You'd be doing me a favor taking some off my plate."

Ethan took a bite. Watching him chew, she was suddenly aware of her mistake. Ethan was a pastry chef. He had been trained at some of the world's best restaurants. His slow and methodical jaw-chewing was telling her he was considering gagging aloud.

"Did you make this?" Ethan asked, his voice low.

"You can spit it out."

"Holy hell, Avi." Ethan started scarfing. "It's so good!"

"It's plain salmon," Avital commented. "Made in an air fryer. Nuked in a microwave two days later. We're both probably gonna get food poisoning."

"It's the best thing I've ever tasted."

She was weirdly fascinated by his response. Also, totally confused. She watched Ethan, mesmerized. All the pretenses of those squared shoulders and straight lines now devolved into straight pleasure. He wasn't pulling her leg. He seemed to really enjoy consuming her food.

What she was beginning to see with Ethan was that he switched. When he didn't know who he was dealing with, he wore a mask. He hid his vulnerabilities. He was all broad shoulders, etched jawlines, confident answers. But when he let his guard down, he was quite sweet. There was a gentleness to him. An innocence.

"I'm actually surprised you like it so much," Avital admitted. "I would think after all your years spent working in top-tier restaurants, your palate would be more refined."

"It's been a while since I had home cooking."

"You don't get home a lot?"

Ethan shook his head, confused. "Excuse me?"

"Your parents," she said, reminding him of their conversation earlier in the day. "In Connecticut. They don't cook?"

He hesitated before answering. "Not really."

"That's interesting," she said, digging back into her plate. "So what made you want to become a pastry chef?"

"Oh," he said, shifting in his seat like it was a difficult question. "Well, to tell you the truth... I never actually wanted to be a pastry chef."

"Really?"

"My original dream was to be Iron Man."

Avital exploded into laughter. She was not expecting the joke, or the serious way he delivered it, but the sight of her cracking up made Ethan smile, too. She couldn't help herself. A fire lit inside her belly. He was gorgeous when he blushed.

"I'm sorry that didn't work out for you," Avital said, knocking her knee playfully into his.

"Yeah." Ethan grinned, returning the touch with a playful nudge back. "I'm still mourning the loss."

Avi was keenly aware that their thighs, and knees, were now completely pressed against each other. She was getting carried away. She stood up, the physical separation a boundary between them.

"So," Ethan said, returning to his food, "did you always want to be general manager of Best Babka?"

Avital scoffed aloud. "Ha! No."

"So what did you want to do?"

Avital met his gaze through the darkened hallway. "I wanted to be a photographer."

"Really?"

She nodded. "I was studying at UCLA. After graduation, I was working at the *LA Times* as an assistant photo editor. My big dream was to eventually take all that photography experience and turn it into my first showing at a real live gallery... but it never happened."

"Why not?"

"Life. IC. Money. Take your pick. I needed something reliable and stable...where nobody would mind that I wasn't reliable and stable. So I came home. I moved back in with my parents and took over as manager."

"You still take photographs, then?"

"Not really."

"Why not?"

"Nothing around here really interests me, I guess," she said, before adding, "Plus, my camera broke a few years back."

"Your camera broke?"

Avital shrugged. "It happens."

She wanted out of this conversation.

She teetered back from him, down the hall, to where they had opened a window to allow a cool breeze to enter the upper floor. Outside, the lunar moon was at a crescent sliver. Avital held herself and swayed, trying to count the stars above the brownstones.

"So why don't you get it fixed?" Ethan said.

Avital turned around to see Ethan standing directly behind her. He had closed the gap between them, unwilling to let her walk away from the conversation. But that was his dichotomy again. One minute, the sweet-natured guy, extolling her air-fryer salmon. The next, the guy willing to call her out on her flimsy excuses.

Avital defended herself. "I haven't had the time."

He raised an eyebrow in her direction. "That seems a bit like a cop-out."

"Maybe it is," Avital admitted.

Ethan met her eyes directly. "If photography is something you love, Avital, you shouldn't give it up. You should keep fighting for it. And you shouldn't wait for permission from other people, either. You should just go out there, put yourself out there. Make it happen. I'm not trying to overstep my boundaries here, but you just told me your disease feels like a joy-robber. Well, here you have something that gives you joy. Something that makes you happy. And the only one stopping you from doing it…is you."

She could feel the heat of his body closing in on her. Her breathing slowed. Pressing back to the window, a cold breeze flitted through the flimsy material of her T-shirt.

"I'd love to see it one day," Ethan said.

"What?" Avital squeaked out.

"Your photography," Ethan said. His voice was low and growly. "Old stuff. New stuff. Whatever you want to show me. I'd love to see what you've spent so much of your life feeling passionate about."

It felt like he was asking for something else.

Avital hesitated on a response. Ethan kept his eyes firmly on her, his lips parting ever so slightly. It was an intimate thing, sharing your art with another person, placing your most honest and vulnerable bits before them for judgment. It was almost as intimate as sharing your body.

"I just—" Avital slunk down onto the wood floorboards beneath her feet "—I don't want you to be disappointed. People have certain expectations, you know? And I don't know... I don't know if I'm capable of meeting those expectations."

Oh, the metaphors. Avital wasn't sure if she was talking about her photography or her vagina.

Ethan seemed to note her hesitation, pulling back from the question, pulling back from her. "How about when you're ready, then?" he asked softly.

Her heart ached. "Okay."

"Good."

Ethan headed back to the place where they had been eating, bending down to clean up the plates. From her vantage point, the moonlight streamed through the windows, highlighting his juxtapositions, the sharp angles in his nose and cheeks, paired with the soft roundness of his thick curls and feminine lashes.

If she had a working camera, she might have even taken his picture.

TWENTY

On Thursday morning, Avital stood in the shower, letting hot water bead down her back. She didn't want to think about Ethan—especially when she was naked—but he was on her mind.

For the last five days, they had been sharing food, and intimacies, on the second floor of Best Babka. But it was something he had said, in the beginning of the week that kept sitting that sat with her. *Well, here you have something that gives you joy. Something that makes you happy. And the only one stopping you from doing it…is you.*

Avital leaned her head against the tiles.

He wasn't wrong.

Standing in the shower—trying not to get shampoo and conditioner in her oversensitive nether regions—she put Ethan and his joy-mongering out of her head, taking a careful accounting of how she was feeling.

The burning she normally lived with was better. Unfortunately, it had been replaced with a pressure far more un-comfortable. She tried to ignore the feeling, but the relentless heaviness became emotionally exhausting. Everything with chronic illness felt unbelievably difficult.

Avital finished her shower. Grabbing a towel and wrapping it around her, she headed to her closet to throw on whatever was clean. Her mind wandered back to Ethan. In her never-ending war with her own body, she had forgotten to connect with and take care of herself.

And so, that morning—unlike every other morning since developing IC—Avital went to the bottom drawer in her bureau and found a tiny plastic crate filled with makeup. Pulling it out, she took a seat on the floor in front of her full-length mirror.

She felt slightly ridiculous putting on makeup now, after all this time. She also couldn't help but think that using two-year-old makeup was a terrible idea. But she took the container full of expired concealers, lipsticks, and blushes and went to town.

She did her eyes all smoky: black eyeliner, and a purple shimmer. She dotted her lips with the color Fire Engine Red. And when she was done with her makeup, she turned back to her closet and looked for something to wear.

She went through her skirts and maternity dresses, all items she had bought to diminish her chronic pain. But putting each item on, none of it made her feel good. All of it reminded her of being chronically ill. And so, pushing through her closet, she found a plastic bin full of clothing she had kept from col-lege. Rummaging through, she pulled out a small black dress.

Back in the Before Times, it was a tight little number she wore to the clubs. Now the dress swam on her. But putting it on, turning to analyze the final product in the mirror, reminded her how much she liked this—playing in her own sensual femininity. Being a woman. She felt beautiful, too. She *was* beautiful.

And Avital was proud of herself. Even in pain, even hurting, she was holding on to the things that gave her joy.

Ethan entered the kitchen of the Lippmann family compound and nearly tripped over his own feet in shock. It was Thursday morning. Before noon. And Randy was sitting at the center island—fully awake and properly dressed—eating a plate of eggs over easy.

Ethan glanced down at his watch. "You're up early."

"Business meeting," Randy said, unfazed.

Ethan hesitated at the threshold. Should he say it? He wanted to say it. *Buying drugs isn't a business meeting, Randy.* But as Ethan had laid *tefillin* this morning, he was feeling more loving, and therefore patient, than usual.

Ethan forced a smile. "Well, good luck with that."

"Thanks, man."

Ignoring Randy—and the fact that he was wearing one of Ethan's shirts—Ethan headed to the counter. Grabbing a pumpkin crumble doughnut from an open Lippmann's box, he took a bite. The sickly-sweet taste of sugar and preservatives overpowered him. Ethan gagged and, grabbing a napkin, spit his mouthful out.

Randy looked up from his eggs. "You okay?"

"These things are really terrible," Ethan mused, staring down at his doughnut. "How come I never realized these things were so terrible before?"

He wasn't sure what had happened. He had been eating Lippmann's baked goods his entire life. He checked the expiration date, before turning the box over to scan the ingredients.

It wouldn't be the first time that Corporate had shifted around a recipe. The current-day iteration of the pumpkin crumble doughnut was almost unrecognizable from the original. With inflation and the availability of cheaper ingredients, the board had approved at least a dozen changes over the years. But looking at both the date and ingredients, nothing was wrong.

"You're getting spoiled, my man," Randy offered up. "You're getting used to eating real food, real desserts, baked by real and loving hands. It's not good. Your taste buds are changing. You're no longer used to the Lippmann's way of doing things."

Maybe he had a point.

"You know," Ethan said, leaving the doughnut to grab an apple from the refrigerator, "Avital has been making me dinner all week."

Randy stared. "So?"

"Air-fryer salmon." Ethan came over to his side. "Sometimes salad. Last night, she made me raspberries with blueberries, too. She washed them, put them in this little Tupperware thing. She even labeled it with a piece of tape and marker that said For Ethan."

Randy looked confused. "Okay."

"I'm just saying." Ethan took a bite of his apple. "It's nice when someone who isn't paid for it cooks a meal for you. It makes you feel…special. Worthwhile, you know?"

Randy considered the statement. "I guess."

"You don't think so?"

"I wouldn't exactly know," Randy said.

With that, Randy departed. Alone in the kitchen now, Ethan worked on finishing his apple. It was sad that his brother had never had anyone personally cook for him. His mind wandered back to Avital—when his eyes landed on Randy's plate of eggs, now abandoned on the counter.

Ethan stopped chewing his apple.

In the past, much like his younger brother, Ethan would have left the plate there for Freya, their housekeeper, to clean up. But that was before he started working at Best Babka. Since then he had learned that, most remarkably, the trash didn't take itself out.

Picking up the plate, Ethan took it to the sink, scraped off the eggs, and rinsed it before placing it in the dishwasher. Then, just like they had taught him to do at the bakery, he grabbed some cleaning spray and wiped down the counter before making his way to work.

But sitting on the bus that morning, his MetroCard at the ready in his pocket, an hour of time to muse, he couldn't help but think back to that off-tasting doughnut. Perhaps it was more than just his taste buds that were changing.

"You look nice, Avi."

It was Tootles who noticed Avital first when she entered work this morning. Looking up from the counter, nursing a freshly made cup of coffee, he smiled in her direction. "You going somewhere special this evening?"

She hesitated. She hadn't expected that question. Though, it made sense. People normally dressed up for work when they were going somewhere special in the evening. What they didn't do was get dressed up to work late into the evening, at a bakery, with a certain member of staff. Quickly, Avital tried to come up with an excuse.

"O-oh," she said, stammering on her reply. "No, I just... the dress. It's old."

"And makeup?" Chaya said, appearing from the back.

"Makeup?" she squeaked out.

"You don't normally wear makeup," Tootles said.

Avital suddenly felt like she was being given the third degree. "I just…felt like wearing makeup."

"Huh," Tootles said, taking a sip of his coffee.

Great. Just great. She took one day off from being a bridge troll, and everybody had comments.

She decided to ignore the insinuation that she was dressing up for any reason other than her own mental health. The rumor mill at Best Babka loved a good romance more than anything. She was determined not to give them fodder.

"If you must know," Avital said directly, "I am taking new efforts to hold on to my joy."

Tootles leaned in to Chaya. "Is that what the kids are calling it nowadays?"

Chaya chuckled. "I guess so."

It was no use. They clearly intended to believe that she had some salacious romance brewing.

"On that note," Avital said, heading behind the counter, "I'm going to my office. You can send Ethan back when he gets in."

"Oh, *we will*," Chaya said.

"Thank you," Avital said, waving them off.

Avital could still hear them snickering as she rounded the corner and made her way down the hall. Obviously, the makeup and sexy dress had nothing to do with Ethan. It was for her joy, her happiness, her pleasure—and nothing more.

SHEVAT

(January–February)

TWENTY-ONE

"Hold it steady," Sara said, peering over Ethan's shoulder.

Ethan steadied one finger against the cellophane. Pulling taut the black ribbon he was holding with the other, he was just about to loop the last bow and secure it, when his finger slipped *again*. The black ribbon on the dessert platter he was tying unraveled. Ethan huffed out a disappointed breath.

"It takes time, okay?" Sara said. "Nobody is born knowing how to make a Tiffany bow."

"I'm sorry, Sara," Ethan said genuinely. "I know I'm holding up your entire delivery."

"Ethan," Sara said, exuding warmth, "you're putting way too much pressure on yourself. Tell you what…" She took the ribbon, cellophane, and scissors away from him. "Why don't you take a break? Go help Tootles at the front counter. I'm going for lunch. Come back in an hour, and we'll start again."

Ethan was happy to oblige. Making his way to the front counter and grabbing an apron, it was quieter than usual. He was now three weeks into his gig at Best Babka, and while it still wasn't always smooth sailing for him, he was finding his footing. Tootles, Josh, and Chaya offered a quick round of hellos, before making room for him at the counter.

"How's it going, Ethan?" Josh asked, helping a customer fill a pink box with cookies.

"Awesome." Ethan smiled. "Except for the fact that I seem incapable of making a Tiffany bow."

"Ugh," Chaya said with a groan, "I hate those things."

"Tiffany bows are the reason we can atone a little less intensely on Yom Kippur," Josh said. "And Tootles said you were a big help on deliveries."

Ethan glanced over to see Tootles, in the middle of helping a customer, wink in his direction. Ethan knew it was a bold-faced lie. This morning, during his first drive ever out to Staten Island, he had nearly gotten them both killed when he had gone the wrong direction onto an express ramp.

"By the way," Josh said, loud enough for everyone at the counter to hear it, "that express ramp used to get me in the beginning, too. I mean...what does *Wrong Way* on a sign really mean?"

The counter broke into hysterics. Clearly, Tootles couldn't wait to get back to Best Babka and regale everyone with his tale of their near-death experience this morning.

"Hey," Ethan said, pointing out the positive, "I got us there on time, didn't I?"

Tootles clapped him on the back. "That's the spirit, little buddy."

"Thanks, big buddy!" Ethan grinned back.

Chaya appeared with a tray of macaroons, glancing between them both. "This buddy thing between you two is getting a little out of hand."

"What buddy thing?" Ethan said, looking over to Tootles.

"You mean…"

"I think she does…"

Ethan turned around. Tootles did the same. When they faced forward again, they were wearing the matching *Little Buddy* and *Big Buddy* hats that Tootles had knitted them after their first delivery run together. At first, he had thought they were kind of weird. But now—and like everything at Best Babka—the people were rubbing off on him.

"You two and those hats," Chaya said, shaking her head.

Ethan raised his eyebrows in Tootles's direction. "I think they're jealous."

"They're totally jealous," Tootles said, returning to the counter.

Ethan did the same, picking up a box to serve the next customer. In the process, his eyes wandered down the hall.

He was looking for Avital.

What had begun as a curiosity now became some strange sort of endless longing. He was constantly searching for excuses to go find her. And his hours at work… Well, they seemed to be growing unnecessarily long.

He knew it wasn't a good idea, getting so close to Avital, allowing their relationship to grow in new ways and to new levels. But his heart was drawn to her. He didn't want to give her up, even though he knew that their time together was finite. For now, he just wanted to enjoy it. Her. He would worry about the rest later.

"Hey," Ethan said, noticing that the front counter was clearing out a little. "Does anyone mind if I go check in with Avital? See if she needs help with anything?"

"Avital, huh?" Tootles said.

"I just want to make sure she's not—"

"Little buddy—" Tootles used his chin to point toward the hall "—get the hell out of here."

★ ★ ★

Avital had been staring at the line item marked *asparagus* for the last ten minutes. She was supposed to be balancing the weekly budget, making sure that all the profits taken in at Best Babka were consistently covering their outgoing costs. Instead, she was thinking about Ethan.

Ethan, bent over moving boxes in the evening, sweat cascading down his neck. Muscles flexing beneath a white T-shirt while he worked, tearing off a strip of duct tape with his teeth, before gently running his hand down the slit of those two cardboard squares. She must have undressed him in her mind a thousand times already today.

A knock at her door drew Avital back to reality. It was Ethan. Usually, when she saw him, her heart soared. But today, she burst into laughter. Ethan was standing at the threshold, wearing a cap with the words *Little Buddy* stitched across the front. She had heard about the hat from Josh, but today was the first time she had seen it. Clearly, Avital wasn't the only person who had found an affinity for Ethan.

At the sight of her laughter, Ethan attempted to search for the source of her amusement. Avital pointed with one finger to her own head.

"Oh," Ethan said, quickly removing it, "I forgot I was wearing it."

Avital took the opportunity to tease him. "What you and Tootles do in your free time is none of my business."

Ethan nodded. "Fair enough."

"How's it going, Ethan?" Avital smiled.

Of course she was smiling. She found that nowadays, she couldn't stop smiling when Ethan was around.

"Pretty good," he said, squeezing the cap between his hands. "Except for Tiffany bows, it's been a quiet day around here."

"Tiffany is giving you trouble, huh?"

"Tiffany is trying to get me fired." Ethan sighed. "I was actually coming by to see if you needed help with anything."

Avital scanned the room. Since Ethan had become her right-hand man, she was ahead of schedule. Not just on her own work, but on the second floor. Ethan was more than a miracle worker: he was an angel.

"Actually," Avital said, disappointed, "I'm all caught up."

"Really?"

"Yeah."

"You don't need me to, like…clean your bathroom or anything?"

"You cleaned it yesterday," she reminded him.

"Oh," he said, rubbing the back of his neck, "I guess I did. Well, I guess I'll go back to failing at ribbons."

Ribbons.

"Actually," Avital said, rising from her seat, "I can help you with that."

"Really?" Ethan turned back.

"I know a trick."

She led Ethan down the hall, back to the room where they made platters. From her vantage point, she could see the front counter. Tootles was working there, but otherwise Ethan was right, it was quiet. Avital was happy to find it empty.

"Sara's at lunch?" she asked innocently.

"Yep," Ethan said. He pointed to a dessert platter of cookies where a black ribbon lay haphazardly in curls at the side. To the left of it, thirty more trays were still waiting to be decorated. "There's a big funeral in Brooklyn."

"I heard," Avital said, picking up the ribbon and unfurling it in front of Ethan.

She motioned with her pointer finger for Ethan to come closer. Ethan grinned a little and, taking one giant step forward, leaned over her shoulder. Their bodies made contact, and a wave of craving ran through her, before she managed to push it away again. They were here to make bows. Nothing more. There couldn't be anything more because after the craving, there was pain. There was always terrible pain, and the reminder that her body was broken.

"The trick to a Tiffany bow," she said, pressing her finger down in the middle, "is in the pressure of your finger. If you hold the bow too tight, you can't spin the package. If you hold it too loose, the entire thing falls apart." She looked up to him. "You see?"

His eyes narrowed. "I see."

"You need to give it enough wiggle room to keep spinning the package." She showed him, repeating the pattern four times. "Spinning, tightening, and pressing…spinning, tightening, and pressing until…voilà! Perfect bow." Avital grabbed a new dessert platter from the stack and pushed it down the counter to Ethan. "Your turn."

Heading to the wall where they kept their various arts-and-crafts supplies for platters, he tore off an appropriate length of black ribbon. Back at the counter, he bent over the tray and got to work.

Avital paced around the room while he worked but otherwise tried not to micromanage him or offer too many suggestions. It was important that Ethan feel confident making a Tiffany bow on his own. It was kind of a signature at Best Babka, along with their pink boxes.

Ethan had one last loop to go. Avital could feel the nerves rising inside her belly. It was the last loop that was the hardest. The final loop and knot required both coordination and precision. Ethan was just about to call victory on his first Tiffany bow when his finger slipped. The entire ribbon fell into a heap of black mess around the platter.

"Oh," Avital said, feeling bad for him. "Well, that sucks."

She was waiting for him to say something, do something, *respond*. Instead, Avital realized…something was wrong.

His shoulders slumped. His entire body seemed to crumble in on itself. But it was when she moved around to the side of the table, came closer, that she saw something that made her concerned…his hands were shaking. Vibrating. This was a side of Ethan she had never seen. She didn't understand it. It was just a silly Tiffany bow.

"I—I'm sorry," he said, stammering.

"Ethan," she laughed, "what are you talking about? That was amazing!"

He blinked, confused. "It was?"

"Come on," she said, picking up the ribbon, pushing the dessert platter back his way. "You can't stop now! You're so close. You show that shiva platter who's boss."

Ethan looked up. Met her eyes directly. "I can't do it, Avi."

She held out the ribbon to him. "I believe in you."

Ethan took the ribbon.

Turning back to the platter, he took a deep breath, pressing his finger down. Avital stood back, giving him space. After three more successive rounds, he found his way once again to the final loop. She stopped pacing, turning on her heel, waiting with bated breath…and then, his finger slipped again. This time, however, he didn't just crumple. Rather, he glanced over his shoulder, back to Avital.

Avital crossed her arms. "Well?"

Ethan huffed. "It's war now."

Avital marched right up to him. "You get 'em, soldier."

It would take Ethan six more disastrous attempts before he could claim victory on that dreaded bow, final knot, and loop. Stepping back, seeing that perfect Tiffany bow staring up at him, his face morphed into delight. "I did it."

Avital nodded. "You did it."

Ethan could not contain his excitement. He pounded his chest like a Neanderthal discovering fire. He jumped up and down, making jazz hands and dancing the Macarena. Avital laughed at his antics, allowing him the celebration, clapping along with his festivities. Finally, he made his way back to her. Ethan teetered back and forth on his loafers, before finally, moving in to embrace her.

"Thank you," he said.

"It was all you," Avital said.

"No," he said, nuzzling his nose into her neck. "It was you, Avi. You're incredible."

His breathing became heavy. His hands lingered. Avital felt her own heartbeat quicken in response. The soft touch of his fingers became a pull. His hands edged downward, to the center of her back, wrenching her closer. And Avital allowed it.

She allowed him to pull her into him, against him, feeling the mass of his form, resting her face in the cotton of his shirt, his metal buckle pressing into her belly—his thighs, the heft of his manhood, up against her scars—because it was the touch, the humanity, *her humanity*, she had been missing so long.

And then, before they could pass that place where they could never go back, that she could never take back, she stepped away from him. And he stepped back from her. And it was awkward. *Really awkward.* But she didn't want to lose him forever.

Later that night, working together on the second floor, Avital brought it up, and Ethan agreed that it was best to keep things friendly. What happened downstairs was just a flirtation, a reckless little nothing, something meaningless and silly—and anything more would be a bad idea.

TWENTY-TWO

"You don't think it looks like—" Avital cocked her head sideways "—vomit?"

Ethan looked up from the box he was packing. Avital waved a hand toward the three hundred tiny swatches of paint color hanging on the wall across from him.

For a woman who showed almost no indecision when it came to any other area of her life—such as the clear declaration she made, after their near kiss a week ago, that she wasn't interested in him—she had remarkable difficulty when it came to what shade the walls should be.

Now, having cleared out the first room of junk, Avital was trying to decide on what color to paint the walls, while Ethan was working on salvaging old boxes of baking equipment from her parents' and grandparents' time at the bakery.

"Which one of those green blobs," he asked, pointing with one finger toward her mess of rectangles, "is the vomit one?"

"It was…" Avital turned back, leaning in to inspect "…I'm not sure."

She fell to the floor. Bending down, she ran her hands through the tiny paint cards she had swiped from every Home Depot in a fifty-mile radius, and he knew what was going to happen next. "Oh God," she groaned, glancing from the floor back to her expressionist work. "I think I've messed the whole system up now."

"You had a system?" Ethan teased her.

She tsked. "Not nice."

That was usually the extent of Avital's temper. She could get moody, but in his entire time at Best Babka, he never actually heard her yell at anyone. Not even her brother. He found that attribute in her, especially considering his family, rather remarkable.

"Avital," he said, shaking his head, "just pick something already."

She turned back to her blotches of vomit. "It has to be right."

"Avital, Avital…" Her name was like a song.

"Maybe I should try a different color?"

He sighed. "You want me to do the paint," he said, trying to be helpful, "and you can work on sorting baking equipment?"

"No," she said sweetly and headed for another one of her stacks of paint cards.

It was unfortunate about the near kiss. The way her denim dress kept rubbing against her rump when she bent in it was causing a serious bulge to form in his pants. Ethan shifted the way he was sitting and, pulling at his trousers when she was wasn't looking, attempted to stay focused on the task at hand.

"Ethan," she said, holding up two paint swatches, "what

should I try next? Honeysuckle Raspberry or Pinkberry Fuzz?"

Ethan blew all the air out of his chest, as if the decision warranted two people stressing over it. "Honeysuckle Raspberry."

"Honeysuckle Raspberry it is," she said, heading for another tin of paint. "The good news is, even though the paint color is taking a little longer than I originally intended, we're still ahead of schedule on the second and third room. The laundry room is basically all done except for new equipment. We're really over halfway there..."

Ethan mumbled, "Less than halfway."

"And I'm sure that once I narrow down the paint color for this room—" she grabbed a brush, putting a bit along the wall "—the other rooms should be much easier."

Ethan stopped untangling wires. He was certain he hadn't heard her right. "Wait...what?"

"The other rooms," she said, a smile on her face. *A smile.*

"You're not using the same paint color for the other rooms?"

"I wasn't planning to." She frowned with her whole face. "Why? Is that a bad idea?"

"Only if you want to get the second floor done before the coming of *moshiach*."

"Ethan." She huffed a little, like he was the one who was being unreasonable. "I want to make sure I get it right." She turned back to the wall, crossing her arms against her chest, to begin the process of obsessing once again. "Paint is expensive."

"It's not that expensive," he countered.

"It's not just the paint," she clarified. "It's putting up shelving and moving everything back in. If I realize three months down the line I hate it, I have to take down the shelving, pay someone overtime...and do the whole thing all over again.

That's what makes it expensive. I just don't want to make a mistake."

Ah, so that was what it was about. Here he was thinking for three days now that she was worried about a color. But for Avital, money was a constant source of anxiety.

"Best Babka seems to be doing well for itself, though," he mused.

"Define *well for itself*," she said.

"You have lines out the door most weekdays."

"We also have a staff of over fifty," she said. "Health-insurance costs. Building costs. City taxes. State taxes. Who knows what could push our business from profitable to closing its doors forever..."

"You really think Best Babka is that vulnerable?" Ethan said, removing a piece of newspaper from what appeared to be some sort of circular blade.

"No more or less than any other small business," she said, directing her gaze back to Ethan. All at once, her eyes went wide. "Oh my God," she said, rushing over to him, picking up the faded piece of yellow newspaper that he had just discarded. "I can't believe it."

Ethan put down the blade to see what she was getting so excited about. In her hand, she was holding a newspaper. Across the top of the page, above a grainy faded photograph of a stage that frankly looked like a tornado had run through it, were the words:

THE GREAT BABKA WAR OF 1958 REACHES
AN APEX

The discovery piqued Ethan's curiosity. Returning to the box, he realized that it was not just filled with old newspaper clippings, but mementos from some long-ago Purim. A *grager*, the noisemaker used to drown out Haman's name on the festive Jewish holiday. A mask, blue and sparkly, used to cover the eyes.

Avital put it on. "How do I look?"

Ethan wanted to say *adorable*. No, what he really wanted to do was kiss those sweet lips angled in his direction. But it was moments like this, finding a box about their long-standing family rivalry, where he was pulled from the fantasy. He remembered that he was really a member of the Lippmann family, and even though he had long since stopped searching for the pumpkin-spiced babka recipe, she didn't know the truth.

He had wanted to kiss her, in that heated, passionate moment in the bakery together. But afterward, knowing how terrible the betrayal would be, he had also agreed it was a mistake. Avital bent down, and exploring the contents of the box for herself, pulled out a small black journal. As she flipped through it, he glanced over her shoulder. It seemed to be a ledger of sales from Best Babka's first year in business. Beside each transaction were the initials M.L. Ethan recognized his grandfather's handwriting.

"I wonder if some of this stuff belonged to Moishe," Avital said quietly.

"It would make sense," Ethan said. "Chayim did throw him out without warning."

Avital blinked. "That's not what happened."

"Oh," Ethan said in an attempt to backtrack. "I guess I must have heard the story wrong. Josh mentioned something about it when I first started working here."

"So no one told you about our sordid family history and the way Moishe Lippmann has been trying to destroy us for over fifty years?" she asked.

Avital might have been the one wearing the mask, but it

was Ethan who kept his cover. "No," he said. "I don't be-lieve so."

"You know that this building has been in my family for five generations," she explained. "For the first two generations, it was a general store. It did well, until industrialization came. Department stores like Sears, Roebuck meant people could get the same products for cheaper... My great-grandparents were at risk of losing everything."

"They needed a new model," Ethan said.

"Yep," Avital said, returning to her story. "My grandpar-ents, Chayim and Rose, who were working in the family business, were hosting Shabbat dinners. And during these din-ners, they started baking. They made all these desserts, bigger and more elaborate, developing recipes for their friends and neighbors. It was a passion for my grandfather, especially... and soon, Chayim became famous around town for his amaz-ing desserts. Everybody wanted them, until people were beg-ging for Chayim to come to Shabbat dinner or asking Rose for an invitation to theirs. And this is when my grandfather got an idea—"

"Turn the general store into a bakery."

"Exactly," she said, "except it's hard to turn a general store into a bakery. You need money. You need to build working kitchens and buy mixers and flour. My great-grandparents and grandparents were already pretty strapped. They didn't have the money to do all that...but they did have a building. So, they decided to go into business with a local man and his wife, Moishe and Lilly Lippmann. So they went to Moishe and said, 'We'll provide the building, and you provide the money, and we'll work together. We'll split the profits right down the middle, fifty-fifty.' It's a good deal, right?"

Ethan swallowed. "I guess."

"So," Avital continued, "they opened the business, and

it thrived. The first month, all those eager Shabbat invites turned into customers. There were lines out the door. And then, six months into this...when Moishe and Chayim were finally turning a profit, Moishe absconded. He walked into Best Babka in the middle of the night, stole half their stuff and all their recipes, and then pulled his money out of the bank. A month later, and right across the street, he opened Greatest Babka in Brooklyn...using all of their recipes."

The problem with Avital's version of events was that Ethan had heard it the complete opposite way. It was Moishe who went to the Cohens and gave them the idea. It was Moishe who saved the Cohen family business. It was Moishe who gave and gave and gave. And it was Chayim—that shark—who ultimately betrayed him.

The part that was throwing him off was about the recipes. *Moishe stole all their recipes.* That couldn't be correct. If Moishe had stolen all the recipes, then he would have the recipe for pumpkin-spiced babka. He wouldn't have needed to send Ethan in to steal it.

Her story had to be wrong. Or, at the very least, there had to be some version of the truth that sat in the middle.

"After that," Avital said, shaking her head, staring down at the article, "the competition for babka became fierce. Soon, each business had to start lowering prices and coming up with gimmicks just to compete. If my grandfather brought in a clown, Moishe brought in two clowns. If my grandfather put up lights, Moishe put up six lights. Before long, everyone in the Jewish community was involved, until even rabbis were taking sides, talking about who had the better babka from their pulpits on Saturday morning."

She sighed, heavily. "It all came to a head, however, when my grandfather decided to throw a Purim carnival. It was there, in front of the entire neighborhood, that the two men came to blows. My grandfather had no choice. Overcome with anger, defending his territory and his family recipes, he broke Moishe's nose. When he came to work the next day, Greatest Babka in Brooklyn had closed. Moishe had fled. The next time we heard tell of him, it was in the form of a yellow-and-blue box on a grocery shelf."

"Lippmann's."

"The one and only," Avital said. "After that, it was lawsuits upon lawsuits between our two families. It went on for years. Decades. He caused both my parents and my grandparents so many sleepless nights. I can't tell you how many times that man almost put us out of business…"

Ethan swallowed. She had taken off the mask now and was staring down at the article in her hands. Ethan wanted to touch her. But he was afraid because he knew the reality of who he was and who she was and that they could never be together.

"So—" Ethan swallowed "—you must really hate them."

Avital turned to him. "Who?"

"The Lippmanns." Ethan said it carefully. Cautiously. "You must wish…all sorts of horrible things on them."

She took a long time to answer the question.

"I don't hate them," she said finally. "Believe it or not, I don't wish ill on them, either. What kind of person would I be to wish ill on anybody?" Another silence passed through the small space. "Not that I could ever say this aloud to any-one in my family, but I always kind of felt bad for them."

"Why?"

"I don't know the whole story. Josh and I were young when it happened, so it was all hush-hush, and no one wanted to talk about it in front of the children. But apparently, after his wife died of cancer, there was some sort of horrible accident, and his daughter died…and the granddaughter became disabled…and the surviving kids are all types of messed up."

"Messed up?" Ethan asked. "How?"

"Apparently, one kid is like a drug addict, and the other is some sort of sociopath."

Ethan grimaced. He did not appreciate her erroneous assessment of him.

"Anyway," she said, concluding her tale, "the lawsuits stopped coming shortly before my parents retired. We haven't heard from Moishe Lippmann in years. I guess, whatever happened to him, he's long since forgotten about Best Babka and Chayim Cohen."

Avital didn't know that the quiet just meant Moishe was lying in wait. He sighed, his heart a mess. "So what do you want me to do with this stuff?" he said, not able to look at her.

She thought it over before answering, "Just throw it out."

Entering the Lippmann family compound, Ethan raced upstairs, straight to his brother's bedroom. The room was dark. Randy was asleep.

"Wake up!" Ethan said, turning on the lights.

"Dude," Randy groaned. "What time is it?"

"Late." Ethan sat down on his bed. "Do you think Grandpa lies?"

Randy squinted. "What?"

"Grandpa," Ethan said, like the question was simple. "Do you think he always tells us the truth?"

Randy blinked three times. "Of course he lies to us, Ethan!" he said without hesitation. "He's lied to us since the day we got here. What the hell is wrong with you? How can you not know this already?"

Ethan didn't know how to respond. Randy sighed and then threw his covers off.

"Hold on," Randy said, annoyed.

"Where are you going?" Ethan asked.

"Where do you think?" Randy said, heading over to his backpack.

Digging into his bag, Randy pulled out a vape pen. Popping the thin end into his mouth, he sucked it back, holding the smoke in his lungs for a good fifteen seconds before exhaling. Satisfied, Randy sat back down on the bed.

"Okay," Randy said, "I'm ready now."

Ethan stared at the floor. "I like her, Randy."

"Who?"

"Avital Cohen."

"Great."

"I have to tell her."

"Uh…" Randy cocked his head sideways. "No."

"Why not?" Ethan asked.

"Because you're a Lippmann!" he said, like the answer wasn't obvious. "And she's a Cohen! And there's not a chance in hell this relationship can work out for either of you."

Ethan crossed his arms against his chest, thinking it over. His brother had a point. Ethan knew he was playing Jenga with pink boxes full of babka. Eventually, his jaunt into the real world, with real people, would come crashing down around him. Whether she wanted to kiss him or not, the lie was beginning to eat him up inside.

"You remember when we were little," Randy said, "when we first got here, and Grandpa wanted to change our names? Said it wouldn't be right, him raising us…with the surname Rosenberg. And you fought him. Hard. You and the old man went at it for weeks, until one day, sitting at the dining-room table, you picked up the mashed potatoes…and bam, in front of everyone on staff…just chucked it full on and straight at his face."

"He was pissed."

"I thought he was going to kill you," Randy said. "I think the only reason he didn't was because this place was so big and you were so little that he just couldn't find you. But when he did finally find you, the old man caved, and he told you that we could all keep our last names."

"With conditions," Ethan reminded him.

"Always."

A long silence settled between the two brothers.

"But that night," Randy said, "you came into my room and you told me that we'd won. You said we got to keep our names. We were gonna stay Rosenbergs. And I believed you. For a long time, I thought we had a chance against the old man. But here's the thing. We didn't win. You didn't win, especially. 'Cause he was never gonna let you be anything other than a Lippmann."

It was a surprisingly sober thought for a man who spent most of his day stoned. Ethan sighed. "I can't keep doing this, Randy."

"Yeah," Randy said sympathetically. "I know."

Ethan was running late to work the next morning. For the first time since starting at Best Babka, he'd made a detour. He hadn't known what to do with the checks that Avital handed him each week. Before that moment, he hadn't actually needed the money. But walking up to the teller in One National Bank, he checked another first off his rapidly expanding list of ventures.

"I'd like to open a bank account," he said, before adding, "under the name Rosenberg."

TWENTY-THREE

Ethan could finally say that they were making progress on the second floor. The first room, once just a mountain of trash in boxes and plastic bags, had now been organized into neatly arranged shelves. There was one section for Jewish-holiday decor, one for stationery, and another for other office necessaries. Across from that, Avital had placed old bakery equipment from when her grandparents had first opened the place, having made the decision to keep the relics for sentimental reasons.

In all their long hours of working together, Ethan had not come across the recipe. Not that it mattered. At some point, he had completely stopped looking for it. As the weeks drifted past, it was easy to forget that was really his mission. It was only when he had to go home—or the temptation of a kiss with Avital came about—that he remembered.

Ethan dug his hands into his pockets. "It looks really good."

"Right," Avital said, coming to stand at his side. "I think it smells better, too."

"Definitely."

His eyes drifted over to her. Her blond curls were a sweaty mess. The silk scarf she was wearing to hold her hair back was out of place.

"Should we get started on the next room?" Avital asked.

Ethan had a better idea. Like the laundry room, the second room had been cleared of all its clutter. Now, most of the work that still needed to be done was cosmetic. As it was the smallest of the spaces, Ethan reasoned you couldn't do much with it in terms of storage, but given the placement, the way the window was pressed up right against the redbrick wall of the neighboring building, he had an idea.

"I was wondering if you would let me handle the second room," Ethan asked.

Avital met his eyes directly. "Why?"

"I have a vision," he said, very confident. "A plan. I think you're going to like it."

"Are you going to tell me what this plan is?"

"No," he said, "but I was thinking I would do it during lunch breaks, so it wouldn't affect our schedule to get the new laundry equipment in. It might even get us ahead of schedule. I'm thinking it won't take me more than a week. Two, at most."

"So," she said, her hands on her hips, "you want me to give you a room in my business to redecorate any way you please, without telling me what you're planning?"

Ethan grinned. "Basically."

He could see her stressing about it. This was the woman who took over a week to pick out a paint color. But he also knew Avital. He had learned that she had this remarkable faith in people, *in him*, even if she sometimes had trouble extending that own faith to herself.

"Well," she said, crossing her arms against her chest and shifting her weight to the other hip, "if you really want to give up your lunch breaks…"

"Great." He smiled, leaving it at that, giving her no time to second-guess herself. Pressing past her, he opened the door to the third room. "After you, my lady."

Avital shrugged, walking past him, the smell of cherry blossoms lingering in the air once again. The realization that they were nearing the finish line, nearing the end of those late nights spent together, sharing meals and conversations, caused his heart to ache. He liked her. But she had drawn a clear line, and he had agreed to it, and before anything else could happen, he would need to tell her the truth.

Avital turned back to him. "Last room," she said, almost sadly.

Ethan nodded. "I guess…we should begin."

And yet, both of them stood hesitating outside the door.

Avital sat in her office, the door wide-open, and saw Ethan and Tootles rushing past in the hallway, carrying wood boards and drills, snickering like two small schoolboys as they passed. Rising from her seat, heading to the door, she stopped them on their way to the second floor.

"Hey," she said, calling their attention back, "whatchya doing?"

The two men turned and, placing the boards and tools behind their backs, acted innocent. "Nothing," Ethan said, raising one eyebrow at Tootles.

"Working," Tootles confirmed.

It had been like this for the last week. Avital, trying to pull some hint from Ethan over what was happening in that tiny second room. Ethan, remaining surprisingly tight-lipped, occasionally pulling Josh or Tootles into his master plan.

"What are those for?" she asked, nodding at the lumber.

"What?" Ethan asked innocently.

"The wood you're holding." She smiled. "It looks like you're planning on building something?"

Ethan shrugged his shoulder at Tootles. Tootles shrugged his shoulder at Ethan. "I don't see any wood," Tootles said innocently. "Do you, little buddy?"

"No," Ethan said. "None at all."

With that, they pivoted and were off, racing up to the second floor. Avital shook her head and returned to her desk. In truth, the antics were making her smile, too. She had been taking care of people so long, putting everyone's needs in front of her own, it was nice to finally have someone step up and take care of everything for her.

She trusted Ethan.

Stranger still, when she glanced out into the hall during her lunch break expecting to find him, she missed him. She knew that their time together, their evenings on the upper floor, were coming to an end. It made her sad. It was strange, and wonderful, how he had somehow managed to infiltrate her heart. But still, she wasn't sure. Beyond not wanting to lose him, she wanted what was best for him. They were friends, after all.

In another life, in another universe, she was certain they could have been more. But for now, she was just too fraught with anxiety about her hurting, broken body and the fact that sex was often the very furthest thing from her mind.

On Sunday night, Ethan came to her office. Presenting a scarf, he was adamant that blindfolding her would only make the surprise better. Not wanting to ruin his hard work, she allowed the game. Turning around, she felt the soft silk pressing against her eyes and forehead as he tightened the knot around her head. The feeling of his hands on her hair, of him touching her, caused the space between her legs to ache once more.

"Good?" he asked, adjusting it gently, whispering into her ear.

Avital bit back her excitement, her desire. "Perfect."

"Careful," he said, leading her from the office into the hallway.

With her eyes blindfolded, she was forced to focus on sensation. There was pain, of course. Always pain. But also... desire. Ethan's hand, those gloriously thick fingers, was wrapped around her own so warm and sweaty. His grasp, firm but gentle, guiding her in a way that felt safe. The scent of him, that remarkable combination of musk and salt and sandalwood, the ocean overtaking her, that incredible and delicious scent of male.

They came to the stairs that would lead them to the renovated floor. Avital hesitated. She was concerned about missing the landing of a step while wearing a long skirt.

"Maybe we should have done this at the top of the stairs?" she wondered aloud.

"It's more fun this way," Ethan reminded her.

Avital swallowed. "Okay."

She attempted to find her footing but faltered. Instead, her Birkenstock came down on Ethan's shoe. "Sorry."

"It's fine, Avi." He laughed. "This is supposed to be fun, remember?"

Her anxiety returned. "I can't do this."

"Avital." Ethan pressed his lips up against her earlobe. Her entire body shivered. "Trust me. It will be okay."

She believed him.

His hands wrapped around her waist as he lifted her up. A surprised squeal escaped her lips in the process, as she gripped his neck in a tight hug, her legs dangling over his arms. "Ethan," she said, bemused. "What are you doing?"

"Carrying you."

"You'll drop me."

"Never."

He began walking up the stairs. One step after the other, she gave in to the feeling of floating with Ethan. She was safe with him. The trepidation in her chest disappeared. Her grip around his neck softened as she leaned her cheek up against him. She could feel the heat of his body, his sweat, beneath the soft wool of his sweater. That woodsy, fresh-cut scent of him, filling up her nostrils.

Arriving safely, Ethan loosened his grip, bringing her down to her feet. She heard the door to a room squeak open, before Ethan took her hand, leading her inside. Without words, he came around her, untying the knot, removing the blindfold.

Her mouth fell open. Avital was speechless. It was not what she was expecting. A twin bed with a delicate lavender comforter rested against one wall. Beside the bed, in front of the window, was a small white nightstand. A tiny potted plant and a maroon laptop, currently plugged in as if waiting to be used, rested on top. Across from that, on shelves made of reclaimed wood, were wicker baskets, cookbooks, and family mementos found during their time cleaning the second floor.

"I know it's not much," Ethan said, excitement peeking through his voice, "but you so often have to work when you're not feeling well. I figured this would be a much better option. There's a bed, a lavender-scented heating pad in the nightstand. In that wicker basket over there, there's some medicine and things I've seen you take over the last few weeks."

"Ethan…"

"And I know what you're going to say," he said, as if he could already intuit her argument. "That you don't need a whole room to yourself. But I figured *you* can use the room when you need to…and if any other employee wants to use it for whatever reason, like if Sara needs to take an important legal call, or if Marty needs a nap, or even if Josh just wants to meditate on some new recipes for this new girlfriend he's dating—" he pointed to a shelf, where Ethan had salvaged cookbooks from her parents' and grandparents' generation "—then, they can use it, too."

"Ethan…"

"I just…" He rubbed the back of his neck. "Before you tell me you're disappointed, and you hate it, and to change everything back—"

"It's amazing!"

"Really?"

"How could you think this place is anything but amazing?" She sat down on the bed, shaking her head. "What I don't understand is how you did all this. The shelving, the bed, the laptop… I only gave you a few hundred dollars."

He plopped down beside her. "I got a good deal."

Their arms were touching. The feeling of him, the heat of his body, caused her to shiver. She no longer wanted to fight the desire that had been building in her. Avital took a deep breath.

"Would you like to see my photography?"

Ethan smiled. "I'd love to."

Avital sat on the bed beside Ethan, her portfolio of photography in her hands. He was trying to pay attention, to listen to the way she described each image. But all he could think about—beyond wanting to kiss her—was that he needed to tell her the truth.

"People look at the image," Avital explained, "and they see a simple black-and-white photo. Nothing fancy. Anyone can take it, right? But if you look beneath the first layer, there's depth. I like juxtaposing things, the lighting against the setting and the subject... Sometimes I like mirroring, too. But I don't ever want an image to say just one thing."

"You're so talented, Avi."

She shrugged. "You're the only one who thinks so, apparently."

"You have to keep taking pictures. Your art needs to be in this world."

She turned to him, her eyes meeting his. Her hand moved from the photographs she was touching to his thigh. His entire body responded. Every instinct he had was screaming at him to take this remarkable creature into his arms and make love to her. He wanted to hear her moan.

The soft touch on his thigh became a pull. The kiss he had wanted, the kiss he had been closing his eyes at night and thinking about forever, was so close now. It took everything he had to pull away. Rising from the bed, catching his breath, he stopped her before they could go any further.

"Avi," Ethan said, "I can't."

Her eyebrows arched. Her shoulders crumpled. A combination of emotions passed across her face in one mixed-up muddle. "I'm sorry," she said. "I must have read the situation wrong."

"No." Ethan knelt in front of her. "You didn't. I like you, Avital. I like you a lot, okay?"

Touching her knees, placing his head at the mantle of her femininity, the urge to lift her skirt appeared again. Oh, how he wanted to reach his hands beneath it, run them from her socks up the length of her legs. He could even imagine the soft wetness waiting there between her thighs, access unhindered, but he couldn't do it without telling her the truth.

"I want to kiss you," Ethan said, desperately trying to explain himself. "There is nothing—nothing—in the world I want more right now than to kiss you. But I need to tell you something first. Something you might not like…"

Suddenly, Ethan's phone vibrated in his pocket. Reaching for it, he moved to turn it off. Instead, he caught sight of the name on the caller ID. *Hebrew Home for Assisted Living.* Great. Just perfect timing. They would not be calling him unless there was a problem.

"Sorry," Ethan said, standing up. "I need to take this."

"Seriously?" Avital scoffed.

Ethan wasn't listening. He was already heading down the hall in order to take the call in a more private setting. Pressing his phone against his ear, he could not believe what he was hearing on the other end of the line. The news was not good.

"You're kidding me," Ethan said, incredulous. "No. I'll be right there."

When he turned around, Avital was standing in the hall.

"I really hate to ask this," Ethan said, "but would you mind giving me a ride upstate?"

"Right now?" she said, glancing at her watch. "To Upstate New York?"

"I wouldn't ask if it weren't important."

He could see she was hurt, confused, by the tears building in the corner of her eyes. But even still, and likely because it was Avital—a genuinely good person—she gave in to his ridiculous request.

"Fine," Avital said, huffing out the word. "But you're paying me back for the gas."

TWENTY-FOUR

The car ride upstate with Ethan was weird. Silent. Despite the many questions she threw at him, Ethan was only willing to offer up crumbs in terms of an explanation.

"Are you at least going to tell me where we're going?" Avital asked.

"To my sister," Ethan said quietly.

"The one who lives in Connecticut near your parents?" Ethan slumped in his seat. "No."

"No?" Avital asked, snapping her head around. "Is there a different sister I don't know about?"

"I mean," he backtracked, getting more nervous, "it is the same sister, I just... I made up a different version of her."

Avital couldn't help herself. Even though it was dark, and late, and flurrying...she kept taking her eyes off the road to look at Ethan. "What?" she said, turning in his direction. "What does that even mean? Why would you even do that?"

"Not when you're driving."

He was scaring her.

"There," Ethan said, pointing to an exit. "Make a left at the light."

Avital did as instructed, finding herself rolling past a stucco sign. Lit up by decorative lights and dotted with ivy, it read *Hebrew Home for Assisted Living.*

"Your sister lives here?" Avital asked.

He nodded. "Yeah."

Avital pulled her car into a parking spot. "I don't understand."

"My sister is disabled."

"Were you embarrassed to tell me the truth because she's disabled?"

"No," he said, adamant. "I love my sister. I would never hide her."

"But you did hide her," she reminded him.

"It's not that simple."

Ethan went to unbuckle his seat belt. Avital tried to follow.

"I actually need you to stay here," Ethan said.

Now she was just annoyed. "Absolutely not!"

"Please." Ethan was begging. "I promise I'll be back in five minutes, okay? And then I will explain everything. I will tell you the truth about everything, too. But just…give me five minutes to deal with this first."

He was looking at her with those big doe eyes, and she hated herself for even giving him the benefit of the doubt.

She waved her acquiescence. Ethan took off. Watching him disappear through the entrance, turning left and heading down a hall, she gave him a grand total of three minutes before deciding she had waited long enough. She was worried about Ethan, and she wanted to know what the hell was going on.

Stepping out of the car and closing the door behind her,

she stomped through slushy puddles in Birkenstocks, mak‐
ing her way inside.

Avital heard the commotion first: a loud wail, mixed with
a cacophony of voices, mixed with something crashing. She
twisted in the direction of the noise. Three nurses rushed
past her in a full sprint. Avital had to step aside to keep from
getting knocked over.

The wailing grew louder. The sound of voices, a mixture
of argument interspersed with calming platitudes, rose in
the hallways around her. Avital rounded a corner and found
Ethan talking to an older woman in pink scrubs. His hands
pressed up against his belt, his voice direct and firm. His back
was turned to her.

"How could you let her throw them out?" Ethan said.

"She's new," the woman in pink said. "She thought they
were trash."

"You know how important those boxes are to her!" Ethan
said, glancing toward the room where the crying continued.
"Where are they?" His tone was clipped.

"The dumpster," the nurse said, exasperated. "Out back."

Ethan disappeared into the room with the nurse follow‐
ing. Avital tiptoed closer. Peeking inside the doorway, she
saw Ethan was sitting on the floor with a woman. Running
his hand down her dark brown hair, he spoke to her softly.

"I'm going to find those boxes for you, okay?" he said,
glancing up at the nurse. "Did you give her anything to help
her calm down?"

"About twenty minutes ago."

"It's okay, Kayla." Ethan kissed her on the forehead. "I'd
be upset, too."

Avital watched, unseen. She wasn't sure what was going
on, but she suddenly felt bad for intruding on what was clearly
a private family moment. She began to tiptoe back from the

door, fully planning to return to the car, when a sign on the door caught her eye. On a whiteboard, next to scribbles of butterflies and flowers, was the name of Ethan's sister.

KAYLA ROSENBERG-LIPPMANN

Ethan turned around.

"Avital." Her name fell from his lips.

She did not give him time to explain. Almost as soon as their eyes met, she was taking off down the hall. Ethan chased after her.

"Avital!" he said, catching up with her midway. "Please. Let me explain."

"You're a Lippmann!"

"No," he said. "I mean... I am, but it's not that simple."

"You lied to me!" The words tumbled from her mouth in a fury. "All this time, all these months...you lied to me."

Her voice cracked and faded. She didn't know how to describe what she was feeling, because she had absolutely no idea what was going on. Ethan Rosenberg was really Ethan Lippmann. How was it even possible? Her mind racing, all she wanted to do was get away from him.

"Look," Ethan said, grabbing her by the elbows, "I know you're pissed."

She yanked herself away. "*Pissed* doesn't even begin to cover it."

"I know," he said, hands outstretched, desperate for something. "But please...please, Avital... Just give me five minutes, okay? I just need to find these Lippmann boxes for my sister, and then I swear I will explain everything. But please... don't leave, okay? Just wait for me. Just give me one chance to explain."

She didn't answer him. Her mind was far too busy racing

with questions to form words. The sound of the woman's wailing returned, and Ethan spun and exited through a side door into the back. Avital stood there, fuming, questioning... before finally saying screw it.

Stomping her way to the parking lot, she got back in her car. Slamming the door behind her, she turned the key in the ignition, prepared to leave him forever. But when she moved to step on the gas, she hesitated.

She deserved an explanation.

Avital stepped out of her vehicle. Huffing her way back inside and heading out the back exit, she found Ethan, crawling around the first of three large dumpsters. Watching him toss boxes and dirt aside, ripping into bags with abandon, she couldn't help but think it was a just punishment. Trash was exactly what Ethan Lippmann deserved.

"So which one are you?" Avital asked. "The drug addict... or the sociopath?"

A piece of spaghetti dangled from his hair. "I guess the sociopath."

"Seems accurate," she said, crossing her arms against her chest. "And I'm assuming you coming to work at Best Babka had nothing to do with wanting to learn the secrets of modern kosher cooking or garnering a better understanding of the kosher market?"

Ethan swallowed. "No."

"So what were you doing at my store, Ethan?"

He sighed. "My grandfather wanted me to steal your recipe for pumpkin-spiced babka. He had plans to take it and mass-distribute it under the Lippmann's brand name. I was there to put you out of business. But I swear, Avital—"

She could feel her lower lip quivering, but she wasn't going to cry. Oh, no...she would not give Ethan Lippmann the pleasure of knowing he had hurt her.

"I swear," he said, his face red, his voice pleading, "I didn't want to do it."

"But you had a choice!" she said, snapping at him. "Every day you walked into my store, you had a choice, Ethan. For three months, during all those late-night conversations—you could have said something. I showed you my photography!"

"I didn't want to lose you," Ethan shouted. "And you're right, okay? I made a bad decision. I made the cowardly decision, too. I lied about who I was, and what I was doing there, and my family history... But all those conversations with you, Avital... Everything I felt, including tonight when I told you I like you, was real. *It was real, okay?* If you want to walk away and hate me forever, I'd understand. But if there's even one small sliver of a chance that you could forgive me... Just give me five minutes to find these freaking Lippmann boxes for my sister, and then I will tell you everything, okay?"

Avital blinked back tears. Groaning, she spun back toward the parking lot, torn between the urge to leave him and to stay.

A thousand thoughts raced through her head. He was a Lippmann. He was the enemy. *He had tried to ruin them.* But then, this other part of her...

The way he had shown up for her when she was sick, taking on long hours, melding with the heart of their Best Babka family. All their shared conversations together, the way he devoured her air-fryer salmon, their discussions about faith and spirituality, his willingness to listen to her talk about her illness. The silly smile on his face, the way his shoulders relaxed when he came to her office wearing his Little Buddy hat. The room he had built for her.

What kind of person would do all these things if they were really a monster?

And then, another realization.

Because she knew Ethan.

She knew him.

Avital shook her head, frustrated. And then, tying up her skirt like a diaper around her lower extremities, she began crawling up the side of the dumpster.

"What are you doing?" Ethan asked.

"What does it look like I'm doing?" she snapped back at him. "I'm coming in to help you find these Lippmann boxes for your sister."

Ethan stammered, confused. "Wh-why?"

"Because," she said, finding her way to the top, plugging her nose up, "I like you, too."

And then, feetfirst and without hesitation, Avital jumped into the dumpster.

TWENTY-FIVE

Disaster averted.

Ethan tucked his sister into bed while Avital watched from the doorway. Kayla's Lippmann boxes had been restored to their rightful place at the side of the room, and he'd placed a sign on the wall above them that read Do Not Throw Out in big block letters. Pulling up her covers, Ethan kissed her good-night. Then, shutting off the light, he met Avital on the threshold.

"I guess we should go somewhere to talk," he said.

"Is there somewhere we can go to get cleaned up first?" Avital asked, glancing down at her skirt. "I'm kind of worried about getting a urinary tract infection."

Ethan paused before answering. "There's a place nearby. We'd have to be quiet...but we can get cleaned up, get you a change of clothes."

Avital nodded, and returning to the car, they took off.

Twenty minutes later, they were parked at the end of the driveway, the Lippmann estate looming in the dark beyond.

"This is where you live?" Avital asked.

"Unfortunately," Ethan grumbled.

"I knew the Lippmanns had money, but this is—"

"Grotesque?" He filled in the blanks for her. "Monstrous? Indecent?"

"I was leaning more toward *incredible*, but sure…we'll go with your interpretation."

Ethan sighed. "I guess we should go inside, then," Ethan said, stepping out of the car first. Avital quickly followed. "Just remember what I said," he explained one more time, leading her down the driveway. "Follow me. Try not to make too much noise. If my grandfather finds out you're in his house…"

"Trust me," Avital said. "I know eccentric grandfathers better than anybody."

Taking her by the hand, he led her inside. Luckily, it was past ten o'clock. The house was quiet. The majority of the staff had gone to bed. Holding her in his grip, he moved briskly but silently.

"Come on." Ethan nodded toward the stairs. "My room is in the back wing."

"The back wing?" Avital mouthed.

His hearing was on high alert as he went, and he felt every ounce of danger as he led her up the stairs. Finally, he made it to his room. Checking the hallway once more for interlopers, he closed the door behind her.

"You okay?" Ethan asked, meeting her eyes directly.

"I'm fine, Ethan."

"You sure?"

"Yeah." She didn't seem to understand why he was so nervous. "Where are we?"

"This is my room," he said.

Avital blinked. "This is your room?"

Her eyes scanned the space once more. He could see she was confused. Ethan didn't have time to explain. Quickly, he turned on the light to a bathroom before heading over to one of the lower drawers of his bureau, pulling out a pair of sweatpants and a sweatshirt.

"Here you go," he said, handing them to her. "You can take a shower in there. There are towels and toiletries in the linen closets."

"What should I do with my dirty clothes?"

Ethan did a quick once-over of the room and then grabbed a liner from a hidden wastebasket in the wall. "Here," he said, leading her to the shower. "Just hurry up, okay?"

"Ethan," Avital said in a whisper. "I can't wear these."

"Why not?"

"Uh," she said, pointing down at the designer label, "probably because they cost more than my natural life. What if I spill coffee on them or something?"

Ethan squinted. "You want a coffee?"

"You know what…" Avital shook her head. "Never mind. I'm taking your sweatpants. I'm not giving them back, either. I'm gonna use them as a down payment on my first house."

Avital disappeared into the bathroom. The sound of the water turning on told Ethan she had figured out the toiletries, towels and waterfall shower situation on her own. Ethan waited, counting down the seconds until he could get them out of there. This wasn't safe. This wasn't smart. He should never have brought Avital home.

The shower turned off. Moments later, Avital appeared, her hair wet. His clothing swam on her tiny body. "I left the garbage bag in the bathroom," she said.

"Thanks," Ethan said, heading into the bathroom and shutting the door behind him.

Throwing off his clothes and tossing them into the bag, he stepped into the shower. It might have been the quickest shower of his entire life.

Swinging open the door, he was expecting to see Avital. Instead, his heart caught in his throat. His grandfather was sitting on his bed, both hands resting on his cane. Ethan scanned the room, but Avital was nowhere to be seen.

Moishe scowled. "Time for a family meeting."

TWENTY-SIX

"Everything okay, Grandpa?"

Ethan played it cool. Walking past the old man, heading to his bureau, he opened a drawer, pulling out a pair of pajamas. When he did, he made contact with Avital's blue eyes, peeking out from inside his armoire. She must have heard Moishe coming up the stairs, coughing due to his asthma, and thought quickly, jumping into the wardrobe to hide.

Ethan met her gaze, letting her know that he had seen her, before turning back to his grandfather.

"By my good graces," Moishe began, tapping on the top of his cane, "Kayla is provided for. Your brother has a roof over his head. And you, Ethan…you have the chance to become king of a baked-goods billion-dollar empire. And what do I get in return for my years of love and kindness? How do you repay me for being there for you…and caring for your siblings?"

"I'm working on it," Ethan said, attempting to defend himself.

"Shut up!" Moishe exploded. "You think that's enough? You think that makes up for all the money, time, and energy I've spent on you? *Useless. Nothing.* Your entire life. Your entire life... You've ruined everything you've touched. *You killed your own parents.* No wonder nobody wants you. No wonder nobody loves you, either. Who could ever love a nothing?"

His grandfather had a gift for finding the places that hurt the most. Usually, Ethan could turn it off, pretend he was somewhere else, and just let the words fade out around him. This time, however, he was being berated in front of Avital. The shame he had felt all his life, the secret he had hidden from everyone at school and in his many failed relationships, was now fully revealed.

"You know what I think, Ethan," Moishe said simply, shrugging his shoulders, "I think the reason you haven't found that recipe is because you don't want to find it. I think...you're getting too close to these Cohens. You're spending all your time with them, you're getting to know them, and you can no longer remember where your loyalties lie. So let me be very clear about what's going to happen if you fail me, if you choose the Cohens over your own flesh and blood."

"I'm not choosing—"

"Shut up!" Moishe said, cutting him off. "I will ruin you. And I'm not just talking about getting you blacklisted from every possible job in business you apply to going forward. I'm not just talking about the joy of seeing you destitute, struggling to make ends meet, with no idea how to survive in the real world. I'm talking about your family. You understand me, Ethan? No more Randy. No more Kayla. You will never have access to them again, you understand?"

Ethan met his grandfather's eyes directly. "I understand."

"Then, don't disappoint me."

Moishe wobbled out of his room. Ethan waited at the door for pin-drop silence, to be certain the old man had departed back down the stairs and reached his wing, before heading to the armoire. Offering his hand, he helped Avital out, bringing her safely to the carpet.

When he finally found the courage to meet her gaze, he didn't like what he saw. Her eyes were red. Her face was pale. He couldn't protect her or Randy or Kayla...because he couldn't protect himself. He heard the words of his grandfather echoing in his brain, sitting there upon his heart.

Who could ever love a nothing?

"Let's get out of here," Avital said.

Avital didn't say anything to Ethan during the car-ride escape from the Lippmann compound. She kept her eyes firmly planted on the road ahead, her hands gripping the steering wheel, while Ethan slunk in his seat beside her. All he could think about was that she knew the truth now: she knew the truth, and he was going to lose her.

Avital found a place to stop—some park, about ten minutes beyond the Lippmann estate, which, given that it was now past eleven, was devoid of people. Finding her way toward a basketball court, she parked beneath a streetlight. A quiet settled over the vehicle, which felt unbelievably oppressive. The sense of being stuck coupled with his shame that he should have known better, should have been able to stop it, but his grandfather was right. He was a nothing, a disappointment, a failure. No one would ever love him.

Finally, Avital broke the silence. "Does he always talk to you like that?"

Ethan shifted in his seat. "Pretty much."

She turned in her seat to face him. "And this is your grandfather?" she asked, like it needed to be confirmed. "The man who raised you after...your parents..."

"After my parents died," he finished the sentence for her. "Yeah."

Because the stories she had heard were true.

Her voice cracked. "Ethan..."

"I don't want your pity."

"It's not pity," she said. "It's concern."

Truthfully, he didn't feel deserving of that, either.

And then, Ethan told her the truth. He told her about the day his parents died, the aftermath, moving in with his grandfather. He told her about all the years since—getting sent to boarding school, coming home every summer to work at Lippmann's, never having a single say over any choice in his own life. He told her that he was an alien—that before coming to Best Babka he had never taken a bus or cooked his own meals or cleaned a bathroom.

Until finally, he told her the story of Moishe seeing that ad in *Jewish World News*. He told her the truth. That he didn't want to do it, that it went against his very core values...but he was stuck. Half-baked. Like one of Chaya's challahs, sitting on a counter at Best Babka, struggling against all odds to rise.

Avital took it all in. Occasionally, she nodded. Sometimes, she looked out the window. Mainly, though, she just stared at her hands, thoughtful and pensive, while Ethan spoke. And when he was done, when all the secrets of his life were laid out before her, he readied himself for the worst.

Who could ever love a nothing?

Who would ever want someone so broken, and fallible, as him?

"Do you really think he would do it?" Avital asked. "Disown you? Put your sister in some state-run home? Throw out your brother?"

"I don't know," Ethan said simply. "I want to believe he wouldn't. That his ramblings are just that—the gibberish of an old and broken man, desperately trying to hold on to his family in all the worst ways. But I don't know, and I suppose that's what makes the threats so terrifying."

Avital was quiet for a long time. "Believe it or not, Ethan... I do understand."

Ethan sat up in his seat. "You do?"

"Yeah," she said, before unbuckling her seat belt, opening the driver's side door. "I need some air."

The sound of it shutting caused Ethan to slink back down in his seat. All the worst thoughts ran through his mind— *This is it, she's leaving me. I'll never see Avital again*—and then, Avital knocked on his window. Ethan rolled it down.

"You coming?" Avital asked.

Quickly, he unbuckled the belt. "Yeah."

Outside their vehicle, Avital made her way to a park bench. Ethan sat down beside her. In the quiet that followed, he disappeared. He stared out into the distance, fading into the trees, going someplace where the words would hurt less, the way he always did with his grandfather. He didn't want to get emotional when Avital dropped the bomb.

"I was thinking about killing myself."

It was not what he was expecting to hear. "Wh...what?"

"The day of the fire," she said, staring into the distance. "I was sitting on this park bench near Best Babka, and I was thinking about how the pain was so bad, and how I had thirteen pills...thirteen goddamn pills to get me through the next three months...and I thought, maybe this is it. This is where I become one of those stories. One of those sad stories you read about in a social-media feed. Some poor, abandoned chronic-pain patient—some beautiful girl lost at twenty-four—who had no way of escaping her pain except to take her own life."

"Avital…"

His heart broke for her. He had this urge to reach out and take her hand, to pull her close to him and hold her forever. But her hands were folded neatly in the center of her lap, and he still wasn't sure that she had forgiven him.

"You know the worst part?" she said, shaking her head, laughing a little at the absurdity. "I don't want to die. In fact, I'm terrified to die. But I was sitting there, and I was thinking…how do I keep living like this? How do I make it one more minute in so much pain? And then, I get this call there's a fire. The second floor is a mess. I have to call insurance, and this awful woman hangs up on me three freaking times… and I was certain it was the very worst day of my life. I was certain I would never be able to survive it. And then, do you know what happened?"

Ethan stared down at his shoes.

"You came into my office," she said. "You told me you were going to help me. You told me you were going to make my life easier. And you did, Ethan. You took that very terrible day, and you turned it into something better."

Ethan swallowed. "You did the same for me, Avi."

"I know."

A peaceful quiet settled between them.

"So now I know the real you," she said. "The broken, messed-up, imperfect you. And now you know the real me. The broken, messed-up, and imperfect version. And I don't know where we go from here, Ethan. I don't know if this thing will ever work out between us. I highly doubt it will… but I know I'm not ready to lose you."

Ethan blinked. "You're not firing me?"

"Not today, anyway." She smiled.

"But what about your family?" he asked, shocked and

amazed that she would even consider lying to them. "What about the business?"

"I'll figure something out."

Her words caused a stone to dislodge from his throat. Ethan coughed, trying to choke back the feelings. He didn't want to cry in front of Avital.

"You think we're so different," she said finally. "But we're not. We're both living in chronic pain. We're both just…trying to figure out how to live alongside the things that have hurt us. And maybe we've both made mistakes in the process. I certainly have. But you're not a bad person. You're good and kind, and just in case no one has ever said it to you before, you didn't deserve all the bad things that happened to you."

It was too late. Tears ran down his cheeks. He had the urge to suck them back, to wipe them away with the back of his hand, to protect himself from the potential of another scar. Instead, she reached over and took his hand, and in the quiet that came after, where no one was shouting or berating him for his feelings, Ethan learned something important.

It was easy to be real when you felt safe.

Ethan met her gaze once more, and his entire body vibrated with desire. He was drawn to the roundness in her face. Her delicate smile, like two tiny petals of pink set against bows of white. He had a desperate, longing urge to run his finger down her cheek. To pull her toward him, taste those lips.

"Avital," he said, his voice heavy with desire.

"Yeah?"

"Forgive me," he said, leaning in closer. "But I'm going to kiss you now."

She lifted to meet his lips. The taste of her, the soft little whimpers emerging from her throat, stoked the heat of his own desire. The taste of her, the soft little whimpers emerging from her throat, stoked the heat of his own desire. It felt like the entire universe was sitting in that kiss. Avital was wind, and sand, and earth, and fire, and tiny little drops of morning dew. She was his, and he was hers—and even if it couldn't last forever, they had shared one healing moment in a lifetime of hurt together.

"Ethan," she whispered, "let's go back to Best Babka."

ADAR I

(February—March)

TWENTY-SEVEN

"Everybody ready?"

Avital stood at the first-floor landing near the staircase. With scissors in hand and bent over a red ribbon, she grinned toward the staff of Best Babka waiting in a half circle around her, ready to toast with their plastic flutes of kosher champagne. Standing beside her, holding a clipboard, waiting to do his final inspection, was Jensen.

The crowd responded to her question with cheers. Her eyes flicked toward Ethan. He looked so damn attractive. He smiled, one eyebrow edging upward, and she knew he was thinking of mischief.

She was thinking about mischief, too.

It had only taken Avital two days to come up with her master plan. She had been sitting in her office, going over the weekly baking schedule with Josh and Ethan, when she landed on Chaya's name. In an instant, the clouds opened up and the closest thing to a mystical moment in her life appeared. She knew what had to be done.

The second floor was nearly done. She could pull Chaya off breads, move Ethan onto it. It made sense. After Ethan's hard work, people would begin to wonder why he hadn't been promoted to baker. The problem being, of course, Ethan Rosenberg-Lippmann didn't know how to bake. She also couldn't exactly teach him in broad daylight.

But by putting him on breads, Avital could kill two birds with one stone. For one, she could teach Ethan the basics of baking. More important, it would give her time. Time to figure out if she were even capable of having an intimate relationship with Ethan, before blowing up both their lives and their families for nothing.

"Come on, Avi," Tootles whined, "the suspense is killing me already."

Avital cut the ribbon. A stampede of employees filed excitedly up the stairs. Ethan and Avital waited at the bottom for everyone to find a space, before following after them.

"Avi," Josh said, incredulous, "this is amazing."

"It doesn't even look like the same place," Jensen responded.

The first room was now carefully allotted for storage. The third room was devoted to paperwork. Across the way, in the laundry room, the smoke damage had been removed, and new washer and dryer units rested against the wall. But it was the second room—the room Ethan had built for Avital, with its little bed and bookshelves made of reclaimed wood—that drew the most attention.

"Holy challah," Tootles said, stepping inside to see the final product. "I might have to move in here."

"It's definitely bigger than my apartment," Sara said, peering over his shoulder.

"It's bigger than my apartment and your apartment put together," Tootles confirmed.

"So," Avital said, glancing over to Jensen, "did we pass inspection?"

Everyone on the second floor fell quiet. With clipboard in hand, and in a very detached and professional manner, Jensen moved from room to room. He checked the wiring, the cables. He examined the windows. He even ran one hand down some paneling, as if looking for dust. And then, making some scribbles on his clipboard, he took a deep breath.

"Well," Jensen said, glancing around the room, "I would say you passed with flying colors. Great work, and congratulations to everyone involved."

The whole room broke into applause at the good news.

"All right," Avital said, bringing the room back to a calm. "Thank you to Jensen for coming in today. If everyone has seen the upstairs, I invite you to meet me and Josh in the kitchen for a very special announcement."

The excitement now shifted to knowing glances aimed toward Ethan. Five minutes later, the staff of Best Babka was gathered around them in a large circle.

"The reason I called you all in today," Avital said, "is that I have something to share with you. As all of you know, no matter who you are when you begin work at Best Babka, we all start at the same place. We make pink boxes, learn how to tie Tiffany bows, work the counter, and if you work hard enough, proving yourself in the trenches, then you get to move to the kitchen."

Avital turned around and, reaching beneath a drawer in the counter, pulled out one of their branded Best Babka shirts. "Ethan Rosenberg," Avital said, holding it in her hand, "would you come over here for a second?"

Ethan did as instructed, taking his spot beside her.

"Ethan," Avital said, "you have become an absolutely invaluable member of our team. You have consistently shown up, and stayed late, making yourself indispensable to every person who needs you."

"Hear! Hear!" Josh said, lifting a glass of champagne.

"The best little buddy," Tootles said emphatically.

Ethan put one finger on his nose, pointing toward Tootles with the other. "I see you, big buddy!"

When the clamor finally settled, Avital continued.

"Beyond all these things," Avital said, "you are a good person. You treat everyone at Best Babka, from the customers to the staff, with kindness and compassion. You have been an invaluable help to us, and you are worth so, so much. Which is why today, I'm honored to promote you to baker and formally invite you to join our family. I'm pleased to announce that starting next Sunday, Ethan Rosenberg is officially going to be taking over for Chaya on bread duty."

Another round of raucous cheers, followed by shouts of praise, went up around the room. Avital handed Ethan the shirt. His eyes creased around the edges as he threw it on over what he was wearing, biting back clear pride.

"Speech!" Josh shouted. "Speech from our new family member."

"Well," Ethan said, shifting his weight where he stood, "I'm not really the best at spontaneous speeches, but I just want to say that working here, meeting all of you, it really has been the best experience of my life. It's been...life-changing. Which I know seems hard to believe, but it's true. So thank you... really, from the bottom of my heart. You all mean the world to me. That's really... I don't know what else to say."

"Great job, Ethan," someone called out.

"Couldn't be prouder of you."

"You rock, Ethan."

Until finally Tootles stepped forward. Wrapping one arm around Ethan, quelling the cheers, he said, "So now that you're officially one of us, I think there's only one question left on everyone's mind. What are *you* making as your specialty dish for this year's Purim carnival?"

Avital knew Ethan had been dreading this moment. He was, after all, supposed to be an overqualified pastry chef.

Ethan let the question linger in the air before responding. "I don't know, big buddy," Ethan teased Tootles in return, "but if I did…I certainly wouldn't tell you. After all, I heard your bourekas are the one to beat."

The crowd devolved into laughter. Tootles beamed at the compliment. Ethan beamed, too. Avital couldn't help herself. She smiled along with them. Watching from the sidelines, it was easy to get wrapped up in the fantasy.

It felt right. Ethan and Josh. Ethan and Tootles. All of them, baking and being together. It was a lovely, and beautiful, daydream. And yet—Avital couldn't help but think it—this was a daydream that would disappear with reality.

TWENTY-EIGHT

"Tonight," Avital said, one hand perched on the edge of her apron, "I will be teaching you how to bake."

Ethan looked up from the notepad he was scribbling instructions in and immediately lost his train of thought. He had never seen Avital in an apron before, and the way it hugged her body was making it hard to pay attention to what she was saying.

"For your very first lesson," Avital said, grabbing the laminated recipe book that hung on the wall of every kitchen, opening it up between them, "we will be making challah. Now, you would think, looking at this recipe, that challah is simple to make. It's just bread, right? Soft and fluffy. Some yeast, oil, flour, honey, sea salt… No way to mess that up, right?"

She angled her weight against the counter, pointing one finger in his face.

"Right." He grinned, pulling her closer.

"Wrong," Avital said, pushing his hands away.

She spun away from him to begin gathering up ingredients. Ethan tried to ignore the throbbing, aching need emerging from his lower belly.

"Now," Avital said, "just because challah looks like a basic recipe doesn't mean it is. There are a zillion ways to a mess up a challah. Chances are, before you make a perfect one... you're gonna screw one up. I'm telling you this because it's normal. It happens to everyone in this kitchen. But eventually, everyone here becomes a challah expert... So just be patient with yourself, okay? You'll get it eventually."

"I appreciate that, Avi."

A heat flushed through him. All he wanted was to be close with her. Avital pulled away. She grabbed three bowls, laying them out before him. Ethan attempted to breathe through his sexual tension and return his attention to making challah.

"So, there are lots of ways to make challah," Avital explained. "Lots of recipes, and versions, too. I'm going to teach you the Best Babka way."

"Sounds good." Ethan smiled.

"Now, with every Best Babka challah you make," Avital explained, "you're going to use three bowls. The little one to create the yeast mixture. The middle one for wet ingredients. And the big one for dry. First, we make the yeast mixture." Ethan watched as she put a few teaspoons into the small bowl, before heading over to the sink.

Avital let the water run a little before taking his hand.

"You feel that?" Avital asked, putting his fingers beneath the stream.

Ethan swallowed. "Definitely."

"That's how hot you want the water to be. We add a cup

of hot water to the yeast," she said, demonstrating, "and voilà! After ten minutes, the yeast will begin to bubble. That means it's activated. In the meantime—" she returned to the counter, taking the opposite side from him, pushing the laminated recipe sheet his way "—I want you to make two bowls. One with all the wet ingredients. And one with all the dry ingredients."

Ethan grabbed the recipe book and began. Avital circled him, keeping enough space between them to maintain a professional atmosphere, while he worked. He got the first part right. He measured out flour and salt into one container. Next, he began on the wet ingredients. He poured in water, olive oil, and honey, before heading to the fridge to grab a carton of eggs. He cracked one open and dropped it in.

"Nope," Avital said, shaking her head. "Start over."

"What?" Ethan said, staring down at his wet bowl. "Why?"

"Gotta check your eggs for blood spots."

"Ugh." Ethan closed his eyes. "I can't believe I forgot that."

"Yeah." Avital sighed. "It's one of those things that has to get burned into your brain here. *Check the eggs for blood spots.* We've had more than one batch that had go in the trash because someone forgot."

Ethan went to the cabinet to find a glass. "I've seen Chaya do it so many times at this point." Grabbing the carton of eggs again, he poured one into the glass. Looking inside, and then raising it to the light, he searched for any tiny specks of brown or red.

"Good?" he said, making his final determination.

Avital glanced over. "Good."

Ethan dumped out the bowl of wet ingredients and started again.

"You must lose a lot of money doing this," Ethan said.

"Tons," Avital admitted, before getting another bowl. "But you would know all about that, I imagine."

"How do you mean?"

"Well, Lippmann's has a *hechsher* on their products, right?"

"We do," he admitted. "But I've never actually been in one of our factories."

"Wait, you've never been in one of your own factories?" Avital asked.

"No, of course I've been in our factories," he said. "What I mean is... I've never really been in charge of overseeing the day-to-day there. The closest I've ever gotten to supervising the actual making of baked goods is digitizing the original recipes for my grandfather."

"Wow..." Avital shook her head. "I can't even imagine. I feel like I was born with a mixer in my hand."

"I am firmly corporate." Ethan smiled. "Numbers, Excel sheets, sales and marketing..."

"Oooh," she said, before adding with a smile, "don't forget corporate espionage."

"Yes, well..." He finished checking his last egg. "We had a saying at Lippmann's."

"What was that?"

"If you miss work on Saturday, don't bother coming in on Sunday."

Avital grimaced. "Ouch."

"It isn't the healthiest environment to work in."

"The way you describe it, working at Lippmann's sounds kind of like a nightmare."

"That's the thing about nightmares," Ethan said, "most people don't realize they're in one until they get out of it."

Avital nodded. "Yeah."

"By the way—" Ethan figured he would throw the question in "—you get that camera of yours fixed yet?"

"Nope."

"Hmm…" Ethan raised both eyebrows at her.

Avital smiled at him but otherwise was more than happy to move the conversation back to making challah.

"Okay," Avital said, leaning over to check his bowls. "Now, that you finished the eggs, I want you to take the now bubbling yeast mixture, add it to the wet, and then slowly mix the wet ingredients into the dry."

Avital demonstrated the first round herself, slowly adding all the wet items into the dry ones, before forming a sticky and floury golden-yellow ball.

"Now," Avital said, grabbing a handful of flour from the bag and flinging it across the counter. "We get to the most important part of our recipe. Any idea what that is, Ethan?"

Ethan considered the question. "Love?"

Avital stopped.

Ethan squinched his forehead. "What?"

She burst out laughing—full-on hysterics—and covered her mouth. "I mean—" Avital gasped, trying to be supportive "—that's very important, too."

Ethan bit back a smile. "But it's not right?"

"No."

Ethan frowned. "Of course."

Avital nudged him playfully with her elbow. "Aside from baking with love…"

"Thank you for that." Ethan blushed. "I appreciate it."

"You're welcome." She smiled, nudging him back with her hip. "Most people think the most important part of challah-making is in the ingredients," Avital said and dumped the ball of dough onto the counter, "but that's not true. You can take any base, for any recipe, and change it up...come up with all sorts of clever alternatives...but the secret to a truly great challah is in the texture of the dough."

"The dough?" he said, leaning in closer to her.

Avital stepped away from him. She placed her hand on a mixer, sitting unused on a side counter.

"Most modern-day bakeries," she explained, tapping on the machine, "use giant mixers. It's easier, quicker, cheaper in terms of labor, blah, blah, blah...but it also gets you a different type of dough when you knead using a mixer. We don't like challah that tastes and feels like you could buy it in any market. We do it the old-world way, the way my grandparents made it, passed down *l'dor v'dor*, from generation to generation. Which is why we make our challah, like all of our products, by hand."

Avital tossed the ball into the center of the counter.

"First," Avital said, "I want you to touch the dough."

"Okay."

"No." Avital laughed, pushing him away playfully. "I mean really touch it. Pick it up. Feel the weight. Roll it around and give it a few good pinches."

Ethan did as she instructed. He picked up that heavy ball of sticky dough. He felt the weight. He stuck his fingers into it.

"Now," Avital said, "I want you to commit the feeling of the dough right now into your memory. This dough... is at a ten."

"A ten?"

"It hasn't been manipulated yet through kneading," Avital explained, leaning over his shoulder. "Which means all those delicious glutinous bits that give handmade challahs their gorgeous yellow stretchy consistency when you pull it apart haven't been created yet. It's just a lump of flour, honey, oil, yeast and water. It's heavy, and if you bake it this way... well, frankly, it's probably gonna be burned on the outside and uncooked in the middle. No good. This dough right here is at a ten. You got it?"

"I think so."

"Now," Avital continued, coming around him again, putting her hands around his waist, "how we change the shape and texture of the dough from a ten to a one, to when it is ready for going into the refridgerator for rising, is through kneading. We apply pressure, slowly. We gently, but firmly, massage our ball until all the air bubbles are released and the dough is fully activated."

She reached her hand into the bag of flour, sprinkling it against the ball.

"Fold and squash," she said, demonstrating the action. "Fold and squash."

Avital stepped out of the way. Ethan took her spot at the counter.

"Fold and squash," he said, repeating the action. "Fold and squash."

"Now, as you're folding and squashing," she said, leaning over to inspect, "you want to be stretching the dough out. I know that sounds convoluted, but basically... How do I explain it? Like a hora. Bring the dough in, stretch it out. In and out. That's the same with kneading challah. It's like a dance. You need to follow the dough, feel how it's reacting...listen to your dough. It's the physical manipulation that develops the glutens in your bread. So you push down, release, pull... good. Fold, squash, stretch...stop, stop, stop." Ethan stopped.

Avital took a piece of the dough off, rolling it around between her fingers in front of him. "You feel this dough right now?"

Ethan took the tiny ball from her. "Yeah."

"How does it feel?"

"Kind of wet."

"That's sticky," Avital said. "Sticky isn't good. Sticky is a five. It's getting there, but it's not stretched and ready yet. Add more flour."

Ethan reached into the bag, pulling out a handful, sprinkling it on his ball.

"Every time you feel that stickiness," Avital said, "add flour."

"Stickiness. Flour," Ethan repeated. "Got it."

Ethan continued kneading. Avital stepped back, giving him room. With each round, he began to understand what Avital was teaching him in the kitchen. The dough reacted to his movements. If he pressed too hard, the dough would get sticky again. *Back to a five.* If he pressed too lightly, it would get dry. *Back to a ten.*

"How long do I do this for?" Ethan asked.

"Usually, it takes about ten minutes of kneading," Avital explained. "But that can change on so many factors. The temperature of the room. The humidity in the air. Even the season can affect how your challah turns out. Which is why a true baker doesn't have to rely on clocks for kneading. They rely on the feeling of the dough beneath their hands."

Ethan continued working the dough. Pressing and pulling. Squashing and stretching. After a few more minutes had passed, he was officially sweating.

"Wow," Ethan said, taking a minute to breathe. "I didn't realize kneading challah took such physical endurance."

"Yeah." Avital laughed. "Bakers need strong forearms... and gentle fingers."

"I hope I'm up to the challenge."

Avital smiled. "I'm certain you are."

Ethan nodded. "This is actually kind of fun."

Avital cupped her cheek, watching him. "You think?"

"Honestly," he said as he returned to kneading, "it's kind of therapeutic."

"Well," Avital said, "maybe it'll turn out you have the bug."

"The bug?" Ethan asked curiously.

"The baking bug. Not everybody has it."

"Do you?"

"Hell no," Avital said. "I hate baking."

"But you're good at it."

"No," she corrected him, "I grew up around it. I know the science. I can whip out those skills and train someone when necessary. But do I enjoy spending hours kneading dough or developing some new recipe? Absolutely not. I don't have the patience for baking like Josh."

"But photography?"

"It's different," she said. "Plus, there's an immediacy to the photo, right? All the rest—coloring, composition, layering—can be done in a computer program. But for me it's not quite the same thing as baking. A photo will last forever. But a baked good exists to get eaten. I guess I've never liked it...the idea of working so hard for something that just disappears."

"Well, maybe you're missing the point of the baked good?" Ethan said. "They make people happy. That's different than art, right? Which can make people happy but also exists to say something, to comment on society, whatever. Anyway, I think that's why Josh loves baking. He likes seeing how it gives folks joy."

It was something he could understand intimately. He felt that same way whenever he made Avital smile.

Ethan took his hands off the dough.

Avital inspected it once again.

"Now," Avital said, placing his hands on top of the dough. "You see how the surface of your dough has changed? It's smooth. It's satiny. It has this big and beautiful round shape to it...like a full moon on Rosh Hodesh. And when you pick it up, it feels a little stretchy, right? It's not too sticky, not too loose, not too firm... This challah is at a one."

"A one."

"Commit this to memory," she said, laying her hands on top of his. "This is what you want every challah you make to feel like. It doesn't matter the recipe. It doesn't matter how long it takes you to knead. It doesn't matter the temperature or the humidity in the room. You want your challah dough to feel like this. A one."

"Okay." Ethan closed his eyes. "I got it. Now what do I do?"

"Now..." Avital said, releasing him. Lifting up the ball, she placed it back in the bowl, before stretching a towel over the top. "We leave it covered and let it rise. Then, you do this six more times, after which we take the first challah out of the bowl, and I'll teach you how to braid it. We'll start with three strands, four strands, and five strands tonight, after which, if you're not totally exhausted, we'll move on to circular and holiday braids."

Avital turned to leave. Ethan grabbed her by the hand. "Hey," he said, not wanting her to depart. "Where are you going?"

"Back to work," she said flippantly. "I've got payroll to deal with and taxes to get in order."

He pulled her back into his arms. "Stay with me."

"Ethan..."

Wrapping one arm around her waist, he pulled her closer, his nose nuzzling into the crook of her neck, kissing her softly. Her body buckled as a light moan escaped her lips. He took her dipping and sighing as acquiescence, that she was just as excited as he was at the prospect of finally moving their relationship from heated kissing into something more.

"Come on," he whispered. "We're alone."

"And," she reminded him, placing both hands on his chest, "if we don't have the challah made by the morning, people are going to wonder."

"Let them wonder," he growled.

"And what about the challah?" she said, pointing to the empty bowl.

"We have all night to make challah."

"And we have all night for making out, too…" she said, returning to boss mode. "But first—" she pushed the bag of flour his way "—challah."

But First, Challah should have been on a T-shirt.

He didn't understand her reticence, but he always gave in to Avital and her wishes. He couldn't bring himself to deny her any request. Whatever Avital wanted, desired, he would do for her. It scared him how much needing her to be happy affected his own joy.

Even though he knew what they had would likely never last, his heart had already become devoted to her.

Despite his own screaming want, he released her from his embrace. Avital flittered from the room, leaving Ethan with more than just the dough rising.

Avital stared at the reflection of herself in the bathroom mirror. Pushing her hair back behind her ears, turning off the running water where she had just rinsed her face, she took a deep breath. It had been two hours since she'd last checked on Ethan. She knew she needed to see how he was managing on the challahs, but she was hesitating.

She did not feel good. She certainly did not feel well enough to engage in any type of sexual activity. Still, she didn't want to make tonight about her chronic pain. She liked Ethan. She didn't want to lose him. Even with the burning, shooting pain spreading through her lower pelvis, she was determined to take her shot at a normal and healthy sexual life.

Gathering her courage, she sought out Ethan. Leaving the bathroom, heading down the hallway, she returned to the kitchen. Ethan was just in the process of pulling a tray of freshly baked challahs from the oven. His perfect tuchus, once again, flexed in her direction.

It was a unique type of torture. Wanting him, physically and emotionally, while simultaneously unsure if that desire could ever be quenched.

Ethan spun around. A happy bit of surprise registered in his eyes when he saw her. "Just in time." He smiled, warm and adorable, in her direction.

"Looks like you've been busy without me."

He laid the loaves on the counter. "I wanted to surprise you."

She was certainly pleased. Over the last four hours, he had made six batches of challah dough to be refrigerated for the morning and learned every type of holiday braid. Now they were doing one final test on his abilities. He had made all the five-strand braided challahs alone, from start to finish, without Avital's help.

"What do you think?" Ethan said, surveying the bread on the counter.

"Honestly," Avital said, shaking her head, "you're really good at this."

Ethan didn't believe her. "You think?"

"I'm serious, Ethan." She thought back on her many years of lessons. "I've never taught anyone who got a challah right on their first try."

He stared down at the tray of perfect golden challahs. "Well," Ethan said and smiled, stepping closer to her, "I had a good teacher."

His hand wandered over to her waist. The feeling of his touch caused her own desire to quicken. Avital melted. Her heart quickened inside her chest, as the desire to kiss him emerged once again. He was so handsome. He was so good to her. But then, alongside that growing sexual attraction, was pain. Another stabbing spasm rolled through her body. She decided to ignore it.

She pressed her body closer to him. Ethan raised one hand up to the side of her face, caressing the space between her lip and her cheekbone. Her entire body prickled with desire.

"You're so beautiful, Avital," Ethan whispered. "You're perfection."

He kissed her. Full lips, gentle and warm, met her own. With soft and delicate strokes, he parted her lips, and his tongue found its way into her mouth.

She moaned. Ethan responded to the sound by pressing his arousal against her. The heat of him, the heft of his chest rubbing against her hardened nipples, sent her into overdrive.

Cradling her fingers around the back of his head, she pulled him into her. And then, more pain. Pain, along with anxiety, which kept growing at each new experience of touch.

"You're perfection, Avital."

She moaned again. "Ethan…"

"You have no idea how much I want you."

"I want you, too," she said, her eyes closing.

Ethan responded. Picking her up, he placed her on the counter. Wrapping her legs around his waist, he trailed his tongue along her neck. "I've wanted this for so long," he whispered. "There's going to be no end to how much pleasure I give you tonight."

She whimpered, hot little breaths against his neck, tearing at his back, nails digging into him. Ethan pulled her closer, kissed her deeper, and she moaned with every new flick of his tongue, his hands moving to explore her body. The firmness of his erection now pressed against her body—but it felt terrible. Like someone attempting to penetrate her with an immersion blender set to full power.

Avital grimaced in pain, but then, feeling Ethan trailing his tongue along her neck—wanting that intimacy so desperately—said nothing.

She could do this. She just had to get through this one little sexual experience. Like a transvaginal ultrasound.

Avital kept her face pressed into his neck, biting back tears, willing herself to get through the agony. Pressing her lips together, she was determined to stay silent. She didn't want to ruin the moment, what they had, and her chance at a normal sexual life.

His hands made the way to the bottom of her skirt. Lifting it, his fingers danced their way up to the insides of her thighs. She writhed beneath his grip. Ethan responded by touching her harder, quicker, determined to give her pleasure. Avital's moan turned into a groan.

"Stop," she whispered.

"What?"

"Stop!" she said, pushing him away. "It hurts! I can't!"

And then—perhaps not surprisingly—Avital disappeared into a bathroom.

TWENTY-NINE

Avital couldn't stop crying. It came in heaving gasps, hysterical and out of control. It wasn't just the pain now, radiating through her lower abdomen, it was all the memories of the last two years, feet wedged into stirrups, biting back fear and pain as some stranger prodded around her pelvis.

It was the catheterization with expansion, the burning and relentless pain that didn't dissipate, despite eight rounds of totally useless, but incredibly strong, antibiotics. It was the nausea, mixed with starvation, mixed with the memory of all those nights, sitting on ice, crying on a park bench, wondering how she would survive. It wasn't Ethan. It was everything else wrapped up into Ethan.

"Avital?" Ethan knocked on the door. "Please talk to me."

"Go away!" she shouted.

"Please."

He sounded so sad, so desperate. She felt terrible for running away from him, for messing it up for them. All they had was time, and she was wasting it fully. She should have known better than to believe her body could function normally.

"I'm sorry I didn't make you feel safe."

Her lower lip quivered. "What?"

She closed her eyes, hating herself even more. It had nothing to do with Ethan. Or did it? He was good. He was kind. She knew who he was despite their whole sordid beginnings. But it wasn't just her body that changed with the onset of chronic pain... It was her. It felt impossible figuring out life with sexual dysfunction at twenty-four. It felt lonely, too. No one ever talked about such things.

"Avi," Ethan tried again.

She spit the words out. "You won't want me anymore!"

"Impossible."

"Ethan," she said as she rubbed her temples, "you're so sweet, but you really don't know what you're talking about."

"Um, Avital," he said directly, "I hate to point out the obvious to you, but despite everything we've been through... I'm still here. I'm still here, okay? And I'm gonna keep sitting outside this bathroom till you come out or you let me inside. Your choice."

He was, once again, the most annoyingly helpful human being she had ever met. Just like he was, once again, saying all the right things. Avital pushed open the door to the bathroom, meeting Ethan's eyes. "I need help."

"Okay."

She began rattling off a list. *Azo, Uribel, water, heating pad, ice in a baggie.* Ethan wasted no time. Leaving her, he ran around her office, digging through drawers, pulling out her medicine, before finally dumping scoopfuls of ice from the minifridge into a plastic bag. When he returned to her with all the items, Avital was past the point of decorum. Fully flaring. Fully burning. Desperate for relief, she grabbed that bag of ice from him, lifted her skirt, and placed it right against her vulva.

"Oh, thank God," she said, closing her eyes.

"Avital?" Ethan said, interrupting her bliss.

"Yes?"

"Your medicine," he said, holding two red pills in one hand and a bottle of alkaline water in the other. She took them. Ethan stood and plugged her heating pad in. "What temperature do you like it on?"

"Six."

He selected the setting before gently laying it across her lap. She swallowed. He took such good care of her.

"Is that good?" he asked, his hands patting her belly.

"Yeah."

"Anything else I can get for you?"

"No."

He slid down next to her, waiting patiently. And he was here, wasn't he? Sitting on a bathroom floor with her...while she pressed ice against her vagina. Gathering her bladder meds and heating pad, keeping her company in her very worst moments.

"I'm not completely naive, you know?" Ethan said, his eyes softening around the edges. "I know this has something to do with your pelvic pain."

Avital sighed. "I told you I have interstitial cystitis, and chronic pelvic pain, and a whole bunch of issues that doctors don't know what they're dealing with. Well, what I've left out of our discussions is that it's more than just having cramps. It's more than just having to pee ten thousand times a day, or going in for ultrasounds and surgery. I tell people that I have chronic pelvic pain because that's the simplest and least mortifying way to describe what I'm dealing with...because I can't have sex, Ethan."

"Can't?"

"I mean—" she backtracked on the statement "—maybe I can. Maybe I can't. I don't know, honestly. All I know is, whenever I even start thinking about sex…it hurts."

She started at the beginning. She explained waking up with pain, thinking it was an infection, countless trips to doctors, and the treatments that never worked. She described all the efforts to stop her chronic pain, all the experimental and holistic treatments—not covered by insurance—and all the missed work, too. She told him about moving home, surgery, changing her entire life around to manage her disease, but waking up to find that the pain was still there.

Then, she told him the truth about her sex life. That it was nil. Nonexistent. That even the thought of someone touching her down there terrified her. That her pain was often so bad, so easily triggered, that she couldn't wear underwear or pants. That she couldn't go in a swimming pool or use scented soap. That everything—any type of touch at all—could put her into a painful flare that would leave her unable to get out of bed for days.

Until finally, because she cared about Ethan as a person, because she wanted the best for him, she gave him an easy out.

"I would totally understand if you just want to be friends," Avital said.

"The last thing I want to be is just your friend, Avi."

"I know," she said sadly. "But chronic pelvic pain *is* my normal. It's my every day, and it's not ever going away, either. So before we go any further with things, I really need you to think about if you want to be with someone like me."

"Like you?"

"Someone who might not ever be able to have sex normally. Someone who might never be able to have sex more than four times a year. You're a nice guy, Ethan, but I don't expect you to be a saint. If you want to take some time to think about it, too... I would totally understand."

"I don't need to think about it," he said definitively.

"Ethan," she argued, "I don't think you're understanding the extent of my dysfunction here."

"Avi!" It was the first time he had ever raised his voice to her. "Stop trying to get rid of me, okay? I already told you, I'm not going anywhere. At least, not until you fire me...at which point, I will happily depart from your life. But until then, I'm going to insist you turn around so I can rub your back."

Avital blinked, confused. "What?"

"Your back," he said, waving with one finger toward the wall. "You're all types of stressed out. It's not good for you. It can't be good for your IC, either. You can tell me all the reasons we won't work out while I'm giving you a massage."

Freaking Ethan. It was nearly impossible to push away a man who wanted to give you back rubs while you were trying to tell them all the reasons they should break up with you.

Still, what kind of person turned down a free back rub?

Avital twisted around. Ethan began rubbing her shoulders. All at once, the tension in her body melted. The fact that tonight was a disaster suddenly didn't seem to matter. It felt good, being between his legs, feeling his fingers massaging in between the blades of her shoulders. It made the thought of losing him—all the odds stacked up against them—even more terrifying.

"Why are you so good to me?" she asked quietly.

"Because you're good to me," he said simply.

Her heart ached. Here he was again, saying all the right things.

"So where does that leave us?" Avital asked sadly. "A

woman who can't have sex, and a man who's lying to everyone about his identity?"

"I don't know," Ethan said, resting his head on her shoulder. "But we'll figure it out together."

THIRTY

Lying in bed that night, Ethan was a man on a mission. Googling interstitial cystitis, he read every wiki, forum, and fact page that he could find. He went on Facebook, joining various patient groups, scanning the members' questions and responses. He even found his way over to Reddit and, posting anonymously, asked for advice from other people with IC on how he could be supportive during sexual activity.

It was also that night when he realized how much she was suffering. He had not understood the full extent of her disease, how disabling it was, how much pain she lived with. He thought back to her comments about foxholes and suicide…and it suddenly made sense. Every post and comment seemed worse than the last, and it broke his damn heart. He hated that she lived with chronic pain. He hated that he couldn't help her.

It seemed a tragedy that someone as smart and as talented as her would be saddled with such challenges.

Suddenly, a familiar skunky smell wafted down the hall, wrinkling his nose. Ethan looked over to his clock to see it was way past midnight. He shook his head, annoyed. Randy was once again partaking in his favorite pastime. It was amazing his brother even existed at all. Then again, Randy was a pro at feeling numb.

Numb.

The thought caused Ethan to shoot up in his bed. Tossing his laptop to the side, he scrambled for his brother's room. Without even knocking, he threw open the door. Randy was listening to music on his bed, wearing only boxer shorts and an oversize tie-dyed T-shirt.

"Randy," Ethan said, hand on the door, "I need you to tell me everything there is to know about marijuana."

"Dude." Randy blinked in the direction of the threshold. "I must be hallucinating."

"You're not hallucinating." Ethan turned off the music, grabbing a chair and pulling it over.

"You want to know about weed?" Randy asked.

"Yes."

"Why?"

"Long story," Ethan said, avoiding the question. "But the point is I need to know how it works. Like what? I roll a joint for someone, they smoke it, and then what happens? They don't feel any more pain, right?"

Randy rolled his eyes. "You know, dude, it's people like you, with your misconceptions and wild lack of understanding, that have made it difficult to get cannabis federally legalized in this country."

"Randy," Ethan said, "I'm serious. Stop messing around and help me with this already."

"Jesus, dude." Randy finally got out of bed. "Fine. Just let me get myself situated first."

Ethan watched as his brother laid out the small green buds onto a small white paper, before rolling it and licking the edge. After which, he promptly lit it up and began smoking it. A large puff of skunk-flavored smoke clouded the air, causing Ethan to cough. "All right," Randy said, moving toward his computer, "what do you want to know?"

"Everything."

"This is gonna be a long night." Randy sighed, before opening up to a document on his computer. On the page in front of him was a photograph of a marijuana plant. "This," Randy said, speaking to Ethan like he was a child, "is what we call a cannabis plant. Now, people like you—people full of misconceptions and prejudice—tend to think of all marijuana as the same. This could not be further from the truth."

"Hold on a second," Ethan said, racing back to his room. He grabbed a notebook and a pen, returning to Randy's side at the desk.

"What are you doing?" Randy asked.

"Taking notes."

"Dude," Randy said, shaking his head, "I really must have overdone it tonight. I mean, my brother, the most straitlaced person in the entire world, asking about weed." Randy bent over and pinched Ethan in the stomach.

"Hey!" Ethan said, pushing him back. "Watch it."

"Oh, crap," Randy said, surprised. "You are real."

"Can we just get on with it already?"

Randy returned to his computer. "So anyways," he said, glancing over to the pad where Ethan was scribbling down details furiously, "this is a picture of a cannabis plant. Most people like you think it's the bud, or flowers, that produce the high-inducing cannabinoid THC...but it's not." Randy zoomed in to show thousands of little spikes of white, oozing from the leaves. "What causes the high-inducing cannabinoid THC is actually in the oil, or resin, of the plant. And this resin can be made into all sorts of products. The flower, of course, which you smoke, but also, oils, tinctures, edibles, even salves."

"Wow," Ethan said. "I really had no idea cannabis was so...extensive."

"That's a good way to think about it," Randy said, switching to an image of an indoor-grow garden, where thousands of marijuana plants were being carefully nurtured in a hydroponic system. "Now, there are two types of marijuana strains, indica or sativa. Indica normally makes you sleepy. Sativa makes you feel more awake. Within these two groupings, *cannabis cultivators*—like myself—use something called terpenes to change the taste, aroma, and appearance of the plant. Terpenes can be found in all plants and animals, and because of this, they also have medicinal and therapeutic benefits."

Ethan got excited at the prospect. "Tell me more about terpenes."

"Terpenes are what give marijuana plants different properties. For example—" Randy reached around to one of his plastic tins, pulling out a green bud, laying it on the petri dish before placing it on the desk in front of Ethan "—this guy right here has a lot of myrcene in him. Myrcene is also found in hops, mangoes, and lemongrass and is known for its sedative properties. Myrcene is great if you want a bud that puts you flat-out on your couch. And if you smell it—" Ethan lifted the bud to his nose "—you'll notice it has an earthy, clove-like smell that might even remind you of your favorite beer."

Randy went back to his plastic bin, pulling out a different bud and laying it on his petri dish. Ethan analyzed the tiny flower in front of him.

"This bud," Randy continued, "has a ton of limonene in it. Limonene is known for lifting mood and being an antidepressant. A lot of people who have anxiety, or who experience panic attacks while taking medicinal cannabis, may choose a strain with lots of limonene, because it's less likely to increase feelings of anxiety. And if you smell this one, you'll notice it has hints of lemon and lime in there."

Ethan put the two buds down next to each other on the desk. Comparing the two, he could see that the buds were different. Not only in how they smelled, but how they looked. The way the flower folded up into itself. The colors in each petal. Ethan began to see that marijuana, or cannabis, was more science than he had ever envisioned.

"This is kind of amazing, Randy," Ethan said genuinely.

"I know."

"I had no idea there was so much science to cannabis."

"It's an art as much as a science," Randy said.

Randy went back to his computer, opening to a large data graph. Then, pulling out a pad of paper from a drawer, he opened to a page where hundreds of notes were scribbled next to dates.

"This is what I've actually been working on the last few years," Randy explained, pulling out a small vial of what looked to be orange-brown crystals. "I call it the Holy Grail. It's a hybrid strain. It gives you a really clean buzz, but it's loaded with limonene so that there's no increase in anxiety. Plus, it actually decreases your appetite...so you don't have to worry about being couch-locked and wanting to eat the house. Ninety-five percent THC. One day, when I find the right grower to go into business with, Holy Grail is gonna be the bud that launches me as the next Jack Herer of marijuana."

Ethan blinked. "You want to find a distributor for the product you've created?"

"That's the dream, anyways."

Randy grew quiet. Ethan suddenly saw his little brother in a new light.

The wild jungle of hydroponics that lined his wall. The plastic bins of buds and notebooks and paraphernalia. The hours he spent devoted to his habit of marijuana. All of it was actually…research. It seemed impossible that for all these years he had seen his brother as a loafer, when in reality he was working hard on developing his own brand and business.

"Jesus, Randy," Ethan said, flabbergasted.

"What?"

"You're, like…smart."

Randy grumbled. "Well, it's not like anyone pays much attention to me, anyways."

Ethan pressed his lips together. Growing up with their grandfather, heart-to-hearts were not really something they did. If a message needed to be relayed, it usually came from a secretary. But now, and thanks to his experience with Avital and her family, Ethan was learning a new way of behaving in his relationships with others. He was learning how to make up for mistakes, too.

"Randy," he said, meeting his brother's eyes directly, "I'm sorry."

"For what?"

"For not understanding," he said genuinely. "This stuff you're working on, it's supercool…and super complicated… and honestly, I'm really proud of you."

Randy was quiet for a few moments. "You know, Ethan, you're probably the only person who has ever really listened to me."

It made Ethan sad. The Lippmann siblings had been granted every privilege in life…except the most important one. Ethan moved to give his brother a hug. The two embraced, before Randy spoke into the crook of his neck.

"This is awkward," Randy said.

"Yeah."

They separated into a more comfortable pat on the back.

"So," Randy asked, "you gonna tell me why you want to know all this stuff now?"

Ethan sighed. "It's for Avital Cohen."

"Uhhh," Randy said, his eyes going wide, "and why are we securing marijuana for Avital Cohen?"

"We're kind of dating...though, that's not really a great word for it right now, either."

Randy's shock morphed into a full cackle. "Dude!"

"It's not funny, Randy."

"You are so freaking screwed!"

"Thanks for that, bro."

Randy shook his head before looking at his brother. "No wonder you both want to get high."

"It's not like that," Ethan said, trying to explain. "She's got a condition called interstitial cystitis. It causes her chronic pain. She hasn't had much luck with traditional medicine, but I was thinking...maybe marijuana would help her."

"Aaah," Randy said, finally understanding, "so what you actually want to know about is medicinal cannabis?"

"Medicinal cannabis is different than regular marijuana?"

"Kind of," Randy explained, turning back to his computer. "The main difference, from my understanding, is that people who use medicinal cannabis don't want to get high. They want the benefits of the cannabinoid for pain relief, anxiety management, increasing appetite during cancer treatments, or whatever, without the psychoactive effects. So medicinal cannabis users will specifically use a high-CBD ratio to a low THC-ratio. As for the strains and terpenes, that will usually depend on what condition they are trying to treat. There's actually a lot of experimentation that usually has to happen."

"That sounds complicated."

"It can be," Randy admitted. "But honestly, Ethan, I'm what they call a recreational marijuana user. I'm all about the psychoactive effects, which means I'm probably not the best person to help you and Avital. Lucky for you, however... I know someone who can help."

"Who?"

"My rabbi."

"Your rabbi?" Ethan rolled his eyes. "Come on, Randy. Stop messing with me."

Beyond the fact that no Jewish clergy person would ever sell medicinal cannabis, spiritual aid was the last thing Ethan needed right now. Randy opened up another drawer, pulled out a Post-it Note, and scribbled down an address in Upstate New York.

"Get Avital," Randy said, handing the slip to him. "Go here. Ask for Rabbi Jason."

THIRTY-ONE

Avital was not the type of person who often felt anxious, but that morning, she couldn't even manage payroll. She was totally focused on one repetitive thought. Ethan had not come into work yet. In his entire time at Best Babka, he had only ever been late once.

She tried not to read into it, but all her worst fears seemed to be coming true. She had told him the truth about her sexual dysfunction, and Ethan had taken off.

She told herself it was for the best. He was a Lippmann, after all. There was never any chance of there being a relationship between them. Still, she couldn't help but be disappointed.

A knock at her door drew her from her melancholy. Josh entered. Right away, he knew that something was wrong.

"What happened?" Josh asked.

"Nothing," she lied.

Josh cocked his head sideways. "Ethan?"

Avital huffed, annoyed. It was no use keeping secrets from her brother. Or anyone at Best Babka, really. Despite her best attempts to keep their flirtation on the down-low, their relationship had quickly become an open secret.

"Come on, Avi," Josh moaned, taking a seat in front of her desk. "I really don't understand why you're being so weird about this."

"I am not being weird."

"You've always been slow to commit...but this is moving at the speed of inanimate."

Avital deadpanned, "Thanks."

"I'm just saying—" Josh shrugged "—everybody knows you two have a thing going on. If you've been trying to keep it secret, you're both terrible at it."

"Nice."

"I mean, seriously, Avi, no one cares that you're our general manager. They love you. They love Ethan. Every single person at Best Babka is rooting for you two to be together. I'm rooting for you."

Except for the fact that no one knows his true identity. Avital couldn't help but think it. Still, her heart was a mess this morning, and Josh was her twin brother, and when she needed a best friend, he was always there.

"Fine," she said, throwing her hands up. "Yes, you're right. Ethan and I have been...*having a thing* with each other over the last few weeks."

"Knew it!" Josh practically patted himself on the back.

"And we were here last night, working together...and we kissed."

"That's great!"

"We started doing some other things, too."

"That... I actually don't need to hear."

She held up one hand, willing him to stop talking.

"And then," Avital said, spitting out the words in one breathless fury, "I flared. Our hot-and-heavy make-out session ended with me having ice down my pants, locked in a bathroom, writhing in pain… And then I told Ethan that I haven't had sex in years, and that I would totally understand if he wants to call whatever this thing we have off, and now it's ten o'clock in the morning and Ethan isn't here."

"Oh." Josh pursed his lips. "Okay."

"Seriously?" Avital grew annoyed. "That's all you have to say?"

"Maybe he's running late?"

"Come on!"

"I'm serious, Avital!" Josh laughed. "Maybe it's not as disastrous as you think, okay? Maybe the dude hit traffic. Maybe he forgot to set his alarm. Maybe he had the squirts! The point being, give the poor man the benefit of the doubt. He likes you, okay? You clearly like him. Whatever the situation, I'm sure you'll both work it out."

Avital frowned. She appreciated his certainty, but he really didn't know the extent of their troubles. She had an urge to tell him the truth—to end the lie and reveal everything—when Tootles appeared at the door.

"Sorry to bother you, Avi," Tootles said, peeking his head inside, "but Mrs. Grossman is asking to speak to you. I've tried to deal with it myself, but you know how she gets on Tuesdays."

Avital sighed. "I should go deal with that."

Leaving her brother behind, Avital headed to the front counter. Mrs. Grossman was, once again, complaining about her latest purchase.

"Avital," Mrs. Grossman said upon seeing her. She picked up a half-eaten black-and-white cookie, waving it in her face. "Taste this. Does this taste right to you?"

Avital pushed the cookie away and tried not to lose her cool on dear, sweet—but also totally annoying on Tuesdays—Mrs. Grossman. The twenty-minute visit was a common occurrence. Mrs. Grossman came in every Friday morning to buy a box of cookies for Shabbat, then walked in every Tuesday to complain about them.

"You know I can't eat that," Avital reminded Mrs. Grossman.

"Well, it's not right," she said, holding it up between them. "Look at the chocolate. It melts so fast. Have you ever seen chocolate melt this fast?"

Avital felt her eyes glaze over. Normally, she was much better at handling the unique joys that came with customer service. But with Ethan still a no-show, her patience was wearing thin.

"You know what?" Avital said, grabbing the pink box from her. "Let me just refund the damn thing."

She was just about to take cash out of the register when the bell above the front door rang out. It was Ethan. Her heart lurched in her throat. He hadn't abandoned her.

"I'm sorry, Mrs. Grossman," Ethan said, stepping between them, physically interrupting. "But I need to talk to Avital."

And then, her eyes wandered down the length of his form. Her newfound smile morphed into a frown. Judging by his harried presentation—and the fact that he was still wearing his clothing from yesterday—she knew where this conversation was heading.

Ethan pulled Avital down the hall, out of earshot of others. He was talking so quickly and so erratically that Avital struggled to keep up.

"So I was thinking," Ethan said, his words trilling up and down with nervous energy, "about last night. I went home and read all about your disease, and—holy crap, Avital—it sounds way more awful than I even realized. I can't believe you live like that. I have no idea how you manage everything you do."

"Just get to the point, Ethan."

"Anyway—" Ethan took a deep breath "—I was thinking about it, and stressing about it, because deep down inside, I just really want to help you feel better...and you know how I have this brother who is kind of a druggie?"

"I guess."

"Well, I thought he was a drug addict, too," Ethan said, before adding with some level of excitement, "but it actually turns out he's supersmart, and he knows all about marijuana. And for years he's been telling me about this business he's building, and how he gets all the weed he smokes from some rabbi, which frankly I never believed because who would believe a rabbi is selling drugs? That's some next-level *Breaking Bad* stuff, you know?"

"Ethan!" Avital stopped him. "Please. I can't stand the anticipation. Just drop the bomb on me, already...and let's call it a day."

"I thought we could try marijuana."

Avital's eyes widened. "Excuse me?"

"Well, technically—" Ethan backtracked "—medicinal cannabis. It's different than recreational marijuana because of the high-CBD content to low-THC ratio, which counteracts the psychoactive effects or something. Anyway, I honestly don't know much about it... But I think it might help, and I figure if you're game, what's the harm in trying it out, right? It's legal now in New York. It might be legal everywhere in America before too long. Time to get with the times, right?"

Avital was confused. But also pleasantly surprised. Ethan hadn't given up on her at all. The rest, however, took her a minute.

Offering her drugs for her chronic pain was unusual, certainly. But what really touched her was that he'd taken time to learn more about her disease. He had cared enough about her, and her struggles, to make them his own.

"I'm sorry," Ethan said gently. "I'm going too fast for you."

"No." Avital laughed. "I think I get the gist of what you're saying."

"Have you ever tried it before?"

"I tried it twice," she admitted. "Once when I was in seventh grade. And another time in college. Honestly, I never really liked it. It always gave me panic attacks."

"I think," Ethan said carefully, "this is a little bit different. There's a real science behind cannabis now—if you know what you're doing. Strains, and terpenes, with different medicinal properties and ways to get the positive benefits without all the negatives like anxiety and munchies. Actually, Israel is on the cutting edge of medicinal cannabis science and technology."

"Wow," Avital said. "You sound like an expert on this."

"I've actually never tried it myself," he admitted, "but my brother—"

"You mean the drug addict who isn't a drug addict?"

"Exactly," Ethan said and smiled. "He's been studying cannabis for years."

Avital considered Ethan's suggestion seriously. She had never been the type of person who was into drugs. Indeed, in high school—at parties and things—she had always been a bit of a Goody Two-shoes. But life had changed. Her needs had changed, too. What would it hurt to experiment with one last thing to treat her chronic pain? It couldn't be half as bad as the limited opioids and other expensive pharmaceuticals she had been put on throughout the years.

"Okay," Avital said, throwing her hands up. "Let's go get high!"

THIRTY-TWO

The place was a dump.

Ethan and Avital pulled into a parking lot in the middle of nowhere. A ramshackle one-story building made of weathered wood, with a sloped roof, stood on the corner lot of four empty and adjacent parcels of land. Beyond the main dispensary, a large fence surrounded a garden and what appeared to be three different types of nearly windowless warehouses.

The entire place would have been completely inconspicuous, except for the fact that it was crammed full of vehicles of all types and makes. In addition, a brand-new sign attached to the roof of the building—adorned by the animated image of a man in a *kippah* smoking a large joint—read *Holy Rollers* in neon green-and-yellow lettering.

"So this is it," Avital said nervously.

"This is it," Ethan confirmed. He recognized the smell emanating from the building after years living beside his brother.

Exiting the vehicle together, they made their way to the

rickety front porch. By the front door, a tiny blue-and-white ceramic placard welcomed them with the words *Bruchim Ha-baim*: bless all who enter. Ethan recognized it as the traditional prayer of greeting in Jewish homes.

A ginormous man wearing a black security jacket appeared. Even though they weren't doing anything illegal, it felt… sketchy. Ethan couldn't help but worry if they were about to be arrested. Instead, the guard shifted his weight around his belt and without offering a smile said, "Identification, please."

Avital and Ethan dug out their cards. He took a moment to scan them into some system, proving that they were over the age of twenty-one and thus legally allowed to buy cannabis under New York State law.

"Okay, Ethan and Avital," the guard said, handing their ID back to them, "do you need to speak with a budtender today?"

"A what?" Ethan asked.

"We've never smoked weed," Avital suddenly interjected.

The security guard rolled his eyes. Clearly, in the wake of legalization across America, he was used to noobs of all types showing up anxious and feeling out of place at his front door.

"Head inside," he said, clearly bored, as if he had explained this ten thousand times already today. "Once you pass through the metal detector, you'll see the main store. Pick a line. A budtender will help you. Cash only. There's an ATM at the end of the hall. Exit out the back."

"Great," Ethan said.

"Thank you so much," Avital said.

Avital and Ethan did as instructed. Making their way through an ominous-looking hallway, they passed a metal detector and one more round of security before finally coming to the store proper.

"Holy moly," Avital said.

The place was packed.

Customers from all walks of life—men in business suits, college-age kids in hoodies and sweatshirts, and a little old woman in walking pants and a visor—spanned the room. Beyond the glass display cases filled with small jars full of marijuana, seven employees wore green shirts embroidered with the word *Budtender* in the right-hand corner.

"What do we do?" Avital asked. "Should we get in line or something?"

"My brother said there's a rabbi we should ask for."

"A rabbi?" Avital was incredulous. "Are you sure?"

"That's what he said…"

"You also said your brother did a lot of drugs."

Ethan frowned. Avital wasn't wrong.

"Menu?" someone said, handing them a large laminated sheet.

"Oh," Ethan perked up at the words. "Thanks."

Avital put one hand on his arm and glanced over his shoulder.

"What should we get?" Avital asked.

"I have no idea," Ethan said.

The entire menu was like reading a foreign language to him. *Grapefruit Kush. Purple Haze. Jack Herer.* Beside the odd-sounding names were even stranger words and numbers. *Hybrid. High CBD. Battery and Cart. 95% THC. 1 Ounce.* Finally, Ethan landed on a word he recognized.

"There's something called the Painkiller," Ethan said.

"Maybe we should just get a gram of that?"

Ethan nodded, thoughtfully. It seemed like a good idea.

"Excuse me," a voice spoke out behind them.

Avital and Ethan spun around. A man in an oversize *kippah* was sporting a wide smile beneath a short brown beard. Four swinging *tzitzith*, worn-out and frayed, peeked out from beneath a long-sleeved graphic T-shirt.

"You both look—" the man searched for the words "—well, more nervous than a firstborn on the tenth plague of Egypt."

"We're kind of new to this," Avital admitted.

"My brother sent us," Ethan explained. "Randy Lippmann?"

"Randy," the man said and beamed. "Of course. I know him well."

"He told us to come here and ask for a Rabbi Jason. Said he might be able to help us out."

"Well, then," the man said, clapping Ethan on the back supportively, "you've come to the right place. I'm Rabbi Jason. Not only am I a spiritual adviser to all who walk through my hash haven, I'm the proud owner of Holy Rollers dispensary and grow farm. Why don't you both follow me into my hash office...and we can figure out what's going on."

Avital wasn't sure what to make of the friendly weed-smoking rabbi who ran a grow farm and dispensary. But there was something about having the blessing of a rabbi on her hunt for pain relief that felt like kismet.

Taking a seat beside Ethan in the rabbi's office, Avital's eyes darted around the room. A mixture of hamsas and Hebrew blessings on tile placards lined the walls. Behind his desk, beyond a stack of pictures and photos of his family, were bookshelves filled to the brim with Holy Rollers product and all manner of Jewish textual books. She recognized a Talmud, opened somewhere in the middle, resting on a *shtender*.

After a brief round of introductions and a quick game of Jewish geography, Rabbi Jason took his seat at the desk. "So," he said, giving Avital his attention, "how can I help you today?"

Avital glanced over to Ethan. She couldn't help being nervous. It was hard talking about such intimate things with any-one, let alone a stranger. Plus, her entire experience with the medical industry had been that people, at best, couldn't help her, and at worst, didn't believe her. She was constantly on guard talking about her body. Like being female meant she was immediately invalidated in some form.

Ethan took her hand. "You can do this," he said gently. "I'm right here."

It made Avital feel better.

"I have a disease," Avital said, finding her courage. "It's called interstitial cystitis."

"I'm familiar with it," he said, before adding, "I'm sorry."

It was such a simple thing to say. But his words—that *I'm sorry*—caused the floodgates to open.

"I'm just a mess," Avital explained. "One day, it's cramps. The next day, it's fatigue and cramps. The next day, I'm up every twenty minutes going to the bathroom, feeling like somebody is running a cheese grater up and down my blad-der. I can't work. I can't sleep most nights. I'm constantly in pain. And when I go to my doctor and try to get pain medi-cation, they tell me they can't prescribe it. They tell me they want to help me, but they'll lose their license, or to come back in three months."

"And then, you have to worry about being labeled a doctor-hopper?"

"It's like the whole system is designed, in a way, to tell me that I don't matter. That my pain doesn't matter. That I should just live with it and suffer...or go off and die if it gets so bad that I can't manage. *But I don't want to die.* And I'm not a drug addict, either! I just want some...quality of life."

The words caused a torrent of emotion to release from in-side her. Despite the fact she barely knew this man and had only just begun explaining all the reasons she was here, she crumpled into tears in front of him.

"I'm sorry," she said, over and over.

"It's okay," Rabbi Jason said gently. "Let it out."

"I shouldn't be crying in your hash office!"

"I don't know how you wouldn't be crying," Rabbi Jason said emphatically, "considering all you've been through."

His kindness and understanding only made her cry more. Grabbing tissues from his desk, she dotted at tears. Ethan kept a steady hand on her back. It felt good to have him there. To share her sorrows with another person.

"Crying doesn't mean you're weak," Rabbi Jason said genuinely. "Crying in front of another person means you're strong. It means you're okay with being vulnerable. Most people pretend they're made of steel, that nothing ever hurts them, that everything is Instagram-worthy toxic positivity. You know what I always say to those people?"

Avital shook her head. "No."

"Our sages tell us, 'The only gate to Heaven still open is the gate of tears.' Not the gate of mercy, not the gate of prayer... or whatever gate there is that God keeps at the entrance to Heaven...but the gate of tears. So I always ask myself, *what it is about tears that God feels is worthy of being heard?*"

He let the question linger in the air between them before answering.

"God doesn't want us to suffer," Rabbi Jason said. "That's why he leaves that gate open. That's why he gives us knowledge, on the very first page of the Torah, in fact, so we have the tools to alleviate that sorrow. God is not looking at you, judging you on high, punishing you with pain and suffering. God is in bed, crying with you. You're not alone in this, okay?"

Avital nodded. "Okay."

"So what else, Avital?" Rabbi Jason asked quietly. "What else do you need help with today?"

Avital glanced over to Ethan, hoping he could take over. It was so awkward, sitting in a room with two men, talking about your broken hoo hah…and your desperate freaking need, your overwhelming desire after two straight years of celibacy, to have sex.

"Well," Ethan said, blushing, "we'd like to…"

"Engage in sexual activity," Avital said.

"We tried, once."

"And then I wound up with ice down my pants, crying in the bathroom."

Ethan squeezed her hand tight. "I was totally okay with that, by the way."

Rabbi Jason folded his hands into a pyramid beneath his chin. "You two are cute together."

Avital blushed, glancing in Ethan's direction. They were cute together. She so desperately wanted this medicinal cannabis thing to work out in her favor. Upside, it was already going better than at least 90 percent of her doctor's appointments. And there were no annoying paintings of women standing in fields of flowers on his wall.

"So now," Rabbi Jason said, clapping his hands together, "we understand the *kashya*, the question, and we can work to find a solution. Let me ask you both something. Is it sex you're looking to have with each other…or intimacy?"

"Is there a difference?" Ethan asked.

"A very important one, in fact!" Rabbi Jason beamed wide. "Now, I can give you guys plenty of products that will help make the physical act of sex easier for Avital. But as a rabbi, and having dealt with this myself in my own marriage—"

"Wait," Avital sat up in her seat, "your wife has pelvic pain?"

"We have four beautiful children," Rabbi Jason said, turning around a photo frame to display them, "but unfortunately, after the birth of the third one, my wife had trauma. It happens to a lot of women, in fact…and more people should talk about it."

"I wish they would," Avital said quietly. "I would feel so much less alone to know there were other women, other couples, going through this exact same thing."

"Exactly," Rabbi Jason said. "Nothing changes without education, without understanding. And what you are dealing with, Avital, affects millions of women around the world. It affects men, too. For some it's pelvic-floor dysfunction. For some it's medical trauma. Sometimes it's menopause or auto-immune disease or fibroids. Sometimes, nobody can find a cause. But Avital, you are not first woman to sit in my office, seeking help for chronic pelvic pain, trying to find a way to be intimate with their partner again…and unfortunately, you won't be the last, either."

"So what do we need to do?" Ethan said. "How do I approach sex—"

"Intimacy," Rabbi Jason corrected him.

"How do we approach intimacy with each other differently?"

"I thought you would never ask," Rabbi Jason said and beamed again, opening a drawer, and pulling out a bong. "I'm gonna tell you something here that is going to blow your minds." Moments later, he was aiming a lighter into the metal opening and lighting it up. "I'm sorry," Rabbi Jason said, pointing it toward them. "Where are my manners? Do you want some?"

"I'm driving," Ethan said.

"Ah, right." The rabbi shrugged and continued. "So where was I, again?"

"You were gonna tell us something that was gonna blow our minds."

"Right!" Jason sat up. "The secret to intimacy…the secret to mind-blowing sex with a partner you love, where your souls merge into one and you feel as if you've been lifted into the Heavens themselves, the secret to intimacy, Ethan and Avital…is boundaries."

"Boundaries?" they said at the same time.

"You're shocked." The rabbi laughed. "I know. But did you know that, according to statistics, married Orthodox Jews have some of the most sexually satisfying relationships around? And do you know what Orthodox Jews do that is different from the rest of the world?"

"*Niddah?*" Avital offered up.

"Excellent, Avital," Rabbi Jason said, before turning to Ethan. "You got a smart one here, eh?"

Ethan squeezed her hand again. "I know."

"For two weeks," Rabbi Jason continued, "out of every month, while the woman is menstruating and afterward, they as a couple…they don't touch. They don't have sex. They don't speak erotic words to each other or hold hands or even lie beside each other in the same bed. The woman takes that time, during her cycle, maybe when she's not feeling so great because of cramps or fatigue or mood swings, to rest and re-cuperate."

"That sounds like a nice break," Avital admitted. "Though, I still don't quite understand how that leads to intimacy."

"Well, think about it," Rabbi Jason challenged them. "You're a couple. You've been married one, ten, fifty years… doesn't matter. And for two weeks every month, you're not allowed to have sex. What do you think those couples do the very second those two weeks are over?"

Avital laughed a little. "Probably jump right into bed."

"They're probably dying for it."

"Exactly," Rabbi Jason said. "After those two weeks, the woman goes to the *mikvah*, the ritual bath, and she immerses herself like a day at the spa…and then, she goes home to her husband, and they are intimate together. For a Jewish couple, it's the boundary that leads to intimacy. It's the boundary that builds the eroticism.

"Now," Rabbi Jason continued, "I'm not telling you that you need to observe the rules around *niddah* or wait until marriage. That's up to you and Avital. But what I am trying to demonstrate is there's a lot of wisdom in Judaism about sex and intimacy. And all of these lessons can help you and Avital. For example, do you know what is guaranteed in every *ketubah*, or marriage license, of every Jewish woman?"

"No idea."

"*Onah*," the rabbi said. "Responsiveness. A woman can request sex from her husband at any time, and he has to engage in it with her. And do you know who can never compel a woman to have sex?"

"The man?"

"Exactly. Judaism allows the woman to create the boundary. The man, however, must wait to be welcomed within that boundary."

Avital glanced over to Ethan. It was interesting, this idea of boundaries building pleasure. This idea that Avital had a right to decide when she felt safe or not, allowing her partner to enter her bed. She had always seen sex as something that was a given in relationships…but perhaps, all the focus on sex was actually impeding true intimacy.

"So," Ethan said, leaning forward, "how do I take these boundaries, and this *onah*, and create an intimate experience for me and Avital?"

"Great question," Rabbi Jason said, standing up, pulling

books from one of his shelves and laying them down on the desk. "So the first thing you need to do is allow Avital to establish her boundaries. Avital—" he met her eyes directly "—I imagine you have days where your pain is worse…and where your pain is better?"

"Yes."

"Do you think you could be comfortable on a day with less pain attempting sexual activity?"

Avital thought about it honestly. "I think so. I mean… I do have some good days. I just haven't tried yet, so I don't really know."

"But you're willing to try?"

Avital did not hesitate. "Absolutely."

"Good," he said, pointing between the two of them, "because it's important that you communicate where you are in your pain. What level? If sex is possible…or not? You need to use your voice, Avital. It's up to you, as much as to Ethan, to communicate pain *and* desire."

"And what about Ethan?" Avital said, looking at him. "What is he supposed to do while…I'm erecting boundaries?"

"Another great question," Rabbi Jason said and pivoted in his seat toward Ethan. "What I want from you, Ethan, going forward…in those spaces when you can't be together…is to build up that eroticism with Avital. There can be a lot of pleasure in the boundaries. So, you're going to talk sweetly to her. You're going to send her loving messages on your phone. You're going to compliment her, whisper secrets to her, and feed her delicious food. I want you to find enjoyment in the longing, eh? And then, when Avital is ready…"

"*Onah*," Ethan said. "Respond."

"Now you're getting it!" Rabbi Jason took another hit of his bong. "Avital is like…like a delicate cannabis flower. Difficult to grow. Totally sensitive to every element. Did you know if we get one single fly in our grow garden, it can kill our entire crop? The resin the cannabis plant creates is actually an insecticide."

"Really?" Ethan mused.

"Think about that," Rabbi Jason said, taking another hit. "Something so delicate and difficult to grow...yet if all the right ingredients are there...you find divinity."

Avital watched the bong bubble up, before dissipating into a large cloud of smoke around them. When the haze faded, she could see there was still something on Ethan's mind. Avital nudged him to ask the question.

"So once Avital is ready," Ethan said, glancing between them, "how do I respond in a way that doesn't hurt her?"

"Excellent question, Ethan. You two are on fire today." Rabbi Jason put the bong down. "Did you know that the *Shekinah*, what we Jews consider the divine omnipresent being of God, is feminine? Which means every time you lay down at the mantle of your love, you are, literally, engaging in an act with the divine presence. You are making love not only to Avital, but in partnership with God."

Ethan shifted in his seat. "I don't think that sentiment... actually makes me less nervous."

"Well, I can give you something for the nerves, too." Rabbi Jason laughed. "But Ethan, you see...this is also why Judaism has so many rules for men regarding sex. The burden for her pleasure, her delight, *is on you*. And you wouldn't rush God, would you? You wouldn't just wham, bam, thank you, ma'am the divine presence?"

"I guess not."

"Of course not," Jason said emphatically. "It's God we're talking about here. And before you enter the *holy of holies*, what do you do? You clean yourself up. You speak sweetly to your love. You adorn her with oils and perfumes and gifts

and jewelry. You build and build and build the excitement...
until God is begging you to come into her tent...until God
is so swept up in your love and adoration that she can think
of nothing else! You understand what I'm saying, Ethan?"

"I think so."

"Look," Rabbi Jason said, pushing aside his bong, "Judaism
is very smart about sex and about couples. It understands that
the more we have something, the less we want it. Your issue
right now is chronic pelvic pain. But one day, God willing,
you might be married. You might have children and busy
lives, and you've been sleeping with each other for twenty
years, and you love each other, of course, but all that excitement you had when you first met, all that explosive chemis-
try when it was new and amazing, has faded.

"These tools for intimacy," Rabbi Jason continued, "they're
not just for Orthodox Jews. They're not just for women with
chronic pelvic pain. They're not just for couples who have
been together for fifty years. They're for everyone who wants
to have a better and more fulfilling sexual life with their
partner."

Avital was beginning to feel better. And she liked it—
knowing that she had the tools to create this erotic space
with Ethan. Knowing that her *boundaries* weren't a negative
but a positive, something that could sustain them and their
relationship, even when sexual activity had to be off the table
for a while.

"You should really write a book about this stuff," Ethan
said.

"I actually throw a Jewish tantric lovemaking retreat every
spring. One week, full nudity, tons of weed. You and Avital
should come."

Ethan forced a smiled. "We'll definitely think about it."

"Good." Rabbi Jason smiled. "Because the key for you two,

beyond eradicating or reducing Avital's pain to a more tolerable level—which we will try to do through various forms of medicinal cannabis—is to learn to find delight in the eroticism. Bask in it. *Bathe in it.*"

"Do I need a prescription or card for medicinal cannabis?" Avital asked.

"It's really up to you," Rabbi Jason explained. "The truth is, where marijuana is legalized for recreational use, there's no real difference in the products we sell. You can walk in and buy medicinal cannabis and recreational marijuana from us today. In New York, you'll pay less taxes on medicinal cannabis. Also, some people like to have their medicinal-cannabis card if they're traveling to another state and planning to buy marijuana there. Many states have reciprocity laws, which means you can use your New York card in a place like Washington, DC."

"That will be good for when we travel," Ethan said.

Avital smiled. She liked the idea of traveling with Ethan.

"Does it take a long time to get your card?" Avital asked.

"It's very easy," the rabbi said. "All you need to do is have a doctor certify that you need medicinal cannabis. I can provide you with a list of doctors who do this, and after they review your medical records and what medications you're on, they'll make a determination on whether or not you can get your card."

"Will it take me three weeks to get an appointment?"

"No." Rabbi Jason smiled. "In fact, you could probably get an appointment this afternoon if you want and take it from your car. You have your medical records online somewhere, or even some prescription bottles with your name on them?"

"I travel with a small pharmacy," Avital said.

"Then, you should be good to go," he said, pulling out a sheet of paper, handing it to her. Looking down, she saw it was a list of doctors who could certify her for medicinal-cannabis usage. "Once a certified doctor has given you the go-ahead, you'll register using that certificate for a medicinal-cannabis license from New York State. Your card should arrive in seven to ten days. You can use their temporary license in the meantime, however."

Avital was shocked. "That sounds pretty easy."

"We *want* it to be easy for patients."

"And what about talking to my doctors?" Avital asked. "I'm on a lot of different medications. How do I know they won't interact?"

"It's important you're honest with your doctors about medicinal-cannabis usage," Rabbi Jason explained. "However, be aware that your current physician probably has very little knowledge or experience with medicinal cannabis."

"How can that even be possible?"

"Unfortunately," Rabbi Jason nodded solemnly, "because it isn't legal on the federal level, there haven't been studies. They also don't teach about medicinal-cannabis usage in medical school. The good news is you'll be able to talk to the doctor who certifies you…and they should be able to guide you on where to start, what to watch out for, and even provide resources if you need to speak with a medical practitioner while using cannabis."

"That would be great," Avital said.

Rabbi Jason smiled. "Do you think your doctor will give you any trouble?"

"I think she'll be thrilled I'm not in her office asking for opioids." Avital laughed at the thought. But then, there was this other, more powerful notion bubbling around inside of her. "Honestly," she said, glancing between both men, "I think it just will feel good to have some control over my own pain management. I'm so tired of having to constantly ask for help, beg for help...only to be left without resources. It's my body, and it should be my choice what I do with it."

"That's a huge part of it." Rabbi Jason nodded sympathetically. "For me, and others in this field, it's not about making money. Legalizing marijuana is a human-rights issue. People should not be in pain. Suffering is not a *mitzvah*."

"Suffering is not a *mitzvah*..." Avital mused on the words. "I like that."

"We sell it on T-shirts!"

Rabbi Jason reached beneath his desk, pulling one out. On the front, a smiley face in *peyos* and a *kippah* was toking a joint.

"Eh?" Rabbi Jason said. "Nice, right?"

Avital was speechless.

Rabbi Jason put the T-shirt back beneath his desk. "Now, before I send you two on your way to begin your journey into the wide and wonderful world of medicinal cannabis, there is one other thing I want to tell you. The mistake most people make about sex, in general, is to focus on the orgasm. From this point forward, Ethan and Avital—*orgasm is not the goal*. In fact, I want you to put the idea of orgasm completely out of your heads. Don't think about it. Don't worry about it. It does not matter!"

Rabbi Jason waved them toward him. Avital and Ethan leaned in closer. "Say it with me," he said, prodding them to repeat the phrase. "Orgasm is not the goal."

"Orgasm is not the goal," they repeated.

"Again!"

"Orgasm is not the goal!"

"Excellent work." Rabbi Jason beamed. "I want you to keep repeating that phrase, like a mantra in your heads. Say it until you believe it. Because for you two, the goal is intimacy. The goal is eroticism. The goal is treating Avital like the divine being she is. Touch each other, talk to each other, linger in her divine femininity. Savor the enjoyment that comes with the building of tension during the periods where she needs boundaries. *Boundaries are not bad.* I would venture to guess, that if you do these things…all the rest will come pretty naturally."

THIRTY-THREE

For the next two weeks, Ethan spent almost all his free time with Avital. In the kitchen, they blew through that laminated recipe booklet on the wall. After he perfected challah, it was lekach, or honey cake, traditionally eaten on the holiday of Rosh Hashanah. Next were macaroons, another staple, made for Passover. From there, it was black-and-white cookies, mandel bread, rugelach, hamantashen, and bourekas.

Every night with Avital ended the exact same way. Upstairs. On the second floor. Lying on the bed together, kissing. Sometimes they would watch a Netflix movie on his phone. Sometimes, her hand would wander down to his pants, and Ethan would find the release he bit back, night after night.

But mainly, he waited for her. He never once pushed Avital. He let her take the lead on all things, building the boundaries, bringing them down, communicating when she was ready or when it was too much.

Perhaps the most surprising bit about it to Ethan was that

it still felt intimate. Not having sex forced them to continue deepening their relationship through communication. He had never felt so close to anyone.

In the meantime, Avital sought out a doctor and got her New York State card for medical marijuana. She also did her due diligence, informing her physicians about her choice, who then confirmed with her—as Rabbi Jason had warned—that they knew absolutely nothing about marijuana usage and that they wished her (and Ethan) all the best in their journey to pain-free love.

Until finally, with the month of Adar II—and Purim—fully approaching, they returned to Holy Rollers. With the help of Rabbi Jason and a very friendly female budtender, who lived with endometriosis, they stocked up on oils, vapes, pre-rolled joints, 1:1 suppositories, and personal lubricant.

When the time came to pay, Ethan pulled out his wallet.

"I can't let you pay for all this," Avital said, moving to stop him.

"Avi," Ethan laughed a little, "I've spent more on a pair of socks."

"Right," she said, touching her forehead, "I keep forgetting you're part Lippmann."

Ethan lost his train of thought. The reminder of what had brought him to Best Babka, and to Avital, caused his heart to ache. He hated the way the name followed him, the knowledge that eventually everything they were building together would fall apart. He was so wrapped up in Avital that searching for the babka recipe felt like another life.

"You know what?" Ethan said, pulling her closer. He nodded at the *Suffering Is Not a Mitzvah* T-shirts hanging up across from the counter. "We'll take two of those shirts, too."

"Excellent choice," Rabbi Jason said, beaming.

Outside Holy Rollers, the sun was still shining. It seemed

to be a welcome departure from the donkey-belly skies that had plagued them all winter, too. Ethan took her hand, and they walked back to her car together, the conversation drifting from the bag of weed she was holding to Purim.

"Have you decided what you're going to make for your specialty item?" Avital asked.

"I have an idea," Ethan said, smiling at her.

"You gonna give me any hints?"

"Nope." He grinned. "Though, I was rather hoping you would help me with the taste-testing part."

She tsked at him. "Don't tease me. You know I can't eat anything."

They came to her vehicle. Avital turned flirtatiously, and leaned back against the door. The temptation of a kiss appeared once again.

"So now what?" she said. "We just pull into a back lot somewhere, get high, and go to town?"

Ethan considered her question seriously.

Of course he wanted Avital. He wanted nothing more than to reach down, pull up her skirt, and discover with his tongue if she was wearing underwear. But sex was not the goal here. Orgasm was not the goal, either. The goal was intimacy. The goal was eroticism. The goal was worshipping the divine in Avital.

"I have a better idea," Ethan said, wrapping his hands around her waist. "How would you like to go away with me for Shabbat?"

ADAR II

(March–April)

THIRTY-FOUR

Avital threw her head back. The wind whipped her hair as she sat in the passenger seat of the red convertible Ethan was driving on the first warm day of spring after what had been a brutal winter. Her eyes closed. Her cheeks hurt from smiling. She felt the freedom of the open road as they drove along back roads in Upstate New York.

"You sure you don't want to sleep?" Ethan asked, glancing over the console at her.

Avital opened one eye in his direction. "You promising me a long night?"

"That's completely up to you."

Avital smiled seductively, but otherwise, offered no hints. Sometimes when she looked at him, she completely forgot he was a Lippmann. Then again—she ran her hands across the smooth leather interior—there were always reminders.

"I can't believe you own this car and you take a bus to work every single day," Avital said, guffawing.

"Technically," Ethan reminded her, "I don't own anything. This is my grandfather's car. I just happen to be allowed to drive it. Besides, I like taking the bus."

"Nobody likes taking the bus, Ethan."

"You know the best part of taking the bus, Avi?" Ethan smiled, adorably, in her direction. "I don't owe anybody anything."

She nodded before reaching over to lay one hand on his thigh sympathetically.

"Where are you taking me, again?"

"I told you," he said, lowering the radio volume, "it's a surprise."

They rounded a corner, coming upon a large lake. The trees that surrounded the water were just beginning to bloom. Tiny white and pink buds dotted the otherwise golden-brown terrain. The earth was coming back to life.

"It's so beautiful." Avital smiled.

"Would you like to stop?" Ethan asked her.

"Do we have time?"

"All the time in the world."

Ethan pulled off on the side of the road. Turning off the music and engine, he jumped out of the car, moving to open the door for her. Taking her hand, he helped her exit the vehicle, then they walked together hand in hand down to the water. They were so far away from any noise now. All the bustle of a life in a busy bakery in Brooklyn had faded away into rural tranquility.

"Actually," Ethan said, holding one finger up to her, "just wait here."

"What?"

"I was going to wait for this part until later," he said, calling back to her from the trunk of the car, "but I figured this is as good a time as any."

Avital laughed and shrugged her shoulders. When he returned, he was carrying a picnic blanket, a juice pitcher, and a basket. She could barely see his head peeking out from behind all the stuff.

"What is—" she gasped, amazed "—what is all this stuff?"

"It's for you," he said, laying down the picnic blanket.

Avital took a seat. Ethan continued unloading his items. Set on china dishes in front of her, there was hamantashen, black-and-white cookies, and two different types of rugelach. He reached for two plastic champagne flutes, before filling them both up with something yellow from the pitcher and handing one to her.

"To us," he said, lifting his glass to her, taking a drink.

"To us," she repeated, but did not drink.

She put her glass of yellow juice down. Ethan sat, beaming at her. "Well, go on…" he said, picking up a plate and handing it to her. "Eat up."

"Ethan," Avital said, confused, "you know I can't eat any of this."

"You can eat all of this," he said nonchalantly, before beginning to point out each item. "Organic pear juice," he said, nodding to her champagne flute. "Fresh squeezed first thing this morning."

Avital lifted it up to her nose. "Really?"

"And—" he moved on to the cookies "—everything you see before you is IC-safe."

Avital felt her mouth go dry. "What?"

"I know you often can't eat the things we make at Best Babka. So I went and found the IC list, and then I asked Josh about it just to be sure—"

"You spoke to Josh?"

"Of course." Ethan smiled, displaying the items. "Everything is gluten-free. I used a combination of tigernut flour—

delicious stuff, by the way—almond flour and coconut. All of it organic. All of it kosher. And I know you guys usually use lemon to give the blueberry compote a kick, but I spent some time this weekend experimenting with mint, basil, and honey...also goat cheese...to see if I could take it up a notch. Anyways, hopefully you like what I came up with."

"Ethan..." She was speechless. In her entire life, no one had ever done anything so kind for her. "I don't know what to say."

"Don't say anything," he said, grabbing a plate. "Eat."

Avital wasted no time. She grabbed one of the hamantashen, taking a bite. Rich blueberry jam, coupled with the taste of the honey and sweetness from the tigernut flour, sent ripples of pleasure over her tongue.

"Oh my gosh," Avital said, her mouth full as she reached for another. "I want more."

He loaded up a plate for her. Avital devoured three more cookies before officially tapping out.

"I want to keep going," Avital said, lying flat on the blanket, fully satiated, "but my stomach is weak and puny."

Ethan laughed.

"You know," Ethan said, wrapping up the rest of the cookies, "it's interesting. You do all this creative stuff at Best Babka, mix traditionalism with modern, but even being a GM with chronic illness, you've never thought about branching into specialty or medical diets?"

"We've tried in the past," Avital admitted, thinking back to when she had first been diagnosed, "and we do some limited specialty items like gluten-free challah or vegan black-and-white cookies. But the truth is Best Babka isn't really set up for that level of specialization. Even within medical diets, patients can have vast differences in terms of what they can tolerate. Like, I can tolerate blueberries on the IC diet, but not everyone can."

"So what are some of the diets?" Ethan asked curiously. "Outside of things like gluten-free, vegan, or peanut-free?"

"Oh gosh." Avital put her now-empty plate down. "So many. Off the top of my head... There's the autoimmune protocol. A lot of people with autoimmune disease go on that one. There's also Wahls. That's for folks with MS, or people who believe they need mitochondrial support. Then there's just people who have allergies and triggers—corn, coconut, sesame seed, whatever. It can get very complicated."

"Hm," he said, folding his thumb beneath his chin in thought.

"You seem very interested in this," Avital noted.

"I need to be." He met her gaze with a steely determination. "Safe foods are going to be my specialty item at the Purim carnival."

"Really?"

"Yep," he confirmed. "I'm going to make a whole bunch of desserts for people who can't normally eat them. It will be interesting to see if there's a market for it, right?"

Avital laughed. He was amazing. What he had done for her was amazing. Ethan lay back on the blanket beside her, their hips touching, their arms pressed up against each other. He smelled delicious. A pressure began building in her lower pelvis. She knew what she was feeling.

"I have to pee," she said all of a sudden.

"Oh." Ethan sat up looking around. "Well, I'm not sure where there is a bathroom."

Avital groaned. "Oh God!" She began freaking out. "I knew this was going to happen! As soon as I took that second glass of pear juice. Doomed!"

"Avi," he said, "what's the big deal?"

"There's nowhere to pee, Ethan!"

He pointed to a tree.

She crossed her arms against her chest. "I'll just hold it."

"Please go pee, Avi."

"No!"

Ethan sighed. Standing up, he walked over to aforementioned tree.

"What are you doing?" she screamed at him.

"Peeing!" he shouted back.

"Why?"

"Because I had to go, too!"

Finishing up, and with just as much ease, he zipped up his fly and made his way back to Avital. Her mouth was half-open, as Ethan pointed to the tiny plastic bottle of hand sanitizer hanging off her pocketbook. "Do you mind if I…"

"Oh," she said, giving him a spritz. "No problem."

When he was all cleaned up, he waited for her to go next. Still, she was hesitating. "Avi," he said, smiling and trying to assuage her fears, "it's no big deal. You're telling me, in all your summers in Israel, you never peed outdoors before?"

"It's not that," she explained nervously.

"Well, what then?"

"I'm wearing a skirt," she explained. "I'm worried that crouching, balancing, and holding it up is just gonna land me in a big pile of—"

"Ah," Ethan said, before offering her a hand. "Well, let me help you, then."

"Oh, come on!"

He laughed. "It's fine, okay? I've already seen your tuchus, and I was with you when you needed ice…"

"I don't need a rundown!"

"I'm just saying," he said and bit back a smile, "consider-

294

ing all we've shared these last few months, I'm not entirely certain why this is the hill you refuse to pee on."

He had a point. Making their way to a tree, Ethan allowed her to balance on him. Squatting down, one hand on his knee, one hand on her skirt, she looked up.

"Well, this is romantic."

Ethan laughed. "I don't know," he said thoughtfully. "I rather like that we've passed a new level of intimacy in our relationship."

"Oh, yeah. I can't wait to write about this on our wedding website."

Ethan raised both eyebrows. "You want to marry me, Avi?"

"That was a joke," she said nervously. "I didn't mean..."

"I like that you said it," he said, before adding, "Honestly, Avi... I really like you."

"I really like you, too."

She felt a weird, inexplicable bond with Ethan. Then again, she was also squatting on the ground, unable to have sex, and their families hated each other...so where was their growing attachment to each other really going to get them?

"Are you done?" Ethan asked.

"Honestly," she said, "I'm too nervous now to pee."

Ethan laughed. "I'll try to be quiet."

"Could you...maybe look away?"

"I can't see anything, Avi."

"Yeah, but," she said, "now I'm worried about peeing on your shoes."

"I wouldn't want anyone to pee on my shoes but you."

"Jesus," she said, shaking her head. "What a pair we make."

"You know," Ethan offered up, "some guys are into this."

"What?"

He clarified. "People peeing on them."

Avital frowned. "Seriously, Ethan?"

"I'm just saying, considering how often you have to go—" he pursed his lips thoughtfully "—you could probably have a very lucrative career if the whole Best Babka thing doesn't work out."

Avital cocked her head sideways. "Are you being serious right now?"

"It's the Lippmann in me. I'm always thinking about other avenues for making money."

"You're looking at me, Ethan."

"Right," he said, angling his head upward, "eyes...on... tree."

Finally, Avital finished. Standing back up, cleaning her hands with some sanitizer, she sighed, relieved.

"Thank you," she said.

"Anytime." Ethan smiled.

"Also," Avital said, flipping her hair back. "Don't ever mention *any* of this again."

Ethan laughed, following her back to his picnic blanket at the edge of the lake. He slid back down next to her. In the quiet that came after, in the sight of the sun edging down to the horizon of the water, her mind raced. She was beginning to have feelings for Ethan, real feelings. And though they weren't having sex, they were getting to know each other in ways that felt more real to her, more intimate.

"Are you cold?" Ethan asked.

"No."

"Are you in pain?"

"Not really," she said, before adding, "Actually, my pain has been a lot better recently."

"Hey—" Ethan crooked his neck in her direction, a genuine smile spreading across his face "—that's great news."

"Yeah."

"Any reason why it might be better now?"

Avital considered the question seriously. "There's no definitive way to know," she explained, taking Rabbi Jason's advice by communicating her experience fully. "It could be where I am in my cycle. My pain often gets worse around ovulation and my period."

She stopped for a moment, glancing over to Ethan. The man did not bat an eyelash at the discussion of her womanly issues. Feeling relieved to be sitting beside a grown-up, she carried on.

"It could also be that Dr. Prikh was right. That I was in a flare and eventually things would get better."

"Things always find a way to get better, right?" Ethan said optimistically.

Avital nodded. He was always so sweet and chipper. Like honey dripping from challah on Rosh Hashanah, his goodness stuck to everything.

"But I think…" she said thoughtfully, "I'm just a lot less stressed out with you around."

"Really?"

"Stress has always been a huge trigger for me," she explained. "I try to meditate, stay calm, do pelvic-floor yoga… but I don't think I realized how stressed out I was working at Best Babka until you came into my life."

Ethan nodded. "It's definitely not an easy job."

"Running a small business never is." She sighed.

"So why don't you stop?" Ethan asked her.

"I can't stop."

Ethan pressed his lips together, concerned. "It doesn't sound like working at Best Babka is very good for your health."

He wasn't wrong.

Best Babka had never been her dream. It had been her safety net. But now, it wasn't even functioning as that.

"I'm sorry," Ethan said, backtracking. "I shouldn't have said anything. It's not my place."

"No," Avital interrupted him. "It's not that. I'm glad you said it. It's just…" Her thoughts stuttered to a halt.

Ethan moved closer to her. "What?"

She shifted in her seat, thinking about the five hundred dollars' worth of weed she had packed in a brown bag in her suitcase. "I just don't want you to be disappointed."

Ethan shook his head, confused. "Why would I be disappointed?"

"What if we can't… What if I can't…" Her stomach turned at the thought losing him.

"I didn't plan this trip so we could have sex."

"But you bought all that weed."

"I bought all that weed for *you*, Avital. I bought it as a gift, in the hopes that it makes you feel better. But I want you to hear this—there are no strings attached to anything I'm doing this weekend. There are no expectations, either. All I want is for you to have a great time."

Ethan took both her hands inside his.

She had never felt more complete, or safe, with anyone.

"Remember what Rabbi Jason told us," Ethan said. "Let's not worry about sex right now. Let's just focus on having fun together, spending time with each other, being together. If something happens, great. And if not…that's okay, too. Because I still get to be with you, Avi. I still get to be here, in the middle of this beautiful location, with the most incredible woman in the world. That's more than enough for me right now."

Avital concurred with a gentle smile. She knew that sex was not the goal…not the focus, not the reason…but she was beginning to think about it all the same.

★ ★ ★

"What do you think?" Ethan said, unloading their bags from the car.

The cabin that Ethan had chosen for their weekend getaway stood on the same lake where he had organized their picnic. Avital exited their car and breathed in the fresh upstate air. It was not what she was expecting. Given her suitor's extraordinary wealth, she was expecting something far grander than the small wooden cabin. But it was delightful, all the same.

"It's beautiful," she said.

Ethan put the bags down at the front and unlocked the door. Stepping inside, she took stock of the place they would be spending their next forty-eight hours together. Large couches flanked the entryway beside shelves full of books and board games. To her left, a large kitchen with wraparound windows overlooked the water.

"Where did you find this place?"

Ethan was in the kitchen, putting food and drinks into the refrigerator. "Actually," he said, turning around, "it was my parents'."

"You grew up here?"

"We used to come here in the summer."

Avital stopped, surprised. Ethan, perhaps noticing her hesitation, paused putting away food. "I'm sorry," he said. "Maybe it was a poor idea to bring you here."

"No," she said immediately, coming over to the counter, which separated the main living area from the kitchen, in order to take a seat. "No. It's perfect, Ethan. I'm so glad you shared this with me." He nodded, seemingly lost for words, before turning back to organizing the fridge. "I'm actually just a little surprised."

"About?"

"I thought you were...richer."

"Well, we weren't poor," he admitted, turning back to her. "My mom worked in finance, and my dad was in conservation. We had a nice apartment on the Upper West Side and a small house on a lake to spend summers in. But I didn't grow up with Lippmann money. Actually, from what I remember about my parents, they were really down-to-earth people."

Avital shook her head. "So all the stories about the terrible Lippmanns I've grown up with over the years aren't true?"

"Are they ever?"

Ethan slid down across from her at the counter. It was interesting, listening to Ethan talk about his family. He lit up when he spoke about them.

"Ethan," she said, knowing she needed to be gentle in her approach, "have you thought about selling this house? The money might help you get a fresh start away from your grandfather. It could even help you get power of attorney over Kayla."

"Can't," Ethan said simply. "After my parents died, all the assets they owned were split equally among their three children. But since Kayla isn't able to make her own decisions, all her assets went to her legal guardian...my grandfather. There's no way to sell the house without all three of us signing off on it, and honestly, I don't really want to. I feel like it would be selling off a part of my soul."

Avital nodded. "That makes sense."

"I suppose the bright side is my grandfather has maintained it all these years. He even sends a cleaning crew in once a season to spruce it up. No one really uses the place anymore, but I appreciate that he's taken care of it for us. He's not all bad. He's just...broken."

Avital couldn't help but think back on her own intergenerational trauma. "It kind of reminds me of my grandfather," she said.

"How so?"

She shifted in her seat, leaning in closer. "I didn't tell you this part of the story because I didn't realize it was relevant at the time...but I do remember something else from around when your parents died. I remember that my grandparents were fighting about contacting your grandfather."

"Really?" he asked, confused. "Why?"

"I think my grandmother... She wanted my grandfather to call Moishe. Or, I don't know, send a fruit basket or something. I remember her saying, 'He just lost Lilly, and now Patricia!' And the saddest part about that, Ethan... I think my grandfather wanted to call Moishe, too. I remember him sitting by the phone in the living room, playing with his bottom lip, just sitting there...for hours. But when push came to shove, I don't think he ever did it. I think he was probably just too scared that after so many years, and so much bad blood, he would make things worse."

"It's interesting," Ethan said, filling in the blanks of the story, "because my grandfather brings it up all the time. How Chayim didn't even bother to call him after Patricia died."

"You're kidding."

"Wouldn't that be ironic?" Ethan said, shaking his head. "If all this bad blood between our families, if all these games and lawsuits, are simply the result of two old men, incapable of picking up the phone or being the one to apologize first."

"I could totally see that happening," Avital admitted.

"But if that were the case," Ethan said, coming around to her side, "maybe there is hope for us, after all."

She cocked her head back. "What?"

"Maybe," Ethan said, pulling her closer, "us getting together is just what this family needs to end three generations of rivalry."

Avital scoffed. She wasn't ready to be as optimistic about

their prospects as Ethan. "Or maybe it's wishful thinking," Avital suggested. "Maybe we tell our families, and you get disowned, and Kayla gets put into a home, and Randy is thrown out into the street. Or maybe Josh hates me forever because I allowed a Lippmann with nefarious intent to continue working at Best Babka."

"All right," Ethan said, throwing his hands up in open surrender. "I get it."

"Or maybe," she said, happy to lay out every worry constantly running through her head, "maybe we can have sex once, twice...but then, you suddenly realize that you don't want to go the next fifty years of your life only getting it four times a year. Maybe, you realize that people are miserable in sexless marriages, in dead bedrooms, and that you want more in a relationship with a woman than peeing on trees together."

Ethan raised one eyebrow in her direction. "But I really enjoyed peeing on a tree with you."

"It's not funny, Ethan."

He sighed, digging his hands into his pockets. She knew he tended to be the more optimistic one. He was chipper and hopeful, whereas she was always in pain and scared. But this time, she felt the need to save him from himself. After all, when you care about someone, you want to see them happy.

If he couldn't have the best with her, she wanted him to have the best with...well, someone. Someone great. And fun. Who could make love to him, the way he deserved.

"Look," she said, taking his hand, her voice veering into sadness, in spite of all her efforts to stay hopeful. "I just think we shouldn't worry about the future. We should just have fun, enjoy ourselves...see where life takes us."

Ethan nodded. "Okay."

She was ready to get swept back up in the fantasy of him. Throwing her arms around his shoulders, she moved in for a kiss. The taste of him, the warmth she felt within his arms, pushed all her concerns to the background once more.

"Actually," he said, pulling back from her, "I have something for you. A gift. I was going to give it to you later, but now that you mention it, why wait for good things?"

With that, Ethan raced from the house and headed back to the car. Avital leaned on one hand, sighing heavily. He was too good to her. She didn't know that men like Ethan existed, someone who cared for her with his whole heart and unconditionally.

Ethan returned to the house. Stepping into the kitchen, he placed a large pink box—wrapped up in the most perfect white Tiffany bow—on the counter between them.

"You got me pumpkin-spiced babka from the bakery?"

"No," he said, grinning, and pushed her chair in closer, "something even better."

Avital opened his gift. Pressing her fingers through tissue paper, she pulled the item out.

It was her camera.

Except, examining the once-broken power button at the top, she realized it was fixed.

"Ethan," she said, overwhelmed. "How did you manage this?"

"I had some help from a little bird named Josh," he said. "I figured that while we were here, in this beautiful and inspiring location, you might want to take some photos."

"I don't know what to say."

"You don't have to say anything," he said. "Just go out there...and find your joy again."

It was such a simple concept. Finding her joy. It was also something she realized had been lost alongside her constant battle with chronic pain.

She had forgotten how to hold on to her happiness. Heck,

JEAN MELTZER

she had forgotten what made her happy. But here was Ethan, her rock, her guide—her knight in shining armor—not bringing her back to herself, but helping her to discover a new normal.

Avital swallowed a thousand feelings, all circling the center of her chest. Leaving the camera on the counter, she threw her arms around his neck, squeezing him tight. He held her, warm and supportive, and she tried to commit the scent of him, the sensation of his arms wrapped around her, to memory. How sad that one day she would have to give him up.

"Look at you," Avital teased Ethan playfully, "tending a fire on Shabbat."

Ethan glanced back from the firepit he was stoking. It was now past eight o'clock. Nightfall had fully settled over their cabin. After a long hike and a delicious dinner that they had cooked together, they'd found their way out to the lake, where a small pit and stone seating beckoned.

Avital wrapped a throw around her shoulders before Ethan returned to her side. In front of their feet, the flames crackled.

"Tell me about them," Avital said quietly.

"Who?"

"Your parents."

"Truthfully," he said, shifting in his seat a little, "I don't remember too much."

"Then, tell me whatever you remember."

His eyes lingered over the water. "My mom was beautiful. And smart. My dad…was really approachable. Everybody liked him. Sometimes, they would fight. But mainly, I just remember them laughing a whole lot. I guess the best way to describe them is that they were a team."

Avital pulled her legs up to her chest, watching him, listening. Ethan smiled.

"What?" Avital asked curiously.

"Just something I remembered," he said.

"So—" she nudged him, wanting in on the joke "—tell me."

Ethan acquiesced. "My mom used to say this thing. 'If your heart is in the right place, it will never lead you in the wrong direction.'"

Avital cocked her head sideways. "That's beautiful."

"Yes and no." Ethan chuckled. "She used to say it about going shopping."

Avital laughed. "Shopping?"

He shook his head. "I had completely forgotten about that, honestly."

Avital couldn't help but point out the obvious. "You don't really talk about them."

"I know."

"Do you talk about them with your brother or Moishe?"

"Never," Ethan admitted. "It was like the accident happened, and we moved in with Moishe, and aside from laying *tefillin* and doing mourners' *kaddish*, we didn't deal with it at all. But it's nice, you know? Talking about them. I thought it would be hard...but instead, it feels good."

"Yeah?"

"It makes it feel like they're still here."

"Well," Avital said and leaned her head against his shoulder, "I'm happy to hear about your family anytime."

She spent another few moments like this, pressed up against him, breathing him in, his warmth enveloping her. She took a careful accounting of her pain. It sat somewhere around a four. Not great...but also not terrible.

"Ethan," Avital said, looking up at him, "I think I'm ready to try some medicinal cannabis."

"Really?"

She nodded.

Ethan went inside the cabin. When he returned, he came equipped, holding the paper bag full of medicinal cannabis products. Avital opened it up. Staring down at suppositories, oils, prerolls, and vapes, she couldn't help but feel overwhelmed.

"The budtender at Holy Rollers said go low and slow," Avital said, reaching for a tiny cardboard box labeled *Chocolate Haze*. "Maybe this one? I think it's what they call a preroll, so a basic joint. Rabbi Jason said it's good for pain relief... and anxiety."

Ethan nodded. "How can you go wrong with that?"

She opened the box, pulling it out. It was smaller than she remembered them being. But thinking back to seventh grade, it felt familiar.

Ethan pulled out a lighter. "Ready?"

"Let's do this thing," she said and placed her lips on the end.

Ethan lit the other end, and Avital took one giant breath in.

She reacted immediately. All at once, she began coughing, hacking, and sputtering, leaning over while rubbing her throat. Ethan quickly took the joint from her and stubbed it out.

"You okay?" he asked, clapping her back.

"Holy—" She couldn't talk.

"That good, huh?"

"I...can't...breathe."

Ethan ran inside to get her a glass of alkaline water. She downed the entire thing in three large gulps.

"How do you feel?" Ethan asked, taking a seat beside her.

Avital analyzed her mental state. "The same."

"Really?"

"I'm not actually sure I even inhaled." Avital sighed, the effect of which caused another round of raucous hacking.

"I tried to, but then I just started coughing...and now, my throat is killing me."

Ethan stared at the snuffed-out joint in his hand. "You apparently need more experience smoking. Your lungs are far too healthy."

"Clearly."

Avital kicked the sand beneath her feet. *Great. Just great.* Medicinal cannabis felt like her last great hope for pain management, and pain-free intimacy, and she couldn't even take one successful hit.

"Or maybe," Ethan said, after considering the situation, "what you need is a snack."

"Seriously?" she grumbled. "You're thinking about food right now?"

"Actually—" he opened up the preroll, dumping three tiny green buds into his hand "—I was thinking more like I'd make you a dessert."

He was an artist.

Avital took a seat at the kitchen counter, while Ethan set about getting to work. Watching him, she marveled at how easily he had mastered baking. He was able to follow recipes, intuiting solutions to problems beforehand, while simultaneously creating his own results. Finding the gluten-free flour, honey, and raspberry that he had brought, he began crafting some new recipe.

In the meantime, she drank her pear juice and enjoyed the show. His biceps flexing while he worked, the apron hugging his perfect frame, her mind was firmly on devouring Ethan. After forty-five minutes, Ethan presented Avital with a plate of fresh-from-the-oven raspberry and medicinal-cannabis hamantashen.

Avital picked up one piece, observing the tiny flakes of green spotting the little triangle cookie.

"How much weed is in this?" she asked.

"According to my calculations," Ethan said, glancing down at a paper where he had scribbled numbers. "It should be a one-to-one ratio of THC and CBD…and each cookie should be about two and a half milligrams."

"So no more than two cookies?" Avital asked.

"Probably a good place to start," Ethan confirmed.

Avital reached for a cookie.

"Bong appetite," she said and took a bite.

THIRTY-FIVE

Avital had never realized how amazing carpet could feel. Rolling around the living-room floor of their cabin, the feeling of those plush threads tickling her skin, she was suddenly aware of a large—and extremely sexy—presence standing over her.

"Avital?" Ethan asked, peering down at her from above.

"Yeah?"

"You okay?"

"Great."

"Are you high?"

"I don't know."

Avital started laughing. There was something about the way Ethan was looking at her, bent over, hands on his hips, eyes all serious, that just seemed ridiculously funny.

Ethan moved his face closer to inspect, and Avital suddenly became entranced by the shape of his nose. It was so long, and pointy, with a jagged little bump right at the top. Truly, she had never seen a nose so spectacular in her entire life. She reached for it, giving it a good honk. "Honk!" she said. "Honk! Honk! Honk!" Before devolving into laughter again.

"Avi," Ethan said.

"Yeah."

"What are you doing?"

She considered the question. "I don't remember."

It was the strangest thing. She remembered being with Ethan, eating a triangle of hamantashen. And then, the long wait. Sitting around in the kitchen, watching Ethan clean up, certain it wasn't working. And then, all at once, she was struck by the feeling of dizziness. A tingling sensation began at the top of her head and worked its way down to her toes.

Avital analyzed the sensations floating through her body. The pain was still there, obviously. It lingered, like a jellyfish vulva, just beneath the surface of the water. But this time, her jellyfish didn't sting. It tingled.

"And how are you feeling?" Ethan asked.

"Different," she admitted. "Weird."

"But better?"

"I'm not sure," she said, blinking up at the ceiling. "I was having a pretty good day to begin with. Though, I might just be so high right now that even if I am in pain, I don't really care."

"Can I lie on the carpet with you?"

"Oh my God," she screamed. "You have to lie on this carpet. It's the most amazing carpet ever."

Ethan reclined on the carpet next to her. "It's my first time making edibles," he said, quite seriously. "I think next time… I'll change up the CBD to THC ratio. Counteract some of those psychoactive effects with a much higher CBD level. We can also try experimenting with different terpenes. See if one helps you out more than the other."

"Yeah," Avital said, not really paying attention. "That sounds like a great plan."

The feeling of his arm, now touching the skin of her own arm, caused that tension in her body to rise again. She wanted him. Normally, she would give in to the fear, her anxiety spiraling over her ability to perform, but tonight, she just wanted to have fun. She just wanted to be normal, and intimate, with Ethan.

"Ethan," she said, grabbing onto his shirt, "let's go in the lake."

"I don't think that's a good idea." He frowned.

"Why not?"

"It's kind of cold out."

"Ethan." She huffed, annoyed. "I haven't gone swimming in over two years. Please... I promise I won't drown."

He swallowed. "Okay."

Ethan stood up, heading for their luggage. "Let me just get some towels and bathing suits for..."

She didn't want to wait for Ethan or towels or bathing suits. Avital sprinted outside to the lake. Tearing off her shoes and socks, feeling the sand beneath her feet, she made her way into the water. It lapped at her toes. Her ankles. Her calves. It poured through her skirt. Ethan was right. It was freezing. But she didn't care.

There were still so many simple pleasures left in her life. She closed her eyes, willing herself to embrace it all, absorbing the goodness. The water. The cold air on a perfect spring night. The stars shining above her, breaking through the clouds. And Ethan—dear, sweet Ethan—coming up behind her.

"Avi," Ethan said, his voice fraught with concern. "Please." He stepped into the water, holding a towel. "You're shivering."

Avital spun around. "I have scars."

Ethan nodded, coming closer. "Me, too."

She swallowed. "I'm afraid."

"I know," Ethan said gently.

"I'm just—"

He repeated the words. "There's no goal here, right?"

"Right."

"If you want me to stop—"

"I don't."

She wanted this.

She needed this.

She took off her shirt, tossing it to the shore. Next, she removed her bra. Unbuckling the latch from behind, she tossed it into a pile with her shirt. Finally, she grasped the elastic of her skirt, pulling it down to the ground, stepping outside of it. She was revealed. All of her. Scars, too. She stood naked before him.

"Ethan," Avital said.

"Yeah?"

"Get rid of the towel."

He tossed the towel to the shore.

Her eyes wandered down to his pants, where a large bulge had formed. His desire was evident. His body angled toward her, longing for her, wanting her—but Ethan didn't move. He waited. He stood there, freezing water lapping at his trousers, seeking an invitation.

"Tell me what you need from me, Avital."

"I need you to touch me."

He stepped forward. Taking her in his arms, he kissed her again. His lips, soft and gentle. His hands, solid and firm against the divot in her back.

Her knees began to buckle. "Ethan."

"How does that feel?" he whispered.

"Amazing."

"How about—" he kissed her neck, drawing upward until his lips tickled the very bottom of her earlobe "—on a scale of one to ten?"

She laughed, stepping back. "What am I...a challah?"

"No," he said, his voice low and growly. "But I want to know how to please you, Avital, and to do that, I need to understand your body. I need to understand what hurts you... and I need to learn how to touch you in a way that feels good and safe. So," he said, bringing his lips back to her neck once again, dragging his tongue along her skin, "on a scale of one to ten, with ten being terrible and one being amazing, how does this feel?"

Avital considered the question. Pleasure was a feeling she had grown unfamiliar with, but now—with Ethan, running his soft lips over her collarbone—she closed her eyes, allowing herself to really focus on the sensation.

"Seven," she said.

His tongue inched higher up her neck, toward her ear. "And now?"

She moaned. "Four."

"And now?" he said, returning to her lips, kissing her softly.

"Three."

"And now?" he said, exchanging that soft kiss for a firm one.

"Eight."

It was strange, using logic to make note of an act that was always supposed to be instinctual. And yet, the careful analysis of her own pleasure in regard to his touch worked. With each number, she understood this new body of hers. She realized things about herself, too.

She liked a slow touch over a fast one. She preferred a firm caress to a gentle one. She hated the sides of her breasts being touched without warning, but she loved—went totally nuts, in fact—when Ethan got down on his knees in the sand, with the moon as their only witness, and kissed the inside of her upper thigh.

"And here?" Ethan asked.

"Eight."

"And here?"

She gasped and melted again. "Two."

With each careful accounting, her desire grew, her body responded. And with it, the memory of those feelings—her femininity, her sexuality, her womanhood—returned.

She abandoned her concerns, sinking into the sensation of Ethan's fingers and lips trailing against her skin. She gave in to the erotic, the intensity of waiting, the pleasure that came from *needing*, until what she had with Ethan was something beyond sex. She rose from her body, all shimmering light and tingles, each breath and sigh searching the universe to find him.

"Four," she whispered.

Ethan responded. "You are perfection, Avi."

"Five."

"I love touching you like this."

"Eight."

"I love pleasing you, Avital."

"Four."

"I want only you."

And so it went, all night, for hours upon hours. Ethan touching a spot. Avital calling out a number. Ethan responding to each touch, each sensation, each acknowledgment of what gave her pleasure, or not, accordingly. Until finally, they had moved from the water and shoreline into the main bed, and Avital no longer knew if what she felt was good or bad, painful or pleasurable, only that the rising tide inside of her had to come crashing to shore.

She needed him. She wanted him.

But mainly, she wanted this for herself.

She gripped his hair, bringing him closer. And it was there, in that space, that her body expanded and opened, and Ethan met her welcome with strong and capable strokes, gentle and rhythmic, loving and passionate, until her body was lifting off the bed and her mouth was angled up toward the ceiling. "One…one…one…"

THIRTY-SIX

The next morning, the sun was shining.

Avital blinked her eyes open to find Ethan dozing in a light slumber in the bed beside her. Noting the tangled sheets between them, her first thought was not of pain, it was of Ethan. It had been a long night. After all his hard work and effort on her behalf, he had earned a proper sleep-in.

Crawling out of bed, she was careful not to disturb him. Heading to the bathroom, she rinsed her face and brushed her teeth before doing a careful analysis of how her body was managing.

There was a strange sort of humming in her lower regions, but the pain...wasn't necessarily worse. It gave her hope for the future. It gave her hope that with time, and support—maybe also medicinal cannabis—she could begin finding a new normal. She was ready to make peace with the thing that had hurt her.

She was just about to make her way to the kitchen and

begin hunting down breakfast, when the sight of Ethan sleeping peacefully caught her eye again. The sunlight mixed with the reflection of the water just outside and painted the walls in a rainbow of angled colors. Avital stopped, leaning against the door frame.

He had one leg thrown over the cover, his arm wrapped around the pillow. His beautiful form, naked, all those spectacular rounded edges, the full depth of him. In some ways, it was a typical image of a man in his prime, experiencing the afterglow of a sexual escape with some lover...except for the items surrounding the bed.

On the nightstand, next to three bottles of prescription pills, sat her bottle of alkaline water. Plugged into the wall, and on the bed next to Ethan, was a bright blue heating pad. A plastic bag full of water sat in a lump on the floor.

She couldn't help but think that Rabbi Jason had been right. She had put so much focus on being able to have a physical relationship with Ethan, but that wasn't the part that made her feel the most connected to him. That wasn't the part that made what they had intimate.

It was the part afterward—Ethan moving around the room, gathering up Azo and Uribel, before running her a shower. He didn't care that the bedsheets were stained. Or that she needed ice between her legs after sex. Or that when she cuddled into him after their evening together, he was holding her *and* a heating pad. He saw her at her most vulnerable, broken self...and still, he cared for her.

Avital found herself reaching for her camera. Pulling it out, adjusting the lens, she snapped a photo. Then another... She shot him from every angle, capturing the way he was sleeping among the accoutrements of her disease, before he began to stir. Rising from his spot wearily, he directed his sleepy eyes in her direction.

"Hey." Ethan smiled.

Avital sat down on the edge beside him. "Hey."

"How you feeling?"

"I'm okay," she said and realized that she meant it.

His eyes wandered down to the camera she was holding. "You're taking pictures again?"

She turned the camera around. Ethan took it in his hand, staring at the image. "It's beautiful, Avi," Ethan said, his eyes genuine.

"I think I'm going to turn it into a series."

"Really?" Ethan sat up a little taller. She could see he was happy about the news. "That's great."

Avital returned to the images in her camera. "I want to explore this idea of breaking boundaries. What it means to overstep bounds, and break tradition, and create space for the walls to come down. I keep thinking of the lake outside, and how water sometimes siphons off into tiny tributaries. It moves without permission. And I guess...that's what I want to start taking pictures of. I want to explore the way boundaries get built up and taken down. I want to explore the spaces between a wall and an opening."

A tight smile worked its way through pressed lips.

"What?" she asked nervously.

"You're a genius," Ethan said simply.

"I wouldn't go that far." She laughed.

"You are," he said, refusing to let her downplay her talents, "the most brilliant—" he reached over, taking her into his arms "—the most talented, the most beautiful woman, the most remarkable person I have ever met."

She lifted her eyes up to him. "I think you might be biased."

"I am totally biased."

Ethan kissed her. Avital melted, folding into his arms. Giving over to the passions of her heart, her whole body sparked. She felt safe with Ethan. Even though she knew what they had was limited...the tension building up between them like pink boxes in a crammed hallway...she didn't want to deal with it.

"You know," Ethan said after a few quiet moments, "I was thinking about that time I came into your office, and you asked me why I lay *tefillin* and keep kosher. I told you it was because there's no such thing as an atheist in a foxhole. And you told me that atheists are created in foxholes. Well, I've changed my mind about that. I think we were both wrong."

"Oh?" She laughed, surprised at the revelation. "Okay."

"Maybe the foxhole isn't there to teach us to have faith in God. Maybe it's there to teach us to have faith in ourselves."

Avital considered his interpretation. "I like that."

Ethan nuzzled his nose into her neck. "Here's the real reason I lay *tefillin* and keep kosher. It's because I don't want to turn into my grandfather. Judaism has rules. It has structures. It provides some sort of guideline for living our life...and that appeals to me, because my grandfather never taught me those things. Because for most of my life, I've just been fumbling around, trying to prove my worth to other people, trying to prove myself to my grandfather. *And then I met you.* And suddenly, that thing my mom always used to say made sense. 'If your heart is in the right place, it will never lead you in the wrong direction.'"

Her heart ached for him.

"I don't know if there's a God, Avi," Ethan said, meeting her eyes directly. "But I know that when I look at you, there's something good in this universe. There's something better, still worth fighting for. You are—" the words caught in his throat "—you're the very best thing to ever happen to me."

"Ethan..."

He pulled her onto his lap. Avital wrapped her legs around

him, pressing her breasts against his chest, their lips meeting with frenetic desire. And Avital gave in to it, her nails dragging up his back while he kissed her, pleasure merging with pain merging with the heat of his own body, pressing against her, pressing into her. She allowed herself to be vulnerable, and remarkable, and broken, and adored. Because Ethan was—he absolutely was—the best thing ever to happen to her.

In order to have intimacy with another person you needed healthy boundaries. You needed walls and fortifications. The ability to say no. The freedom to communicate when something hurt you. You needed to have your limits respected. But just as important, she realized, sitting there, her soul merging into Ethan's, was knowing when to bring the ramparts down.

THIRTY-SEVEN

"Rise and shine, little brother."

Ethan pushed open the door to Randy's room with one foot. His hands full of cookies, he struggled to turn on the light switch with the tip of his nose before heading toward Randy. "Come on," Ethan said, plopping onto the edge of his bed, laying out four plates across his bedspread. "Wake up," he said, getting up to open the blinds. "I got something for you."

"Dude," Randy said, shielding his eyes with one hand. "Seriously. It's, like...not even noon."

"I brought you breakfast."

"What?" Never the type to turn down food, Randy sat up. Gawking in the direction of the four plates of baked goods, he looked totally—and rightly—confused. "What the hell is all this?"

"Well," Ethan explained, pointing to each item. "Those are IC-safe blueberry and tigernut hamantashen. These are paleo coconut macaroons. This plate was supposed to be gluten-free raspberry rugelach, but between you and me, I don't think I have the flour right just yet. And this plate—" Ethan pushed a stack of gooey double-fudge brownies his way "—this plate I made specifically with you in mind. I call them Brownie Bombs. They have caramel and chocolate and marshmallow inside them. They also have ten milligrams of THC...so, you know, you may want to go slow."

Randy blinked, twice, in Ethan's direction. "You made me weed brownies?"

"Yeah."

Randy shook his head. "Why?"

"Because," Ethan said, sitting back down on the bed, "you really helped me with Avital. And just, I don't know, man... I'm grateful to you, you know? You're a great brother. You deserve to have someone do something nice for you."

Ethan waited for Randy to say something. After a few silent moments, he picked his chin up off the floor and came back to reality. "Sorry," Randy said, shaking his head. "I'm just...still on the fact that you made me edibles."

"Well, don't be surprised, man," Ethan said, clapping his little brother on the back. "Eat up."

Randy shrugged and, reaching over to the plate of brownies, took a bite. All at once, his eyes went wide. His chewing slowed, his hand covering his mouth, a tiny moan of pleasure escaping through his lips.

"Good, right?"

"You made these?" Randy asked, disbelief spreading across his face.

"Yep."

Randy shook his head again. "Holy hell."

Ethan bit back a smile. He knew he was good at it. He had some natural instinct for baking that he didn't quite understand. But he enjoyed the process. He liked how things were simple when it came to recipes. A chemical reaction between ingredients. A specific and allotted time for flour to rise. Baking was simple. At least, compared to life.

Ethan reached over, squeezing Randy's knee, before rising. Randy, confused, called out to him at the door. "Hey," Randy asked, "where are you going?"

"Work, of course."

"You don't want to eat any of this?"

Ethan glanced back to the plates littering Randy's bedspread. As it turned out, Ethan's favorite part of cooking wasn't actually developing the recipe. Or even eating the food himself. It was the joy he got from seeing others revel in his tasty creations. At Best Babka, he had learned that food was more than just sustenance. It was an expression of family. Of love.

"It's cool, bro," Ethan said, nodding back at the plates. "I made it all for you."

"Sister." Josh grinned, poking his head through her office door. "You're looking most lovely this morning."

Avital looked up from the box of office supplies she was unpacking and narrowed her gaze on him suspiciously. Josh only ever used the moniker *sister* when he wanted something from her. Stepping inside her office, he dropped into the seat across from her desk, his face red as a cherry.

Avital stood, placing her hands on her hips. "What do you want?"

"First—" Josh leaned forward "—how was your weekend?"

He was practically salivating at the chance for some salacious gossip. No doubt he'd immediately share it with everyone on staff. Her and Ethan's relationship was now a full and open secret, with everybody speculating on their next steps. They weren't fooling anyone. Apparently, they hadn't been for some time.

Avital smirked. "My weekend was good."

"You and Ethan..." Josh let the words linger.

Avital took the seat across from him. "We managed."

"Just managed, huh?"

She bit back a smile.

"Oh," Josh said, raising his brows. "Okay."

"He has wonderful hands."

"That's good."

"Firm," she said, suddenly enjoying the opportunity to make her brother uncomfortable. "And, if that weren't enough to make our weekend together *explosive*, he also has the biggest, most beautiful, most perfect-looking..." She was waiting for Josh to interrupt her. Say something snarky. Instead, he raised both brows, daring her to finish the sentence. Avital huffed, annoyed. "You're no fun."

Josh laughed. "Go on. I'm already totally jealous of his relationship with Tootles, so you know, he might as well be *shtupping* my beloved twin sister, too."

Avital shook her head. "You are so crass."

"You started it."

The banter, like always, was all in jest. After a few more minutes of childish back-and-forth, followed by the tossing of a pencil eraser, Josh softened. "Hey, Avi, I'm happy for you," he said genuinely.

"Thank you."

"Speaking of love interests," Josh said, clapping his hands together, "I need a favor."

Avital rolled her eyes. "How did I know?"

"I want to introduce Mom and Dad to my new girlfriend."

"Okay."

"And I was thinking—" he pulled his chair closer "—that

maybe we could do it at the Purim carnival? And maybe to take the pressure off…you and Ethan would be there?"

"Mom and Dad haven't met Ethan." She shifted in her seat, confused. "At least, not in any official way."

"So—" he chewed one fingernail nervously "—I was thinking, since we're both dating people we like, people we're both clearly getting serious with, maybe we could do, like, a dual introduction?"

Avital scoffed outright. "Absolutely not."

"Come on, Avi!" Josh was full-on begging now. "You know how overzealous Dad gets whenever one of us brings someone home. And Mom will start talking about bakers making the best lovers. And God forbid someone brings up Moishe Lippmann. I can't put this one through that, Avi. I like her. I don't want her to know how *meshuggener* our family really is…without easing her into it first."

Avital folded her head into her hands. "Jesus."

"Please, Avi."

"We're not at that point, Josh."

"What do you mean you're not at that point?" Josh was incredulous. "You spend all your free time with the man. You went away with him for a weekend. He fixed your camera. I really don't understand why you're being so weird about this."

Avital bit back the words. She wasn't being weird. It was a terrible idea, introducing Ethan to her parents as her official boyfriend. It meant adding layers, and complications, to their already very problematic relationship. But she loved her brother. She couldn't deny him the chance at love—the chance at happiness—simply because her own relationship was built on lies.

Avital pinched her eyes shut. "I'll talk to Ethan."

"Really?"

"And only if he agrees to it," she said, pointing one finger at Josh.

His relief and excitement bubbled over, forcing all doubts to the back of her mind.

PURIM

THIRTY-EIGHT

"Chag Purim Sameach!"

It was a perfect morning for a party, and the entire neighborhood around Best Babka had been transformed. Tables lined the street, each one hosting a Best Babka employee showcasing their specialty item. Between them, clowns, face painters, and a magician wearing colorful costumes performed to the delight of children. At the end of the street, on a large stage that had been set up the previous night, klezmer music was playing on a large speaker system. Shushan had come alive in Brooklyn. The Purim carnival had arrived.

Ethan was just putting the finishing touches on his own booth when he realized that the voice wishing someone *Chag Purim Sameach* was directed at him. Turning, he saw a little girl, dressed up like Queen Esther, holding a plastic bag filled with two tiny hamantashen—the triangle shaped cookies traditionally eaten on Purim.

Ethan instantly recognized the bag as a *mishloach manot* of-fering.

"Chag Purim Sameach," Ethan said back, attempting to bend down on one knee.

It was more difficult than usual. The giant felt hamantashen costume he was wearing gave him limited mobility.

Purim commemorated the story of Queen Esther who saved the Jewish people from extermination during the Achaemenid Empire in Persia. Now, all over the world, Jews engaged in Purim festivities by reading the Scroll of Esther, giving gifts of food, dressing up in costumes, and donating to charity.

Ethan took the gift. "Are these for me?"

The little girl nodded repeatedly, before sticking her fingers in her mouth. Behind her, an older woman, talking to an apparent friend, was holding a wicker basket filled with similarly shaped *mishloach manot*. The woman looked over, and Ethan raised one hand in acknowledgment of the gift before returning his attention to the little girl.

"I like your costume," she said.

"Thank you." Ethan smiled. "You know what I am?"

"A hamantashen!"

"That's right," he said. "But can you guess what kind of hamantashen?"

She stuck another finger in her mouth. "Raspberry?"

"No."

"Apricot?"

"No."

"Chocolate?"

"Are you ready?" Ethan teased her. "I'm a...*person*-tashen."

The little girl laughed. Ethan pointed to his table. "Would you like a hamantashen?"

She glanced over his booth. "They're not made with peo-ple, are they?"

Ethan laughed. "No."

"What about peanuts?"

"No peanuts, either."

She went to reach for one, when a woman—whom he assumed was her mother—came racing over.

"Lara!" she shouted, pulling her hand back. "No. You know you can't have that! I'm sorry," she said, her attention now turning to Ethan. "She's deathly allergic to nuts."

"Well, I have good news for you," Ethan said proudly. "My specialty for this competition is creating medically safe desserts. I have nut-free hamantashen, IC-safe hamantashen, AIP-safe hamantashen. And, in about fifteen minutes, I'll have soy-free, gluten-free, and lactose-free hamantashen, as well."

"Wow!" she said, glancing over the table. "Well, would you mind if I buy all of the nut-free ones?"

"Really?"

"My daughter can never eat with the other kids," she said sadly. "It's always such a struggle, and she comes home crying from almost every holiday event."

Ethan frowned sympathetically. "I can only imagine how hard that is on you both. I also care about someone who can't eat a lot of foods. That's actually why I started making them. Mainly for her, but...also so she could enjoy food with the people she cares about. Eating is a social activity, after all."

"Especially when you're Jewish," the woman said.

Ethan laughed. "Too true."

"So what do you say?" the woman said, digging out all her cash, flashing it to Ethan. "Would it be truly terrible of me to buy all your nut-free hamantashen?"

Ethan considered the question. "I mean...considering this entire event is for charity, I don't see why not."

"Thank you," the woman said, gathering them all up, throwing mounds of cash at Ethan. "And by the way, if you ever think about starting your own business with these baked goods or running a pop-up, I will be the first customer at your door."

"Thank you," Ethan said, waving the cash as she departed. "Thank you so much!"

Ethan dropped the three hundred dollars into the *pushke*, or charity tin, at the front of his booth. Watching the woman and her daughter walk away, he couldn't help but think about what she had said. *I will be the first customer at your door.*

"You know," Avital said, appearing behind him, "our sages tell us, 'Purim is when we take the masks off.'"

"So what does it say that I'm dressed up as a hamantashen?"

"It says," Avital said and shoved three dollars into his *pushke*, "that you secretly want to be a vagina."

Ethan crooked his neck back. "What?"

"You don't know?" she asked seriously.

"Apparently I'm out of the loop."

"Outside of the whole triangle-hat thing they teach you in Hebrew school," she said, leaning on his table flirtatiously, "some believe that hamantashen were originally fertility cookies. Hence the whole oozing cherry filling coming out of the middle of said triangle."

"You're kidding me."

"Thankfully," she teased him, "you have the cutest clitoral hood I have ever seen in my whole life."

"Well, I appreciate that, Avital."

Heat rose in his cheeks. He wanted to kiss her. But glancing toward the stage, he could see Avital's parents—and grandparents—waiting for the event to start. Though he had met them peripherally while working at the bakery, he didn't feel right engaging in hard-core PDAs with their daughter. At least, not until he was given the official introduction as her boyfriend.

"And what about you?" Ethan asked. Avital was wearing an all-white dress. "Are you in costume?"

"I am."

He cocked his head. "An angel?"

"No."

"A bride?"

"I am..." Avital said dramatically "...a photograph waiting to be developed."

Ethan laughed. "Clever."

"It felt appropriate for Purim this year."

"Indeed."

After their trip together, Avital had continued taking photos. Sometimes she even brought her camera to work. Though she had not yet developed those photos, Ethan was proud of her. He couldn't wait for the entire world to see her, and her talent, the way he did.

"Hey," Josh said, clapping Ethan on the back, *"Chag Purim Sameach."*

"Chag Sameach," Ethan said, turning around. Josh was dressed like a giant hot dog, a trail of mustard and relish running down the middle.

"This is quite the impressive lineup you got here," Josh said, his eyes wandering down Ethan's table. "Avi, you see what the man did for you?"

Avital beamed. "I see."

"So where's the muse?" Ethan asked, searching the festivities for Josh's mystery woman.

"At work," Josh said simply. "But she'll be here later tonight for the after-party at the bakery." He glanced back in the direction of his parents. "And I really appreciate you both being there to play backup."

"It was about time, anyways," Ethan said, wrapping one

arm around Avital, pulling her closer. Her blue eyes reached into his soul.

"And who knows?" Josh said, playfully punching Ethan in the shoulder. "Maybe this time next year, we'll be getting ready to celebrate a joint wedding."

With that, Josh departed, making his way to the front stage, in order to get the carnival properly started. But his words—the discussion of the future—forced them both into an awkward silence. There wouldn't be a future because they were lying to everyone.

A speaker squealed, drawing their attention away from the inevitable. Josh stepped up to the microphone on the stage and announced the opening of festivities and the beginning of the Purim carnival Best Babka Bake-Off competition.

Ethan spent the next five hours hawking his medically safe version of Ashkenazi baked goods. Throughout the carnival, and even with stiff competition from other members of the Best Babka staff, he was doing quite well in sales. But more surprising—and moving—were the stories customers shared with him at the table.

A man told Ethan how he'd developed food sensitives after being diagnosed with Lyme disease. A woman with breast cancer could no longer eat soy. Another got migraines whenever she ate corn. And after each purchase, Ethan heard the same refrain. *If you ever think about going into business, I'll be the first customer at your door.*

He didn't know if the interest would be enough to make a business economically viable in a place like Brooklyn, but he could feel a seed of an idea taking root inside his mind. Finally, at three o'clock in the afternoon, with the competition drawing to a close, Josh collected up all the Pushkins and went to the stage. Avital reappeared at Ethan's side.

"How's it going?" she asked.

"Great," Ethan said. Save for six small plates of ha-mantashen, he was completely out of product. "Though, I doubt I'm gonna beat Tootles."

Across from Ethan, Tootles beamed, leaning on an empty table. The line that had formed all day for his creative take on bourekas had finally dissipated with a knitted sold-out sign he had come prepared with.

"So you heard about the salmon bacon boureka?" Avital asked.

"Heard about it?" Ethan said, patting his belly. "I already ate six."

Ethan wasn't upset. Tootles's creations were sheer genius.

"I could not be more pleased to announce the winner of this year's Best Babka Bake-Off competition," Josh said. "Tootles, with his specialty item, salmon bacon and cream cheese bourekas!"

The crowd went wild. Tootles burst into tears. Pulling a knitted handkerchief from his pocket, drying his eyes and blowing his nose, he made his way to the stage to accept his award.

"Congratulations, man," Josh said, laying one hand on his shoulder. "You want to tell us where we'll be donating to-day's proceeds?"

"Knit and Chill," Tootles said, leaning into the micro-phone. "It's an organization that makes blankets, hats, scarves, and mittens for people in homeless shelters. They also set up knitting classes for free all around New York. And the reason I chose them is that after I got out of prison, before I started working at Best Babka, I was homeless. Knit and Chill— like all of you, my family, at Best Babka—gave me a second chance at life. So thank you," he said, crying into his knitted hanky. "Thank you so much."

The competition was over. For the crowds, there would be two more hours of live music on the stage, and a *megillah of Esther* reading, but for the staff of Best Babka and the Cohen family, it was time for the after-party.

"I guess I should officially meet the family," Ethan said.

"I guess so," Avital said.

Most everyone on staff at Best Babka had beaten Ethan and Avital to the after-party. Tootles was raising a glass of kosher champagne. Family and friends flooded the front entrance. Most of the voices, like the laughter, Ethan recognized.

Avi took Ethan's hand and, leading him down the hallway, searched for the Cohen family. They found them, standing huddled in a circle by the back door, where the parking lot was, excitedly welcoming someone with hugs and handshakes.

"Ethan," Josh said, waving them over. "Avi. Come here and meet my girlfriend, Melinda."

The crowd parted like the Red Sea. All at once, Ethan's smile faded. His heart stopped beating inside his chest. His entire relationship with Avital flashed before his eyes, and time slowed. Josh's mystery girlfriend was none other than Melinda Shankman, his friend and the nurse who worked the front desk at Hebrew Home for Assisted Living.

"Melinda," Josh said, beaming widely, totally ignorant of the situation, "this is my twin sister, Avital, and this is her boyfriend—"

"Oh my God," Melinda squealed excitedly. "Of course I know Ethan Lippmann. Ethan comes in almost every Shabbat to visit his sister, Kayla, at the center where I work."

Melinda attempted to embrace Ethan. Sheepishly, he returned the favor, patting her on the back. Meanwhile, the Cohen clan had gone drop-dead silent. Mouths open and angled to the floor, they cast confused and sideways glances at each other.

"I'm sorry," Melinda said. "Did I say something wrong?"

"You mean... Ethan *Rosenberg*, right?" Josh asked, still incredulous.

Ethan's gaze wandered over to Avital. Her eyes were focused on the linoleum floor, her lower lip quivering. He knew what he had to do. This was her family, her business, the people she loved, and her community. As much as he wanted the dream to go on forever, it was time for both of them to face reality. Ethan stepped forward and took full responsibility.

"Actually," Ethan said, clearing his throat before continuing, "Rosenberg was my father's name, and it's my legal name. But socially, and for most of my life, most people know me as Ethan Rosenberg-Lippmann...because Moishe Lippmann is my grandfather."

THIRTY-NINE

Avital could barely hear herself think over all the shouting. There were threats. Wild accusations. All manner of Yiddish and English curse words. But the truth had come out. Ethan Rosenberg was a Lippmann. He was the heir and grandson of Moishe Lippmann, mortal enemy of the Cohens. Worst of all, he had been sent by his grandfather to steal their world-famous pumpkin-spiced babka recipe.

It was an unforgivable crime, made all the worse by the fact that the staff of Best Babka—previously enjoying the spoils of an after-party with Tootles—was now leaning out the doorways of their kitchens, overhearing every unflattering word.

Avital had an instinct to explain—to describe the way Ethan had helped her renegotiate her life with chronic pain—but no one was giving her the chance.

"Call the police," *Zeyde* said, growing flustered.

"You can't call the police," Avital said.

"Everybody," Grandma Rose shouted, "please calm down."

"It's corporate espionage," Josh offered. "It's a felony."

"It's not," Avital said, trying to raise her voice above the *meshuggeners*. "He used his legal name. Also, I've known who he was for a while now...and I chose to let him continue working at Best Babka, okay?"

"You think that's better, Avi?" Josh screamed at her before turning his rage on Ethan. "And you. Taking advantage of my poor, sick sister."

"I don't want to fight with you, Josh," Ethan said, raising both hands into the air.

"I'll fight with you," Avi said, stepping between them. "And I am not some charity case, okay? I wanted to be taken advantage of."

Josh threw his hands up. "Now I know he's messed with your head!"

"Call the FBI," *Zeyde* screamed, wrenching at the collar of his shirt. "Call the rabbi. Avital, Avital...how could you let this happen?"

The broken, betrayed sound of desperation in her grandfather's voice pulled her back to herself. Her heart sank at his words. All the feelings that had been swirling around her, all the doubts that came with choosing Ethan over Best Babka—over her own family—faded with her grandfather's words. How had she let this happen?

"Please," Ethan said, trying to defend her, "this is all on me, okay?"

"It's not on Ethan," Avital yelled.

"I swear," Ethan pleaded. "I care about Avital and Best Babka very much. If you would just give me ten minutes to explain what happened—"

"Explain!" Her grandfather grabbed an umbrella from a bin by the door. "Explain with this."

"*Zeyde,*" her mother said, cutting him off at the pass.

"I'll kill you," *Zeyde* said, desperately trying to poke Ethan with the umbrella. "You and Moishe and the entire Lippmann clan!"

With the threat of violence now fully engaged, every Cohen was attempting to wrangle the weapon from their grandfather's hand.

"Chayim," Rose said, "calm down."

"Give me that umbrella, Grandpa," Avital's mother said.

"Toss it over here, Grandpa," Josh said, waving at him from across the hallway. "I'm happy to finish him off."

It was no use. The old man's rage could not be contained. "May his name be wiped out," *Zeyde* shouted, his entire face turning beet red, one hand raised in open defiance, the other still clutching the stick end of the umbrella. "A curse on you and Moishe and all the children who come after you—"

"Your heart," Rose cried, before turning to appeal directly to Avital. "Please, take him outside. Take him outside before your grandfather kills himself...or somebody else."

Avital snapped back to reality. Grabbing Ethan by the arm, she began dragging him down the hallway, heading outside. She was just about to exit onto the street when she looked back. Her grandfather was clutching his chest, tumbling to the floor. The last words she heard sent a shiver down her spine.

"Call an ambulance!" her mother said. "Josh! Now! Call 9-1-1."

FORTY

Avital spent the rest of the night at the hospital. With each passing hour, the news only got worse. *Zeyde* had experienced a heart attack. *Zeyde* needed emergency surgery. *Zeyde* was in the ICU, on a breathing tube, to see if he would wake up. After five hours, her parents went home to get some sleep, while her brother dropped Melinda off at home, but Avital, wracked with guilt, remained behind.

Ethan appeared at the end of the hall. Dressed in a pair of slacks and a white button-down, he had removed his hamantashen costume. He had a cup of something hot in one hand and a plastic bag in the other. Ethan took a seat beside Avital on the bench.

"How is he doing?" Ethan asked.

"He still hasn't woken up."

Ethan nodded. Putting the cup down and sifting through the bag, he began pulling out items. "I got you some low-acid coffee," he said, trying to be helpful. "And some dinner.

There's salad, and a tuna sandwich… I did my best to find you IC-safe stuff…but there weren't many options around the hospital."

She put the coffee and the food to the side. Truthfully, the last thing she felt like doing was eating. All she could think about was her grandfather, lying in a hospital bed, his very last thoughts being that his own granddaughter had betrayed him. *Avital, Avital…how could you let this happen?*

Ethan moved to take her hand. Avital pulled it away. She couldn't bear to look him in the eyes. Ethan read the room and, leaning back in his seat, sighed.

"I guess this is when I finally get fired, huh?" he asked quietly.

She nodded. "I wish it could be different."

"Me, too."

Avital took a deep breath. In the silence that passed over them, she could hear machines beeping, ventilators pumping—the grand finale to a great affair that was dead on arrival.

"I wanted to tell you," she said quietly, "how much these last few months have meant to me, how much getting to know you has meant to me. You took my whole world and you changed it for the better, and I want you to know that I appreciate the joy you brought back into my life."

Ethan swallowed. "We don't have to give each other up, Avi."

She touched his cheek. "Yes, we do. You need to go home and figure out what to do with your family. And I need to stay here and figure out what to do with mine. I'm asking that you give me the time to do that, Ethan. That you respect me enough, and the difficulty of this decision, to not contact me again after tonight."

Ethan pressed his lips together. "If that's what you want—"

"It's what I need, Ethan."

"Well, Avi—" he choked on his words "—when have I ever been able to deny you?"

Tears gathered in the corners of her eyes. She blinked them back, looking away. Down the hall, two nurses were laughing at something on a cell phone.

There was still one thing Avital needed to do. Reaching into her pocket, she felt for the neatly folded piece of scrap paper she had borrowed from a nurse earlier that evening.

"So now what?" Ethan said, his voice quivering.

"Now," Avital said and met his eyes directly, "we say goodbye."

"Would it be terrible of me to ask for one last hug?"

Avital laughed, tears fully coming now. "No. In fact, I would like that very much."

They rose from the bench. He wrapped his arms around her. She breathed him in, trying to commit his touch to memory, trying to hold on to his scent, before finally slipping the piece of paper into his peacoat pocket.

"Avital Cohen," Ethan whispered, "you go and have the best damn life."

She nodded, pulling away from him. Ethan let her go. Moving backward, a bittersweet smile splashed across his red cheeks, he offered a wave goodbye. Avital touched her heart and, with a gentle nod and a shrug of their shoulders, they both accepted it was over. Ethan turned from her, his shoes making a squeaky sound against the hospital flooring, and walked away, as promised, through the door and down the stairs, without so much as glancing back.

FORTY-ONE

"Good evening, sir."

Outside the hospital, Stephen was waiting by the limousine. Now that Ethan had been found out and everyone knew he was a Lippmann, there was no point in continuing the con with grand efforts such as public transportation. In full view of any person walking by or even looking out a window, Ethan dipped into the back seat.

Stephen took his position at the front.

"I was surprised to hear from you this evening," he said, glancing up to speak to him through the rearview mirror. "Even more surprised to be picking you up from the hospital. Hopefully everything is okay?"

Ethan huffed a sad little puff of air through his nostrils. "Not really."

"You're not ill, are you, sir?"

It was nice of Stephen to be concerned for his well-being.

"No," Ethan said, unbuttoning his jacket. "I was actually there for...a friend."

"Well, I'm glad to hear you're all right." Stephen smiled. "And where will I be taking you tonight, sir?"

Ethan ran through his options. He could go to a hotel. He could go to a bar. But it was late. Ethan was emotionally and physically exhausted. For now, all he wanted to do was sleep.

"Just take me home," he said.

"Of course."

Leaving the hospital, the limo snaked its way through the streets of Brooklyn. Ethan sighed and, staring out the window at the city, tried not to let the hurt, pressing against his chest, overtake him. But he was going to miss her. She was the best thing to have ever happened to him.

Slinking down in his seat, he tried to get comfortable. It was weird. It had taken him forever to get used to taking the bus to work. But suddenly, it was the limo that felt strange and impractical. He couldn't get comfortable. He switched seats, before taking his jacket off entirely, tossing it into the seat across from him. In the process, a slip of paper fell to the floor by his feet. Bending down, he picked it up, reading the words scribbled across the front. He switched seats, before taking his jacket off entirely. He tossed his wool peacoat to the seat across from him, and a small slip of paper fell to the floor by his feet. Bending down, he picked it up and read the words written in blue block print across the front.

Because I Know Who You Are

It had to be from Avital.

Hands shaking, he opened up the scrap paper. And then, Ethan completely lost it. The emotions he had held back tonight—the emotions he didn't want to share with Avital, because he knew it would hurt her—rose to the fore. His chest spasmed, caught. His stomach roiled. Because there, hastily written down on the inside of that page, was the Cohen family recipe for pumpkin-spiced babka.

"Avi," he said, running his hand through his hair. "No..."

It killed him. It smashed him like the glass at the end of a Jewish wedding—a million disparate pieces, a thousand unanswered questions, running through his mind. Why would she do it? Why would she even risk handing over something so precious? Didn't she know he was a disaster, a failure...a nothing? But then, turning the piece of paper back over, he read the words on the front one more time.

The urge to tell Stephen to turn the car around was overwhelming. All he wanted was to go back to Avital, find her in the hallway, make her reconsider. But he had also learned from their journey together that love wasn't safe unless it came with good boundaries...and so he squelched the impulse.

Turning the paper over and scanning her recipe again, he read the ingredients. It was your typical babka recipe. Nothing that special or surprising outside of the bananas. The recipe called for a ton of bananas, in fact. Almost four per batch. Ethan couldn't help but think back on his trip to the wholesale market with Josh.

He should have guessed. People didn't realize that bananas could often be used as a good replacement for sugar. Aside from making a product moister, the taste was often completely eradicated thanks to the addition of other, more prominent ingredients. In this case, and in this recipe, it was the pumpkin and chocolate. He knew it was possible, because before changing bananas out for a cheaper brand of white sugar, Lippmann's had done the same exact thing with their pumpkin crumble doughnut.

His mouth went dry at the thought.

No. It couldn't be. Could his grandfather have had the recipe for pumpkin-spiced babka all along? It didn't make sense. Why would his grandfather set him up in such a horrible way? And yet, comparing the stories that Avital had told him, knowing the old man, it seemed more possible than ever. Still, Ethan needed to be sure. Popping up from his seat, he lowered the privacy divider.

"Actually," Ethan said to Stephen, "change of plans. Would you mind taking me over to Lippmann's corporate headquarters?"

"Of course, sir," the driver said. "Planning on a late night?"

"Possibly."

"Well," Stephen said, meeting his eyes in the rearview mirror, "it's nice to see things getting back to normal."

Normal. The word caused Ethan to bubble with rage. Stephen found an exit and, taking the ramp, headed toward the lights of Manhattan. Ethan settled into his seat, his fatigue fully lifting, and prepared himself for the fight of his life.

FORTY-TWO

"Good morning, Grandpa."

Ethan had been waiting at the head of the dining-room table when Moishe, having just awoken and looking for breakfast, wandered past. Turning on the light, squinting across the large table, Ethan could tell that Moishe had not expected to see him.

"You're up early," Moishe said.

"Technically," Ethan corrected him, "I'm up late."

Ethan had not slept that night. After going to Lippmann's headquarters, he'd found the original recipe for the pumpkin crumble doughnut and confirmed his sneaking suspicion regarding the old man. After which, he promptly came home, packed a bag full of clothing and other necessary items, and took a seat at the dining table.

"Huh," Moishe grunted, unfazed, and moved toward the kitchen.

"I wouldn't bother," Ethan called over his shoulder. "I told

Freya to take the morning off. If you want breakfast, you'll have to make it yourself."

"Why would you do something like that?"

"Sit down, Grandpa," Ethan said, folding his hands calmly in front of him. "You and I need to have a family meeting."

He was somewhat surprised that the old man actually obeyed. Moving to the table, Moishe took a seat at the far end across from Ethan with his eyes gazing out the window, sitting sideways with an arm draped over the backrest of his chair. Ethan couldn't help but notice that all his body language seemed to want to avoid this confrontation.

Ethan let the silence linger between them, before digging into his pocket. Pulling out the recipe from Avital, he held it firmly between two fingers.

"I have it," Ethan said.

"You have...what?" Moishe barked.

Ethan did not jump. "The Cohen family recipe for pumpkin-spiced babka."

Moishe grumbled, shifting in his seat a little. It was interesting how his grandfather responded. There were no accolades, taunts, or threats. Indeed, judging by the way he slumped in his chair, waving one finger in Ethan's direction while searching for words, it didn't seem like his grandfather even cared.

"Well," Moishe said finally, "good for you."

"That's it?"

"What do you want me to say?"

"I don't know," Ethan said and shrugged. "That you're happy?"

"Of course I'm happy," Moishe said, pivoting in his seat toward Ethan. "So, come on... Hand it over."

"I don't think so." Ethan put the recipe away. "Everything in life is transactional, right? Isn't that what you always taught me? Why give something away for free when you can get something better in return?"

"You want to play games, boy?"

"I want a fair deal."

"I'm your grandfather!" Moishe shouted.

Ethan shrugged again. "Business isn't personal."

Moishe played with the bottom of his chin. He could see the old man's wheels turning. He thought he was smarter than Ethan, better than him. He thought Ethan was a chump who could be easily manipulated.

"All right." Moishe smirked. "I'll play. What do you want?"

"I want you to give me power of attorney over Kayla."

Moishe's response was immediate. He scoffed. "Absolutely not."

"Why not?" Ethan said. "You're always saying she's a burden and a chore. You barely visit her. So I'm giving you an out, Grandpa. I'm giving you two things you've always wanted. You can have the recipe…and I'll take over responsibility for Kayla's care. Win-win situation. We both get what we want."

Ethan could see the rage building in splotches of red across his grandfather's cheeks. Because he was caught, cornered at the end of the table. All the lies, all the benefit of the doubt that Ethan had given him, were now being brought into the light.

"What's the matter, Grandpa?" Ethan asked.

"I'm not giving you Kayla," he shouted.

"Why not?"

"Because she's my granddaughter!"

Ethan remained cool and collected. All his years of dealing with the old man during rage-nadoes had given him an epic poker face.

"But don't you want the recipe?" Ethan asked. "You told

me it was the only way to save the company. You told me it was revenge for all the wrongs that Chayim Cohen and his family had done to you over the years. Isn't garnering this recipe the most important thing?"

His grandfather swallowed. "Fine," he snapped. "Give me the recipe, and I'll call the attorneys after breakfast."

"Call them now."

"It's seven o'clock in the morning, Ethan. The offices aren't even—"

"Call...them...now."

He rose, wobbling over to the adjacent room, where a rotary phone sat on top of an antique console. Picking it up, he began dialing the number. Even though the ringing on the line was distant, it cut through the silence. It rang once, twice, three times...before Moishe slammed down the phone. Standing there, he huffed, eyes cast down.

"What's the matter, Grandpa?"

"The matter?" he snapped. "You're a failure. A disaster. What do you think you can do for her, huh? You have nothing. Nothing, Ethan. I'll hand over control but will still be paying for her care. How is that fair to me, Ethan? When I've given you everything. When I'm made you the man you are today. Everything you have, everything you are...is because of me."

"Actually," Ethan said, "it's the opposite."

"What nonsense are you talking?"

"Everything I am, everything I have...it's in spite of you."

His grandfather was stunned into silence.

"Take a seat, Grandpa."

Reluctantly, Moishe left the phone behind and wobbled back to the table.

"You don't remember it," Ethan said, shrugging slightly. "Then again, why would you? It was just another summer to you. I was fourteen years old, and you decided I was going to work at Lippmann's headquarters, learning the ropes. Do you remember what my first job there was, as an intern, working twelve-hour days?"

Moishe pursed his lips but remained silent.

"Again," Ethan said simply, "why would you? But I remember. You sat me down in a room full of boxes, which were full of old papers from the fifties and the sixties, and you told me to digitize and record every page, creating a database. You know what was in those boxes, Grandpa? You know what I typed up and saw, over and over again? The original Lippmann's recipes..."

Ethan reached into his pocket, pulling out the recipe from Lippmann's. And then, finding Avital's recipe, he held them both up for comparison.

"They're exactly the same, Grandpa," Ethan said, before pushing both recipes across the table. "Yours was modified for a longer shelf life, obviously...but the pumpkin crumble doughnut is basically a small version of their babka. And you had to have known that. Because who else puts bananas in a recipe that calls for pumpkin spice? So of course... I'm sitting here and asking myself, did Moishe steal the recipe, or did Chayim?"

All the color drained from Moishe's face.

"But it's not so simple, is it?" Ethan said. "Because then, I took a walk over to the legal department. Lucky me. I spent a summer working there, too. And I started pulling out all those old lawsuits and depositions between you and Chayim Cohen. And do you know what story those documents told, Grandpa? It told the story of two old men, best friends since childhood, who had created those recipes over Shabbat with their wives together. It told the story of two men, constantly in competition with each other, who'd had a falling-out."

"You don't understand," Moishe defended himself. "He kicked me out of the business. He took everything I had and—"

Ethan ignored his rambling and instead pulled out his phone, scrolling to the image he had collected while hunting through Lippmann's for the truth. "Actually," Ethan said, "I wrote this part down just so I would have it. I believe the judge referred to your conflict as 'the most immature and irritating that has ever graced my courtroom, and if I had the power, I would throw you both in jail for wasting so much of the court's valuable time.'" Ethan sucked back air. "That's quite an indictment, Grandpa."

Growing more agitated, Moishe's voice shattered into a staccato of pieces as he spoke. "It's not true. He stole that recipe from me. He gave me no choice but to open Greatest Babka across the street."

"Well," Ethan said, putting his phone away, "the truth usually lies somewhere in the middle. The only thing I know for certain is that there are no good guys or bad guys in this story. Just a whole bunch of broken, messed-up people...some better than others at living with the things that have hurt them."

"You don't understand." Moishe turned red. The quiver in his speech now sounded like the coughing, choking spasm of oncoming tears. "We were friends. We were best friends... We built that business together, and he didn't even call me... he didn't even contact me after your mother died!"

"Finally," Ethan said, sighing heavily. "The truth. All the bickering and hatred—all the myths that eventually devolved into frivolous back-and-forth lawsuits—sending me into Best Babka on this ridiculous mission. All of it came about because two old men, who were once best friends developing recipes in a kitchen together, couldn't admit how much they missed the other."

"Ethan…"

"You could have just picked up the phone, you know," Ethan said.

"Just hear me out."

"No," Ethan said, cutting him off. "No more lies. No more games."

"Please."

"Your love is so toxic," Ethan said, shaking his head. "You have no boundaries. You're a bully, and a tyrant…and the saddest part about that, Grandpa, is you've created the very thing you fear. You have no one left. You're alone in this world."

"Stop." Moishe began to weep. "No more."

"Believe it or not," Ethan said, "I'm not saying these things to hurt you. You and I are different in this way. It doesn't make me feel better to see you upset. It doesn't lessen my hurt, either. But I'm telling you these things, rather than just leaving, because there's some hope in my heart that you and I can work on healing from this point forward. Because I do love you, Grandpa. I will always love you. But I'm not going to permit any more of your abuse in my life."

Ethan rose from the table. Grabbing his backpack from the floor, he headed toward the door. Moishe lifted his red eyes in Ethan's direction. "Where are you going?"

"I'm leaving."

"What?" Moishe said, rising to his feet. "You can't leave."

From there, it was his typical onslaught, followed by threats and promises. Ethan didn't hang around to hear them. Leaving his grandfather behind, he sprinted away, racing through empty rooms full of expensive antiques, landing in the foyer.

He was just about to leave, walk out the double doors of that haunted mansion forever, when someone called his name. Randy was standing in the middle of the staircase. White socks pulled up to his ankles, frizzy hair all disheveled, he glanced toward the dining room where Moishe was still screaming for Ethan to come back.

"Got your note," Randy said.

"I didn't want to wake you."

Randy came down the stairs. "Finally told the mean old goat off, then?"

He nodded. "Yep."

Randy smiled. "'Bout damn time."

Ethan couldn't help but laugh. It felt like they were little kids again—two brothers, innocent and hopeful, them against the world.

"Do you know where you're going?" Randy asked.

"No idea."

"But you're not coming back?"

"No."

Randy nodded, and then, opening his arms wide, he moved in for a hug. The two brothers spent a few moments locked in a tight embrace.

"I'm proud of you, bro," Randy said.

"You know what, Randy?" Ethan said, looking at his little brother, finally seeing him fully. "I'm proud of you, too."

Randy swallowed, overwhelmed. And then, Ethan left the Lippmann compound for good.

Standing on the driveway, gazing out past the trees and forests, he felt as if the whole world welcomed his arrival. Despite all the uncertainty—the very real lack of a path spread out before him—he found himself, for the first time in his life, able to breathe.

FORTY-THREE

Ethan awoke to the painful sensation of someone smashing a vacuum cleaner into his ankles. Blinking his eyes open, pulling his legs up and out of harm's way, it took him several seconds to remember that he was currently couch-surfing at Kayla's, and Tony—one of the custodians on staff at Hebrew Home for Assisted Living—was not at all pleased to see him.

"Sorry, Tony," Ethan said apologetically.

Tony responded by pulling out the vacuum plug and heading to the next room. Ethan didn't mean to be a burden, but since leaving the Lippmann compound, he was desperately trying to figure out next steps…all while saving money.

Sitting up from his less than restful sleep, cracking his aching lower back, he scanned the room for Kayla. She had taken a break from building her Lippmann cardboard-box city in order to eat breakfast.

Ethan smiled. "Morning, Kayla."

It always made him feel good to see her. Kayla responded

to his morning greeting by dipping her waffle into a plastic cup of maple syrup.

She was a bright spot in his life, a constant source of love and cheerfulness. Beyond all these things…she had a couch and didn't seem to mind him crashing on it. Unfortunately, the staff at Hebrew Home for Assisted Living didn't share her sentiment.

"Ethan," Melinda whispered, peeking her head through the threshold, "you're still here?"

"I'm still here," Ethan confirmed unhappily.

He had debated using his savings to get a hotel room. Or even heading out to rent an apartment. But he had learned a few valuable lessons while working at Best Babka.

The first was that, in the real world, every penny counted. He also really didn't want to spend money without some sort of a game plan. What if he needed those ten or fifteen dollars later on down the road for something more important? He thought back to the way Avital had agonized for days over paint colors and suddenly understood the depth of her trepidation.

The other part, of course, was that some part of him was still waiting for his grandfather to retaliate for what had happened in his dining room.

Ethan hadn't checked his bank accounts, because he was determined not to take a cent from his grandfather ever again. But he had come to Kayla's room, in part because he wanted to be there if Moishe suddenly ordered them to toss her on the street. Thankfully, it had been three days, and bills for Kayla were still being paid.

"Listen," Melinda said, stepping into the room, "I know you're sort of in a situation right now, what with the whole being a Lippmann thing, and Chayim Cohen in the hospital, and Avital dumping you… But you really can't keep sleeping here. My supervisor is coming back from vacation this week, and the custodial staff is complaining about you making their jobs harder."

He had figured that out by the vacuum-bashing he received.

He bit back the urge to ask Melinda for more information on the Cohens and, by extension, Avital. He had made a promise to her, after all, and didn't want to overstep boundaries. Plus, inquiring would put Melinda—now Josh's official girlfriend—in an awkward position.

"I promise," Ethan said, "I'll be out of here by tomorrow."

"Thank you, Ethan."

Melinda flitted from the room. Ethan sighed, looking back over to his sister. She had finished her waffle and was now happily picking at her scrambled eggs.

He wasn't sure how much she understood of the situation, how much she could garner from his conversations with Melinda—or what he had told her, directly—but at least she was a willing ear. Ethan laid his head on her shoulder.

"What am I gonna do, Kayla?"

Kayla responded by handing him an apple.

"Thank you," Ethan said, taking a bite.

With a happy trill, she left her tray of food. Returning to her arts-and-crafts project on the floor, she grabbed a pair of scissors, cutting another rectangle from the inside of a Lippmann's box. For the last three days, Kayla had been doing nothing but cutting out tiny rectangles, before scribbling a cross—or a *t*, he wasn't sure—inside each one. Everywhere Ethan looked, rectangles with crosses inside of them lined the room.

Still, Ethan was nervous. At any point, Moishe could take Kayla away. He didn't want Kayla to think he had abandoned her if his grandfather suddenly decided to deny Ethan visitation. Taking a seat beside her, he tried to break the news gently.

"Kayla," Ethan said softly, "can you stop making rectangles for a second?"

Kayla responded by handing him a rectangle.

"No, Kayla," Ethan said, ignoring her, "I need you to listen to me, okay? This is important. I might not... I might not be able to come visit you for a while. But I want you to know that even if you don't see me for a while, I love you, okay? I love you so darn much."

Kayla responded by handing him another rectangle.

"Kayla, please..."

Another rectangle.

Ethan sighed. Maybe it was pointless. Maybe he was so desperate for understanding, for a friend, after all these years, he was simply reading into the tiny gurgles and paper cutouts. And then, Kayla picked up two handfuls of rectangles and tossed them at his chest.

"I know," Ethan said, pressing his lips together. "I see that you're making rectangles."

Kayla huffed.

"You want me to help you?" he asked, moving to pick up the scissors again.

This time, Kayla slapped his hand away. The smack caused Ethan to take notice. Kayla had never tried to get his attention in such a personally physical way.

"What?" Ethan said. "I don't understand."

She picked up another rectangle, forcing it into his hand.

"Kayla..." Ethan rubbed his left temple. "I don't..."

And that was when he saw it.

The project his sister worked so hard on wasn't a hodge-podge of shapes or some way to process trauma...it was Flatbush Avenue. Rudimentary, of course. Certain aspects clearly developed from her imagination, based on all the things Ethan had told her over the years, but it was definitely Flatbush in Brooklyn.

The pathway going down the middle was the road. The large rectangles scaling up the side were buildings. Even her periodic colors and tin foil—they were trees and mailboxes. And the rectangles he was holding in his hand, the ones with the crosses scribbled in them, they were windows. Until finally, he figured out which of the rectangles was Best Babka...

"Oh, Kayla," Ethan said, his heart filling. "I understand."

He wrapped one arm around her, pulling her closer to him. All this time, all his visits where he had confided in her every aspect of his life—all the times the doctors said she was incapable of understanding or communicating... Kayla had been listening. She had heard every word.

Ethan picked up one of her windows.

"When God closes a door," he said, holding it between them, "find a damn window, right?"

Kayla nodded happily, putting one of those windows between her lips, before returning to her art project.

Ethan's heart landed in his stomach. His sister had so much faith in him. Avital had so much faith in him. Really, what he needed now was to find that same faith in himself. It wasn't easy...pulling yourself out of a foxhole.

His gaze returned to Kayla's miniature city. From the storefront Best Babka, across Flatbush Avenue, to the construction-paper building representing Greatest Babka, which had sat empty all these years.

The rest happened in an instant. A flash of an idea. A million different pieces, combining into one perfect plan...at least, a potentially perfect plan. He needed a phone. Unfortunately, Moishe had cut Ethan's cell phone off—along with all access to any family money—shortly after Ethan left the Lippmann family compound for good.

Standing up, racing to the nurses' station, Ethan found Melinda in the middle of a conversation with another nurse. Ethan interrupted. "Can I borrow your phone?"

"What?"

"Your phone," Ethan said, waving toward her purse. "Please! I wouldn't ask if it weren't important."

Melinda didn't hesitate. Digging her cell phone out of her purse, she handed it to Ethan. He wasted no time calling his brother. "Randy," Ethan said, the moment he picked up, "it's me. Ethan. Listen, I have an idea. Don't tell anybody where you're going. Don't tell Grandpa, especially. Just meet me at Hebrew Home for Assisted Living."

"I mean," Randy said, stalling, "I was just about to get high."

"Randy!"

"I'm kidding, dude," Randy said. "Of course I'll be there. We're brothers, right?"

Ethan allowed that lump of feeling in his throat to remain. "I love you, Randy."

"I love you, too, bro."

Ethan hung up, handing it back to Melinda, before pointing at printer paper and pens from her desk. "Do you mind if I take this?"

"I guess not," Melinda said.

"Thank you." He gathered the items and sprinted down the hall, turning to call back to her, "Thank you for everything. You have no idea how much you've helped me."

Ethan returned to Kayla's room. Landing on the floor beside her, spreading out the papers, he grabbed one of her crayons, before beginning to sketch the edges of a large graph. Kayla watched him curiously, fingers in her mouth. "You know, Kayla," Ethan said, looking up from his own art project now, "I wish you would have mentioned earlier that you were a genius."

Ethan and Randy spent the next six hours splayed out on the floor of Kayla's room. Together, they tallied up costs. Anticipated difficulties. Figured out numbers. They argued a lot, too. Until finally, with the sun setting over Hebrew Home for Assisted Living, Ethan gathered up a stack of loose-leaf pages into one document, stapling them together. They were done. Now, the only thing left to do before putting their plan in place was to say good-bye to their sister.

Ethan and Randy both took a seat on the floor.

"Hey, Kayla," Ethan said, taking the windows out of her hand in order to attract her full attention. "Randy and I might have to go away for a while. If that happens, we might not be able to visit you as much as we have."

Kayla turned her nose upward, concerned.

Randy jumped in. "But we promise you, okay?" he said, reaching over to take her hand. "We're gonna come back for you. We're not forgetting about you or leaving you behind. You're always gonna be our big sister. And we're always, always gonna take care of you." Randy turned to Ethan, his entire face wrinkling with concern. "Right, Ethan?"

Ethan didn't hesitate. "Absolutely."

"We love you, K," Randy said finally. "I love you."

Kayla seemed to understand, because she leaned over, pressing one hand each to their knees, as if giving them permission. The brothers took that as their cue. Randy put his hand on Kayla's shoulder, and Ethan did the same, the triangle they made on the floor a shared promise between them.

"Well, look at that," Randy said, his lips edging into a faint smile. "The Rosenberg siblings, back together again."

Ethan laughed. Kayla beamed. Randy turned red in the cheeks. But with all their good-byes spent, the two brothers headed out, eager to begin putting their plan into place.

The future was unknown and terrifying—but it was theirs. The Rosenberg siblings would no longer be bound up in the whims and abuses of their grandfather. Wherever their parents were, Ethan was certain they were proud.

FORTY-FOUR

"Randy," Ethan whispered through the darkness in knee-high grass, "maybe we should come back in the morning?"

Randy spun around and aimed his flashlight directly in Ethan's eyes. "It's fine," he said, once again attempting to alleviate his brother's fears. "Why are you so freaked-out, anyway?"

Ethan shielded his eyes from the light. It was one thing to be creeping up on one of New York State's largest cannabis dispensaries in broad daylight, but he didn't feel great about creeping up on a weed grow in the middle of the night.

"I— It's just..." Ethan stammered.

"What?" Randy said, annoyed.

"This seems like a great way to get shot."

Randy huffed, annoyed. "Rabbi Jason is antiviolence." He turned back to his path through the overgrowth. "Besides, your way is more likely to get Lyme disease out here."

"Great."

"Come on," Randy said. "Rabbi Jason lives just beyond that fence."

The fence was over six feet high and was surrounded by barbed wire. A small rounded door with a latch hook greeted their arrival. Ethan grimaced. This did not look like a fence designed to welcome visitors, especially those trailing through two-foot weeds in the middle of the night. Unconcerned, Randy went to open it.

Ethan put out a hand, moving to stop him. "Randy."

Randy jumped. "Dude!" he said, clutching his heart. "Can you stop acting so nervous?"

"Sorry, but do you really think that's a good idea?" Ethan said, nodding to the gate.

Randy rolled his eyes, pushing the door open. "He never arms it."

Ethan frowned. "Seriously?"

"For real, man," Randy shook his head. "If you're gonna be in the drug trade, you need to calm the hell down about crawling through tick-infested unknowns at two o'clock in the morning."

His brother had a point.

"Anyway," Randy said, "we're almost there, *thank freaking God*. We just gotta go through the fairy garden."

Ethan mouthed the words *fairy garden*.

It was, indeed, just that. A miraculous little farm of triangle-shaped plants, growing in neat and tidy rows, for several hundred feet. Interspersed between the flowering plants were fairy lights, tiny mobiles of Jewish stars, and stained-glass hamzas.

"Wow," Ethan said. "So is this his grow garden? It's nice... but it doesn't look like one hundred and forty thousand square feet of bud."

"Dude." Randy stopped. "No. This is his own personal stash."

"Oh."

"That," Randy said, shining his flashlight into the distance, where three giant warehouses stood illuminated by lights. "That is the Holy Rollers grow garden. It is a place of epic majesty that only the luckiest of cannabis advocates and distributors can enter. Also, bro...don't call it bud."

"You call it bud," Ethan reminded him.

"Yeah, but I'm the drug guy. You're the business guy. It sounds weird...drug terms...coming out of your straitlaced mouth. It keeps freaking me out."

"I'll try to remember that."

They approached a small, but equally charming, wood-framed house. A black cat sat on a seventies-era rocking chair and greeted their arrival with a loud meow. Randy responded by giving the kitty a scratch behind the ears.

"Hey, Mooshie," Randy said. "Your owner home?"

The cat responded by jumping off the seat and wedging his body between Ethan's legs. Ethan was just about to bend down and introduce himself, when the front door of house flew open. Rabbi Jason was standing there—in nothing but a white T-shirt, *tzitzith*, and a *kippah*—holding a twelve-inch purple bong in one hand.

Rabbi Jason seemed unbothered by the lack of modesty in the midst of a surprise visit. Waving the bong around as he spoke, his Hebrew National hot dog kept peeking out from beneath his shirt. Ethan attempted to avert his eyes.

"Randy." Rabbi Jason smiled. "Ethan. What a pleasant surprise. I see you've met my guard cat."

"Sorry to bother you so late, Rabbi," Randy said.

"For you—" Rabbi Jason beamed "—it's never too late. I was just finishing up a workshop on tantric lovemaking.

You've arrived at the perfect time." A naked woman—breasts exposed, belly full of curves and ripples—walked by in the background.

"Oh, dear God," Ethan said, covering his eyes.

Rabbi Jason, unfazed, took a long inhale of his bong. After blowing out three perfect ringlets in the direction of the sky, he angled his purple monster at Ethan. "You want some?"

"Unfortunately," Randy said, interrupting the offer, "we're not here to get high."

Rabbi Jason grew concerned. "Why ever not?"

Randy dipped his chin toward Ethan, who took that as his cue. Pulling out their proposal—ignoring the fact that their only hope for independence was both super high and half-naked—Ethan began his spiel.

"Actually," Ethan said, displaying the document before them, "we're here with a business proposition."

"A business proposition?" Rabbi Jason asked curiously.

"Something that will benefit us both," Randy said.

"Something you've been wanting to do for a long time," Ethan said, leaning in for the hard sell. "A way to help those in our community. A chance to engage in social justice and *tikkun olam*, all while educating the public about the medical benefits of cannabis. This here…is the chance do good deeds together, build goodwill in the community, and turn a profit."

"*Tikkun olam*, you say?" Rabbi Jason stroked the bottom of his beard. After a few thoughtful moments, he stepped back from the threshold. "Well, all right, then," he said, welcoming them both inside, "let's see what you two have for me."

NISSAN

(April–May)

FORTY-FIVE

"Thank you so much, Mrs. Grossman!" Avital waved from the doorway. *"Chag Pesach Sameach!"*

Avital waited just long enough for Mrs. Grossman to disappear halfway down the block before closing the door, turning the lock, and placing the sign that read Closed for Passover firmly in the window. Spinning around in her spot, she found Josh, along with the entire staff of Best Babka, waiting for her to make the call, eyes eager with anticipation.

"I am pleased to announce—" Avital smiled, reaching behind her back to remove her apron "—that we are, officially, on vacation."

"Let the feasting begin," Josh said, popping a bottle of kosher champagne.

A round of cheers exploded from the room.

The holiday of Passover celebrated the Israelite exodus from slavery in Egypt. In a rush to escape, the ancient Israelite people did not have time for their bread to rise. In commemoration of this event, modern-day Jews abstained from eating chametz, or leavening, for seven days in Israel, and eight days in the diaspora. Because the commandment also included removal and possession, Jews often spent several days thoroughly cleaning their homes and kitchens to make sure that all containers and kitchen tools were free of chametz.

As a kosher bakery, it was too much work to *kasher* all their kitchens to receive a proper *hechsher*, or seal of approval to sell kosher for Passover products. And so for the holiday of Passover, everybody got the week off. Best Babka would be closed for nine days. As such, it was a tradition to pull out and eat all their own chametz for one final send-off before the holiday started.

Avital laid her apron on the counter, while the rest of the Best Babka staff made their way to the back kitchen.

"You coming, Avi?" Josh said, waving her to follow.

"I'll be there in a minute." She smiled. "I just have a few things to finish up in my office."

"Well, don't take too long," Tootles warned her. "We're running low on my salmon bacon bourekas."

Avital heeded his warning before returning to her office. Taking a seat at her desk, she put the finishing touches on her Passover post for social media, reminding everyone that they would be closed for the holiday. She went to the bathroom. And then, straightening up piles of paper and making sure she had a neatly defined list of to-dos for their return, she headed for the door, taking one final glance at the place. The office was spotless. Not just like she was getting ready to go away for a week…but like someone planning to leave.

"Avi," Tootles said, beckoning to her as she entered the kitchen, "come on. Sit down over here."

Tootles made room at the table, and Avi slid down beside him.

"We were just talking about Ethan," Chaya said.

"Ethan." Avital met Josh's eyes across the table. "Really?"

"We were wondering if you've heard from him," Sara said.

It had been nearly a month since Purim, and Avital had not heard one single peep from Ethan. Of course his name came up. *What happened to Ethan? Ethan made really good hamantashen. I wonder where Ethan is now.* Once, Josh had even caught Tootles crying hysterically into his Little Buddy hat. But to Avital, all of it seemed irrelevant. Ethan was gone. From what she could tell, he had disappeared off the face of the earth.

"I'm afraid I haven't heard anything," Avital said.

"I still can't believe he was a Lippmann," Tootles said.

"And a gazillionaire," Chaya offered up.

"You would have never guessed," Tootles mused. "Such a down-to-earth guy. What's that word you used for him, Marty?"

Marty was happy to translate. "He was a mensch!"

"Yeah." Tootles sniffed. "To think...all of this drama for some recipe he didn't even need to steal."

The table fell into an uncomfortable silence. Avital couldn't help but notice that all eyes—except for Josh's—were going in her direction. Her twin brother wasn't engaging in the out-loud pondering. Instead, he was staring at his plate, not eating.

After that night in the hospital with Ethan, a lot had happened. Josh had been furious with her. Avital had been wracked with guilt. Her grandfather was still in critical condition in the hospital. She went to work, each day, dreading the uncomfortable tension that met her in the hallways. The tension that came because she had risked it all...and for what?

She wasn't prepared to use the word *love*. But the experience had forced her to do some serious soul-searching.

And then, one Shabbat, with Chayim still in the hospital—and her brother still furious with Avital—Rose Cohen broke through the awkward silence ruining their Shabbat dinner.

"Go right on ahead and hate Ethan Lippmann," she had said, pointing an accusatory finger at every single one of them. "But your grandfather is in the hospital, the grandchildren are caught in the middle, and this *meshuganas* has gone on long enough!"

As it turned out, there was no pumpkin-spiced babka recipe to steal. Moishe and Chayim, along with their wives, Lilly and Rose, had developed it together, back in one of those small shared kitchens, when they were hosting Shabbat dinners.

"Oh, you would never believe it," her *bubbe* had said. "Growing up, those two were inseparable. But also constantly in competition with each other…neither one knowing when to call a draw. Cards, checkers, grades, girls. I tell you, one couldn't take a piss without the other pulling out his *shmeckle* and trying to outshoot him."

There were other interesting parts of the story, too. Like Lilly and Rose, hanging out for years as besties unbeknownst to their husbands, frequently sneaking off to have a girls' night together, and once even going on a cruise.

"She hated it as much as me," Rose had said, thinking back on their lives together, "but what could we do? These men… they were our husbands. Different times back then. You did what your husband said, and you kept quiet about it."

For the Cohen family, the news was earth-shattering. All of them were now forced to reevaluate the stories that had carried through all their lives. But after her grandmother's Shabbat confession, things returned to some version of normal.

Her grandfather got better and was eventually able to go home. Josh stopped being angry at her. And as was so often the case with these things, people began forgetting why they were even angry at Ethan to begin with and simply found themselves missing him. If Avital were being honest with herself, she missed him, too.

"Have you tried to call him, Avi?" Chaya asked gently.

Avital slumped. "I did."

"And?" Tootles's eyebrows lifted in anticipation.

Avital shook her head. "It's just…over."

Once the truth was revealed to all, including the staff at Best Babka, Avital had tried to call Ethan. She wanted him to know what his grandfather had done, but the line had been disconnected. Avital took the dead dial tone as a sign that he had fully returned to his life as Ethan Lippmann.

"Well…" Tootles said, breaking through the sadness spreading through the room. Standing up from his seat, he lifted his glass of kosher champagne high. "Let's all raise a glass to Ethan Rosenberg-Lippmann. The nicest rich dude I've ever had the pleasure of meeting. Wherever he is…I hope he's happy."

The room responded with shouts of *Hear! Hear!* All except Josh. When Avital looked up, his eyes had shifted from his plate on to her.

Avital sat on the second floor, in the tiny bedroom that Ethan had built for her, staring at the reclaimed shelves. Downstairs, most all of the Best Babka staff had finished their party and gone home for the holiday. The only person left was Josh, and Avital realized she was waiting for him.

"Can I come in?" Josh asked.

"Of course."

Avital slid over, making room on the bed for her brother. He sat down beside her. A long silence settled between them. Ethan's Little Buddy hat was resting on the shelf across from them.

"You thinking about Ethan?" Josh asked.

"Ethan," she admitted. "Life. Honestly, I'm a whole jumble of deep thoughts nowadays."

Josh rubbed the back of his neck. "I can't help but notice

you've been quiet the last few weeks." He pressed his lips together, staring at the floor. "And that your office is basically the cleanest I have ever seen it. Maybe I'm just reading into things, but as your twin brother, the person who shared a womb and bunk beds with you until the age of eight, I can't help but wonder if something is going on."

Avital nodded. "I'm thinking of cutting back my hours."

"Oh, wow."

She swallowed, gathering her courage. "And I was thinking of training Tootles to take over as general manager."

Josh responded to the news with a heavy, choking gasp.

Avital squeezed her eyes shut. "Don't cry."

"I'm not," Josh said, crying.

She squirmed in her seat, fists balled up at her sides. "I'm not going to be able to do this if you cry, Josh."

"Sorry," he said, blinking back tears. "Sorry. I got it—" he took one deep breath, blowing all the air out of his chest "—under control."

"And after I train up Tootles, and get everybody at Best Babka situated for the future," Avital said, reaching over to take his hand, "I've decided to leave Best Babka. I'd like you to buy out my share of the business, and let me go, Josh. I need you to let me go."

Growing up, their parents had gifted each child eleven thousand dollars a year into a special business trust. When the time came for them to retire, Josh and Avital used part of this income to purchase the business from their parents.

Along with that purchase agreement were smaller details drafted by the lawyers in regards to their partnership. If one of them should decide to walk away, any buyout agreement would be spread out over several years.

Josh was quiet for a long time. "Is it because of what happened with Ethan?"

"No," Avital said quickly, before backtracking a little. "I mean...yes. But not for the reasons you think." Josh gave her space to find her words. "You were right, you know? From the very beginning, Best Babka was never my dream. I'm here because chronic pain derailed my life plans. I'm here because I felt like I had no choice. And because it was never my dream, I made decisions that put everyone at Best Babka in jeopardy. I made decisions that placed my own needs above the needs of my employees and staff."

"Oh, Avi," Josh said sympathetically, "you're being too hard on yourself."

"I appreciate that, Josh, but let me finish." She took a deep breath. "I feel like there was a demarcation point in my life. There was the Avital before chronic pain—who could wear pants, and work reliably, and have loads of amazing sex. And then one day, I woke up...and that Avital was gone."

"You're still the same Avital to me," Josh said.

"Stop," she said, cutting him off. "Stop saying that. Because it's not true. People always say, *Don't make your disease your identity.* And you know what, Josh? I hate that statement. I think it's the most ableist thing I've ever heard. The very definition of *chronic* is that it's every day. It's something I will have to negotiate, and manage, for the rest of my life. It touches everything. The clothing I wear, the food I eat, the career I take on, my ability to have sex...my future, my faith. It touches every aspect of these things that make us human, that make us understood to other people..."

Avital squeezed his hand. "And you know what, Josh? That makes it part of my identity. Acknowledging that isn't a moral failure. It's not me trying to get attention, or wanting to be depressive, either. It's simply me describing the reality of my life. Of my day. *It just is.* And I have to acknowledge it, Josh.

I have to accept it as part of who I am going forward in order to make peace with it."

She met his eyes directly. "The Avital I was before is gone. I've been trying to get back to that person, sending out old photographs like some lifeline to the past...and it's pointless. She's never coming back. There's never going to be a future for me without chronic illness. I need to grieve who I was, all the losses that came with that demarcation point, so that I can begin to move on. And I'm telling you this, Josh...because it's okay."

Josh swallowed. "Yeah?"

"Yeah," she said, the emotion overwhelming her. "Because what I learned from my experience with Ethan is that even on the bad days...there can be good."

She reached over, taking her brother's hand across the bed. "Best Babka isn't good for my health. It's too many hours. It's too much stress. I need to focus on my health right now. But also, I want to figure out who I'm going to be in this new body, moving forward. I've realized there's still this whole amazing world out there, just waiting for me to come and discover it. But mainly, the most important thing I've realized is that if I'm going to be in pain the rest of my life, then it's even more important that I hold on to my joy. I need to create the life that makes me happy. So that when the bad days come, because they will keep coming, Josh...they don't hurt me as much."

"You are a warrior, sis."

She smiled. "I am."

And then, her twin brother—her best friend—let her go. "So," Josh said, "what are you gonna do...after I buy you out of Best Babka?"

She laughed, tears coming to her eyes. "I'm not entirely sure, yet."

KISSING KOSHER

"Seriously?"

"I was thinking of just taking some time off at first. Maybe experimenting with different jobs, see if anything really appeals to me or works better with my health issues. I'll have the money from the buyout, too, so that gives me some freedom to explore."

"Are you still going to be doing photography?"

"Definitely," she said. "But part of this next stage for me is trying new things. Who knows? Maybe I'll come to find I really like advocacy work or coloring or dog-sitting... Heck, maybe I'll come to discover I have a passion for knitting streetlamp cozies like Tootles."

Josh nodded. "You always did love a good cross-stitch."

"True." Avital laughed, thinking back to her Camp Ahava days.

"And what about health insurance?" Josh asked.

"My plan right now is to enroll under the Affordable Care Act. I looked up some rates, and it should be doable. Besides, there's always medicinal cannabis when I'm having rough days. I don't need to go to the doctors for that."

She knew that the news was hard for Josh, but Avital had never been so excited. There was a whole world out there, countless joy and reasons to continue living. Avital was ready to find it.

"So," Josh said, staring at his feet. "When do you think you'll want to be out of here by?"

"I was thinking by summer, actually."

Josh sighed. She could tell by the way he sounded, disappointed but resigned, that he had been hoping for more time. "Can I still rely on you to show up," he asked quietly, "if I ever need help with anything?"

"Oh, Josh," she said, turning to face him, "you can always rely on me."

The tears started coming again. "Gosh, Avi, how am I gonna function here without you?"

"You've never needed me here, Josh," Avital said, taking his hands in her own. "Best Babka has always been your baby. And I know you will do a great job, bringing up that baby for the next generation of the Cohen family. Also," she said, feeling the need to point this out, "remember the rule. One item at the wholesale market, under ten dollars. Bring Tootles with you if you need to."

"No kosher ham hocks for me."

"No."

She laughed. He laughed. Soon, they were devolving into childish antics, playfully pinching each other on the bed. "Let's get out of here," Josh said.

Heading downstairs, they did one final sweep of the storefront. They made sure all the trash was put out and that none of the sinks were leaking, then checked that all the lights were off and the doors locked, before heading to the parking lot together.

"So," Josh said, placing his key in the back-door lock, "this Passover we will be celebrating the Israelite exodus from Egypt…and Avital's exodus from Best Babka. I really don't think a story could feel more appropriate."

She nodded. "How else do you get to the Promised Land?"

With that, Josh locked the door behind them, and Avital took her first steps into her new and joyful life.

SIVAN

(June—July)

FORTY-SIX

It was a beautiful day in summer. Avital stood at the front counter of Best Babka, feeling the sun kissing her skin through the windows. She had officially left Best Babka as general manager and part owner over a month ago—and her return to the front counter as a favor to Josh felt like a lovely reminder. Though she was no longer a daily part of the Best Babka family, she would always be a welcome visitor.

"What are you smiling about?" Chaya said, coming to refill a tray of marzipan rainbow cookies beside her.

"I was just thinking how lovely today is," she said, shrugging her shoulders, breathing in the scent of baked goods being made in the kitchen, mixed with familiar smells of the city in summer. "You can almost smell the joy in the air."

"That's the trash," Tootles said from the back. He was in the middle of eating a boureka, lifting it in Avital's direction. "You can smell the dumpsters three miles away in the heat."

"Well—" Avital beamed, unwilling to have her good-mood bubble shattered "—it's wonderful. I love everything about being back at Best Babka."

"Girl," Chaya said, shaking her head, "I don't know what you're on these days, but whatever it is…please share it."

Avital laughed. Though she was planning on partaking of some medicinal cannabis later, her good mood was simply the by-product of a life lived in contentment.

She had started small, donating all the clothing that reminded her of being sick, buying new makeup. She also stopped being so strict on her IC diet. Sometimes she engaged in activities she knew might increase her pain, like eating one of Tootles's salmon bacon bourekas, simply because she knew they would also make her happy. And though she still wasn't sexually active—she'd had no real interest in getting down and dirty with anyone since Ethan—she had started taking baths and even went swimming at the local JCC.

Of course, she still had pain. But when the bad days came now, she didn't fight it. *She didn't have to fight it.* She got into bed, loaded up on rescues, and disappeared into a good romance.

She began to look at her chronic pain as a sacred whisper from the universe to slow down. She built a rampart, protecting both her physical and emotional health. And when Avital looked in the mirror, saw those dotted thighs and pink scars, she called them beautiful. She was not merely a warrior but a creator. She loved the woman she was becoming.

"Apparently—" Tootles chuckled a little at the thought "—leaving us behind was the best thing Avi ever did."

"Come now," Avital said, looking between them, "you know my decision had nothing to do with you. You, and Josh, everyone here at Best Babka were actually what made it so hard to leave sooner."

"We know," Chaya said, embracing her with one arm. "And we're always happy to have you come back and visit us."

"Amen to that," Tootles agreed. "We missed you, Avi."

Avital smiled. "Me, too."

Tootles went back to lunch, leaving Chaya and Avi to once again staff the front counter. Though, in all honesty, and glancing back out to the empty storefront, she wasn't entirely sure why Josh had been so adamant about having her help out. It had been relatively quiet at Best Babka. Partly because it was the beginning of July and half the city had departed for their summer homes or on vacation.

But she figured that Josh wanted someone around just in case something did go wrong. After all, it was looking to be a big week for him. He had taken Melinda upstate and was going to propose to her. Perhaps having Avital there meant there was one less thing for her twin brother to worry about.

Avital sighed and, leaning back on the counter, picked up the cross-stich she was working on. It was one of the hobbies she had taken up in the wake of her joy-finding, along with jewelry-making, and thrifting. As for her photography, she was still working on that, too. But instead of sending her artwork to galleries, letting other people decide on the value of her work, she made it available direct to market.

Now, in addition to an Etsy site, her favorite photographs taken over the last four months lined the walls of Best Babka, a price tag on a cue card beneath each image. And while she had only sold a few images, she was happy. She was being paid for her art, doing what she loved on her own schedule, and no one could take that away from her.

The bell above the front door rang out. Avital looked up from her cross-stitch over to Chaya. Seeing that she was busy washing a pan, Avital put her handiwork down and moved to help the late-afternoon customer.

"Hello," she said, before her tongue caught in her throat.

For a moment, she thought it was Ethan.

It was an honest mistake. The young man standing in front of the counter had the same sort of build. Tall, with a V-shape at the waist, and brown curls piled all over his head. But just as quickly, she realized it wasn't him. For one, he was much thinner than Ethan. His waist and legs, especially. And when she really looked into those soulful brown eyes—she realized he was younger, too.

Shaking it off, Avital forced herself to get a grip.

"How can I help you?" she said.

"I heard the pumpkin-spiced babka is out-of-this-world good here."

"You heard correct."

"Hm," he said, looking through the display case. "Well, then, I'll take two of them."

Avital loaded the order into a bag, before turning back to the young man. "Anything else?"

"How about a box of those macaroons?"

"Another good choice," Avital said, adding them to his tally. It went like this for another few minutes, before she headed to the cash register to ring him up.

"What's a Shirley Temple at the Jersey Shore Ice Cream?" he asked.

"Oh," she said, glancing toward the whiteboard where it was written. "That's our specialty item of the week. My brother and another employee invented it." She didn't want to get into the whole sordid story about Ethan. "But basically it's a cherry and vanilla ice cream with swirls of white chocolate."

"Sounds amazing."

"It's pretty good," she admitted. "Especially on a hot summer day."

"I didn't realize you guys made ice cream, too?"

"In the past, we didn't…but the new owner likes to experiment."

"Hm," he said, thoughtfully. "Well, I'll take a cone of that, as well."

She grabbed him a cone, before bagging up the items. The young man paid, taking his purchases. She was expecting him to leave, but instead, he lingered in the front area, licking his cone, staring up at one of her photographs. It was the photograph of Ethan. Though, out of respect for the modesty requirements of their more religious clientele, they had covered up his naked tuchus with his Little Buddy hat.

Avital moved to make a sale.

"Would you like me to take it down so you could get a closer look?"

"No need," he said, smiling at her. "I'll take this one."

"Really?"

"But," he said, with all seriousness, "I'm not paying thirty bucks for it."

"Oh." She grimaced at his words. She should have known the man was going to drive a hard bargain. She prepared herself for a battle.

"This photograph is worth at least fifty dollars," he said.

Avital laughed. "Excuse me?"

"Yep," he declared defiantly. "I'm not paying anything less for it."

Avital was thrilled. "You know what?" she said, clapping her hands together. "Fifty dollars."

"Much better."

The man dug into his pocket. Avital waited while he pulled out a messy wad of crumpled-up cash. She had never seen so many one-hundred-dollar bills in one place—like the man was a drug dealer, or a very popular male stripper—but she didn't feel it was her place to ask. The exchange complete, Avital grabbed a stepladder and took the photograph off the wall.

"Actually," the young man said, apologetically, glancing

at his watch, "I hate to put this on you, but I need to run to a business meeting, and I already locked up the store. Would it be possible for you to bring it over next week?"

Avital didn't understand. "Bring it over?"

"Yeah," he said with a wry smile. "I'm your new neighbor. My partners and I just bought the building across the street."

It took Avital a minute to fully grasp the details of what the young man was saying. *Moishe Lippmann had sold Greatest Babka.* After three generations, and over fifty years, it had finally happened. She was still choking on her tongue, trying to make sense of his words, when he began heading for the door.

"Wait," she called out. "When should I bring it?"

"How about Thursday?"

"Thursday is…great."

"Great." He smiled, pushing open the door. "I'll see you then."

With that, the young man disappeared from view. Avital stood in the front entrance of Best Babka and, still in shock over the young man's revelation, quickly moved to text Josh. Then stopped, realizing that texting Josh about Moishe Lippmann would only feed into the war they were all trying so hard to forget. She was better than that. More important, it wouldn't make her happy.

Putting her phone away, she made a mental note to tell Josh as an aside when he came home from his trip with Melinda, before putting it in her schedule to bring the photograph over next Thursday. Still, glancing back out the window, she couldn't help but wonder about who had bought the building across the street and what they were planning to do with it.

FORTY-SEVEN

Avital arrived at Best Babka on Thursday and found that who-ever had bought the building across the way had begun doing construction. A large tarp covered the front entrance, offer-ing no clues about the new owners. Still, she would find out soon enough. Taking her photograph off the wall, wrapping it up in tissue paper and including a small note of gratitude for the purchase, she was interrupted by Josh.

"You heading over there?" he asked.

Avital glanced up from the bag she was packing. "Yep."

"Well," he smiled back at her, "good luck."

Avital wasn't sure what she needed luck for. Then again, her brother had been in some sort of love bubble—head fully in the clouds and not all there when you talked to him—ever since returning from his trip with Melinda. She had, unsur-prisingly, said yes when he'd popped the question. Avital par-ticularly liked the idea of gaining a sister.

She headed across the street. Ducking beneath the construction rafters and tarp, she pushed open the door of what used to be Greatest Babka. A small bell attached to the top announced her arrival. Despite only just starting the remodel, they seemed to be making progress.

Whoever had bought the place was certainly investing good money in it. A gorgeous reclaimed-wood counter, with a glass section for showcasing products, sat toward the back. Above it, the white walls had been decorated by shiplap, and acrylic shelving had been put up. Near that, a box full of mason jars was in the process of being unpacked.

The space itself was filled with a variety of mismatched tables, chairs, and large couches, giving the impression that the disorganization was a carefully made stylistic choice. But in one of the corners, on a colorful carpeted play mat, were children's book and toys. She could smell paint...mixed with something buttery and fragrant—definitely someone baking—but also, something that smelled skunky. Her first thought was that someone was opening a café.

"I'm sorry," a voice came from the back kitchen, "we're not open—"

Avital nearly dropped the bag she was holding as he stepped through the doorway.

It was Ethan.

Wearing a green apron, he held a tray of bite-sized hamantashen in his hands. Her heart landed on the floor between her feet. It was him. He was here. And holy pumpkin-spiced babka...he looked amazing. It was like the man had gone up ten points in hotness since the last time she had seen him.

"Avital," Ethan said, putting his tray down.

He came closer, meeting her immobility with steps of trepidation. Soon, they were standing just a hand's width apart, and the urge to reach out and touch him, feel his arms around her again, was completely overwhelming.

"I—I was—" she stammered, "I was coming over...to drop off this photo."

"That was me." Another voice sounded from the back. Avital looked toward the kitchen and immediately recognized the young man who had bought the framed photograph from her last week. "I'll just, uh... I'll just give you two a minute to catch up."

The young man departed.

Avital shook her head, confused. "I don't understand what's happening here."

"That's my younger brother, Randy."

"The drug addict?"

He smiled. "Not quite."

All at once, her phone began vibrating in her pocket. Grateful for the intrusion—still trying to figure out what the heck was going on—she scrambled to pull it out.

"It's a text message from Josh," Avital said.

"What does it say?" Ethan asked.

"'Don't be mad at me.'"

She glanced back through the windows, toward Best Babka, but the construction tarp covered her view. Still, she imagined Josh—and Tootles, and all the rest of the folks at Best Babka—with their noses pressed up to the glass.

Ethan moved to explain. "Josh reached out to me."

"Of course he did."

"I told him that you had been very clear with me about your expectations." Ethan rubbed the back of his neck. "But then, Josh brought up the possibility of a loophole. If I couldn't come to you...then, maybe, we could get you to come to me?"

She bit back laughter and tears. "How very Jewish."

"I hope you're not mad at me."

"No."

How could she be mad at him? Seeing him again after all this time, the only thing she felt was gratitude. She had missed him so much. Maybe, in her quest for joy and a new life with chronic pain, she hadn't allowed herself to acknowledge how much it had hurt to lose him.

Ethan swallowed. "Would you like to talk?"

Avital nodded. "That would great."

Quickly, he cleared the packing tape and boxes off one of the tables, offering her a seat. Avital took it, and Ethan slid down in the seat beside her. His entire body angled over the small patio table, his hand lingering precariously close to her own heart.

"How have you been?" Ethan asked.

"Actually," she said, considering the question, "I've been good."

"Yeah?"

"Yeah."

He nodded. "Good."

"And you?" she asked.

"Oh man," he said, running one hand through his thick hair. "Where do I even begin?"

"Oh my gosh," she said, grabbing him by both elbows. "I forgot. You don't even know." Touching him again brought memories of their passionate night to the fore.

"Know?"

She explained about her grandmother, and Moishe and Chayim, and the secret pumpkin-spiced babka recipe that he had had all along. "Can you believe it, Ethan?" she said, the words pouring out of her like water. "There wasn't even a recipe to—"

"I know," he said, trying to assuage her concerns. "I figured it all out the night you gave me the recipe."

He told her how seeing the addition of bananas triggered a memory from his youth. "From there, it was a simple trip to Lippmann's offices…where the truth was pretty evident. I confronted my grandfather the next morning, and I haven't seen him since."

"Wait," Avital said. "Does that mean—"

"Randy and I have both gone no-contact."

"Wow."

He nodded. "It's weird because…some days, I miss him. And then I have to remind myself that he was never the grandfather I wanted him to be. But I always have hope that there will be some sort of reconciliation. For now, though… I'm just working on healing from past wounds, breaking patterns, and basically protecting my boundaries."

She squeezed his wrist. "I'm proud of you, Ethan."

"And what about you?" he asked.

"Oh," she said, chuckling a little. "I haven't been doing anything."

Ethan laughed. "Come on."

"No, seriously, Ethan… I left Best Babka. Josh bought me out of the business, and I've been using time to just…focus on my health and figure out life in this new body. Mainly, I've just been bumming around, taking on odd jobs and hobbies. Honestly, considering how little actual responsibility I have right now, it's been the best few months of my life. I feel like a whole new woman."

"And you're still taking pictures?"

"I am."

His eyes caught hers. She looked away, her heart landing in her throat. "Speaking of which," she said, reaching down to the photograph at her feet, "this is yours now. I hope you're not mad I've been selling a photo of you partly naked at Best Babka."

"Mad?" he said, rising from his seat, taking the photograph toward the glass counter. "Heck, no. I'm gonna hang this right here, above the counter, so that everybody who walks in sees it. After all, this photo right here...this is what we're all about."

Avital blinked. "I'm sorry. I don't understand."

He left the picture, returning to the table, placing one hand on her wrist while he spoke. She had no inclination to move away. Sitting beside Ethan, feeling the heat of his skin pressed up against hers, made her happy.

"After the confrontation with my grandfather," he said, "I had this idea. Holy Rollers makes most of their money from recreational-use marijuana, high-THC products with no CBD. And that's great for making money. But what I learned from you, Avital, is that medicinal cannabis patients may need a bit more specialization in the products. Not just helping them find the best ratio and strain for their own individual bodies but creating better methods of delivery for patients.

"For example," Ethan continued, "let's say you have someone with celiac disease who has no experience with medicinal cannabis. We'd make them a high-CBD, low-THC gluten-free hamantashen. Or let's say you have a child who needs medicinal cannabis for epilepsy management. We'd make them a medicinal cannabis juice box—something that can easily be tolerated in the morning."

She glanced over to the tray of hamantashen. "So, you're not opening a bakery right across the street from Best Babka?"

"No." He bit back a smile. "Though, Josh and I have spoken about working together to create Best Babka products for people on special diets since our kitchen is better equipped to handle allergens. We are, technically, a medicinal-cannabis dispensary. Though, we prefer to describe ourselves as medicinal-cannabis compounding pharmacy."

Avital blinked. "How do you know all this?"

"Oh—" he laughed at the question "—I've been living with Rabbi Jason."

Avital laughed. "No way!"

"Yeah," Ethan explained. "He wanted us to really immerse ourselves in the world of marijuana before going into business with us. So we lived with him and worked beside him...and I learned everything, from what it takes to operate a grow farm to how to best help medicinal cannabis patients. I'm actually a certified budtender now."

"Wow."

"Yeah," Ethan said thoughtfully. "It's been a really good experience for me. I even came to appreciate all the nudity and tantric lovemaking courses he holds in his living room."

Avital nearly choked on her tongue. "Excuse me?"

"Let's just say that any woman I wind up with is going to have a very satisfying sexual future. *Anyway*—" Ethan smiled, refusing to drop any additional hints "—we worked there, learning everything, and when Randy and I had some savings, plus enough understanding of running a dispensary, we negotiated a deal with Rabbi Jason where, over time, we would buy him out of the business. From there, Rabbi Jason approached my grandfather about selling this building."

"And your grandfather just sold it to him?"

"Well," Ethan admitted, "he didn't know we were involved. Plus, Rabbi Jason gave him a hard sell about how Yom Kippur was coming up, and how good deeds and charity can change God's decree about being written into the Book of Life...and I think, considering what happened, he was looking for some brownie points with God. Either that, or he loved the idea of someone opening what he saw as a drug den across the street from you."

"I'm going with the latter," Avital said.

"Either way, here I am."

A question mark lingered in the air. Her entire heart was pressing against her chest.

"I wanted to thank you, Avital."

"Me?"

"You were the inspiration for this store," he said, standing up.

Offering his hand, he led her back outside. Ethan brought her to the sidewalk and pulled down the tarp. She looked up to find a large placard on the front of the building. On a white board, in pink lettering and surrounded by cherry blossoms, were the words.

What the Heart Kneads

"You always talk about what you need, Avital," Ethan said, holding her hands. "You need pain relief. You need money. You need safety and security. I don't know if I can give you those things, but I will spend the rest of my life trying to provide them for you...if you let me. Because I know what I need, Avi. And it's you. *You're what my heart needs.* I was wondering...if you'd be willing to give me another chance."

Avital couldn't breathe, couldn't move. She only knew that she loved him. Oh, how she loved him. Her voice did not waver when she answered. "Yes," she said, brows pinched, pressing her chest into his. "Now, enough with all the talk, and just kiss me, already."

Ethan, as always, obeyed, taking her into his arms and pulling her to him. Their lips met. It was a moment that seemed to rival every happy moment before it. Her heart melted. Her knees buckled. She saw her past and her present and her future, and it all included Ethan. They were meant to be together.

They stood on the sidewalk—the summer sunshine beating down around them—locked in a kiss that seemed to go on forever. And as they kissed and kissed, she was not at all surprised to hear a round of cheering coming from across the street.

EPILOGUE

One Year Later

The couple sitting before Avital in the back office of What the Heart Kneads were new customers. And yet, glancing down at the intake form before her, the story that Austin and Leah were telling her this afternoon was a familiar one. They had found their way to Brooklyn, and Ethan's medicinal-cannabis compounding pharmacy, in a last-ditch effort to relieve chronic pain.

"I hurt all the time," Leah cried, as Austin wrapped a supportive arm around her. "My joints, my skin…everything feels like it's on fire, and no one seems to be able to help me."

Avital nodded. "It's okay. You let it out."

The woman continued, telling her story. Avital listened, occasionally jotting down notes in her file that would help Ethan and Randy develop the right combination of product for her later.

They didn't use titles at What the Heart Kneads. Both Ethan and Randy had felt some hierarchy of employment went against the spirit of what they were doing, but Avital liked to think of herself as a Chief Happiness Officer. Her job, aside from welcoming new customers, was to offer hope. When the woman was done telling her story, Avital handed her a tissue.

"Before we begin developing a plan to help lessen your pain," Avital said sympathetically, "I want you to know that I believe you. The story you're telling me I've heard countless times in this office. I want you to know that what you are experiencing is real. You have nothing to apologize for and nothing to be ashamed of. You know your body better than anyone."

Avital had come to learn how important these words were. *You're not alone. It is awful. I believe you.* The last thing a pain patient needed was guilt on top of an already-difficult battle.

"Secondly," Avital said, "I want you to know that I'm also a chronic-pain patient."

Leah looked up. "Really?"

"Actually, it was developing disabling and severe chronic pelvic pain that led me to discover the benefits of medicinal cannabis myself. And while we try not to say here that medicinal cannabis is a lifesaver, what I can tell you, from personal experience, is that there is hope. From this day forward, you are not alone in your battle. We will work with you, and your doctors, for as long as it takes to lessen your pain. We will not give up on you."

The words made a difference. Before long, Leah had stopped crying. Avital finished up her intake. Bringing them out to the front, she handed off the young couple to Randy, who was working behind their pharmacy counter.

"Leah," Avital said, looking directly to her. "This is Randy, our pharmacist. I'm now going to explain your case to him. If

I get something wrong, please feel free to correct me, okay? He'll likely also have questions for you as well, after I leave."

Leah glanced at her husband. "Okay."

She had learned the importance of this, too. Actually talking to a patient, behaving like they were a real person sitting in the room.

"Leah is experiencing all-over and constant pain, which she described as her skin constantly being on fire," Avital said. "She's been to multiple physicians and specialists, all of whom have no idea what is going on. Some think its fibromyalgia. Some think it's a type of neuropathy. One diagnosed with her atypical MS. What she needs from us is something to lessen her pain. Right now, her most disabling issue is lack of sleep. She would also like to be able to contribute again to helping with the household chores—cooking, cleaning. She especially misses gardening. She's new to marijuana and has never smoked. No food allergies. No history of anxiety."

"Oh," Randy said, smiling in the direction of Leah and her husband, "well, you're easy."

Leah laughed. "Really?"

"Yep," he said, waving her over to a counter. "Come on. I have just the thing to help you. Tell me, do you like milkshakes?"

"I love them!" Leah beamed.

"Well, then—" Randy smiled "—I am about to make your day."

The three set off for the café section of the store. The woman, who just thirty minutes ago had been crying, totally distraught in Avital's office, now walked with shoulders lifted.

Avital sighed. Looking back at that woman laughing, seeing the store she had inspired, with its small café decorated in pink-and-white cherry blossoms, with delicate glass jars of bud lining the wall, she was proud of the work she was doing. Her artwork—black-and-white photographs of intimate spaces, both breached and erected boundaries—adorned the space. The worst part of chronic pain had never actually been the disease…it was the lack of hope.

Avital made her way to the kitchen. Ethan did not hear her come in. Like always, he was fully immersed in a baking project. It turned out, that old adage about marrying your father was, at least and in her case, partly true. Ethan loved baking. He had a passion for creating new recipes that rivaled…well, it almost rivaled his passion for her.

Hopping up onto the counter, she could tell by the way he sat there, thumbing his lower lip, staring through the glass of the oven, that he was obsessing over the babka he was making. She waited for Ethan to calm down, and then realized it was unlikely. Tonight, they would be making their engagement official with a party.

"Last customer of the day," she said.

Ethan spun around. "Hey, you." He left his babka, coming over to give her a kiss. When he pulled back, his eyes angled downward on her own. "I love you," he said.

Avital didn't hesitate. "More."

He kissed her again, and she melted, feeling the safety and warmth of his two strong arms enveloping her own.

Maybe it was all those tantric lovemaking lessons that Ethan had been privy to while living with Rabbi Jason, but over the last few months, both the sex, and the intimacy, had been amazing.

"Ethan," she whispered flirtatiously, "I need you to know something."

"Yes?" he said, breathing heavily.

"I'm not wearing underwear."

Ethan groaned, and reaching for her waist, pulled her closer. She could feel him, his heat and need for her, pressing against her own wanting body. She responded by kissing him deeper, longer, pouring her whole heart and soul into his.

"That's it," Randy said, entering the kitchen. "We are, officially, closed for the day."

Ethan stepped back from Avital. She readjusted her skirt. They both blushed, caught and embarrassed. Randy huffed. "The only reason I'm not saying something snarky right now is because we're celebrating your engagement today, but otherwise...gross."

Avital laughed. "Sorry, Randy."

"Seriously," he said, shaking his head, "it's bad enough I have to stare at Ethan's naked tuchus all day."

"We actually get a lot of compliments on that photo," Ethan reminded him.

"In fact," Avital said as she beamed proudly, "his naked tuchus currently hangs in thirty-six homes in America."

"And two in Israel." Ethan grinned.

Randy sighed. "It's pointless against you two."

They laughed. The joking was all in good fun, of course. Randy had become as much a part of her family as Ethan. Perhaps it was not the future any of them had foreseen when Ethan had first gone undercover at Best Babka, but it was a lovely future all the same.

"On that note," Randy said, clapping his hands together, "I put the closed sign up with a note that we're hosting a private party. The kosher champagne has been chilled, and the pear juice has been squeezed. Anything else you two lovebirds need from me?"

"Ethan is obsessing over the babka," Avital told Randy.

"I'm not obsessing," Ethan said. "I just want to make sure this all goes okay."

Avital knew his anxiety had very little to do with the babka. It had been Avital's idea to give Moishe Lippmann a chance to reconcile with his grandsons. Of course, that reconciliation had come with some tough rules and a whole bunch of conditions.

As for her own grandfather, she knew that inviting Chayim and Moishe into the same space, after so many years and bad blood between them, had a strong potential to end in disaster. But Avital and Ethan were moving forward with their life. There was going to be a wedding, and maybe one day, even children. Her *zeyde* had a choice. Either get with the program or, frankly, get out of the way.

"Look," Avital said, her voice firm, "they both know the rules. If neither of them can behave…what do we do?"

"We throw them out."

"That's right," she said, for both her own and their benefit. "We've established clear boundaries. If they cross those boundaries, they have to leave. This is our day. Not theirs. Besides, if they can't even sit in a room and be cordial with each other, it's better we know before the wedding."

Randy grumbled. "I just think you're gonna be disappointed."

Avital could feel his sadness. Randy was in a different place than Ethan when it came to their grandfather.

"I know," Avital said, reaching out to squeeze his hand. "But for the time being, I'm going to tip the balance in their favor and have faith."

Randy nodded, just as the bell above the front door rang out. From the front, she could hear her brother, Josh, entering with what sounded like the opening act to a circus. "Yo, Avi," Tootles shouted from the entrance. "Where the heck are you?"

"And that would be Best Babka." Avital smiled.

Ethan glanced down at his watch. "Right on time."

"I'll go deal with everyone," Avital informed him. "You let me know when the babka's ready."

"It's a deal," Ethan said.

In the meantime, Avital handed out drinks and caught up with friends and family.

In the meantime, Avital handed out drinks and caught up with friends and family. All of Best Babka had shown up for their engagement party. Josh had brought his wife, Melinda. Her parents arrived shortly after all of them and, with the help of Grandma Rose, parked *Zeyde* Chayim in a chair, where he now waited quietly.

"Ethan," Avital's mother said, kissing him on the cheek, "good to see you again."

"Thank you."

She squeezed him on the arm sympathetically. Her mother had taken Ethan under her wing when he returned to Avital's life, and that motherly love—combined with both group and individual therapy—was helping him heal from his early trauma.

"Whatever will be," she said, looking between them both, "will be. But we have your backs, okay?"

"Thanks, Mom."

"And just so you know," she said, tapping on her purse, "I brought a Taser."

With a proud smirk, her mother flitted off to the side of the room. Ethan turned to Avi. "Do you think she actually…"

Avital answered honestly. "I don't think so… Maybe?"

"*Oy.*"

"Come on, Avi," Josh called from the side of the room. "You're killing us here. When do we get to kick this party off right?"

Avital glanced over to the clock. It was one minute before four thirty, exactly…and Moishe Lippmann had still not arrived. Avital sighed, looking toward Ethan. She could tell by the way he was staring at the door longingly, he was still holding out hope that his grandfather would appear.

"Ethan," Avital said gently, "we can wait if you—"

"No," he said abruptly. "Rules are rules. Let's do this thing."

Ethan quieted the crowd, calling everyone to join him in a circle. Avital took her place by his side. Ethan wrapped one arm around her waist protectively, lifting a glass of champagne into the air for a toast.

"First," he said, "I want to thank you all for coming today. As you know, Avital and I have come through quite the journey to get here."

The bell on the front door interrupted his speech. Ethan stopped, and with the interruption, the crowd around them parted. Moishe Lippmann was standing in the entrance.

He had also not come alone.

Ethan almost didn't recognize him. It had only been a year, but during that time, Moishe Lippmann had grown feeble. Now, not only did he need a walker to enter the store, but an aide. But standing next to the aide, wearing a purple dress and matching headband, was Kayla. She stared up at the walls of their business, mesmerized by the photographs.

Ethan swallowed. After Ethan and Randy had started their business, Moishe had cut off visitation to their sister. And though they were still able to get updates from Melinda, the sight of his sister in the threshold, looking well and healthy, completely overwhelmed him. He had missed her so much.

"I'm sorry I'm late," Moishe said, nodding to Kayla. "Your sister wanted to look extra pretty for today. Plus, we stopped for ice cream."

Ethan stood silent. He knew he should say something, but

the sight of Moishe—Kayla beside him—brought back every feeling from his childhood. Simultaneously, there was rage. And sadness. And hurt. So much hurt.

He had an instinct to toss the old man onto the sidewalk, when Avital reached over, taking his hand. She brought him back to himself. It was not just their hurts that they shared now, but their strengths.

"I was wondering," Moishe continued, "if I could talk to you all alone."

"I was just about to make a toast."

"It's important," Moishe huffed. "I have something to say to you, and Randy, and Avital, too... The toast can wait." Moishe shifted uncomfortably behind his walker. "Please."

The word surprised Ethan. It gave him hope, too.

He glanced over to his brother. Arms crossed against his chest, Randy's anger seeped off him like the smell of weed. He knew that the only thing keeping his brother from storming out was that they had sent the old man the terms for being allowed back into their lives. At least for now, and with the appearance of Kayla, he seemed to be meeting them.

"Fine," Ethan said. "We can talk."

Leaving the party behind, the group made their way to the kitchen. Avital took her place beside Ethan, waiting wordlessly. Randy chose to watch from a safe distance, leaning against a countertop. Moishe, Kayla, and the aide shuffled after them.

"You wanted to talk to us about something, Grandpa?" Ethan asked. His voice was firm but clear.

"I wanted to let you know that I've considered your offer," Moishe said, pausing before continuing, "and I'm here to tell you that I've agreed to your terms."

A small gasp of excitement escaped Avital's lips.

The three of them had been fighting with Moishe for

Kayla for months. They had denied him access to their lives, making their wishes known through certified letters and attorneys, while simultaneously working hard to become financially independent. They had done most of it while planning for a long and protracted legal battle with their grandfather, because none of them ever expected the old man to yield.

It was the closest thing to a miracle that Ethan had ever experienced.

Moishe reached into a bag that hung off his walker, pulling out a file. "This is the paperwork to give you power of attorney for Kayla," Moishe said. "All you need to do is read it, sign it in front of a notary, and file it with your lawyers… Then she's yours."

Ethan took the document from his grandfather. Flipping through it, he confirmed that it was, indeed, power of attorney for Kayla.

"I appreciate you meeting us on this," Ethan said.

"The only thing I ask," Moishe continued, "is that you still allow me visitation. Kayla and I have gotten close over the past few months. She likes ice cream, you know? Pistachio is her favorite."

Ethan couldn't help but ask, "You've been visiting her?"

"Every day," Moishe confirmed.

Despite what had happened between them, he was happy to hear that. Perhaps his absence—and Randy's, too—had made Moishe realize how much Kayla had to offer. He looked to his sister. She did not seem upset by the idea.

"If Kayla is okay with it," Ethan said, "then I am."

"Good," Moishe said.

"Well, if that's it," Ethan said, clapping his hands together. He was eager to get to the party. He especially was not interested in hashing out the details of their past or all the work left between them that still needed to be done.

The old man had met their terms. He had given them power of attorney for their sister. For the time being, he could attend their engagement party. And if he could keep behaving, not say nasty things or start fights with others, he might even garner a wedding invitation.

"There's one other thing," Moishe said, interrupting him. "It's not on the list, but I did it anyway."

Ethan turned cautiously. He still didn't trust his grandfather. But the rules were clear now, the boundaries laid down. If there was one hint of cruelty, one inkling that he was playing some game, the old man was getting tossed straight out. He was not just protecting himself and his siblings now, but Avital, too.

"I've established a trust in each of your names," Moishe said. "There's one for you, Ethan...one for you, Randy...and one for Kayla."

"We don't want your money," Randy interrupted.

"Which is why," Moishe said, as if intuiting the argument, "neither of you boys will come into the money until after I die—"

"Oh, goodie," Randy said with a smirk, "two reasons to celebrate."

"Randy." Ethan glanced over his shoulder, at his brother. "You're better than that."

One of the things they were both working on in the wake of leaving their grandfather's home was not saying hurtful things when they were hurt themselves. It was hard, breaking a pattern. Biting back your anger in order to find the space to say how you really felt. But it was necessary. He was worried that if he and Avital had children, the words he had been raised with would fall inadvertently from his lips.

Randy pulled back on his open animosity. Moishe was clearly not happy with the insult, but made himself continue.

"My point being," Moishe grumbled, "the trust is established. The paperwork done. There's no way for me to take it back or lord it over your heads to control you. It will be there for you...even if you cut me out of your lives."

"You think that makes up for what you did to us?" Ethan asked genuinely.

"I'm not saying it does," Moishe snapped back. "I'm saying it's yours. You want to let it sit in a bank untouched, that's your prerogative. You want to give it away to charity, fine. You want to use it to support this drug business of yours, be my guest. But I'm telling you this because the trust for Kayla will open up to her the minute you sign those papers."

Ethan swallowed. "What?"

"You can use the money for her as you see fit. If you want to keep her at Hebrew Home for Assisted Living or move her somewhere closer to you. My hope is that it takes some of the financial burden off you and your future wife...and also makes sure Kayla keeps receiving the best care."

The whole room went silent. Nobody knew what to say.

"I know I did things wrong," Moishe said finally. "I thought...if I could give you everything, it would be enough. It could make up for the things I lacked, the things I didn't know how to do. So I raised you the way my parents raised me. Tough. And I'm sorry. Not having you around has been terrible. But I'm willing to do whatever it takes to be part of your lives. Because I do love you. All of you... I love you more than my own life."

Ethan glanced back to Randy, seeking his input.

"It's your wedding." Randy shrugged.

Ethan returned his attention to his grandfather. "If you can continue behaving yourself, if you can continue meeting every single condition we set forth, without abusing anyone in the process...we're willing to let you back into our lives. Slowly."

"Thank you," Moishe said, relieved.

"Come, Grandpa," Avital said, taking Moishe's arm. She nodded toward Ethan, giving him a minute alone to decompress with Randy. "Let's find you a nice spot to sit in the main area. Have you ever tried organic and freshly squeezed pear juice?"

Ethan waited for Moishe, Kayla, Avital, and the aide to leave before turning back to Randy.

"You okay?" Ethan asked.

"No," Randy said.

Ethan nodded. "What are you going to do with the money?"

"My first thought was honestly to just take a match and light the whole thing on fire."

Ethan smiled. "Seems like a waste of a fortune, though."

"Probably," Randy said, before his thoughts drifted. "Do you think people can actually change, Ethan?"

Ethan considered the question seriously. "I think," Ethan said, "people change when they want to, when they want to put in the effort to be different. I don't believe people change overnight. Or that some epiphany happens that turns a bad man into a good one. But everyone can make a choice to be better. Maybe, if you make that choice enough times, over enough days of your life…you become better, too."

"Hm," Randy said.

"Should we start getting the babka ready?"

Randy concurred. Ethan pushed himself off the counter, grabbing two oven mitts. Heading to the oven, he pulled out two pans of warm CBD-babka. Randy began cutting, placing the layered cake on plates, when a commotion from the front interrupted their work.

"Do you think…?" Randy asked, eyes wide.

"Chayim."

Ethan wasted no time. Putting down the babka, he raced to the front.

Avital found herself smack-dab in the middle of a standoff. One arm still clutching Moishe—Kayla and the aide behind them in the hall—she had just entered the main room, when Chayim stepped in front of them.

"Not so fast," Chayim said.

Moishe ripped his arm away from her. "You!"

Her heart sped up in her chest. They had just made significant progress with Moishe. The last thing she wanted to deal with was two old men devolving into fisticuffs.

And then the strangest thing happened. Chayim began crying. It started out as a quiver in the lower lip, but quickly morphed into an uncontrollable sob. Before anybody knew what was happening, Moishe was crying, too.

"Moishe," Chayim wailed.

"Chayim," Moishe cried out.

The two men threw their arms around each other, locking each other in a tight embrace. Sobbing into each other's shoulders, pounding each other on the back, they seemed to be in competition with each other on who could be louder.

"It's been too long, my friend!" Chayim said.

"You have no idea how much I missed you!"

"Impossible," Chayim said. "I missed you every day, every second of my life!"

Ethan appeared out of breath beside Avital. "What happened?" he said, his voice trilling with anxiety. "What did they do now? Please tell me no one is bleeding."

"No one is bleeding." Avital laughed.

"Then, what?" Ethan asked again.

Avital shook her head. "I believe we've just witnessed a happy ending."

With peace now found between the two families, the party returned to normal. Randy passed out flutes of kosher champagne and IC-safe pear juice, followed by slices of CBD-infused babka, for those who wanted to partake in it, before Ethan moved to finish his toast.

Avital stood beside him. Resting her hand on his heart, her engagement ring cast rainbows on the walls around them.

They were two people, surrounded by the things that they loved and the things that had hurt them. For though there was pain, great harm shared between them, scars both physical and emotional, there was also joy.

Life was a mission worth living.

And Avital was happy. And Ethan had learned an important lesson. For together, they had uncovered a most valuable secret. The best recipe for love, intimacy, and babka is the one you bake yourself.

★ ★ ★ ★ ★

ACKNOWLEDGMENTS

This is, without a doubt, the scariest book I have written to date. It is deeply personal and deals with things not often spoken about aloud in our modern society. For all these reasons, it makes the people who supported me through this process invaluable.

First and foremost, my utmost gratitude goes out to my editor, Dina Davis. Dina—it's a bit like an old-fashioned Jewish *shidduch* to find yourself suddenly paired with a new editor. I was nervous, shy—*we barely knew each other*! But at every stage of this journey, you put me at ease.

Thank you for your keen editorial eye, responding to my emails quickly, your absolutely awesome brainstorming sessions, your great ideas. Thank you for allowing me to be both fully Jewish, and chronically ill, in my storytelling. I adore your sense of humor. Beyond all these things, you have pushed me as a writer. I said when we started working together that my goal is always to grow and learn as an author. I'm grateful that I'm doing both under you.

Because this book began under another editor, I would also like to acknowledge her here. Thank you, Emily Ohanjanians, for your constant support and friendship. Also, to Nicole Brebner, Editorial Director and my publisher at MIRA. You are often the unseen part of my journey, but I'm well aware that my dreams came true, and this book will exist in the world, because you are championing it. Thank you for believing in me and my work.

As always, I am so incredibly grateful to my two literary agents from Transatlantic Agency, Carolyn Forde and Marilyn Biderman. I count my lucky stars every day that you were the people I queried and can truly not imagine a better agents, or agency, in the biz. Thank you for three books' worth of dreams, always checking in with me, loving my many (many) ideas, and working so darn hard. Thank you for always reminding me that I belong here and belong in the room. I'm so excited for the future together.

Thank you also to my incredible film agents, Addison Duffy and Jasmine Lake at UTA. Thank you for falling in love with my stories, and working so hard to see my super-Jewy and chronically fabulous books become films.

I am also incredibly grateful to my publicist at Harper-Collins, Laura Gianino. Laura—I'd be drowning without your help. Thank you for helping me manage my schedule, arrange interviews, and field all manner of publicity requests. Thank you for your creativity, your tremendous organizational skills, and your kindness. Every time I get an email from you after hours, I wish you wouldn't work as hard as you do… But please know, your efforts on my behalf are beyond appreciated.

To the rest of the incredible team at MIRA, thank you.

Many of you I have not gotten to meet personally, but I know that your hard work and diligence behind the scenes contributes to the success of this book. For your efforts, and your many talents, thank you.

In editorial, thank you to Evan Yeong, Tamara Shifman, Gina Macdonald and Vanessa Wells. Books are never the effort of one person, but a whole bunch of people, working together to craft the best story possible. Thank you for your edits, your belief in me, and all your countless hours of hard work on my behalf.

If you're reading *Kissing Kosher* right now, it's likely due to the efforts of sales and marketing. In marketing, thank you to Ana Luxton, Ashley MacDonald, and Puja Lad. In channel marketing, thank you to Randy Chan and Pamela Osti. In digital marketing, thank you to Lindsey Reeder, Riffat Ali, Hodan Ismail, and Ciara Loader. Brianna Wodabek, thank you for your friendship over the last year.

In sales, thank you to Heather Foy, Colleen Simpson, and Prerna Singh. Thank you for working so hard to sell and uplift diverse books like mine.

Thank you also to the awesome people behind the incredible cover for *Kissing Kosher*. Thank you to the Harlequin art department. Thank you to Alexandra Niit, who directed the cover for *Kissing Kosher*, and to Ana Hard for the beautiful illustration. Thank you to Erin Craig and Denise Thomson for your creativity and talent on my behalf.

I am forever grateful to the subrights team at Harlequin, who works so hard to make sure that international versions of my books are available around the globe. Thank you to Reka Rubin, Christine Tsai, Nora Rawn, and Whitney Bruno.

In every organization there are people in leadership who steer the ship. Thank you to Loriana Sacilotto, Amy Jones, Margaret Marbury, and Heather Connor. I know that the books at MIRA are often a team effort, and my utmost gratitude goes out to you for believing in my books, and working tirelessly to make *Kissing Kosher* a success.

My gratitude also goes out to Katie-Lynn Golakovich in production.

People don't often think of research going into romance novels, but many folks donated their time in order to help bring this book into correct and proper fruition.

Thank you to novelist and pastry chef Louise Miller for providing inside information about working in a kosher bakery. Thank you also to Rebbetzin Nechamie Fajnland of Chabad Reston/Herndon for her classes on Jewish intimacy and love.

I am especially grateful for the help of the Rabbi Jeffrey Kahn and Stephanie Kahn, Takoma Wellness Center, Washington, DC. As well as to Rabbi James Kahn, Executive Director, Liberty Cannabis Cares at Holistic Industries, Strategic Advisor at Takoma Wellness Center, and Strategic Advisor at R&A Health. Thank you for taking the time to teach me about the important history, both spiritual and political, regarding medicinal cannabis. Your contributions to this book were invaluable, and for your time, expertise, advocacy, and all you do for medicinal-cannabis patients, I am incredibly grateful.

During the writing of this book, two incredibly painful things happened in my family. First, we lost my father, Dr. Jeffrey I. Meltzer. Shortly thereafter, we lost our little beacon of hope, my nephew, Baby Boy Chesney. This paragraph is to acknowledge those loses.

Thank you to the people who keep me upright, and keep me fighting, who love me through every day—Leslie Meltzer, Evelyn Meltzer, Howard Cohen, Elissa Cohen, Jared Cohen, Dr. Danielle Meltzer Chesney, Michael Chesney,

Rose Chesney. To my extended family, and especially, my mother-in-law, Karen Maskuli. Also to Erin Sager, world's best reader. Thanks for coming over and massaging root balls with me during writing breaks.

Thank you also to my dearest friend Rabbi Aviva Fellman, for double-checking my Hebrew (*like always*)—despite having four children and working as a full-time rabbi, you're always available for all manner of help, information, support and, most importantly, laughter. Thank you for driving a zillion hours to sit shiva with me when my father died. Thank you for sending me all manner of inappropriate gifts and memes over a decade of friendship. Thank you for bearing with me, and loving me, when I'm too tired to pick up the phone and talk. I don't know what I would do without you in my life.

As always, there is no one more important in terms of support than my husband, Xhevair Maskuli. Jev—I never imagined I would be adored so completely. Thank you for taking care of me through every bad day, for being my best friend, for supporting me in my dreams, for keeping me fighting. Thank you for telling me to get into bed and rest when all I want to do is keep working. Thank you for accompanying me to every event and to every doctor's appointment. Thank you for being the partner that every person deserves. I am able to write romantic fantasies for chronically ill people because you have given me the template of a hero. I love you so damn much.

Thank you to everyone at Jewish Book Council and the Association of Jewish Libraries, including Suzanne Swift, Miryam Pomerantz Dauber, Arielle Landau, Evie Saphire-Bernstein, Rebecca Levitan, and Rachel Kamin. Thank you for working so hard for Jewish books and Jewish authors. You all are my tribe and my community, and I truly do choke up every time you say something nice about one of my books.

Stories have the power to change the world, and so my gratitude also goes out to everyone who works in the world of books. To bookstagrammers, book bloggers, and book reviewers, thank you for all your reviews, follows, reads, notes, shout-outs, and more.

Thank you to our amazing libraries, and librarians, for making this book available to every reader. Thank you to our bookstores, and all our hardworking booksellers. Thank you for choosing to read my book, stock my book, inviting me for events, and making my book available to the wider world.

Thank you also to Andrea Peskind Katz at Great Thoughts, Great Readers for her unwavering support since the publication of my first book. Thank you to Renee Weiss Weingarten and Renee's Reading Club for always welcoming me (and the hubby!) and where I always have the best time.

My gratitude also goes out to everyone in Jewish Bookstagram. We live in a time where antisemitism is growing more prevalent, especially on social media. Your courage, your dedication to lifting up Jewish books and modeling Jewish pride keeps me fighting. I know I'm going to forget some people here, and this list is by no means exhaustive, but I hope it encourages you to continue doing such great work for our world and community.

Thank you also to Kayla Plutzer at KaylaReadsBooks on Instagram, Jamie Rosenbilt, and Melissa Amster for always reading and uplifting Jewish books so proudly, including my own. Thank you to Pearl Adler Saban, who has written reviews and who has become a friend during the last two years of this journey. Here's a ♥ just for you. Thank you to everyone involved in Matzah Book Soup Club, including Lilli Leight and Amanda Spivak. Also to Courtenay Joseph for just always making me laugh.

Thank you also to all the authors, and friends, who have

lifted me up during this journey. Jenna Blum. Lynda Loigman Cohen. Jenni Bayless. Pam Jenoff. Debbie Macomber. Lisa Barr. Felicia Grossman. Jules Machias. Elyssa Friedland. Haley Neil. Zibby Owens. Noelle Salazar. Salam Kabbani. MJ Rose. Amanda Elliot. Rochelle Weinstein. Also, to Brett Gursky.

Finally, and though I am a writer, I feel completely incapable of expressing my gratitude to you, dear reader. Many of you whom have become my friends over the last two years. I wish I could name so many of you personally, but my publisher assures me there is a limit on these things, and I fear forgetting someone.

Thank you for the emails, the likes, and the comments. Thank you for reading, loving, and shouting about my stories. Thank you for all the Friday schmoozing on Facebook. (My absolute favorite!) Thank you for helping me create a community through my books. I love you all so much!

Finally, thank you to every person who has shared their story with me—each one reminding me that books like *The Matzah Ball*, *Mr. Perfect on Paper*, and *Kissing Kosher* are meant to do more than just entertain. That they have import, and that Jewish people, but especially in the case of this book, chronically ill people deserve their own types of romantic fantasies.

I said at the end of the Author's Note in *The Matzah Ball*, that no matter what happened next, my heart was full. Well, here we are three books later, and my heart is still full. To every single person who has supported me on this journey, thank you.

KISSING KOSHER

JEAN MELTZER

Reader's Guide

1. Avital lives with interstitial cystitis and associated chronic pelvic pain. What did you learn about IC and chronic pelvic pain while reading this book? Did anything about her experience surprise you? Do you, or anyone you know, live with chronic pain? How has this experience changed them?

2. Ethan sees his grandfather's emotional abuse as a by-product of Jewish transgenerational trauma. Do you agree with Ethan's assessment? How has the way Ethan was raised differed from Avital's childhood? How has Moishe's emotional abuse affected both Ethan and Randy as adults?

3. A long-standing rivalry leads Moishe Lippmann to send Ethan undercover into Best Babka in Brooklyn to steal their world-famous pumpkin-spiced babka recipe. What is the best dessert you have ever eaten? Do you have any secret family recipes that you keep guarded? Are you a pumpkin-spice person?

4. Ethan lays *tefillin* as a way to make sense of himself, and his own value system, in the midst of increasing pressure from his grandfather to steal the pumpkin-spiced babka

recipe. Do you have any rituals or traditions that you rely on when you are going through tough times?

5. Avital lives with disabling chronic pelvic pain. At one point in the story, she says that Ethan also lives with chronic pain. What do you think she means by this? How can chronic pain be both physical and emotional?

6. Avital feels frustrated navigating the medical system with chronic pelvic pain. Have you ever had an experience with a doctor where you felt that your needs were not being met? Do you believe that being a woman changes how you are treated?

7. Avital's journey with chronic pain leads her to discover medicinal cannabis as a source of relief. What do you think about this choice that Avital eventually makes? Do you know anyone who has used medicinal cannabis for pain relief? Do you think medicinal cannabis should be legal for chronic-pain patients? Why or why not?

8. One major theme of this story is that boundaries are necessary for healthy interpersonal relationships. Do you agree with this assessment? What are some examples of boundaries you have created in your own life?

9. Rabbi Jason believes that intimacy is different from sex. Do you agree with this assessment? What does intimacy mean to you? Have you ever had to relearn, or renegotiate, your body after a trauma in order to experience sexual pleasure?

10. Avital eventually learns to live alongside chronic pain by focusing on her joy. What are some things that make you joyful? Does it help you to focus on these things when times are hard? Why or why not?